VICISSITUDES
OF
WAR
A MALCOLM MACPHAIL
WW1 NOVEL

ISBN 978-94-92843-500 (trade paperback edition)
ISBN 978-94-92843-517 (e-book edition)

Published in the Netherlands in 2020 by Esdorn Editions

Cover design by JD Smith Design
Interior design and typesetting by JD Smith Design

Cover photographs acknowledgement: Canada Dept. of National
Defence/Library and Archives Canada: *Canadians advancing near Remy.*
France, August 1918 (PA-003059); Canada Dept. of National Defence/
Library and Archives Canada: *Sir George Perley visits the Canadians on
Vimy Ridge.* France, September 1917 (PA-001771)

This book is a work of historical fiction. The names, characters,
events and dialogue portrayed herein are either the product of the
author's imagination, or are used fictitiously, except where they are an
acknowledged part of the historical record.

www.darrellduthie.com

VICISSITUDES OF WAR

A MALCOLM MACPHAIL WW1 NOVEL

DARRELL DUTHIE

Esdorn
Editions

Also by Darrell Duthie in the Malcolm MacPhail WW1 series

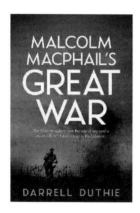 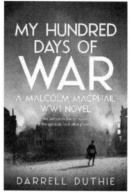 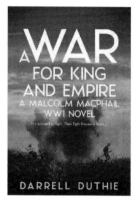

Malcolm MacPhail's Great War – Book 1 (1917-1918)

My Hundred Days of War – Book 2 (1918)

A War for King and Empire – Book 3 (1915-1916)

PART ONE

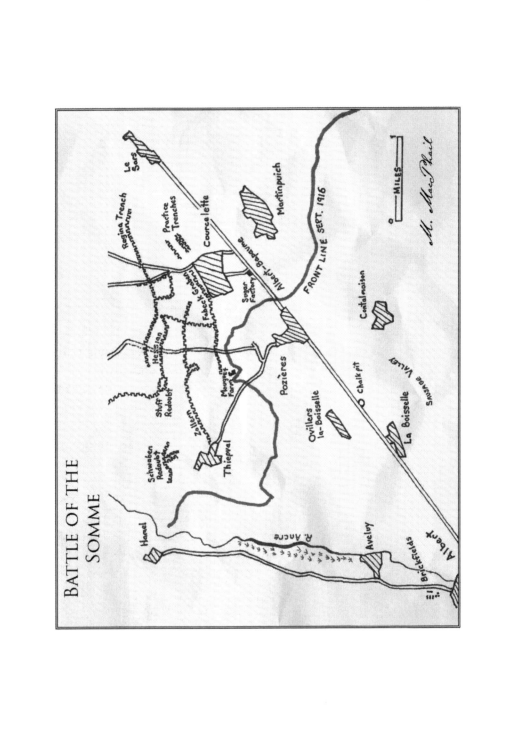

BATTLE OF THE SOMME

Hamel

R. Ancre

Aveluy

Brickfields

Albert

Schwaben Redoubt

Thiepval

Zollern

Stuff Redoubt

Hessian

Mouquet Farm

Fabeck Graben

Regina Trench

Practice Trenches

Courcelette

Le Sars

Sugar Factory

Pozières

Ovillers la-Boisselle

Chalk Pit

La Boisselle

Sausage Valley

Albert-Bapaume

FRONT LINE SEPT. 1916

Contalmaison

Martinpuich

MILES

0   1

M. MacPhail

CHAPTER 1

5th of September, 1916
Albert, France

'Take a look at that,' I sighed. 'That's precisely the sort of thing that's starting to give me a really bad feeling about the Somme, Roy.'

Dundas didn't reply. His eyes like mine were glued on the soaring heights of the once grand basilica of red brick and white stone.

Admittedly, Albert was a small village and in these early autumn days of 1916 there wasn't much of anything to see apart from the village church. Fritz had taken well care of that. If truth be told I'd never really appreciated churches prior to arriving on the Western Front and seeing the great cathedrals for the first time. Our enemy, despite his God-fearing reputation, appeared even less enthralled – he'd battered most into leaning towers of rubble. The average church may not have been much to look at anymore but this one caught my eye straight away. Through the falling rain of a slate-coloured dawn sky, a miracle of sorts was on display.

Baby Jesus held aloft, both the Virgin Mary's arms were clasped in a bow above her head. A classic pose. Wrought in brilliant gold. Less classic was Mary's erect body tilting horizontally, the soles of her feet affixed precariously to the steeple's heights. She was seemingly contemplating a dive into the muddy ruins below, no doubt to escape the wanton fury of the shells. Irreverent Australians – I'd yet to meet any other kind – dubbed her Fanny Durack, after their famous swimmer. For all her accomplishments even they would have to acknowledge that the real Fanny had never faced a dozen German gun batteries out for her head.

'They say the war will be over when she falls,' remarked Dundas, at length.

I sidestepped a particularly large puddle in the road and, shortly thereafter, a heap of horse dung, still steaming. 'Really? That sounds promising. It looks to me like Fanny will be making her exit awfully soon. Especially if one of those Aussies so much as belches in the wrong direction. Did you notice, by the way, how quick they were to move out? I thought we were getting the better end of the bargain, swapping the Salient for the Somme, but I'm beginning to wonder if we weren't somehow short-changed.'

Dundas turned to me, wearing a frown of puzzlement.

Hurriedly I continued. 'You heard what that peasant woman in the field said when I told her where we were heading: "*C'est un mauvais endroit. Très mauvais.*" You really don't have to know much French, Roy, to know that's not good.'

'How bad a place can it be, Mac? I for one am mighty glad to see the last of Ypres and the Salient.'

I nodded. 'Amen to that. Can't disagree with you there.'

'Even if there is a big new offensive planned.'

'New offensive,' I sputtered. 'What do you mean? Did you hear that officially? A new offensive here? They only just finished an offensive. Or was it two?'

'Officially!' he snorted. 'What do you think? You know as well as I do they don't let us in on anything. But don't tell me you actually believed they sent us here for a change of scenery?'

'Hmm,' I prevaricated. I could feel the lines in my brow tightening. 'Well, it's a good thing I've made my acquaintance with Fanny then. Apparently, I'll have to put all my hopes on her.'

On cue, a couple of the dozen-odd 10th Battalion officers and NCOs in our reconnaissance party crossed themselves. It was a sentiment I could appreciate.

Silently we trooped past the church in double file and carried on up the Bapaume road. That's one of the things I really liked about

Dundas. He wasn't one to dwell unnecessarily on bad news. He grasped that a sensible man had to ration his words this early in the morning, particularly when the news was anything but good. Few others in the army were ever so accommodating.

While Dundas was a newly-minted sergeant and I was a newly-minted lieutenant, a disparity in rank which the wearisomely hide-bound British Army took *terribly* seriously, the two of us carried on as we always had. Fortunately our branch of the British Army, the Canadian Corps, had a more liberal attitude towards fraternization between the ranks, even if discipline had tightened remarkably this past year. Regardless, I tend to think Dundas and I would have been close friends whichever army we were in.

Our morning reconnaissance proved to be surprisingly brief. After walking past the 8th Battalion, who were in the process of moving into the bivouacs at Tara Hill, and along the dusty red-brick ruins of La Boisselle village and to the Chalk Pit beyond – barely two miles from Albert – we soon established a couple of salient facts.

First, the ground underneath the thick veneer of Picardy mud was made up of the same stuff as the cliffs of Dover, white to boot. Not at all like the gluey brown muck of the Salient where water began seeping up from below after you'd barely managed to dig to waist level. Even with the recent rain the trenches we were to occupy were a good deal drier than the ones we'd left behind. There were distinct nods of approval when the lineage of those old trenches became clear. They were German. The best trenches usually are; certainly no one in their right minds occupied an old French trench unless there was no other possible choice. That had been one of my first lessons as a soldier.

The second observation, and the more important one, was that the real trouble was only a short jaunt northeastwards. In brigade reserve or not, we all cast anxious eyes at the shells falling in rapid succession in the communication trenches a couple of thousand yards distant, the flashes illuminating the dreary sky. The sound of their concussions rolled ominously across the fields.

I glanced over at Dundas.

His greatcoat was soaked. Water dripped from all sides of his helmet. The scene reminded me of my boyhood home as the neglected eaves began to buckle in the midst of a sudden, torrential downpour, and not long before my father summoned me to hold the ladder. Water trickled down Dundas's nose to its tip. There, a teardrop had formed, hanging for an instant until it disappeared under its own weight, immediately replaced by another. For all his bedraggled appearance his eyes were alert, however, keeping a close watch on the fall of the shells lest their pattern change. That he and I were still alive, and part of the dwindling band of old "originals", may not have been down to our wits. But I liked to think wits didn't hurt.

Dundas caught my look and shrugged.

'The Somme reminds me a little of Salisbury Plain,' I mused, thinking of the bitterly cold and absurdly wet winter months we'd endured last year after arriving in England. That had been our first rude awakening that the war was not quite as we envisaged.

'A lot more Fritzs here than on Salisbury Plain,' grunted Dundas.

'Very true…' I replied. 'In retrospect maybe it wasn't as wretched as I thought. Funny how perceptions can change.'

When the shells began to land 500 yards away the battalion adjutant, Major Lefebvre, decided we had reconnoitered quite enough. It was a decision I had no quarrel with. My stomach was growling, I didn't much like what I saw, and nobody ever received a medal out scouting a reserve trench – not even when it involved a close encounter with a Jack Johnson, which the Germans were dropping liberally all over the front-line trenches.

8th of September, 1916
Trenches near La Ferme de Mouquet, France

After a couple of fine days in which the skies cleared, the afternoon sun beat down with a warm brilliance, and the men engaged in "Practice Contact Aeroplanes", new orders arrived. Not that anybody tipped me to the arrival of new orders. However, when sixteen officers and a handful of NCOs including both Dundas and myself were rounded up for a 5 a.m. reconnaissance of the front line, it seemed a fairly safe assumption.

By the time we approached Mouquet Farm the sun, such as it was, had begun to rise. The weather had taken a distinct turn for the worse. Today was dawning dull and sullen, an unbroken procession of thick grey clouds inching ponderously across the sky. As the light inexorably grew, so too did the sobering realization of where I found myself.

Around was an endless wasteland. Muddy fields seemed to stretch forever, dotted with holes, most of them filled with water. In places where the chalk was close to the surface white streaks ran through the mud. It was a landscape more barren and desolate than any I had ever seen.

Marching towards the Somme days before, the boys had cheerfully belted out *Pack all your troubles in your old kit bag* as we passed by the verdant fields of Picardy, resplendent in their vibrant golds and greens, crops of rapeseed, wheat and corn swaying rhythmically with the breeze. Red brick villages, pretty in their unpretentious simplicity, lined the road and copses of trees spotted the rolling farmland. We had left Ypres behind and were glad for it.

Crossing the Ancre, a small tributary of the Somme, we neared Albert. As we approached, the ravages of war steadily took over. The ground became uneven and muddy, the debris of war everywhere, everything enveloped in a whitish-grey dust. After a mile or two on the dirt roads we were caked in it. Of the villages and trees, precious little remained apart from mounds of stone and brick, and the occasional spindly, barren stump.

But here, here at this spot less than five miles from the centre of Albert, there was nothing. Not a building, nor a tree, not even a single, solitary blade of grass.

For some time we trudged after the guides, unspeaking, veterans of war temporarily bereft of words. Then ahead I heard a couple of officers begin talking amongst themselves. 'So what's this all about?' asked one, a captain. Clinkskill was his name. He'd arrived with the last draft but it's not a name you're apt to forget, which is the only reason I probably took notice of him in the first place. After 18 months at the front you become a little inured to yet another round of fresh faces come to replace the ones that aren't around anymore.

'The 3rd Brigade is being relieved,' said the other officer. 'No prizes for guessing who's to do it.'

'Relieved? So soon? They only relieved the Aussies themselves a couple of days ago. What happened?'

There was a long pause. In the distance a shell went off. 'Casualties happened. Apparently they lost close to a thousand men,' came the answer.

'One thousand men… in three days? Manning the line?'

'Yep.'

At this revelation Captain Clinkskill thought better of questioning further for he began shaking his head. Perhaps he had more experience than I gave him credit for. Many times it's best not to know what you're getting into.

Glancing over at Dundas I saw that he too had heard and was also wearily shaking his head. Roy was definitely experienced. For a brigade to lose a thousand men in a few days was unheard of. Christ! That was a man in four. Simply to hold a trench?

'Welcome to the Big Push,' I muttered.

Dundas ignored me. Naturally he'd read the newspapers too. We all had. After the offensive kicked off on July 1st – Sir Douglas Haig had chosen Dominion Day for the biggest attack of the war – the headlines were triumphant; "OUR CASUALTIES NOT HEAVY" they blithely reassured. As time passed exuberance gave way to a tone of detached neutrality until the "Big Push" was no longer a headline, relegated to the pages behind. However, each day for many weeks after, a few pages further behind, column upon column of alphabetized names spoke of a far grimmer truth. I think we all realized the campaign was not the breakthrough to Berlin everyone had hoped for, although it is not in the nature of soldiers to dwell on such matters – particularly when you're trudging into the midst of it.

'Stiles is back.' Dundas's words came as a rifle shot through the half-light of dawn.

My head whipped round to face him. 'Stiles?'

He nodded. 'He's a captain now. Arrived with the latest draft.'

I was uncharacteristically silent. Then I took a deep breath. 'Stiles… you're certain? He's a captain, you say?'

Dundas nodded.

Softly I cursed under my breath. 'I rather hoped I'd seen the last of Sam Stiles. But I guess there is one small consolation…'

8

Dundas looked at me quizzically.

'At least he's not a general.'

Dundas groaned. 'Yeah, well, as long as you don't forget his pa's connections you'll be fine, Mac. So don't go looking for trouble. I know you.'

I grunted noncommittally. The foremost of his pa's connections, the Minister of the Militia, I'd already met. Dundas hardly needed to remind me. Regardless what I thought of the imperious Sir Sam Hughes, he was not a man to be crossed. Half by accident I'd done that once and for my troubles was demoted in front of the entire battalion. The humiliation was unbearable when Stiles appeared shortly after wearing my stripes and an attitude to accompany it, the beginning of his dizzying ascent through the ranks. I was keen to avoid a repeat of the whole sordid affair.

'Hopefully someone will find Stiles some stores to count to keep him out of the way...' I said. The rest of my words were lost in the explosion.

Past the quarry, less than 300 yards down the communication trench in the direction of the front line, the shell went off with a deafening crash. It was so loud it felt like I'd been hit on the head with a hammer. Dirt and smoke filled the air. The blast was even bigger than that from a Jack Johnson, so I figured it was one of those 250-pound monstrosities that an 8-inch howitzer could lob six miles. Then as the humming between my ears softened, there was another blast; the characteristic rumbling approach far too brief to adequately prepare. Not that preparation did any good if one of those giants had your number.

In retrospect, the thuds in the distance had been a signal to the wary. But if you were going to duck at every single thud you heard on the front they might as well consign you to an asylum; as with thuds there was no shortage of asylums in France.

'They're taking a pounding,' someone shouted. Belatedly we scrambled for cover in the trench.

And a pounding it was. The trenches opposite Mouquet Farm, the very ones we were assigned to take over, were being pummeled.

After several minutes in which we crouched low, listening and praying the gunners weren't about to abruptly shift their aim to the rear, it became obvious that this was more than the usual wake-up call. The reconnaissance would have to wait.

It was a quiet and subdued group that made its way back to the battalion at La Boisselle. I think everyone realized it could have been us up there. The next day we learned that the Germans had followed up the barrage with several attacks – one with as many as 200 men – but were rebuffed. We also learned something else, and this time I *was* privy to the orders.

The battalion was to assume the left sector of the line that very night.

CHAPTER 2

10th of September, 1916
La Ferme du Mouquet, between Pozières and Thiepval, France

It was 9.20 a.m. Our first morning in the front lines of the Somme.

'Lieutenant!'The soldier was calling to me from behind the parapet, helpfully dabbing his finger in the direction I was to look. I stepped up onto the fire-step to join him.

A little more than 100 yards in front of Point 77 small groups of the enemy could be seen. We were facing roughly north. The Germans were rushing laterally from left to right across our field of sight, dashing from hole to hole. They were from the legions garrisoned at Thiepval no doubt. The German fortress a mile to the left on the westernmost tip of the Pozières Ridge had stubbornly defied capture for more than two months.

'Do you think they're heading this way?' asked Lieutenant Rutherford

'No, more likely the farm,' I said. Rutherford began shouting orders.

Due to his seniority – he'd been a lieutenant six months longer than I had – he was in charge. Ostensibly this was his domain, even if the Germans failed to acknowledge it. As domains go Point 77 was hardly remarkable. Its defining feature consisted of three craters at the T-junction of Zigzag Trench and another. A few hundred yards up an uneven and muddy slope lay the rubble heap of Moo Cow Farm; a

11

deceptively innocuous name if ever there was one. The past month the Aussies had suffered a terrible beating trying to take it. As we'd taken over their line, I had the awful suspicion we were the next slotted in to try.

While I continued to survey the scene to the north, Rutherford was in action. He was mustering the defences. P.77 was likely his first independent command and he wasn't taking any chances.

Our two Lewis guns started to rattle furiously.

Within minutes the Germans dispersed, many fleeing to ground. Machine guns tended to have that effect. My experience of machine guns this war had largely been at the receiving end so this was a welcome reversal of roles. Our rifles kept up a sporadic fire but the Emma Gees went quiet for lack of fresh targets. Across the turned earth, ploughed by Heaven knows how many shells, plaintive cries of 'Krankenträger!' could be heard. I didn't understand much German – few of us did – but the tone spoke for itself.

Rutherford's face was normally one of blue-eyed earnestness, befitting a former druggist and son of a Methodist minister. Presently he looked deadly serious.

I went to him where he stood peering through the trench telescope. 'That should make them think twice before they venture this way again,' I said. 'The last thing we need are more Boche in that bloody farm.'

He lowered the telescope and peered down at me from the firestep. For all the carnage, his eyes now flashed a boyish and most un-Methodist excitement. 'Yes. Let's hope so,' he replied.

Rutherford had been sidelined for much of the summer after getting hit at Mount Sorrel in mid-June. In the aftermath of that battle our OC, Colonel Rattray, had unexpectedly promoted me to lieutenant. There weren't a great many lieutenants left in the battalion at that point. The colonel must have figured beggars can't be choosers and I ascended to the lofty ranks of the commissioned officers. Returning to the battalion following a spell at Officers' School I was astonished at how many of the faces were new ones. Months later, regular drafts of men were still appearing.

Unfortunately, in my absence the colonel was promoted and left. His successor, Major Thomson, was less obviously charmed by my abilities. In fact he didn't seem to know what to make of me, if anything. I was a *supernumerary* as the army described it. With all the real positions filled, I was a spare player of sorts, about as critical to the team as the third goalie in hockey. I was shifted from company to company, seemingly on a whim, to serve as adjutant to some newly-arrived captain. It felt a cruel fortune that had seen me promoted only to land in a position where I was entrusted with absolutely nothing. Not that I minded helping Rutherford out. He seemed a decent fellow.

At the shout I glanced first at my watch.

That was another thing I'd done since becoming an officer. I'd bought a watch, a gleaming new Borgel. Paradoxically most of my recent seven-day leave had been devoted to traipsing around London in search of things for use back at the front, including new uniforms and other accoutrements such as a watch – all at the best possible prices. Were it not for the Scottish blood somewhere (and thoughts of Granny shaking her wizened head at my extravagance) I might have forgotten the few shillings saved and actually enjoyed myself. I didn't once contemplate spending the contents of my breast pocket however. Dundas had called me a 'piker' when I told him how I'd spent my leave. The Borgel now revealed that it was 9.30 p.m.

It had taken the Germans a mere twelve hours before they returned. This time they were coming from the direction of Mouquet Farm and from Point 54.

Dusk had since given way to a semblance of night. Which was probably what they were counting upon, even if it was seldom completely dark on the Somme. Invariably, at any given time, somewhere on the front a gun was being fired. Their speckled flashes left a fleeting glow on the horizon like that of the embers of a fire nearly extinguished. Far overhead the luminous whiteness of a solitary, lingering star shell carried far. For miles the ground was shorn of anything standing. The sentry to his credit was quick to spot the intruders.

It was a row of ink-dark figures silhouetted against a background shaded purple and black. When the sentry called out, I didn't hesitate. I peered over the parapet in a way I never would have done by daylight, safe in the knowledge that I was indistinguishable from the rugged contours of the ground. As I spotted the murky shapes through the gloom I shivered. I knew they could be only one thing.

Nor, after a further moment spent observing, was there any question where they were headed.

I turned. In my best *sotto voce* voice I shouted, 'Rutherford!' There wasn't any particular need for silence except that for every step closer they came, the better the odds we might surprise them. General Haig may not have felt the need for surprise on July 1st, but most soldiers would assure you that surprise is one of the keys to ensuring your side comes out on top.

It took only an instant before the lieutenant appeared at my side, breathing heavily.

'Fritzs. Rows of them,' I said. 'They're coming this way.'

Briefly he glanced over the parapet to see for himself.

'How many do you figure there are, Malcolm?'

'I count three rows. Twenty a piece. That's at least sixty, maybe more.'

Softly he whistled. 'Sixty…'

'Look. I'll go alert the others. Give me two minutes and then send up a flare. We'll give them a rousing welcome.'

Rutherford looked at his watch and nodded. I tore over to the craters to get every man I could find, primed and ready. I took special care to alert the boys at the foremost Lewis gun.

The Australians had battered themselves senseless against Mouquet Farm. Six times they had thrown themselves against the deep dug-outs and fortified positions of the old farm, and six times they had been beaten back. Every successful advance had been met by a German counterattack, every yard bitterly and savagely contested. Precisely one week earlier, it was the 3rd of September, the Australian 13th Brigade had made their final attempt. They were supported by our own 13th Battalion. However, the gains were meagre save a 300-yard stretch of the Fabeck Graben, the enemy trench which curled around behind the farm and ran northeast another 2000 yards in the direction of Courcelette. But Fritz was not content to let things rest. He wanted the ground back.

There was a muffled report, more like the dull popping of a bottle being opened than the sharp crack of a rifle shot. The glowing

Christmas bulb of a flare raced up into the night, erupting in a dazzle of bright light. Beneath it the German attackers were caught in an eerie, shifting glare. There were three rows of them, one impossibly regimented rank after another. They were stumbling at a fair pace across the uneven ground in our direction.

I fired at the first man I saw and missed. There was the rattle of a long burst from the Lewis gun in the crater beside me. Behind me what sounded like a whole battalion's worth of rifles went off. My heart was pounding with the excitement. I forced myself to take a deep breath before slowly exhaling. Then I steadied my arm and lined up another figure in the revolver's sights. The barrel bucked like a young colt and again I missed. A curse, a third try, and to my relief I saw him go down. The first row of Germans was gone. The rows behind it were wavering, buckling under the torrent of lead.

Guttural shouts could be heard, words of futile encouragement from their officers and NCOs. Futile because they were caught in the open, we were dug in and ready, and no amount of encouragement was enough to carry them over 75 yards of rough ground in the face of forty rifles and two machine guns. It lasted barely two minutes. It seemed longer.

Their disciplined formation had dissolved. Lone men could be seen scrambling away, climbing up and down through the shell holes, sometimes on their hands and knees. The flare fell to the ground and went out with a fizzle.

I lowered the revolver. There were scattered shots still, but I heard Sergeant Hiller order the Lewis gun nearest me to stand down. Hiller was a steady hand, a veteran of enough fights to realize we might need the ammunition before long. In the heat of battle the new lads tended to forget that. Then Rutherford appeared, diving into the wet dirt beside me, his eyes flitting from left to right counting his men. He too had his revolver in hand, the lanyard hanging down uselessly, almost touching the ground.

A curt nod to greet him. 'I have the distinct feeling it may be a long night,' I said.

He pursed his lips thoughtfully. 'Yes, I fear you're right, Malcolm.' He went to holster the revolver. 'I'm going to double the sentries. We don't want them slipping up on us.'

15

'Good idea,' I said. I raised my hand with the pistol still in it. 'I don't suppose you have a rifle kicking around? This thing may be alright in a trench fight, but it's about as useful as throwing sticks at any kind of range.'

Rutherford grinned. I wasn't sure if that was because he agreed. Perhaps he was simply a better shot. He promised he'd look for a rifle though.

Their artillery found our lines shortly thereafter. Or they tried to. A trio of whistles blew shrilly, seconds before everything shook and a string of deafening blasts led us to dive for cover. Luckily, they were firing short, either not entirely sure where we were and sounding out our positions, or the gun barrels were simply shot out after too many hours of use. There was some pleasure to the thought that Germans, or German steel at the very least, was susceptible to the same fallibilities as our side. Regardless, you couldn't accuse them of lacking in resolve.

Thirty minutes later the German infantry came streaming down the slope from Mouquet Farm again.

'No wonder the Aussies couldn't take that bloody place,' I grumbled to myself. 'There must be an entire battalion camped out up there.' The private beside me was listening attentively but didn't say a word. A flare went up.

There wasn't exactly a battalion approaching, more like a company of 200, although I confess to losing count when I realized that the few sections and supernumerary lieutenant Rutherford had assigned to him were outnumbered by a factor of five. That's likely why we dispensed with the element of surprise and instead began shooting at anything we could hit. It wasn't a feeling of desperation as much as a reflex. There was no doubt in my mind what would happen if we didn't.

I lay prone with the long barrel of the Webley resting on a length of wood I'd found – no surplus rifles had turned up – and that seemed to improve my marksmanship somewhat. The range was so far as to be hopeless. I was pretty sure I got one though before I had to duck down, emptying the chamber on the ground and pushing in another six-round clip as fast as my fumbling fingers could manage the trick.

It was then that I happened to glance over at the far side of the crater. I was in time to see the second man of the Lewis gun crew fall backwards. I expect it was a lucky shot. Despite their superior numbers the enemy were not in a position to be doing much shooting, let alone aiming.

The gunner himself was oblivious to the fate of his partner. He was methodically sweeping the ground a couple of hundred yards out in short concentrated bursts. However, when the ammunition ran out one of our two machine guns would effectively be out of action. As there's nothing quite like a machine gun to keep Fritzs at bay, it was a serious matter.

I hesitated, then sighed. There was nothing else for it. It wasn't as if anybody was awaiting my brilliant tactical insights. The Webley and I were hardly the backbone of the defence. I stuffed the pistol back in its holster.

'Keep at it,' I said to the private, and clambered to my knees. 'You're doing great. I'm going to help out on the Lewis gun.'

The soldier murmured a 'Yes, sir,' and had the good sense to ignore me and concentrate on his shooting while I scrambled ignobly across the crater, trying to keep low.

The gunner didn't notice when I slipped in behind him. His mate who was down, was apparently only wounded. He grinned awkwardly when he saw me. Sprawled up against the edge of the crater, he was holding a dressing clamped to his side, in obvious pain. 'Over there, sir. The pans are in the box.'

Then, like that, the rattle of the Lewis gun ceased. A hand appeared over the gunner's shoulder impatiently motioning "come on".

Thankfully it was only a question of ammunition and not a stoppage. I'd been on a Lewis course many months before, but expecting me to disassemble a machine gun to fix any of the fifteen different malfunctions that the manual enumerated was expecting altogether too much. I could change a tyre on a car if hard pressed, however that was it for me and things mechanical. As it happened, I'd just got my hands round a new pan. It was surprisingly heavy, despite containing only 47 rounds. A Lewis gun could fire up to 600 of them a minute so I was lucky the gunner was aiming first. Among other factors the 600 depended on a crew knowing what they were doing. That too I'd learned at the course.

'Damn it all, Mike.' The gunner swirled round, infuriated at the delay. Seeing me his face twisted in confusion. 'Sorry sir,' he mumbled. 'I didn't expect you.'

Without responding I leaned past, neatly replacing the empty magazine with the full one. 'It's all yours, Corporal,' I said, feeling puffed I'd managed it.

The gunner put a hand under the pan and wiggled it – double-checking I hadn't screwed up I expect – then bent over and pulled the trigger.

It was fortunate he did. Over his shoulder I could see an alarming number of the enemy pressing forward. The Lewis gun chattered fiercely. A cluster of men in their centre went down. Everywhere rifles were firing. I heard two short bursts from the other Lewis gun cleave effortlessly through the din. The smell of gunpowder and cordite hung thick. Flares burned overhead, the horizon was lit by distant shellfire. All around muzzles flashed. The Germans from Moo Cow Farm were dropping like gophers.

When it came to replace the magazine for a fourth time, the gunner motioned I should hold up. 'I think they've called it quits, sir,' he said. At which news I crawled up to lie beside him at the crater lip.

A wary glance confirmed that the danger had passed. I exhaled in relief. 'You can't fault their bravery. I wouldn't have wanted to be in their boots.'

'No, sir,' said the gunner grimly. 'But then if they'd stayed at home instead of tromping all over France and Belgium in them very boots they wouldn't need to be brave.' The man had a point.

Across the crater I spotted the young private who I'd lain beside. I hadn't recognized him at the time and therefore assumed he must have come up in one of the drafts this summer. This had likely been his very first battle.

He must have noticed my stare for he flashed me a train track of brilliant white teeth. In the dark of a Picardy night they could have done double duty as a signalling lantern.

I smiled in return and gave him a thumbs-up.

'What's his name?' I asked the gunner. The gunner had the steady bearing of a man who'd been in the thick of it more than once.

'Duncan.'

'Yes, I know that. But his first name?'

He grinned. 'Fritz. But we call him Fred.'

'You must be joking. Fritz? Really?'

'Yes, sir. He's not so bad, our young Fritz Duncan. A little wet behind the ears. But then he's not the only one!'

I laughed. 'No. I suppose not. He handled himself well.'

The corporal nodded. Whereupon I went in search of Lieutenant Rutherford to report we had a man wounded but that the position was secure. I'd been in worse scraps.

However, I groaned when twenty minutes later all hell broke loose.

It was in the battalion's right sector, five hundred yards away and immediately south of the farm.

A small group of Germans in the trenches near Point 54 made a desultory attempt to move on us. They quickly abandoned the attempt once we began firing. To the east the action was heavier. When I heard the *whoosh* of the mortar rounds from the brigade's Stokes battery at the quarry I knew it was serious. This went on for ten or fifteen minutes, a steady thumping. Round after round was finding its mark – until it ceased. Anxiously we lined up on the parapet wondering if our flank had held.

Word eventually came that it had.

Later still there was a gas alarm when the Boche threw a few lachrymatory shells into Pozières and surrounds. We were spared the tear gas. By that stage my eyes were watering of their own accord. It had been an abbreviated night's rest. Not only had we relieved the 8th Battalion in the midst of a midnight bombardment, we'd spent an entire day fending off Fritz. So much for our quiet introduction to the Somme. But as Dundas had made clear, we were here for our own Big Push. That meant it was unlikely to get any quieter than this. For once the Salient didn't seem quite so bad.

CHAPTER 3

13th of September, 1916
The Brickfields, Albert, France

The Brickfields to the north of Albert on the far bank of the Ancre, were once the location of a thriving brick factory. As such they were probably never very attractive to the eye. These days the factory grounds were downright desolate. An ambling dirt road ran through the site in the direction of the village, and makeshift wooden signs helpfully pointed out the direction of Howitzer Bridge, Crucifix Corner and the trenches; if you wanted to avoid any of those you presumably went the other way. The attraction for the army, in any event, was obvious. A whole assortment of low-slung, tumbledown brick buildings sprawled across the rough terrain, now covered in weeds. They offered endless possibilities to billet the cold, wet and generally miserable sods who by chance or design had earlier followed the direction "trenches". So crowded was the place that they said a stay was by reservation only. Perhaps due to the view.

You could easily make out Albert and the steeple of the Basilica towering above it. Unfortunately, from my vantage point, Fanny didn't appear to have moved an inch.

Other than breakfast, consisting of a hearty portion of fried bacon and rather decent as a result, the big event that morning was the arrival of the Royal Canadian Regiment, one of the storied regular army battalions who marched up in predictably smart order. We knew them lovingly as the *Shino Boys* – after their buttons of similar brilliance – though some, those more cynically minded, preferred the moniker *Rocking Chair Rangers*. By chance I'd already made acquaintance with the RCR, when they first arrived in the Salient, at Plugstreet, almost a year earlier. Their colour was healthy at the time, having come from an onerous stretch on garrison duty in Bermuda, so most sported a god-like bronze tint. Regardless, the men in the platoon had muttered disparagingly about how 'green' they were. Regular army or not, in those days the RCR had a few things to learn about the technicalities of modern warfare, otherwise known as life in the trenches. As civilians not long before we found it rather amusing, even heartening, that we knew our way around better than they did.

But that was more than a year ago. These days the RCR looked as hard-bitten as the rest of us. When I heard they were coming I was curious whether I'd encounter a familiar face. I had one in particular in mind. After confirming that the last of the bacon was well and truly gone, I ambled over to their corner of the bivouacs.

By the time I arrived the third heavy shower of the day was dumping its load. I was beginning to wonder if my curiosity had gotten the better of me, in the fearless example of my black Labrador whose nose led her into all sorts of fixes I invariably had to fix.

A voice came from behind. 'Mac! Is that you?'

Normally I'm as tone-deaf as a doorknob. More so even. Yet the deep baritone and the very peculiar French-Canadian way he'd mutilated 'that' told me everything I needed to know. He was precisely the man I'd been hoping to see.

'The good sergeant Benoît DuBois, I presume?' I swivelled round to make certain.

He stood there, several inches taller than me and as broad as a barn door, not that I'm especially short or scrawny even if I felt that way looking at him. Underneath an officer's cap large enough to shelter a family of geese, his face rimmed by both beard and moustache, he was grinning exuberantly. '*Ben oui, c'est moi.* How are you?'

'I was hoping I might run into you,' I said, my mouth curling into a smile. 'I see they've made you a lieutenant no less.'

He extended a hand and we shook.

Most of what I knew about DuBois came from a cold night bailing trenches with water to our thighs, commiserating in our misery. Despite that, or perhaps because of it, I felt I knew him better than I really did. I think he felt the same.

Ushering me over to the nearest building to get out of the rain, he proffered his water canteen once we'd shaken ourselves off. 'Here, a little drink to warm up,' he said.

Having been a lawyer you get a feel for certain things. I suspected the contents of that canteen contravened every regulation in the entire colourful history of the British Army. As any other red-blooded soldier from the colonies would I reached out and seized it. 'You've upgraded your flask since last we met. This must be the bigger, better size to accompany your bigger, better rank?'

He grunted.

I took a deep swallow. And a second smaller one to chase it down.

'Oof,' I sputtered, as the fire in my throat subsided. Then I breathed deeply which only inflamed matters. 'What is this stuff, anyhow? If you'd held a match under my nose I swear I could have duelled it out with a *flammenwerfer*.'

'Come. Let's sit,' he said. So we did, on a couple of bunks opposite each other, in the corner of the room beside the door. We were close by the windows, not that I had any desire to see the rain transform the path outside to mud, only that there were certain tactical advantages to an unencumbered line of sight. An hour passed before that became relevant.

In the meantime we talked about the war and our experiences, and much else. Contrary to what you might guess, it was a cheerful, animated discussion. Sometimes I thought there was more laughter at the front than at home. The average soldier was a surprisingly cheery chap for all his woes. And DuBois was cheerier than most, though a certain seriousness now settled over him.

'For the life of me, I don't understand what we're doing here, Mac.'

'Oh, that's easy, I said glibly. 'Attacking Fritz.'

He sighed. 'Yes, yes, I know. I know it's helping the French out at Verdun. But why here?'

In lieu of giving an immediate answer, one I didn't have if I was honest, I scratched at my chin. Finally, a few words and some nascent thoughts surfaced. 'I've been wondering that myself, Benoît. Unfortunately, Sir Douglas hasn't found the time to enlighten me or anybody else I'm acquainted with. The one thing I know for certain is that the British and French armies adjoin at the Somme. I guess as this was to be a joint effort... a real *Entente Cordiale*... the generals found this a logical spot.'

'Because the British army and the French army happen to bump shoulders, the whole offensive is here? I've been looking at a map and I don't see much to fight for.'

'You just arrived, Benoît, but out there,' and I jerked my thumb in a north-easterly direction, 'is Mouquet Farm. Now Mouquet Farm isn't much, but apart from shell holes and Fritz that's all you're going to see at the Somme. Brace yourself, you'll be seeing plenty of those.'

Out of the corner of my eye I spotted someone crossing the dirt road in our general direction. The wind was picking up and the rain with it.

I squinted. He was an officer. There was no doubt about it. He was headed in our direction, his gait oddly familiar. Just off the road he looked up. Loudly I groaned.

DuBois frowned. I could see the question mark burning in his eyes. 'A fellow I know,' I explained.

He peered at the figure who was making an undignified dash for the door whilst holding his cap in place with one hand, and his flapping greatcoat with the other. 'Hmm. A captain,' said Benoît.

'So I'm told. Stiles is his name.'

For some reason I hadn't yet seen him and I'd been wondering when he would finally make an appearance. Knowing Stiles he'd arranged a spot of leave in the interim: Deauville, or somewhere equally pleasant. I still couldn't get past the fact he'd turned up at the Somme. Sam Stiles was the kind of warrior who was to be found in the thick of the war effort, so long as the war effort was far removed from the front lines. He'd disappeared a year ago with my sergeant stripes and a bad case of pneumonia and had reappeared wearing three pips and an air of good health. Evidently the battles in the rear were not quite as taxing as those in the front.

Bustling through the door he stamped his flashy polished boots, fastidiously shaking the water from his cap. He'd obviously not been near a trench anytime this year. In fact, everything about him had the appearance of being spanking new. I stood and called out: 'Stiles!'

Blinking he looked our way. Then the recognition clicked in. 'MacPhail!'

He was beaming as he strode over. 'Isn't that something? After all this time. My old corporal Malcolm MacPhail!' Then he noticed my lieutenant pips and he regained his composure. 'I've been promoted too as it happens,' he said, with an exaggerated stage wink.

It's the sort of haughty behaviour that can cause the veins in my head to pulse very rapidly. 'Congratulations Captain, I hadn't realized,' I said, and winked back.

DuBois meanwhile was wrestling with the makings of a grin. He had the good sense to put a covering hand in front of his mouth.

Stiles hesitated before eventually clearing his throat. 'Yes, well, now you know. Best we're clear about where we stand, don't you think?' he said pompously.

'Yes, sir. You must be pleased to be back in the real war?'

Stiles eyed me suspiciously. 'Yes, it's good to be back,' he said guardedly. 'I'm afraid I may be too pressed with other duties to spend as much time with you fellows in the trenches as I'd like however.'

'I can see how that might be a worry,' I muttered under my breath. Stiles was fortunately preoccupied, having taken notice of Benoît for the first time.

'Let me introduce you,' I said hastily. 'Captain Stiles this is Lieutenant Benoît DuBois of the RCR. Lieutenant DuBois, this is Captain Sam Stiles, presently of the 10th Battalion.'

They shook hands. Stiles frowned. 'DuBois. Is that French?'

DuBois was about to respond when Stiles spoke again. 'Well, no matter. As Pa always says: "it's not the ones in uniform you have to worry about".' At that he chuckled.

My mouth was open but the words were caught in a jam behind the lines.

Stiles had no such difficulties. 'Listen, I'd love to stay and chat a little longer, but I really must run. Thought I'd pop in here and dry off for a moment. Great seeing you, MacPhail.' Conspiratorially he lowered his voice. 'I have some important messages from Brigade to the OC. There's something big brewing for the battalion in a couple of days. Remember, not a word fellas.' With that he was gone.

Benoît looked like he needed a *flammenwerfer* of his own.

'His pa is best buddies with the Minister of the Militia,' I said.

'Ah, so that's why he hates French-Canadians.' Sir Sam Hughes was a notorious bigot, so Benoît wasn't completely fishing in the dark.

'Oh, I wouldn't necessarily say that. Mainly it's just work and danger Sam Stiles hates. Which is where you and I come in. Or me, at least, seeing as how we're in the same battalion. Why do you think he was so overjoyed to see me? You he may insult; me he'll have out on a late night working party and up in time to lead the attack... or worse.

'Besides, before you get too worked up, did you hear what he said? That something is brewing. Trust me, Benoît, that's what you should really be concerned about.'

CHAPTER 4

16th of September, 1916
Albert, France

We stood-to on the 15th, the deep rumbling of the opening barrage audible even in Rubempré far to the rear, the battalion prepared to move forward on two hours' notice. And early the next day we did, marching eight kilometres to Contay, through a countryside un-touched by war, past thick hedgerows and rolling green fields dotted with yellow flowers. There a row of double-decker, open-top busses stood waiting to return us to Albert and the Brickfields; a short pause, I presumed, before we would be marching on towards Pozières and action. Mouquet Farm was the place I was betting on.

Upon arrival at the Brickfields, I sought out an officer who might know more. I found him in the form of Major Marriot. He stood observing the men as they settled into our open air bivouacs, what the Americans so appropriately called pup tents: two men under a rubberized groundsheet with barely room to roll over.

But I didn't broach the subject of our orders directly. While army doctrine tended to favour mass frontal attacks, since early 1915 I'd had enough experience of mass frontal attacks to know that a more circuitous route was often advisable. 'Sir?'

The major turned, casually acknowledging my salute. 'Yes, Lieutenant.'

'I was wondering, sir, if the men will be needing their full packs? After all, if we're going into the fray they'll simply weigh us down.'

Major Marriot looked at me curiously. 'You haven't heard, have you?' Whereupon it became evident that Stiles's tip-off was about as reliable as the rest of him.

'We took the Sugar Factory and Courcelette yesterday,' he said, grinning broadly.

'We did?'

Nodding he went on to explain. On the far right of the Corps front the 2nd Division had captured the Sugar Factory and the series of trenches behind it so quickly that it was decided to push on that afternoon. By day's end, General Turner's men had succeeded in capturing the village. It was quite a coup. More than that, really. Courcelette was close to a mile past our starting line, up the road towards Bapaume, and the approaches and the village had been stiffly defended. It had taken two months of bloody fighting before the Aussies succeeded in grabbing Pozières, and Pozières was only two miles from the British lines of July 1st.

'That's wonderful news, sir,' I enthused. 'So I gather we won't be needed anymore?'

'It is good news. But don't get too carried away, Lieutenant. Someone will have to relieve the 2nd Division. If that's us, we'll be needing those packs. The Boche won't take this sitting down, I can assure you.'

In that he was right, of course. The Germans, if what I'd seen at Mouquet Farm was any indication, would be throwing everything they had at Courcelette.

Dundas saw it similarly when I met up with him. The initial heady thrill of the news proved fleeting. 'Holding the new line is going to be no fun at all,' he said. 'Fritz is sure to make life miserable. You realize in addition, Mac, Mouquet Farm, Thiepval and most of the ridge are still in enemy hands?'

The grin I'd been wearing melted away. 'In other words, holding a trench may be the least of our concerns?'

'Don't get me wrong, it's wonderful news.' He paused. Roy Dundas with his thin clean-shaven features, strawberry-coloured hair, and the mildest, soft-spoken manner was nothing like you'd picture the quintessential soldier to be. Most of them had already fallen, certainly the ones who'd arrived in the first contingent like Dundas and I. But ironically few who looked the part were half the soldier he was. I liked Dundas not for his soldierly qualities but for his wit and his honesty. We'd known each other for what seemed like forever. 'I think this is only the beginning for the Corps,' he went on. 'Don't you?'

'Put like that there's not much I can say,' I replied. 'Whatever happened to basking in the moment? You're always accusing me of being the sourpuss.'

'You're right… I think it's rubbing off.'

We continued on down the dirt lane in the direction of Albert. In the distance echoed the sound of shellfire, neither heavier nor lighter than it ever was, none of it directed at the village. It was dry for a change, the air cool and crisp, the nip of autumn to it. Several observation balloons could be seen in the sky. They were ours almost certainly, for darting amongst them and venturing off Fritz's way to take a peek while the weather cooperated were aeroplanes of the Royal Flying Corps. Compared to the Salient that was one of the things that surprised me most about the Somme – just how many of our aeroplanes there were. It shouldn't have done, because for many months men and material had streamed south in preparation for the great attack. Nothing was being spared for the offensive that many had hoped would end the war.

Dundas and I had an hour before dinner and loitering around the weary desolation of the Brickfields didn't hold much attraction. Albert was not a pretty sight either; there wasn't a building that didn't exhibit the traces of war, but it was a sight better than anything to be found in the old factory grounds. Near the centre of the village we clambered over the Ancre on a stone bridge broken by shells, the river beneath little more than a trickle – I would scarcely have noticed it were it not for the sign announcing its presence – and headed for the crossroads and the basilica.

Approaching the Bapaume road, I was surprised at the traffic. Most of it came from the left, from the northeast. Small groups of soldiers in dusty olive green trundled along, no more than a half-dozen at a time, some of them visibly nursing wounds. Then came longer winding rows, two abreast, of German prisoners, all clad in field grey and caked in mud with an icing of whitish-grey chalk, many wearing their characteristic round, cloth trench caps. A few had helmets, the new iron *Stahlhelm*. Unlike our own fish bowls, these were molded over the ear, which seemed a sensible construction. The prisoners made a downtrodden impression. There were ambulances too, most of them motorized, hastening with an audible impatience to the clearing stations in the rear. The stunning victory at Courcelette had not come without cost.

Beside us Fanny seemed little perturbed by the commotion. She'd seen worse, no doubt.

'What in Heaven's name is *that?*' exclaimed Dundas.

There was no question to what he was referring. Lumbering down the road towards us was a mammoth steel behemoth, rhombus in form, its carapace daubed in a motley pattern of drab earthen tones. It was taller than me and probably as long as two lorries parked end-to-end. Huge tracks to either side were wrapped around its entire length, propelling it slowly forward in a cacophony of clanks and rattles and the coughing rumble of a powerful engine.

'I have no idea,' I replied.

We stood and gaped as the monster rumbled past. White smoke bellowed from its topside and it smelled strongly of gasoline. *HMLS Crème de Menthe* was stencilled on the rear in white letters. A large training wheel trailed incongruously behind, although it appeared to be broken.

'Whatever it is,' I said, 'I'm glad it's on our side. Did you see all those guns sticking out?'

Dundas clucked in agreement. 'With any luck we'll have a few of those helping out when our turn comes. They might be useful.'

22nd of September, 1916
Near Courcelette, France

The next day I breathed a sigh of relief when I heard that 3rd Division had taken Mouquet Farm. If I'd had my wits about me I would have realized they'd find something else for us to do.

Sure enough, a day later the 1st Division relieved the 2nd near Courcelette. Three more days were to elapse before it was the turn of the 10th Battalion. The orders arrived in the person of Sam Stiles. It wasn't the only news he brought.

'One more thing, MacPhail, as of now you're attached to C Company. 11 Platoon is yours,' he said.

I was of two minds about this development; pleased to finally have a platoon of my own, even if I suspected it was because my predecessor had departed on leave. About the timing I was less certain. The prospect of a spell in the line at Courcelette held few attractions and apparently I was to do it in command of fifty men I barely knew, and with no time to prepare. I had one other concern. 'What company are you assigned to, Captain?' I asked.

'C Company, of course.' He looked guileless enough. There was no overt indication he'd arranged the whole thing simply so he could have me at his beck and call – although I had my suspicions.

On the way to the trenches that night we passed masses of artillery lined up almost wheel-to-wheel at Sausage Valley near La Boisselle. Otherwise little had changed. It was the same bleak featureless wasteland of a week earlier. At Pozières we turned off onto the little road that passed by Kay Dump and headed in the direction of Mouquet Farm. Just past the cemetery we went northeast again up Tom's Cut, a large communications trench, passing through Piccadilly Circus and along a sunken road towards the Fabeck Graben Trench. Instead of relieving the 1st Division we were to relieve a battalion of General Lipsett's 3rd Division. They'd had a tough go of it apparently.

I knew General Lipsett after a fashion, from when he was my brigade commander, but few others in the division aside from DuBois.

In no time the Corps had gone from two divisions to four; and with all the reinforcements most faces were new. The war carried on even if the old originals didn't.

Past Fabeck Graben, which cut from east to west across the front, the high embankments on the sides of the sunken road began to level off. At that precise moment, right as we emerged into the open, the German barrage came thundering down.

'Keep going fellows,' an officer in the lead echelons shouted.

When the first shell landed the long line of men ahead wavered but kept going, obediently following orders. Three other shells went off. They were dangerously close to the road and in near unison, the flashes so bright and unexpected that I blinked. The air smelled of battle, the atmosphere completely transformed. There were more shouts. And more blasts.

'Fall out! Fall out!' I roared. 'Look for cover!'

Amidst the deafening crashes the platoon scattered. Barrages were like that; if for some reason you weren't terrified yourself, you tended to run in pursuit of those who were. Some went left, some went right. I chose left, in the direction of the narrow length of trench astride the road that I had glimpsed earlier. There wasn't much else in the way of cover. All around shells were exploding, more terrifying by night than by day due to the flashes, the noise so overwhelming it was hard to think straight.

I ran for the trench, my heart and my head pounding, five or six others in my wake. It was perhaps 20 yards away. Not far. But it seemed further.

We piled into it, mindful only of the blasts that echoed to either side, rushing desperately from the one that had blown at our heels. It was little more than a ditch, but even a ditch offered reasonably good protection against the shrapnel and the flying shell fragments. It was another matter entirely if a shell landed too close. Shortly another handful of men joined us. Then a few stragglers appeared, by which time I reckoned there were roughly a dozen men assembled, close to a quarter of the platoon.

'What should we do, sir?' asked one of them. The lad was a barely a week at the front and seemingly oblivious to the fact he might not make it to a second week if he didn't duck, close his trap and stop gawking.

'For Christ's sake, get your head down,' I snapped. 'Listen to the corporal. He'll tell you what to do.'

The corporal was familiar to me. He was a dependable man and I thought rather highly of him. Once, back in the Plugstreet trenches, Wiley had cleaned me out at poker. But he hadn't made an ostentatious show of it as he might have done. Ever since I'd shunned poker, and seldom carried much money. I touched now at the small bulge in my breast pocket, a nervous tick I'd had of late.

As the barrage was moving off I rose up on my elbows, got to my knees and looked over. I could see I'd caught his eye. 'I'd better go find the rest,' I said. 'You keep a watch on this bunch.'

BOOM!

The ground shook and dirt showered over us. Through the dust and the darkness, I heard Wiley's measured words. 'If I were you, sir, I'd wait a bit. No sense stepping into that.' When it cleared I saw him watching me, the bowl of his helmet covered in dirt, his face placid and calm.

'Yes,' I mumbled. 'Perhaps I should.'

I'd been in plenty of barrages so I really ought to have known better. But I'd never been responsible for fifty men before, and I didn't want said of me what was said of certain officers: the well-dressed ones who dapperly led from behind with a batman in tow. With my nerves settling down, and the initial excitement passed I concluded that nobody would be saying *anything* about me if I stepped in front of a Jack Johnson on my first day in command.

As we lay there in the trench, listening to the storm battering the entire swath of ground between the Chalk Mound and Fabeck Graben, an officer jumped over the parapet, batman in tow. It was Captain Stiles. He looked harried, which was not entirely surprising. For a moment he glanced uncertainly at us cowering against the earthen walls. Then, spotting my uniform, hastened over and crouched down.

I nodded at him and he nodded back. As the fog of war cleared so too did his face.

'MacPhail!'

'I didn't expect to see you here, Captain,' I said.

'I didn't expect it myself. But the major insisted we go up with the men. So here I am.'

'Bad luck,' I replied, doing my best to sound empathetic. 'It's a pretty heavy barrage.'

'You have to get your men going,' said Stiles. 'We have a relief to carry out.'

'You must be kidding. We'd be sitting ducks in the midst of this.' The last words were drowned out by another explosion, this one only thirty feet away.

'I'm not kidding at all, MacPhail.'

'No one is going to be relieved if we all get killed, sir.'

The lines in his face tightened. 'Look. I don't want to be here, so for once would you just do as you're bloody well told.'

'It's suicide,' I protested.

'MacPhail, I thought you understood the pecking order. See the three pips? Look close. I'm a captain. You're a lieutenant. I give the orders. You carry them out. Do you understand?' He glared at me. 'The sooner you do, the sooner I can tell the major.'

Stiles was developing quite a knack for expressing himself in ways I never take well to. Possibly, it was also what he was saying. It may even have been that I was on edge because of the barrage. Either way I'm seldom at my best being bossed around by a twat in a position of authority – it was hard to believe I was into my third year in the army.

'I'm sorry, Captain. If we were discussing paper clips I'd defer to you, but we're not. I know exactly what I'm doing. What I'm absolutely *not* doing is running through a barrage with fifty men for no good reason. We'll wait it out here, then we'll move up.'

Stiles stared at me. Speechless for once. But his eyes were afire.

Suddenly realizing the ramifications of what I'd done, a twinge of nausea swept over me. I may not have liked his manner, but to the army manners were wholly irrelevant when it came to the issue of lawful orders given by a superior officer. The penalty for disobeying one was penal servitude. Or was it death?

'It's not like it makes any difference to the 52nd whether we arrive now, or in an hour's time, Captain,' I said hurriedly. 'Better to arrive whole than not at all, don't you think, sir?'

CHAPTER 5

23rd of September, 1916
Front line west of Courcelette, France

'MacPhail…' Stiles had his mouth open, winding up to unleash what threatened to be a deadlier barrage than the one we were in, when out of the darkness a man tumbled into the trench. He virtually somersaulted over the lip and landed on the bewildered lad who'd accosted me earlier. He was an officer, and clearly wounded.

'Jesus!' exclaimed Stiles.

We moved to take a closer look. The startled young soldier underneath gave the impression of being in worse shape than the officer, although that was visibly not the case for the officer was bleeding rather profusely.

Over his shoulder Stiles murmured, 'It's Major Lawless.'

'Guide from the 52nd is he?'

'Yes and no. He's also their OC.'

As we got down on our knees to see how we might help, Stiles motioned that I should take his spot. Heaven knows why. There were several reasons I'd chosen to go into law, one of the most important being that it wasn't medicine. Dissecting frogs in high school biology had been a harrowing experience, though at that time I was blissfully unaware it would pale beside what life in later years brought. Stiles, on the other hand, probably figured that if the Officer Commanding the 52nd died he could always blame it on me… on top of disobeying orders.

Major Lawless was in a bad way but didn't appear to be dying. After we'd extricated the last limb of the hapless private underneath, I did the only thing I could think of, recalling my mother as she tended to my grazed knee after a fall from the bicycle. I removed his tie and shoulder belt, and began unbuttoning his tunic and shirt.

'A dressing,' I hissed at Stiles. 'I need a dressing.'

He took his time doing it, but eventually found one and handed it over, which I then applied to the major's shoulder. 'You'll be fine, sir,' I assured the major.

Gamely the major attempted to speak, however only a gurgling cough emerged. At the effort he grimaced.

'That's alright, sir. Save your energy.'

We had made the major as comfortable as possible with his back to the trench wall when two stretcher bearers turned up. Major Lawless, as I'd correctly diagnosed, had been hit in the right shoulder. However, he was having great difficulty breathing.

'I think he got it in a lung,' I heard one of the bearers mutter to the other.

By the time they put on a fresh dressing, injected him with something or other, and had him ready for the trip to a dressing station, I'd almost forgotten about Stiles. More to the point, Stiles appeared to have forgotten about me. I knew that wouldn't remain so.

Bracing myself I took a deep breath. Then I went over to him. He sat on a wooden stool being administered to by his batman. 'Captain,' I said cautiously, 'I think it's safe to move now. The barrage appears to be lifting.'

The batman was dabbing furiously at Stiles's outstretched sleeve with a white handkerchief. Both looked up. 'Get on with it then, MacPhail,' Stiles snarled. 'It took you bloody long enough.'

I called out to Corporal Wiley and after a lot of running between shell holes, and from ditch to ditch, we finally assembled the platoon. There were several casualties in the battalion. Given the intensity of the shelling I was surprised there weren't more.

By 3.00 a.m. the relief was complete and I detailed Wiley and Sergeant Hatfield to make a duty roster. Then instead of diving into the nearest dug-out and going to sleep as I ought to have, I set off down the trench in search of Dundas.

'You *are* aware he could have you arrested? There's a decent chance he still might. What on earth were you thinking, Mac?'

'That's the problem, I wasn't thinking. And when I did it was too late.'

Dundas was holding himself erect with one hand on a wooden post by the dug-out entrance, the other rubbing his forehead, which he was shaking wearily back and forth. He looked exhausted.

'Admit it. You're still peeved Stiles got your sergeant's stripe back in the Salient, aren't you?' he said. 'For Pete's sake, let it rest. You're a lieutenant, Stiles is a captain, and the whole thing is ancient history. You'll just have to live with the fact he has far better connections, a somewhat higher rank, and considerably nicer boots.'

I had the feeling Dundas wasn't taking me entirely seriously. 'Perhaps,' I said. 'But let me tell you what really bothers me about Sam Stiles, beyond the fact he's almost gotten me killed more than once. He likely would have succeeded this time if I hadn't said anything.'

Dundas groaned. 'Can't this wait 'til morning?'

I ploughed on. 'I always had this bizarre notion that a man earned his rank, not just in the army but in life. In the army we respect a rank because it's supposed to mean something. Not that someone's pa happens to know the minister allowing him to cavort around like a modern day Caesar with a Sam Browne belt, a revolver stuck in it, and the finest calfskin leather on his feet.'

'Mac, you have no idea what Stiles has done. Maybe he earned his promotions the hard way.'

'From sergeant to captain? Fifty miles behind the lines? Right. Next thing I know you're going to tell me Kaiser Wilhelm's men ended up in Belgium in 1914 because they took a wrong turn –'

Dundas sighed. 'Mac, it's been a very long night. But if you're looking for advice, my advice is to get some sleep and concentrate on matters at hand. In case you hadn't noticed, there are a few hundred Germans yonder way who'd love to see your head on a post.' He waved in the direction of the Zollern Trench, invisible in the darkness, 200 yards distant to the north. 'And should that not get your attention, a buddy of mine at Brigade tells me they've received warning orders. According to him we're to attack in the very near future.'

25th of September, 1916
Chalk Pit near La Boisselle, France

At the time I'll admit to having thought it a trifle fantastical; the very idea we'd be involved in an attack. We'd barely finished moving into the front-line trenches. But it proved no idle talk on Dundas's part. The next evening word came that we were to be relieved in order to prepare. Unfortunately, Fritz caught sight of the relief winding along in a long column of bobbing helmets and put up an S.O.S. of red flares. For two nights running we dodged a bombardment. That put paid to any feelings of relief I might have had about being relieved.

However we managed it with few casualties. A day later I was listening attentively to Major MacDonald, the OC of C Company, in a dark and dingy dug-out in the Chalk Pit near La Boisselle.

'Gentlemen, we have it easy,' he was explaining, 'we won't be going in with the 5th Battalion in the first waves, but rather to mop up afterwards.'

Which sounded fine on the face of it. On the other hand I'd made a point of carefully reading and rereading the training instructions GHQ had issued in May:

> In many instances experience has shown that to capture a hostile trench a single line of men has usually failed, two lines have generally failed but sometimes succeeded, three lines have generally succeeded but sometimes failed, and four or more lines have usually succeeded.

Thus aware of GHQ's preference for brawn above brains, my concern was that despite Major MacDonald's breezy assurances, the mopper-uppers would probably be in the third and fourth lines of the assault. And MacDonald's words notwithstanding that wouldn't be easy. As GHQ's instructions made abundantly clear, on them the success of the attack would hinge. So either we'd succeed or we'd get killed trying. Alternatively, we might get out with our necks intact only to be blamed for the attack's failure. When I thought about it, there was a fourth possibility – being killed *and* blamed. They were the sort of odds that had led me to give up poker.

The mood in the dug-out after MacDonald's short briefing was remarkably upbeat, so I kept my dark musings to myself. Most of the officers and NCOs of the company were keyed up at the notion of chasing Fritz out of his trenches. But then, not only were they unfamiliar with the tactical precepts guiding our attack, most had never seen any real action. Stiles hadn't either, although he looked glum at the prospect. I think he'd been counting on holding down the Chalk Pit dug-out. However, MacDonald was clear on that score; the entire company was following the 5th in, with the possible exception of the cook, which seemed prudent. Experience had shown that my appetite was never bigger than in the aftermath of an attack.

I was outside studying the map the major had lent me when Dundas appeared. He popped his head out of the dug-out entrance and clambered up the stairs. Seeing me, he ambled over, the heels of his boots kicking up an exhaust of white dust. 'So?' he asked.

'Three trench lines: Zollern, Hessian and Regina. All on high ground,' I said. 'It may only be a 1200-1300 yard walk, but it's ambitious. And that assumes the wire's cut.'

He reached out a hand and I passed him the map.

For the British armies, the geography of the Somme battlefield could be likened to a box, seven miles high by seven miles wide, with us occupying the left side and the bottom, and the Germans the top and the right. In the southwest corner of the box was the village of Albert, with the Bapaume road shooting diagonally upwards to the northeast. Almost six miles further south streamed the Somme River. Astride the river the French Sixth Army was engaged in its own fierce struggle.

3 ½ miles north of Albert a long, low ridge cuts more or less eastwards across the battlefield. It begins at the fortified village of Thiepval, which itself overlooks the Ancre valley to the west and the original British trenches of July 1st. The ridge stretches on for miles, threading between Courcelette and Pozières, all the way to Ginchy and Morval, far to the east. It was for possession of that ridge, high ground and home to the German second line, that we were to fight.

'What do you think? Will they take it this time?' Dundas asked, looking up from the map.

At this I paused, not immediately catching the reference. 'Do you mean the British at Thiepval?' He nodded. 'I hope so, Roy. I sincerely hope so.'

'It's impossible that in three months an entire army hasn't managed to capture that place.'

'Yes, although by all accounts it's a fortress. Don't forget it's not simply Thiepval they need to take. This whole thing has to work like clockwork. If the 11th Division don't capture Stuff and Zollern Redoubts, not to mention Mouquet Farm, Thiepval will be the least of our concerns. I saw Zollern and Stuff you know. They're at the high point of the ridge, high enough that a machine gun can shoot east almost all the way to Courcelette. We'll be enfiladed if they don't grab them.'

Dundas was frowning. 'You mentioned Mouquet Farm. I thought the 2nd CMR captured that more than a week ago?'

'They did. Built trenches all around it. Then handed it over to the Dorset Regiment, who promptly lost the keys to the Germans their very first night in the line. So now they have to start all over again.'

'A muck up in other words,' he snorted. 'Only fitting they get to clean up their own mess.'

'So long as no one mucks up tomorrow,' I said solemnly. 'And there is a very definite chance of that.' Dundas's eyebrows shot up.

'Stiles has been put in charge of my platoon.'

CHAPTER 6

26th of September, 1916
Zollern Trench, west of Courcelette, France

The morning had come cool and clear, a perfect, crisp autumn day. Of other signs of autumn there were none. No majestic trees creaking and swaying to the rhythm of the wind; no showers of leaves cascading down, painted crimson and gold; no squirrels running amongst them, or leaping fearlessly from branch to branch, nor birds cavorting above. Only a blue sky and an endless horizon of shell-pocked dirt, rising slightly as it climbed to the crest of the ridge. Here and there the ground was coloured by chalk or enlivened by the spindly and tortured remains of a tree, or the fenced posts of a line of wire from the enemy trenches that loomed ahead. The land was churned and holed, littered with debris.

As the hours passed, the temperature rose in accompaniment to the sun. An hour before ZERO Hour it was warm and sunny, which was when the artillery bombardment reached a new crescendo. The heavy guns thudded, pounding the enemy positions in Regina Trench and to the rear. Roughly an hour later, on the far side of noon, a quiet order was passed along: 'Fix bayonets!' Then, as the minutes raced past – my watch showed it to be 12.34 p.m. – the massed machine guns of the Corps took up their rattling chatter. More than a thousand yards away, behind Regina Trench, a hailstorm of lead descended, a deadly barrier through which no hurried reinforcements could pass – or so it was hoped.

Machine guns fired like artillery, in arcs above our heads. It was something new. As was the artillery barrage which began a minute later. They were calling it a creeping barrage, a storm front of whirling steel and high explosive. It crept towards the enemy lines in 100-yard leaps, the long rows of infantry to follow closely in its wake. There was absolutely nothing new about the long rows of men. For 150 years the British Army had known nothing else. Rigid lines of men marching shoulder-to-shoulder, forward into war. One line followed by another. In these modern days, soldiers were clad in khaki, not red, and the enemy was Wilhelm, not Napoleon, but the concept hadn't changed a great deal in a century and a half. With a mere year and a half of modern war under my belt, it seemed to me that the strategy was in need of renewal.

From ahead in the kick-off trenches and shell holes, whistles blew. Their shrillness was barely audible above the chatter of the machine guns and the crashing roar of the barrage, the latter so loud my eardrums were ringing.

In the assembly trenches behind the fire trench, the men packed in close were girding themselves, clutching their rifles and exchanging looks and words of false bravado. We were all nervous. Each face as white as the next. I tried to keep it out of my voice. I was the old veteran in their eyes, and an officer no less.

'Move up,' I shouted. The sergeant and Corporal Wiley began shepherding the men forward.

The first wave was already over the parapet, rushing towards the barrage and Zollern Graben. The second wave would leave on their heels, with enough time in between to leave a proper gap between the lines. Then it would be our turn. As I'd feared, we were in the third wave.

I glanced at Stiles. He stood casually, his arms crossed in front, gazing forward as if there were actually something to see, which there wasn't from our position. Taut lean lines to his face, a smart, well-groomed moustache, and a bulbous red nose that seemed a touch out of place. He wasn't tall, nor was he short, but trim and solid. A soldier's soldier. He'd even polished his boots for the occasion, or his man servant had. Mine were coated in a slimy film of greyish-white dust so thick they would have left even Stiles's batman feeling perplexed.

For all his scheming wiles I disliked Stiles less than I let on with Dundas, or so I assured myself, though a voice at the back of my head found this mildly delusional. Stiles was shallow and superficial, the type who never did any of the work but invariably emerged with the air of one who'd led the charge. I hadn't lied when I said he'd almost gotten me killed… more than once in fact. Yet Sam Stiles had a remarkably infectious charm when the mood came upon him. Usually it was reserved for his chums, though I couldn't help noticing that since his return as a captain his attentions had shifted to other officers, particularly those who might have a say in his further advancement.

Above the reverberating crash and thud of the shells, whistles shrieked. The second wave was going over the top. A moment passed and orders were barked. There was a clattering of equipment and a shuffling of boots, and the company moved forward cursing and fumbling. Strands of communication wire that had come loose from the trench walls caught on rifles and webbing.

Then our turn arrived. Stiles pivoted and caught my eye. I looked down, studying my wrist, watching the seconds tick past. Time seemed to slow interminably and I was conscious of the thumping in my chest, my forehead pulsing in tandem, much faster than the rotation of the thin little hand. I followed it on its steady relentless journey, until it pointed due north. At that moment I looked up at Stiles and nodded, an exaggerated up and down bowing of my head so there would be no mistake. I think I said something as well. He blew at his whistle, his face reddening. Other whistles sounded.

It was a mad scramble. I sprang onto the fire-step on the heels of the man in front. Rifle in hand I pulled myself over the parapet and onto my feet.

The blue sky was now pocked with smoke. Shrapnel shells were bursting in mid-air, and a picket line of white and black plumes, the eruptions too numerous to count, marked out Zollern Graben 300 yards distant. Red flares scurried into the air. Very soon the barrage would move on.

Hurriedly, the company assembled into a long row and began moving forward; dogs straining at their leashes. Sergeant Hatfield was bawling at one group to hold the line. He knew what to do, so I ignored him and concentrated on what lay ahead. There was the crackling of small arms fire but not many machine guns. If you've ever been at the wrong end of an MG-08 it's a sound you don't tend to forget. Fortunately, those I heard were some distance to the left. From Zollern and Stuff Redoubts, I guessed.

I didn't think we had much to fear from those two redoubts, not quite yet at any rate. With the 11th Division storming dead at them, and the 8th Battalion advancing between us and the Brits, Fritz would have his hands full for a spell.

The waves of 5th Battalion men were visible in front, two extended rows of figures that seemed to roll up and down like a piece of rope caught in an ocean swell as they advanced across the age-old folds in the earth, and the countless shell holes carved more recently. The sniping had thinned out the ranks of the first wave quite considerably.

We were less than halfway to the trench when the first wave disappeared from sight. They'd reached their objective. The air was filling with smoke, which drifted back from the barrage and swirled around us; harsh and acrid it bit at the throat. The ground was littered with bodies, some of whom were wounded. We passed by without pausing.

The last 50 yards we took at a run, or as much of a run as we could manage across the pulverised ground. Everyone's blood was up and it was as well it was, for the enemy counter-barrage came thundering down with a crash to the rear. It had taken them almost ten minutes. They were late.

By the time we reached Zollern Graben the first two waves of the 5th Battalion had merged. With the exception of Regina Trench, Zollern was one of the longest in the entire German second system, stretching all the way from Courcelette to Thiepval. The survivors of the first two waves stood in the trench, readying themselves to race onwards to Hessian Trench. The mopping up was to be left in our hands.

Upon reaching the trench, the company fanned out left and right. I went left with Stiles and the others from the platoon. It was unusual to have a captain in command of only fifty-odd men, especially as several companies four or five times that size were being commanded by mere lieutenants. Furthermore, Corporal Wiley had told me that the OC insisted I tag along. Two officers in a platoon was equally strange. For this Major MacDonald had his reasons, no doubt. The lack of any relevant experience on Stiles's part being an obvious one. So, with his three pips Stiles led, and I with my two tried to make sure we didn't screw up.

To a casual observer, or the average red-tab from the staff, that might sound rather easy in a trench that had already been captured. It certainly looked captured. The trench was in bad shape from the artillery bombardment, whose devastating effect was underscored by the sight of dead German soldiers, barely recognizable as such, sprawled in the dirt. However, when a barrage descended on an enemy line or threatened to do so, most of the garrison would have fled to the deep dug-outs that they were such masters at building. Until the barrage stopped. Then they would re-emerge, rifles and machine guns in hand, eager to use them.

On this occasion Zollern Trench was occupied before they had had the chance to come up. The few remaining snipers, and sentries sent out to test the post-barrage waters, lay crumpled on the ground. Bayonet wounds for the most part. But the ones in the dug-outs would be chomping at the bit, aware the trench was occupied and crowding nervously around the steps and ladders, peering up. They'd be anxious to leave their cramped underground confines, perhaps thinking of springing a surprise from behind – with the attackers lined up on the parados looking north. The smarter of them, and the more experienced, would also be a trite fearful, lest we catch them below like fish in a barrel. Which was more or less my plan.

'Get your bombs ready,' I told the assembled men, 'Single file. Two men with bombs, then two bayonet men, then two bombers. And so on. If the dug-out's occupied throw a bomb or two and keep going. The rest of us will be behind you. Whatever you do, don't stop. Leave the prisoners where they are. We'll sort it out later.'

'Sir, can you pass your bombs to the boys in front?' I asked Stiles, and I passed ahead my own so he wouldn't think I was accusing him of not knowing what to do – although I don't think he did. The operational orders dictated that we were to carry two Mills bombs each, in addition to 170 rounds of small arms ammunition, rations, sandbags, haversacks and a full water bottle. The orders hadn't explicitly stipulated how we were to fill the water bottle. It was a near certainty Stiles's was filled to the brim with the treacly dark rum he'd expropriated from a SRD jar. His breath was what gave him away. If the bombs ran out, we could always empty the bottle down a dug-out hatchway and throw a match down after.

'Hang on, MacPhail. Shouldn't we wait for support from one of the other platoons?' asked Stiles.

I shook my head. 'No, sir. We're first in line and we have to move.' Stiles looked uncertain. 'I've seen this before,' I said. 'There's no time to waste. We have to consolidate before they know what hit them.'

'Fine,' he grumbled. 'It's on your head, MacPhail.'

It was not entirely the wholehearted support I was looking for, but it would have to do.

I turned to the excited faces behind. 'Let's clear the trench, boys.'

The sergeant and the corporal looked first at Stiles, who slowly nodded, then at me.

'What are you waiting for?' I snapped.

We dumped the haversacks and set off at fast trot – still a little slow for my taste – but the men in the lead were understandably reticent about charging pell-mell down an enemy trench, even though I had told Wiley that was precisely what I expected. Of course they were the ones who would be caught on the proverbial wire if we ran into a party of Fritzs. But I wasn't kidding with Stiles or the corporal; speed was essential. Every second counted. If the enemy emptied his dug-outs we'd be in a scrap I wasn't sure we could win. Better to bomb them out, like rodents in their holes.

'Faster!' I shouted, impatient now.

The dull bang of a grenade went off, just ahead.

Rounding the traverse I saw whispers of smoke floating up from a dug-out.

Wiley was in front, looking back over his shoulder, not convinced this had done the trick. And it may not have done. However the men behind would deal with it. 'Keep going!' I shouted. 'Move it, Wiley.'

We'd gone more than fifty yards east, past several dug-outs, the lads bombing with enthusiasm, when a machine gun began to zip. *TUF-TUF-TUF.* A long burst that I felt in my chest. It came from around the next bend. The firing stopped. I kept going.

The German gunner and his assistant were on the fire-step, almost level with the parapet, and had been able to swivel their gun around just far enough to catch the lead men as they rushed round the bend. Two of ours were on the ground, including Corporal Wiley. He lay a couple of strides further, in a mangled heap, riddled with bullets. The leading two bombers had made it past on the strength of their speed and surprise. But by then the gunner had his finger on the trigger. Veteran of countless battles, and a good guy to boot, Wiley hadn't had a chance.

One of the bombers stood fifteen feet away, dazed, uncertain what had happened. The other was bounding up the fire-step towards the wall of sandbags and the gunners, his rifle still strung over a shoulder. He could easily have thrown a bomb but he had other plans. The German gunners were scrabbling for a weapon, aware that the machine gun was of no use anymore. It was simply the wrong angle; they were pointed at eight o'clock and he was coming from four. Then I saw a pistol emerge.

'Hey!' I roared at them and I saw the heads spin back to eight o'clock. The bomber was yards away, still fumbling with his rifle, defenceless. I leapt towards them, almost tripping on the fire-step, but the momentum kept me going. I had the Lee-Enfield firmly in two hands, chasing the gleam of the bayonet.

At the very last moment, the gunner shouted '*Kamerad!*' and threw manacled arms into the air. A pistol, an instant too late in making the same traverse as his head, tumbled out of upturned hands. There was a loud *clang* as it dinged the machine gun on the way down.

I had already thrust the rifle forward, my shoulder well into it. The gunner didn't have a chance. He knew it and I knew it. His commander must have known it as well as he'd been chained and padlocked to his post. The gunner's mate, equally chained, took a thrust from the bomber, who'd finally untangled his rifle. He sagged forward. There was no denying their devotion to duty. So why the chains?

By the time I reflected on the cruel absurdity of the situation, and caught my breath, the trench behind was filled with men.

Exasperated, I barked, 'Don't just stand there. Keep going!'

One man didn't move. It was Stiles. He was looking at Corporal Wiley and the other soldier sprawled face first on the battered duckboards. I recognized the soldier. It was young Fritz Duncan from Point 77. Slowly Stiles raised his head and his eyes met mine, accusingly. He didn't say anything. He just stood there. Then I saw his head shake slowly back and forth. Still he didn't say anything. He didn't have to.

Uneasily I gulped.

Several minutes later a winded Sergeant Hatfield reported back. He addressed himself to me in the absence of Stiles, who had returned down the trench to ensure there weren't any 'hiccups'. 'We've cleared our portion of the trench, sir. In fact, we ran into D Company,' he said, grinning. D Company was lending a helping hand to the 8th Battalion on our left. It was most excellent news.

All things considered it had gone smoother than I had expected. For a second I thought guiltily about Wiley and Fritz Duncan. But with an effort I pushed that thought from my mind; our casualties were light. The 8th was on our flank and we held Zollern all the way to the right boundary with the 15th Battalion. Furthermore, I counted 70 prisoners.

In the absence of escorts we told the prisoners to carry our wounded and pointed them in the direction of Fabeck Graben, to pick their way back – no small feat given that their countrymen were shelling the ground in question and our rear lines as well. We had amassed a considerable pile of stick grenades, ammunition, rifles and other equipment. The bombs were a particularly welcome prize. I'd seen more than one attack fail after the supply ran out.

'Fill your pockets,' I told the first man from the platoon I saw.

He looked at them sceptically. 'They work the same as ours,' I assured him. 'It's just a long wooden stick with a bomb on the end. A potato masher. Pull the string and chuck it. Surely you must have thrown sticks when you were a kid?' At this he nodded and grinned. 'See. I knew it. A natural talent.'

Dundas turned up at my side and I was glad to see him. But then Stiles was in my face demanding a report. Major MacDonald appeared just as I was getting started. That did spare the effort of a repeat performance. Worse, I could have been standing two paces back while Stiles made a Maconochie stew of my words in his own report to the major, a weak broth full of things you couldn't identify. This way

I could swing the narrative a little in my favour before Stiles poisoned the well. MacDonald listened attentively, asking no pointed questions. This led me to think he was reasonably satisfied, so I asked one of my own.

'Sir. How is the attack on Hessian progressing?'

MacDonald rubbed at his chin. 'Touch and go, I'm afraid. They lost a lot of men going in. I expect they will be needing some help.' He turned to Stiles. 'Captain, I want you to stand by with the platoon.'

The only possible response to such a request being, 'Yes, sir,' which Stiles dutifully gave. He frowned, however, when the major turned to leave.

I stood primly before him. I kept my mouth shut as Dundas always advised, awaiting his orders. 'You heard the man, MacPhail. Get on with it. If you're lucky you may find an Emma Gee to rush.'

Once Stiles pushed off, Dundas looked at me quizzically. 'Emma Gee to rush?'

'We lost Corporal Wiley and Private Duncan to a machine gun,' I explained. 'Stiles is convinced I unnecessarily rushed things. On top of which he's still peeved about that time when we were shelled during the relief and I refused his orders.'

'Did you? Rush things?'

'What do you think? Fritz wasn't going to stand around picking his nose while we organized a leisurely mid-day stroll down his trench. I did what needed to be done. Whatever Captain Sam thinks.'

Dundas grimaced.

Before I could ask him about the significance of that, Major MacDonald reappeared, breathing heavily. He'd been running. His orders to us were brief and tersely delivered, but not unexpected. He left immediately in search of the next platoon.

Whereupon I shrugged resignedly at Dundas. We'd speak soon enough when this was all over. In the meantime duty called.

CHAPTER 7

26th of September, 1916
Hessian Trench, west of Courcelette, France

The first thing Major MacDonald had said was unambiguously good news; Hessian Trench was captured. But at the urgent request of the 5th Battalion he was ordering three platoons forward, including 11 Platoon, to help consolidate. It was a quarter to two in the afternoon. A mere seventy minutes had elapsed since the attack began and already we'd captured the second objective, an advance of 800 yards. However, we weren't done yet by any means.

Back in relief I'd calculated that since the Big Push began the daily average advance of the British armies was less than 80 yards. If anything that was an optimistic estimate. Therefore, despite the anxious impression the major made, it struck me that things were going swimmingly, at least by the standards of the Somme. This idea solidified in my mind when it was discovered that Captain Stiles was nowhere to be found. 11 Platoon – his platoon – stood assembled and waiting.

We couldn't afford to wait long, so we left without him, leaving me chuckling at the thought of how he would deal with this in his post-battle report; the commander gone missing while his platoon trooped into action. Of course, if we didn't make it back he would be the one chuckling.

500 yards distant, on the far side of the first of two roads that wound

northwest from Courcelette to Grandcourt, was Hessian Trench. In between was another depressing swath of upturned dirt pitted with huge holes, broken stones, wilting fence posts and decapitated trees.

We reached the trench in less than ten minutes – slow by the standards of a town dweller bustling along a paved sidewalk, astoundingly rapid by the standards of a shell-torn Picardy. That we were so quick owed everything to the absence of gun fire. And the disquieting thought that it might not last. The gunfire I did hear was far to my left, from the direction of the two redoubts. Behind us came the steady thump of shells punishing Zollern Graben, the Germans evidently aware it was no longer theirs.

Barely into Hessian Trench and a captain from the 5th Battalion beckoned to me. 'Lieutenant, can you take your platoon and assist D Company?'

'Yes, sir,' I replied. 'Is there a problem?'

'We're some distance ahead of the 8th Battalion. Our left flank is completely in the air.'

'I see. So, it's best if we hurry?'

The captain wiped his grimy hand on a grimy brow and said, 'Yes, if you would?'

Hastening down the trench to the west, I realized the captain's words had also left in the air the question whether the open flank meant immediate trouble, or only potential trouble. With a degree of relief I discovered it was the latter.

D Company had completed the clearing job. The prisoners were being relieved of their weapons and herded into small groups, the task of consolidation already begun. A runner tooled off to request additional reinforcements and a machine gun or two. We started to dig in as well, helping throw up a block to keep the Germans at bay until the 8th Battalion could take the adjoining section.

There was one other issue that loomed large, and soon I was gathered with the other officers and NCOs to discuss it: the final objective, Regina Trench. Actually, there was little discussion involved.

'We're going to send some patrols ahead first,' announced the commander of D Company, 'to see the lay of the land.'

The lay of the land seemed fairly clear to my eyes, slightly uphill to the crest of the ridge with Regina Trench on the reverse slope, a continuation of the same bleak and shell-turned fields we'd walked across all day. 350 yards of mud, but drier today than it had been. Naturally what the captain intended was to reconnoitre the trench, on account of it being on the far slope, and consequently out of sight.

Then the captain pulled the pin on a bomb and tossed it my way – figuratively speaking.

'Lieutenant, I'd like you to accompany the patrol. You have some experience, I understand.'

I couldn't deny that. Although the experience had taught me that such experiences were best not repeated. 'Yes, sir,' I said. There was no need to say more. The captain nodded his approval. He wasn't to know that the mask of stoic imperturbability I was wearing was at total odds with my gut.

Twenty minutes later I found myself crouched in a deep shell hole a hundred feet from a fenced line of wire so wide and dense it could have kept out the entire Reserve Army. Behind it was another line, equally thick: coils and coils of the stuff. As the 5th Battalion plus C Company were but one miniscule part of General Gough's Reserve Army this portended little good.

Impossibly the sun was blazing down. It didn't look in the least like a day for war. The sky to the north was a pristine robin's egg blue, untainted by the steady crash of German shells falling unabated on Zollern Graben. You could see forever. Almost all the way to Vimy Ridge to the north where the guns pounded night and day. Aeroplanes droned over in lazy buzzing passes and four sausage-shaped observation balloons – ours I reckoned – ponderously kept the guard off near Auchonvillers and Mesnil to the west. But as it was a day for war, I kept my head very low.

There were five of us. A lieutenant, two sergeants, a corporal and myself. Each in a hole of his own, all staring at the swathes of wire entanglements and the parapet of Regina Trench not far beyond. Prime targets for any sniper who'd foregone his midday snooze.

The good news was that there didn't appear to be many Fritzs in the trench, a few bucket helmets at most. Although as I'd lectured the men of the platoon only this morning, it only takes one. Nevertheless,

Regina Trench looked ripe for the taking – were it not for the wire, the *accursed* wire.

Lying there, my chin in the mud – I'd rubbed some on brow and cheeks for good measure – I methodically moved the field glasses from left to right, searching for gaps. You could tell it was autumn for the sun was already shaking its limbs prior to calling it a day. Fortunately, it was off to my left (the west), and hence I didn't need to worry about a reflection from the glasses giving me away.

Shells had breached holes in the wire barricade in places. But the gaps were narrow, and there weren't many of them. One might have been enough for a well-trained party of raiders able to zig-zag a passage by night through the entanglements, but not for an entire battalion. Certainly not for a battalion lined up in rows of a hundred, one man abreast the other, all stumbling across the uneven terrain knowing but one direction – forward. And definitely not in daylight.

In frustration I sighed and glanced over at the lieutenant. Eventually he lowered his own glasses and caught sight of me watching. He threw his hands out to either side, palms open – the universal gesture for "what now?" I stabbed my finger over my shoulder a couple of times. *The rear.* He nodded.

We made it nearly 100 yards back up the slope towards the ridge-top when a rifle cracked. Instinctively I dove to the ground. Vaguely aware of the din from the guns I awaited a second shot. Hearing none I cautiously glanced around. The others weren't far off and appeared to be unharmed.

A hand signal to motion that we carry on. We took it in short sprints, all at once, calculating that multiple targets would confuse a single man with a carbine. Diving from one hole to the next, a quick pause to breathe, and then another frantic scramble and a dive ahead. Invariably a shot came, but each time five men got up again and scampered a few yards further.

At the crest of Pozières Ridge we passed out of sight of Regina Trench. Only then did I notice that the lieutenant was cradling his left arm in his right.

'You alright?' I asked him.

'Got it in the arm,' he said, gritting his teeth. 'It's okay. I'll make it.'

I walked beside him to be certain, and we discussed what we'd seen.

Approaching Hessian Trench, the two sergeants and the corporal joined us. The consensus was unanimous.

As the lieutenant was being tended to by a stretcher bearer, I was the one to give the report. And as the captain was eager to pass the report along, I accompanied him to the battalion HQ at an unfinished German dug-out near the Chalk Mound. Due to an unforeseen change in landlords the building efforts below had seen a delay, resulting in the 5th Battalion staff having to encamp on a steep, still unfinished stairway in lieu of better. Coming from farming communities like Brandon, Moose Jaw and Red Deer, I suspect some of them found this the height of luxury. The battalion OC, Lieutenant-Colonel Dyer, deftly ignored the surroundings and listened patiently to my report. He did interrupt once or twice.

'You say the trench was lightly manned, Lieutenant MacPhail? I find that hard to believe.' The colonel was gently pulling at his moustache. The moustache enveloped his upper lip as completely as the wire had Regina Trench and any more yanking looked like it might cover his mouth completely. A nervous tick I expect. 'Are you certain?' he asked.

'Absolutely, sir. One of the tell-tale signs is the number of sentries. In the stretch we observed there were only a couple even though our attack has been ongoing for several hours. Nor did I see a single officer. No, sir, I'm convinced Regina Trench is all but empty.'

'Remarkable,' said the colonel. 'However, your patrol found no breaks in the wire?'

'Not entirely, sir. There were a few spots where one line or the other appeared to be cut, but there was no straight path through. Definitely not that. If the plan, sir, is to send in three waves of men it won't take many Boche to make Regina Trench a very costly breakwater. I wouldn't want to imagine what would happen if they had a machine gun or two.'

'No, indeed, Lieutenant,' murmured the colonel. 'No indeed. Thank you.'

By the time I'd had a bite to eat, squatting outside chewing my iron rations, the matter had been debated and decided. Colonel Dyer felt the wire would need to be first cut before we advanced, a point of view I could empathize with.

'Besides,' added the officer who told me – with the supreme self-assurance of someone on the staff – 'from Hessian Trench we command the valley and the ridgetop as well as from Regina. We can afford to wait.'

It was typical of many a decision made in the heat of battle. Understandable in the circumstances. Sensible even. Especially as the Imperial 11th Division hadn't come up on the left flank. That left Zollern and Stuff Redoubts commanding the open ground for thousands of yards to the east with their machine guns. Easily within range of any massed charges up the ridge. As to the 5th Battalion there were already hundreds of men down and I don't think the colonel felt they could lose any more. Nevertheless, in the light of what was to come it would prove regrettable. A missed opportunity. A blunder even? Not that any of us, least of all me, realized that at the time. Nor did we have any realistic alternative at hand. It was the sort of thing a certain Prussian general by the name of von Clausewitz had once written about.

However, I didn't dwell upon it and, after hearing what I heard when I reached Zollern Graben Trench *enroute* to the platoon, my thoughts were elsewhere.

'Lieutenant.' A soldier had presented himself in front of me, a grimy, sweat-streaked face from C Company, demanding my immediate attention.

'Yes. Lawson, isn't it?' I felt a surge of pride that at the end of a long day I could still match a name to a face.

'Yes, sir, that's right.' He paused. 'The lieutenant asked me to tell you. He said you would want to know...'

A few hundred yards down the trench a salvo of shells landed.

'What! What would I want to know?' I snapped, eager to be on my way. I'd had quite enough of the German guns.

'It's just this, sir. Sergeant Dundas is unaccounted for –'

CHAPTER 8

26th and 27th of September, 1916
Hessian and Zollern trenches, west of Courcelette, France

My first thought was that it simply couldn't be. Missing? Not Dundas.

He wasn't the type to prance around with the brazen, self-assured airs of a Sam Stiles, but he had a keen eye and an even keener mind – neither of which could be said for Stiles. Moreover, he had a fine-ly-tuned nose for trouble, which so far had kept him largely out of it. He'd gone into the exacting and unforgiving business of banking before the war, fitting in like a sow might in a warm bath of mud. So naturally there had to be a mistake. Perhaps he'd ended up at another spot in the line with a different unit, his platoon as yet unaware of his whereabouts. It wouldn't be the first time that had happened in battle. I took up the idea with Private Lawson.

'Perhaps, sir. Anything's possible. All I know is that the lieutenant sent Sergeant Dundas and a patrol forward to scout out Hessian. He expected they were going to send us forward. The lieutenant was right about that; we're to move up shortly. But it's been hours since the three of them left and the 5th Battalion reported they never arrived.'

'Very strange,' I said. 'Thanks for telling me. I'm sure they'll turn up soon.'

They didn't.

Though I only discovered that early the next morning back in

Hessian Trench, when the lieutenant from Dundas's platoon careered around a traverse and nearly bowled me off my feet. He was scurrying down the duckboards with an urgency that suggested either Fritz was overrunning his little squad, or the company OC had summoned him.

'Sorry, Malcolm,' he breathed, 'I wasn't watching where I was going. I'm on my way to the major.'

'Ah. Then I won't hold you up, but have you heard anything from Sergeant Dundas and squad?'

A brief shake of the head. 'No, not a thing.'

'I was thinking; maybe they veered left and ran into the 8th Battalion? It would be easy enough to do. It's not like there are a lot of landmarks out there.'

'Well, if they did, they're taking their sweet time to report back,' he said. 'That's not at all like Sergeant Dundas.'

'No,' I said slowly, 'You're right, it's not.'

'I think they must have got caught in the shelling. It began about that time, very heavy. We had our heads down in the trench, but out in the open –'

'If they got hit by the shelling,' I protested, 'surely someone would have found them by now?'

'Not necessarily.'

The sad thing was it was the unvarnished truth. One shell at the wrong spot and the wrong time; there would have been little left of Dundas and the other soldiers. Mangled bodies like I'd seen in Hessian Trench, or worse. In that case it would be futile even if you combed the ground with an entire battalion.

The lieutenant excused himself and rushed off. With a weary heart I went back to my duties. During the momentary lull in the shelling, supplies were being brought forward and the wounded sent back. For the most part these duties consisted of jabbing a finger in one or the other direction; muttering a word to a stretcher bearer headed the wrong way. Little thought was required. That was a good thing as my head was buzzing with other thoughts, a gnawing fear having taken root in me. The lieutenant's words about the shelling kept replaying in my mind.

To the rear one of our guns cleared its throat. And then another. It was 11 a.m. The artillery began to bombard Regina Trench in an attempt to destroy the wire. Shortly thereafter the Boche artillery retaliated. By 11.45 a.m. we were being bracketed by high explosive, deafening explosions to either side, dirt raining down from above in thick heavy clods. The ground shook in commiseration.

For the first time I could ever recall I didn't find the barrage so harrowing. There was something oddly liberating in the sensation of standing there, my head cleansed of the ability to think, able only to react. To my right there was a huge *CRASH*. The trench walls gave way and splinters flew. Earth poured in like the sea finding its way through a dike. It swept over the two soldiers sheltering there.

We dug them out with our bare hands, grasping theirs as we unearthed them and pulling for all that we were worth. They emerged dirty and shaken, but alive. The bombardment thundered on. Beside me a man began to shake uncontrollably. He threw off his helmet and clamped his hands to his ears. It was the sound that was the worst. A continuous thumping and banging that drove men mad. Even those who'd lived through endless bombardments could suddenly find themselves losing their nerve. I was too dumbed by recent events to notice any of it.

Eventually the guns slackened off. The German counter-attack everyone expected didn't come. And that night we were relieved by the 1st CMR. It was a disorganised scramble to the rear, each man for himself. While I suppose I should have cared about the disorder, I didn't. At the crossroads at Pozières an army chaplain offered a cup of hot tea and I accepted it gratefully. Then I trudged down the dark road to Albert. Behind me the guns flashed and the star shells lit the ground.

28th of September, 1916
Albert, France

Head in my hands I sat on a rickety old wooden bench on the rue de Bray. We were billeted there, and I was commiserating with myself about Dundas, of whom there was still no word. I half expected he'd turn up in Albert with a big grin and an even bigger story. But by then it was mid-afternoon and there was no sign of either him or the others.

'Ah, MacPhail,' exclaimed a familiar voice.

Two polished calf-high leather boots stepped into view. The owner of the boots sounded like he was rather pleased to see me. As I wasn't doling out rum or other favours this was curious. The boots were curiously familiar as well – the Somme not being the ideal stage to flaunt a new attire, even if a rich merchant father was underwriting the shopping excursions in London. I raised my head to a shiny Sam Browne belt and a spotless tunic.

'What do you want?' I grumbled.

Sam Stiles took it on the chin, even managing a wry grin.

'I was thinking,' he said.

Pointedly I said nothing.

'I have to complete my report today. The OC wants them all on paper this time around.'

'Can't help you there,' I interrupted.

A pause. 'What do you mean?'

'With paper. I don't have any.'

Stiles had the expression of a man completely befuddled. He wasn't a difficult man to befuddle.

'Lost my notepad somewhere between Hessian Trench and Regina Trench,' I said. 'So, no paper. You'll recall it was pretty rough ground there. Oh, no, you wouldn't recall that... would you?'

Without really thinking about it I was working myself into a hole deeper than the Lochnagar crater.

Stiles ignored me. 'Yes, that's sort of what I wanted to talk to you about.' Shiftily he darted his head from left to right like he had something confidential to say.

'Ahh...' I said slowly. It was as if I'd spotted a curvaceous woman in a hobble skirt for the very first time. Unfortunately, there the comparison ended. But I had a suspicion what Stiles was up to.

'Yes, well, if you hadn't dashed off with the platoon,' he said, 'I would have been there with you. But I was preoccupied with other responsibilities.' I raised my eyebrows. 'I'll have you know, MacPhail, it wasn't exactly a day off in Blighty sitting there in Zollern Trench.' Once again I said nothing. If I kept this up it might even become a useful habit.

'It's just...' he continued, searching for the right words.

Helpfully I provided them. 'It's just that the OC and several other officers in the brigade and the division may wonder why you weren't with your platoon in the front line rather than holding down a dug-out in the rear.'

He pulled a face. 'It wasn't exactly the rear,' he said, 'but something like that.'

'Quite a dilemma,' I sympathized.

'Less than you might think,' he replied. An edge came into his voice. 'It's not like your own washing is so bloody spotless, MacPhail.'

I glanced at my sleeve. He had that right. My sleeve was heavily chalked in dust and dirt, underneath which were a few dark matted spots, probably dried blood from the young lieutenant with whom I'd reconnoitered Regina Trench. Barely a few months old and already in tatters.

Stiles shook his head in exasperation.

'Oh!' I said, after a stretch. 'You're referring to that small incident during the relief a while back?'

Stiles nodded gravely. 'Refusing to obey the orders of a superior officer is no "small incident", MacPhail. Most would call it a very serious affair. I could have had you arrested, you know.'

'That has puzzled me a little, I'll admit,' I said. 'Why didn't you?'

'One never knows,' he replied, a smirk beginning to form.

'Yes, I'm beginning to understand. In other words, if I go along with the fiction that you were leading the platoon in Hessian Trench, that small incident between you and I never happened?'

The smirk turned to a grin.

'What about all the men who saw you in Zollern Trench? Surely they'll undermine your story?'

'But they aren't officers,' he said confidently, as if that were the only thing that mattered. It probably was. No corporal, let alone a private, was going to take it up against an officer, not for no particular gain.

'Fine,' I said. 'Write your report however you wish. I won't say a word.'

'Good. I'm glad that's settled. Oh, and in case you were wondering, I won't mention anything about that muck-up of yours that got Wiley and the private dead. Not for the moment, at least…'

The threat hung there like a cloud of gas, and me without a mask.

History was repeating itself. Stiles had pulled the same stunt last year in the Plugstreet trenches, and I became his virtual slave for a month. In addition to all the menial work that fell on my shoulders, my neck was on the line twice as often too: once for him and once for me. I was damned lucky I still had one.

'I already said *fine*,' I snapped. 'What else do you want to hear?'

'To you, MacPhail, it's "*fine, sir*".'

'Whatever.'

'What's with you, anyhow?' he asked.

Grim-faced I glanced at him. Uncertain whether I should reveal what was really bothering me. But I could think of no reason not to.

'Roy Dundas is missing,' I said.

'Dundas…' he said, hesitating. The cogs upstairs were turning over at their usual lackadaisical pace. Finally: 'Oh, that buddy of yours? The sergeant?'

I nodded.

'I'm sure he'll turn up. It's not as if there are many places to go out there in No-Man's-Land.' Then he chuckled at the thought.

I didn't chuckle. There was no point explaining to him that missing was also a euphemism for dead but not yet found.

'Well I'm off,' he pronounced. 'A report to write, you know.' He had the cheek to wink as he said it. 'Oh, and get the platoon assembled. We're marching to Bouzincourt in an hour.'

Before I had a chance to reply he was gone.

'Yes, sir,' I murmured to myself. It began to rain.

CHAPTER 9

1st of October, 1916
Montrelet, France

We spent a couple of days marching. First to Bouzincourt, where we were billeted overnight in an astonishing labyrinth of caves forty feet underneath the village, it being impressed upon us that we should mention nothing of their existence. Then on to Rubempré, and finally to Montrelet and a barn filled with more lice than straw. The marching was tiresome. Thirty miles or more all told, up hills and down, on hard *pavé* roads in full pack and weary feet. The only good thing about it was that with every step we took the front was a step further behind. As an officer I wasn't expected to carry a pack, so that was a saving grace. But it had been quite a month. And it wasn't just my feet that were weary.

In the interim the casualties from the attack on Pozières Ridge had been tabulated. They numbered precisely one third of the battalion roll call a few days previous, regardless that we'd only been "mopping up" in support.

These past weeks at the Somme I'd gotten to know the many new men in the battalion as best I could – in hindsight a futile exercise if ever there was one. While most of those wounded would eventually return to the battalion, others would be bedridden for months, if not longer. There would be new faces to replace those that brief weeks earlier had been new themselves, and yet again new names to learn and new acquaintances to make. It seemed that with every passing day the battalion bore less and less resemblance to the one I'd enlisted in.

Then there were the men who categorically would never return. Like Captain Clinkskill. He joined the 10th Battalion only a few weeks earlier and was buried yesterday. Neither could I help thinking about the other category: the missing. According to Lieutenant Miller, who worked for the adjutant and was in a position to know such things, there were 46 of them. Which seemed a lot for a 700-man battalion that wasn't in the leading waves. Some I knew, some I didn't; one name preoccupied my thoughts when I allowed it to. I asked about him whenever I had the chance. But no one had heard or seen anything.

During the morning church service I went so far as to address my concerns to the supreme commander himself. Though even I felt my appeal lacked a certain credibility. I'd day-dreamed too often during church parade to be mistaken as a devout follower, and after all the Big Pushes there must have been an even bigger waiting list seeking his attention.

Only slightly lower in the army hierarchy was the brigadier. He addressed us after the divine service and spoke of the good work done by the battalion. I'd seen Brigadier-General Loomis on a handful of occasions, but I must confess he hadn't made much of an impression, and I even less on him. Nevertheless, I briefly debated whether I should approach him about Roy's case. Fortunately I came to my senses before I did anything rash. After all, there were hundreds of men in his brigade dead, wounded, or missing. What was one more? Then I heard something that left no room for daydreaming.

'Our divisional commander visiting? General Currie? Are you certain?'

Stiles assured me he was. 'Right after lunch,' he said. 'I was going to have a bite myself, but we'd best see that the platoon is looking sharp. The general's a bit of a stickler as you probably know. We wouldn't want him to be disappointed, would we, MacPhail?'

'No,' I said, '*we* definitely wouldn't want that. I'll get on with it, Captain. Enjoy your lunch.'

Stiles flashed a winning smile. He must have known precisely how I felt about him, but so long as I did as he bid he was remarkably good-natured. Irritatingly so, as if to rub it in.

One thing Stiles wasn't prepared to do was get his own paws dirty – not with me available to pick up the loose ends, and certainly not while lunch awaited – but his intelligence proved spot on the mark this time. Major-General Arthur Currie, commander of the 1st Division, rolled in a couple of hours later in an enormous, mud-caked staff car. He was a big man, as tall as I was at six foot two but with the advantage of several inches in girth, so the size of his staff car owed as much to necessity as rank.

Montrelet itself was not a large place, effectively a mere hamlet and a worn down one at that, nestled in the nape of a wooded valley. It had a two-storey stone Mairie of the sort that endowed every village in France, but not even a church; for that you had to walk a mile down the road to Fieffes. The road came to a T intersection near the Mairie, each branch lined by humble plaster and brick houses, and a smattering of larger farm buildings. Behind the buildings were small irregular plots – one could hardly call them fields – and beyond the plots, the tree line with hills rising to either side. Consequently, there was little room for an entire battalion to muster and parade, even one at less than two-thirds its normal strength. So we did the same thing we had that morning and lined up on the narrow strip of dirt in front of the town hall, the ranks spilling over onto the road. A few elderly villagers watched in curiosity from a safe distance.

I was pleased at our appearance. Someone had found a bristle brush and the last vestiges of mud on boots, puttees and tunics were almost gone, the buttons tarnished but clean, and the rifles well-oiled. Generally I cared little for keeping up appearances, but I'd learned the hard way the importance of a well-oiled rifle. There wasn't a man in the platoon who hadn't heard my thoughts on the subject.

I wasn't particularly concerned therefore when the general, with Major Thomson in tow, halted in front of Captain Stiles and myself. 11 Platoon stood rigidly at attention.

'A fine turnout,' said General Currie.

'Thank-you, sir,' we responded in unison. Army protocol dictated that Stiles alone should have responded, as platoon commander. But other than turning out himself, he hadn't exactly been a bastion of support. I guess this was my way of making that clear. Also I wondered if the general would recognize me.

Currie eyed us seriously. 'What were your impressions of the attack?' he asked.

'Excellent, sir,' piped up Stiles, before I could get a word in edgewise.

I rolled my eyes. I may even have groaned softly. Unfortunately, the general noticed. Major Thomson definitely noticed for he looked ready to put a foot of cold Sheffield steel in me.

'You don't agree, Lieutenant?' said General Currie.

'Well, sir…' I said, hesitating.

'Please, speak your mind, Lieutenant. I value officers who are observant and willing to speak frankly. If we're to improve we must learn from our mistakes, and that begins with an honest appraisal of each operation.'

'Well, sir,' I began, 'the creeping barrage seemed effective, at least initially…'

The general had his hands clasped before him, waiting, unflinching brown eyes fixed on me.

'I was in the third wave, sir, and by the time we all lined up at the tape and got on our way, the barrage was moving on. It looked impressive, but I don't think it could have been that heavy as there was a lot of sniping out front. And at Hessian Trench the barrage was lighter still. The boys had a tough go of it. As to Regina Trench, sir, we didn't stand a chance. With or without a barrage.'

'No? And why do you say that?' The general stepped closer, so that he stood directly in front of me.

'Because I was there, sir. Reconnoitering. And it's a damn shame too, if I may say so. Because when I saw it the trench was virtually unmanned. However the wire in front was still intact. Fence lines of it, with that loose concertina wire dumped on top. Even with a handful of defenders it would have been suicide going in. Not to mention with the 11th Division not up on our left, the Boche machine guns at Stuff Redoubt and along the Grandcourt road would have enfiladed us something terrible.'

The general nodded thoughtfully. I had a suspicion I wasn't telling him anything he didn't already know. The general may have known but it was patently obvious that others in the army didn't – the Reserve Army staff, for instance. I'd heard that prior to the attack they once more assembled the cavalry for the "breakthrough", meticulously mapping out distant objectives. All that work left them no time for petty details like artillery concentration. As a result, most of the strongpoints and the forests of wire were still there when the infantry went in. The cavalry might as well have remained in their stables. But then the Reserve Army's commander, General Gough, was a cavalry-man. So was his superior General Haig. That no doubt explained the choice of priorities.

General Currie was examining me. 'For some reason you seem terribly familiar. Have we met before, Lieutenant?' *He did remember!* Up until that moment he hadn't shown a flicker of recognition.

'Yes, sir. I met you in the Salient in '15 during the gas attacks. In fact, you spoke with me on several occasions.'

Currie began to nod. 'Yes, I thought it must be something like that. I'm afraid I don't recollect your name, however.'

'MacPhail, sir. Malcolm MacPhail.'

His eyes narrowed. 'April last year. You weren't an officer back then, were you, MacPhail?'

'No, sir, I was a private and later a corporal. You were my brigade commander.'

'Yes, well, it's fine to see you, Lieutenant. The battalion did good work on the ridge. And thank you for your observations.' Two steps behind, Major Thomson looked slightly mollified. In any event the daggers in his eyes had disappeared.

I don't recall much else from the inspection, the general's short speech, or the pay parade after that... it wasn't often this war I had a major-general soliciting my opinions.

That evening a soldier appeared at my billet. The officers in the barn had been reassigned to a musty-smelling, albeit more comfortable house down the road. Someone had conjured up two bottles of red wine after dinner and, for the first time in quite some time, I found myself welcoming the prospect of a normal conversation.

'MacPhail!' came a shout. Lieutenant Rutherford of B Company barged through the door and into the kitchen where a group of us were seated round a wobbly round table, the air blue from the smoke and ringing with voices all speaking at once. At the interruption the mouths now clapped shut. Heads lifted. The grandfather clock in the hallway could be heard ticking away the seconds. Behind Rutherford a soldier shuffled into view, cap in hand. Awkwardly his eyes darted around. Recognizing the den into which he'd stepped, he pulled himself up straight.

'This fellow's looking for you,' said Rutherford. Then to the soldier: 'That's him.' Helpfully, he pointed a finger at me. He meant well by it, but it reminded me a little of my days in a courtroom when the witness was asked to point out the accused.

I cleared my throat and straightened my shoulders. 'I'm Lieutenant MacPhail. You're looking for me?'

'Yes, sir.'

The clock's slow ticking filled the silence. *Tick... tick... tick...*

'May I ask why?'

'Oh yes, sir. Major Thomson would like to see you. "Straight away," he said.'

With that the room was no longer quiet, an atmosphere of levity taking its place. 'Shame to see you go, MacPhail, but we'll take good care of the wine. Won't we boys? Good luck with the major, eh.'

Someone chortled.

'Alright,' I said to the private. Pulling myself to my feet I grabbed for my cap. As I passed underneath the lintel of the kitchen doorway a voice behind say, 'Perhaps he's to be promoted?' Whereupon there was a great deal of laughter.

No, I was not going to be promoted. That much was certain. Not at seven o'clock in the evening. And not as a lieutenant who'd only been one since June – a mere four months. It would be something to do with Stiles, I thought. Or maybe Dundas. At the thought of him I felt a pang in my stomach. Any news at this late stage was not likely to be good. Not that no news was any better. I put on a sprint to keep up with the private.

The battalion OC was installed in a farmhouse a hundred yards further up the road, the smell of damp neglect virtually indistinguishable from the house I'd just left.

'Ah, there you are,' said Thomson, distractedly, when I presented myself a minute later. He was seated at a small table in a drawing room, illuminated by the yellow glow from a lantern, a thick sheaf of papers before him. As I watched he dashed off a signature and thrust the paper, without looking, over his shoulder at a soldier who stood waiting. 'That'll be all for the moment,' he said to the man. 'Close the door behind you, would you?' No response was required, and he didn't wait for one; he was already addressing himself to the next sheet.

Gently I coughed. 'You asked for me, sir?'

Thomson ignored me and continued reading. When he was finished he glanced up. 'What? Oh, yes. I'm sorry, Lieutenant. Trying to catch-up on all the paperwork. Applications for leave, new commissions, equipment to be signed for…' He sighed. 'It's enough to wish we were back in the trenches.'

'I wouldn't wish that too hard if I were you, sir.'

'No, I suppose not,' he said, and took a sip from his teacup. He grimaced. 'Oh, bugger,' he muttered, 'the damned thing's cold.' I had some sympathy with the tea; he'd left it waiting at least as long as he'd left me. But outwardly I maintained the look of studious neutrality that is expected of fledgling lieutenants when speaking with their commanding officer. Eventually he spoke again. 'The reason I summoned you, MacPhail, is that I've had several messages from divisional headquarters. We've been warned the division is to go back into the line.'

'So soon, sir?'

'It won't be immediately. In a couple of days I expect. The 2nd and 3rd Divisions attacked Regina Trench today. Unfortunately from what I hear they weren't able to capture it. So I imagine that's more or less what our assignment will be.'

I frowned.

'However, that wasn't the only message. I've been asked to provide an officer to help reconnoitre, which leads me to believe the battalion will most probably be in reserve.' Whereupon the drawn lines of his face softened, and mine relaxed into a broad grin. Reserve wouldn't be so bad.

'As the 10th is one of the battalions which knows the ground it was felt we could offer some useful assistance preparing for the next operation,' he added. 'I've already replied I would send someone tomorrow morning.'

'Well, there are several men you could pick, sir,' I said slowly.

'Actually, a name has already been put forth, Lieutenant.' I felt myself frowning again. 'For some reason yours was the one division came up with.'

'Me! They want me?'

Thomson shrugged. 'Yes. General Currie himself made the request I'm told. It appears he took a bit of a shine to you this afternoon. Heaven knows why.'

'I see,' I said. 'The only explanation I can think of, sir, is that the lines between division and heaven are shelled out at the moment.'

Thomson allowed himself a tepid smile. 'You're to report to Divisional headquarters sharply at 8 a.m., Lieutenant. They're in Canaples at the moment, just down the road.'

'Oh, don't look so grim, MacPhail. I've arranged a car for you.'

I was grateful for the car, although Canaples was only four kilometres away according to the sign outside town, so blistering feet aside I could have walked it with ease. But I didn't anticipate I would be staying at headquarters for long – Regina Trench was summoning me. The battalion might miss the action, but apparently I was not to be so lucky. Which made me think of Dundas.

Normally this would have been the sort of thing I would have talked over with him. He had a calm and reasoned way of looking at the world. He was also the only one willing to sit and listen while I got whatever was eating me off my chest. Without him I'd lost my compass.

I studied the major, hoping he might say something about Roy and wondering whether I should venture to ask. But surely he would have mentioned it had there been news? Nearly six days had passed. However I chose to think about it, it was increasingly difficult not to fear the worst. And to make matters worse, my own immediate prospects were looking none too promising.

Thomson had returned to studying his papers. Sensing my look, he glanced up. 'Oh, that'll be all, MacPhail.' After that I didn't dare ask. I made myself scarce and turned in early.

Had I known I was leaving the 10th Battalion for good I would have sought out the others in the kitchen.

CHAPTER 10

2nd of October, 1916
Canaples, France

The Divisional GSO 2 scratched at the crown of his head and looked puzzled when I was brought before him. He would have looked even more puzzled had Major Thomson not arranged the car for me. The morning was cold, misty and wet, and while I hadn't much experience of visiting divisional headquarters I did suspect a certain decorum was expected, a decorum incongruent with being soaked to the bone and looking more like a drenched trench rat than an officer in the King's army. Thanks to the car, though, I was proper enough.

'MacPhail, you say...?' The staff major mumbled to himself, and went on to flip through some papers, hesitating with each one to wet the tip of an index finger before rifling further.

'Yes, sir. Malcolm MacPhail of the 10th Battalion. I was told to report here by Major Thomson, the battalion OC. He said I was to help out with reconnoitering Regina Trench.'

The major continued to look puzzled – until enlightenment sprang from the page he was holding. 'Ah, of course, that's it,' he said. His eyes rose to meet mine, along the way making a closer examination of the materiel he'd been sent. He didn't comment upon it and continued his discourse without pause. 'Plans have changed, Lieutenant. As your commander suspected our orders are to capture Regina Trench.

However the division will be going in on the right, northeast of Courcelette and closer to the Bapaume road. The 3rd Division on our left will be moving through the ground you're most familiar with. For that reason we've decided to make you a liaison officer between them and us. Silly of me, really, I should have remembered.'

For all the bland innocuousness of the title, a General Staff Officer 2 is an important position. The right hand man to the right hand man of the divisional commander as it were. That he didn't recognize the name MacPhail was not altogether surprising. But I suppose those were the sort of details that a staff officer is expected to know. And monotony aside that sure beat having to crawl through No-Man's-Land on a regular basis.

'I have other matters to attend to but I'll let you know the details as soon as I can,' he assured me and sent me on my way.

That gave me a few hours hanging around headquarters, fantasizing about how swell it was to be a liaison officer mixing with generals and the staff, safe, dry, enjoying my second breakfast of the day, and miles from the front. Then reality intruded and I was given my initial assignment: a nighttime reconnaissance of Regina Trench.

I was mildly apprehensive. And to think that was some days before I heard the bitter tally of the first attack on Regina Trench – 2000 men down for virtually no gain.

3rd and 4th of October, 1916
Regina Trench, northwest of Courcelette, France

The first hint of trouble came from the report of a rifle – not far away. Fifty yards at most, which was pretty much where I'd calculated Regina Trench to be. Even before I heard it I saw the pinprick flash and made like Fanny Durack the instant I did.

Unlike Fanny my own passage to solid ground was unhindered. The ground however was anything but solid, and there was a loud wet *smack* when I landed in the mud in a soldier's rendition of a belly flop. It was all I could do to avoid smashing my chin on the stock of the Lee-Enfield, which I'd been holding crossways with two hands in front before I dived. My chin missed the mark, but with the rifle and my arms outstretched to avoid that danger, it left me with nothing to cushion the blow to body and face… nothing apart from a cold puddle of blubber. As it had rained the greater part of the day, and most of yesterday, and what seemed like all of the day before that, it was less a puddle than a mire.

Wiping the worst of it from me, I peered anxiously to either side, in search of the others.

It was remarkably dark, the moon buried behind thick clouds, and I had to squint before I could make them out. The bowl of their helmets protruded above the shell holes and quickly I counted them off. A second count confirmed there were five, and they were all right, so the bullet had apparently gone wide. But not so far wide that we might be lured into underestimating the danger we were in. One of the sentries, or more likely a sniper, had spotted our mid-night reconnaissance party. If it hadn't been so dark we would have been easy pickings for anyone in Regina in possession of a single good eye and a Mauser.

One of the helmets crawled up next to me.

Another shot rang out.

'Well?' said the captain. Burke was his name. He was from the 58th Battalion and in command of this modest mixed patrol of officers from the 1st and 3rd Divisions. Seeing as I was the one who theoretically knew where we were and what we were looking at, Burke had come looking for answers. Not that I had many.

'The Boche are plenty alert, sir,' I said. 'That's for certain. And you saw yourself the wire is still heavy. In fact, I can't see that the artillery has cleared barely any of it. It's possible however we may find a stretch of trench that's still lightly manned.'

'Do you think so?' he asked, a hopeful note creeping in. Whereupon the German marine regiment opposite made a mockery of my words. Along an entire length of trench one rifle after another went off in rapid succession. I had the sensation of being at the far end of a rifle range with a whole company lined up, banging away.

'Forget I said that,' I murmured. 'It appears they've reinforced.'

'You don't say…'

Then matters, as they inevitably tend to in such circumstances, proceeded to worsen.

A white canopy flare soared up into the night sky and burst directly above us. A piercing bright light that wavered back and forth with the wind as it slowly descended. Soon there were two more hanging there, every furrow in the ground for yards around lit up as if the harsh lights of a sports stadium had been illuminated. The coiled lines of wire entanglements – reaching the height of a man where extra coils of loose concertina wire had been stacked on top – glinted in their light. Beyond the wire the dark-etched line of the Regina Trench parapet was visible. Those were not the only things visible. Ten feet to my left, the officer who was on his knees in a shallow hole looked like he'd been caught in a spotlight.

'Get down,' I shouted at him. 'They can see you in Berlin.' Sensibly he took my advice.

'Sir, I don't think there's much else we're going to see now,' I said to the captain, squirming uneasily.

'Oh, you've shown me more than enough, MacPhail. Let's get out of here.'

'Excellent idea, sir.'

By this time the remainder of the marine regiment had heard the call for "all hands on deck" and the fire became something atrocious. Not only was each hand firing a rifle, they'd rounded up at least two machine guns to supplement them.

Captain Burke raised his head and hollered, 'PULL BACK! PULL BACK!' I heard someone repeat the call.

While there were few other options at hand the army is such that an order – even one as blatantly obvious as this – is to be awaited in patient obedience. I wasn't the only one relieved to be on our way, however. Unhelpfully the captain had made no mention how this was to be accomplished.

Cautiously I lifted myself up in order to take a look around – one of my less inspired moments. Almost immediately bullets began plucking at the ground a few feet in front, and I felt one whizz past, perilously close to my ear. I fell prone again. Standing was out of the question.

'You got us here, MacPhail,' said Burke. 'How do you propose to get us out?'

'I think we'll have to crawl and roll, sir.'

'Crawl and roll?'

'Follow me.'

I crawled to the edge of the hole, slung the rifle over a shoulder and began laboriously slithering with all four limbs across the uneven ground in the direction of our lines. I didn't bother checking on Burke. It was a movement all boys mastered at some point in their lives.

The going was slow and arduous and after a couple of feet I was breathing heavily, when I spotted another shell hole to my left. Rather than changing direction, I simply turned into a log and rolled into it. A few seconds later Burke landed on top of me.

'You've got the technique down pat, sir,' I wheezed.

There was a groan. 'Is there anything you don't joke about, MacPhail?'

Behind another zipping burst from a machine gun sounded. Neither of us looked. The Germans may have had no shortage of men, guns or ammunition, but as long as we stayed low that didn't matter.

It took the better part of thirty minutes before the captain and I reached the relative safety of the opposite slope of the ridge. There we were out of sight from Regina Trench and could rise to our feet and stretch limbs that were aching. I was exhausted. Burke looked a shambles. There was some irony to the fact that on the way in we'd walked the same distance in only minutes.

When the other four officers emerged shortly after, muddied, tired, but alive, I grinned at the captain. 'All's well that ends well,' I said cheerfully.

'I wouldn't be so upbeat yet,' said the captain. 'You and I are still expected at Tara Hill: with a full report.'

'So as long as I'm not required to do any typing we should be fine, sir,' I said.

We walked south – overland – there being no pressing reason not to as the big guns were quiet. Darkness had fallen once more and, while no one spoke it aloud, I think we were all keen to put some miles between us and the front. Not that the going was easy. Mud sucked greedily at our boots and it demanded a remarkable concentration not to slip, or step by accident, into one of the many holes – some treacherously deep – that kept appearing out of the gloom a footstep ahead. Eventually we came upon the sunken road leading from Grandcourt to Courcelette and followed it southeastwards towards the village. Or what remained of it.

Since its capture Courcelette had been transformed by the German guns into little more than a barren crossroads. Mounds of red brick and plaster debris ground fine, a few timbers, and a crumbling wall or two were all that was left. Here we said goodbye to the other officers, solemnly shaking hands before Captain Burke and I proceeded towards the road in the direction of Albert.

Even at this late hour the modest thoroughfare was bustling. But then I was used to the nocturnal activity – ever since those first baffling days in the trenches near Ypres in the spring of 1915. Whenever the sun went down the working parties had swarmed forth, running out saps or digging new dug-outs, replacing and repairing the wire and the telephone lines that were forever being cut – any one of a hundred things that needed to be done, the night cloaking this industry from Fritz's eyes. And while the night's role hadn't changed much in the intervening year and a half, there was a significance to the traffic tonight. And it had little to do with the daily grind.

Captain Burke knew it too. 'They're preparing the attack,' he said grimly, as we tottered along the shoulder, a wary ear for traffic from behind.

To which I grunted. Hastily, we both sprang to one side as a lorry with engine roaring battled a rut and threated to veer off the road towards us.

Motor lorries and ambulances, and all manner of horse-drawn carts and limbers were moving forward. Almost as many were making the return trip to the rear.

Passing the Sugar Factory, the ground to either side littered with debris, I noticed some field guns being manhandled into position in the lee of a high embankment. That the debris on the plain of Courcelette consisted of more than just broken structures was obvious, for the air reeked of it. It was a ghastly smell. We put our heads down, walking quickly, anxious to leave this valley of death.

Shortly thereafter an entire mule train passed by, the beasts plodding forward, weighed down by wooden boxes and slotted canvas bandoliers over their backs holding shells for the guns, each shell in a separate pocket: four pockets to a side. With all the shelling, the traffic, and the wretched weather, it was a wonder how the engineers kept the road open. But I didn't have long to marvel at this. Other matters soon took precedence.

'Damn it all,' I cursed. Turning to look as a lorry bore down upon us from behind, my foot had slipped off the road and into a deep water-filled hole, soaking my leg to the knee. Only some last-minute acrobatics spared the rest of me. 'Why don't we just commandeer one of those things?' I muttered to Burke. 'We're both officers. Wave your Webley around if you have to, sir. Otherwise you and I are going to end up in the ditch like some mule.' The analogy sprang to mind as one of the poor beasts lay mangled to one side, its head twisted awkwardly, staring in our direction with bulging, lifeless eyes. In the case of the mule however it was probably not an out-of-control lorry that had done it in.

Burke found it a fine idea and before long the two of us were squeezed in beside a taciturn driver on the narrow, wooden front bench of a battered open-top Autocar. That the driver was mute, beyond a wary 'hello sir' when I nestled in beside him, was of little concern. Neither Burke nor I had the inclination to chat, and by the way the man wrestled with the wheel on the slippery, potted surface of the road I was glad he didn't feel the need to entertain.

3rd Division headquarters at Tara Hill were to be found in some of the deeper dug-outs carved in the chalk and in wooden huts on the hill. The bivouacs of the simple camp for the battalions were laid out in the shallow valley beyond.

Arriving at Tara Hill going on 2 a.m., it was dark and uninviting, the bustle of the road a world away although it couldn't have been more than 300 yards distant. I thought I heard voices further along but there was precious little to see.

'What now?' I asked.

Captain Burke looked around uncertainly. He was a field officer and evidently had as little experience with divisional headquarters as I did. Yet not only did he outrank me, it was his division we were visiting so I wasn't about to go bungling around in the dark waking up cantankerous colonels I didn't know to ask, 'pray, which dug-out should we be in?'

Just as Burke was setting out towards one such dug-out, a loud voice filled with authority called out behind us: 'Halt! Who goes there?'

'The High Seas Fleet,' I grunted, turning. A sentry stood five feet behind. 'Who do you think? Just point us the way to headquarters and we'll be gone.'

There was a chuckle. 'Pass, the High Seas Fleet,' came the response. 'Keep going straight, sir.'

So we did, and almost immediately we spotted a man approaching.

He appeared to be an officer. While the details of his uniform were lost in the darkness, his confident bearing gave him away. Entirely too casual to be a sentry and too self-assured to be a soldier sneaking in from an illicit evening out in Albert.

'Ah, we'll ask that fellow,' said Burke. He'd spotted him as well.

'Excuse me,' he called out. 'We were looking for divisional headquarters.'

'You are?' replied the man, stepping into view.

Even without the gold braid on his cap and the red collar patches on his tunic, I recognized him instantly. So did Burke. Which was not entirely surprising as he was from his own division – Major-General Louis Lipsett, GOC of the 3rd Division.

'We were told to report to the GSO 1, sir,' stuttered Burke. 'On the results of our reconnaissance.'

'And where precisely did you reconnoitre, Captain?' inquired the general.

'Regina Trench, sir.'

'Ah, you did? Well then, you two had best come with me. I'd very much like to hear what you saw.' He glanced over my way and without so much as raising an eyebrow, said, 'Hello, MacPhail.'

'Hello, sir,' I gulped, and went through the hurried motions of a salute.

'The lieutenant and I know each other, Captain,' the general explained to Burke. Burke was shifting uneasily from foot to foot, visibly having the same difficulty I had in finding the correct posture to assume. 'I was the lieutenant's brigade commander,' he went on. 'In fact, I seem to recall I was the very one who pinned those two pips on him. Only back then he and I were in the same division, so I'm intrigued what he's doing here. Walk with me, both, would you?'

'Yes, sir,' I said. Off my left flank an echo came from Burke's direction.

On the way to the dug-out I was able to satisfy the general's curiosity about my presence, and he shifted his attentions to the captain, questioning him about some rather trivial-sounding details of the 58th

Battalion. They were the kind of details I hadn't expected a major-general to be familiar with, let alone care about. But at that point I wasn't very familiar with General Lipsett and his ways.

Arriving at the dug-out, the general threw aside a curtain and began clambering down a steep stairway, motioning that we should follow. Step for step we descended until we must have gone thirty feet or more underground, where we emerged into a sizeable room panelled in planed boards and lit by electric light. There were several pieces of handsome hardwood furniture that wouldn't have looked out of place in a fine manor. 'Wow, the Boche sure know how to construct a dug-out,' I whispered to Burke over my shoulder.

A duty lieutenant, a signaller and a private awaited us. All sprang to their feet at the sight of the general. The duty lieutenant greeted the captain and I respectfully, the signaller nodded politely from a corner table and, after a brief word from General Lipsett, the private scurried up the stairs in a terrific hurry. Within minutes we were joined by a haggard-looking Lieutenant-Colonel Hayter, who I took to be the senior staff officer, the GSO 1. Incredibly, Lipsett and staff were getting even less sleep than I was.

We were invited to sit down, the map before us, while Burke gave what I found to be a rather cursory report. His wind was up no doubt. Being interrogated by your divisional commander and the senior staff officer can have that effect.

'So, in other words, beyond confirming that a large force of the enemy occupies Regina Trench your reconnaissance had little result, Captain,' concluded the colonel.

The steep climb down into the dug-out and the late hour must have addled something upstairs as I now felt the urge to speak my bit. 'It wasn't entirely without result, sir. If you had seen the fireworks show they put on when they spotted us... they used up half a dump of small arms ammunition. So we know they're adequately prepared. And not to forget about the wire we saw, sir. It's ten feet thick in places.' To illustrate I leaned over and slowly traced my finger along the stretch of Regina Trench we had observed. 'Knowing that, sir, you may want to inform the artillery. The way things stand now there's no hope of a getting battalion through to the trench.' Quickly I added: 'In my opinion, sir.'

The colonel frowned. 'Yes, Lieutenant…' It was a toss-up whether the colonel was irritated, intrigued, or just plain couldn't recall my name.

'It's MacPhail,' the general said helpfully.

Colonel Hayter's drooping, weary eyes settled on me again. 'Yes, the wire –' There was a pause. I had the distinct impression that uncut wire was a topic the colonel heard a lot of. 'Well, thank you both for your observations, gentlemen.'

Whereupon we were excused.

Climbing the stairs in pursuit of Burke, I heard a faint voice say: 'He does have a point, sir. We may not be ready.'

'General Gough is pushing extremely hard. He insists we keep up the pressure,' said another voice. 'You'll recall, Ross, he refused to postpone the attack on the 1st in similar circumstances. I don't expect he'll view this any differently.'

Climbing another step I heard something akin to a groan. 'No, I suppose not. We'll just have to do our best in that case, won't we, General?' Then I climbed out of earshot.

On the eve of a major attack it wasn't the most inspiring exhortation I had ever heard.

CHAPTER 11

8th of October, 1916
Regina Trench, northwest of Courcelette, France

The attack was to commence at 4.50 a.m.

A week earlier during the first assault on Regina Trench, the middle of the afternoon hadn't proved overly auspicious. So changes were made. This time ZERO Hour was to come before the break of dawn.

Had our army commander solicited my opinion I would have told him that changes besides the kick-off time were advisable. But then I don't think a man with a name like General Hubert de la Poer Gough was a man much given to taking advice. He hadn't up until now, not according to the scuttlebutt. If he wasn't going to listen to the divisional commanders, let alone our Corps commander, Lieutenant-General Byng – who was not only English nobility but a cavalryman to boot – I had to concede my own chances of convincing him would have been about as slim as us breaking through to Berlin. In true cavalry style General Gough was fixated on a singular goal. "Charge!" was a word they knew well in the cavalry. That the casualties piled up and that they came in the infantry, well… that was only to be expected… and neither that nor the lack of any meaningful ground gained reflected on the brilliance of the strategy.

Other than the hour everything else about this morning's attack was more or less as it had been a week earlier. I don't think I was the only one who wondered about this.

When I inquired at 3rd Division headquarters, the staff officer I spoke with rolled his eyes and grimly shook his head when asked if the wire had been cut. 'Do you think they'll call it off?' I said hopefully. Resolutely he shook his head.

If I was in any doubt about the state of the preparations, when I arrived at the 58th Battalion HQ the adjutant Major MacKay informed me that their last patrol had seen wire all along the front. He was none too pleased about it. In the hope of more uplifting reports I left to "liaise" with the neighbours from my own division, the 13th Battalion. Unfortunately they told a similar story.

Returning to the 58th bearing my grim tidings and a growing sense of foreboding, I then proceeded to the jumping-off trench. It was going on 4 a.m.

'Chilly, eh?'

My reverie disturbed, I looked up.

The mountain of a man to my left had his hands cupped together and was alternately blowing into them and rubbing furiously. General Byng's best intentions notwithstanding, the appropriate application of the term "sir" had yet to percolate down to all ranks of the Corps. Having been in the private's size twelves not so long before it was an omission I found easy to overlook.

'Yes, it is,' I said. 'But that's what they invented rum for. Shouldn't be long now.' This was a response that greatly pleased him. I didn't feel the need to mention the uncut wire.

The night skies were ink dark, a cold rain pelting down. As I stood waiting amongst the assembled troops I shivered, water cascading off my helmet. The shivering was from the cold I reassured myself – self-delusion and valour two sides of the same coin.

These past days the troops had laboured day and night in the drenching rain. Through a few feet of mud, past a layer of flint, and into the hard chalk below they had carved out this new jumping-off trench from where the attack would commence. The trench itself had little to commend it. Trenches seldom did. It was nothing more than a ditch, but its real benefit was that it allowed the battalion to assemble with only moderate risk to our heads should Fritz shower us with a bombardment.

'Do you think they'll be there?' asked Lieutenant Howard, the commander of "A" Company.

It wasn't hard to guess what he meant and why he was asking. I was the 1st Division in his eyes. 'The Highlanders are as ready as anyone can be,' I replied. 'They'll be on your flank. Don't worry about that.'

Howard nodded and left to join the men at the ladders.

We were on the divisional boundary, with the 58th Battalion of the 3rd Division left, and the 13th Royal Highlanders of the 1st Division, right. As the furthermost extremity of the 3rd Division consisted of Howard's "A" Company, I think he was feeling the pressure. Coordination was always a problem when two different divisions bumped shoulders – different commanders… different ways of doing things. Communications were usually also a problem. In fact, when I thought about it, the potential for problems was endless. So I understood Howard's apprehension.

When I first learned I was to liaise between the two divisions I had a fleeting vision of shuttling between Tara and Usna hills, conferring with Generals Lipsett and Currie and their respective staffs, sipping tea and gravely studying maps. That may have been hopelessly naïve on my part, but I also had myself to blame for where I found myself. It had occurred yesterday during the final conference in the 3rd Division dug-out at Tara Hill.

'There is one thing, sir…' I said slowly, after Colonel Hayter asked if anyone had anything to add. No one else did and Hayter looked vaguely amused when my head popped up above the parapet. He nodded me on. 'I wonder if we should rely on the contact aeroplanes alone, sir, to determine where the battalions are. When it's dark, or if the weather's bad, they'll be of little use. A few extra men forward with the battalions keeping an eye and communicating back on the progress might be a useful backup.'

Hayter was agreeable. So agreeable that in addition to ensuring that the wheels were greased between the 13th and 58th Battalions, I found that I'd become one of the implements to implement my own suggestion.

The minutes were ticking by now.

Then, finally, it was time. The barrage opened, a deafening roar that was as reassuring as it was loud, for the shells were ours. Above the night sky pulsed, flashes of orange and crimson speckled the horizon, the wet air tainted with the acrid smell of gunpowder and smoke.

The whistles went off so close in unison as to make no difference. The first wave, consisting of most of "A" Company were already over the top, marching across a No-Man's-Land lit by flashes from the explosions, up the slippery, uneven slope towards Regina Trench 400 yards away.

Eight minutes the barrage was to last. But long before it ended the next wave was also on its way and I was clambering out after them, the rain pounding down even harder. As the liaison officer I was not expected to be in the assault, but Colonel Hayter's orders were explicit; it was critical HQ learn whether the battalions had reached their objectives or not. What he didn't say, but was a fair guess, was that if there was a cock-up between the 1st and 3rd Divisions in the field a certain lieutenant from the 10th Battalion might as well remain in the field. Whichever way I looked at it, I couldn't do any of that cowering in a jumping-off trench. Therefore, off I went.

The two Lewis gun teams of the company were with me, accompanied by a gaggle of sappers. All of whom would be sorely needed, if and when the time came to consolidate.

Long before we reached the top of the ridge the machine-gun fire was tearing a rift in the night. Rifles cracked. Every so often a spot on the crest ahead would pulse, the flash of a muzzle or a bomb or a shell exploding streaking the rain-swept sky, the light lingering for an instant afterwards.

Approaching the ridgetop, I motioned to the others to keep low. A young lieutenant commanded the Lewis guns. He was an earnest lad, fresh from cadet school and home not long before that, eager to please and amusingly deferential about my front-line experience. He hustled over.

After hearing me out, he had his men virtually crawl over the crest. Which was perhaps a trifle overcautious. 'I feel like a bloody tortoise,' grumbled one of the young fire-breathers in our party. However, it was no idle paranoia on my part. What the fire-breathers didn't appreciate was that the location of Regina Trench, midway down the ridge's reverse slope, afforded it an enormous advantage. As attackers crossed over the ridgetop they were silhouetted against the sky. Tonight it was the glow from our own guns to the rear we had to fear.

Having navigated the muddy crest we were soon galloping downslope; that is to say walking as fast as a man can be expected to walk in the dark, whilst trying not to slip and dodging holes at every step, a 28-pound machine gun slung over a shoulder. I found it tough going with just a Lee-Enfield. Admittedly, I was straining my eyes, trying anxiously to gauge whether the first wave had made it to the trench.

It was difficult to draw any conclusions. There were men scattered around, some moving forward, others in shell holes – small groups, but hardly a company full. The small arms fire was still quite heavy. With each step inert bodies of our men began to appear; I nearly tripped over one. But, again, not an entire company's worth. That made me think that perhaps they'd done it.

However, off our left where the other two companies of the battalion were advancing, the air was literally singing with bullets, a hailstorm so thick that advance seemed impossible. Neither were the sounds on our right any more promising, where the 13th Battalion was advancing.

'Is the first wave through, do you think?' I demanded impatiently of the lieutenant. He was a footstep ahead. 'Because if they're not...'

'Don't know,' he replied, falling back to join me. 'Wait... I think perhaps they are. Look, there's the trench.'

I saw what he was pointing at and I saw also the unmistakeable signs of fighting. Bombs were going off, the flashes emanating upwards out of the trench. It was a safe bet they weren't German. Someone had made it through! Then the wire loomed into sight. 10 yards away. 25 yards out from Regina Trench.

Coils and coils of densely concertinaed barbed wire, lightly staked to the ground, four feet high and at least as many feet deep barred the way. There was no way round or through an obstacle like that. Not when the trench behind was packed to the gunnels with hardened German marines and half a boatload of Maxim machine guns, each one capable of firing five-hundred rounds a minute.

'Oh, Christ,' cursed a Lewis gunner at the sight, as he knelt down on his haunches. There was no need to tell anyone that prancing around in the open would only attract unwanted attention.

I looked left and right, then again more slowly, praying I'd spot a path the artillery had cleared. There wasn't a gap to be seen. Of course, in the dark and the turmoil, the open avenues were not so easy to spot. 'Damn,' I whispered to myself. I suppose the guns had given it their best; but a field gun firing shrapnel is not the ideal instrument to gap a thicket of wire, not least because the shells either exploded too soon, too late, or not at all. Not at all was a particularly big problem at the Somme.

When I'd enquired at headquarters why the guns weren't using high explosive to blast a way through, I was told it would cause too many obstacles for the infantry. As if a few extra shell holes to navigate made any difference. But that was the problem with the staff, they seldom had any first-hand experience but were loath to acknowledge it, a flaw of character that only increased the further they were from the front.

'Through here, sir!' A soldier was waving an arm from a shell hole twenty feet away.

I rose to my feet and sprinted over, keeping low.

If he hadn't called out when he did I suspect the whole crew of us would have gone west there and then, facing down the wire and the remorseless machine guns behind.

I jumped into the shell hole beside him. 'Simmonds found a sally port,' he said excitedly. 'The rest of the company made it to the trench. Lieutenant Howard ordered me to stay here to guide the rest through.'

'Smart man your lieutenant,' I said.

Gathering the others was the work of a hasty minute, and before another passed our group filed into the gap, following a narrow path through the entanglements. Private Simmonds, whoever he was, had proved his weight in gold.

Then as the wire fence lines abruptly ended the objective appeared in front. The longest single trench on the entire Western Front: Regina Trench. Deep and well-constructed said the intelligence reports, obviously well-wired, and for the past week manned by three regiments of the redoubtable Marine Infantry Brigade of the 4th Ersatz Division. The Germans were resolved to hold it, General Gough equally resolved to take it, and the Canadian Corps found itself in the middle – between the hammer and the anvil, so to speak. Not for the first time this war.

'Would you look at this?' I muttered, after we crossed the parapet in a heady rush and sprang down into the trench. 'The artillery didn't even touch it.' Which revealed another major advantage of the trench's location. Being both out of sight and on the wrong side of the ridge, the artillery had the greatest difficulty hitting it.

'No wonder the machine-gun fire's so heavy,' said the lieutenant.

As promised, Regina Trench itself was deep and wide, its walls revetted with neatly woven branches as was the German custom. The log-framed entrance to a dug-out looked a good sight sturdier than most mine shafts I'd seen. Fortunately, of Germans there was no immediate sign. Of fighting, however, we could hear plenty. To both sides the machine guns were chattering fiercely.

Lieutenant William Wallace of "A" Company appeared round the bend. 'In the nick of time, MacPhail.' Wallace was clean shaven, something I'd remarked upon when we met in the jumping-off trench a few hours earlier. Then his eyes had twinkled and he'd said, 'All the best men usually are.' Wallace's eyes now bore into me with great intensity, his long rectangular face drawn and pale.

'What's the situation?' I asked, after finding a quiet corner.

'We're holding a hundred yard stretch to the right,' he replied. 'We got as far as a bombing post, but we can't get past. I'm hoping the 13th will turn up soon.'

Inwardly I groaned, thinking of my earlier, breezy reassurances to Lieutenant Howard and feeling guilty as a result. 'There's no sign of the Highlanders, then?'

Curtly he shook his head. 'The rest of the company including the lieutenant and a few fellows from C Company hold the trench left. They're at the junction with the communication trench. But they've run into a lot of opposition. The rest of the battalion is not yet up on their flank, so they're on their own.'

I winced. 'In other words the company is out on a limb, with the Boche to all sides. Is that what you're saying?'

'That's one way of putting it. Another would be to say we have our heads under one of those guillotine thingamajigs the French like so much. All the Hun need do is let fly.'

From the expression on his face I could see there was little to be gained by asking more.

'I'd better have a look,' I said, 'before I report back. I'll come with you.'

One Lewis gun crew and a couple of sappers went left with the young lieutenant to support Lieutenant Howard, and the other crew went right with Wallace and me. The trench twisted and turned every few feet – from above in the aerial photographs it looked uncannily similar to the battlements of a castle. After several sharp turns we reached Wallace's men. A platoon-sized squad were assembled, all crouching, rifles in hand. The sky was growing imperceptibly lighter by this time, and the barrage had ambled off northwards, before it ceased with a few parting coughs.

'There!' Wallace instructed the Lewis gunners, indicating the next traverse. 'Set up at the corner and you'll have a line of sight if they try a rush.'

They didn't. At least not immediately. Instead Wallace insisted on another bombing expedition of his own – the third of the morning. He and a party of bombardiers raced off down the trench.

It didn't go well. There was a lot of rifle fire and shouting, accompanied by the dull bangs of bombs going off. Minutes later the first bomber reappeared round the bend in the trench, followed by the others. Wallace had taken a bullet in his right thigh, was in obvious pain and only able to walk with difficulty. He brushed off my admonitions that he get himself to the rear while he still could. 'It looks pretty nasty,' I said to him. Then we were interrupted. The Boche were letting fly.

The bomb went off twenty feet away, a mere Christmas cracker compared with the blast from even the smallest of the field guns, but not to be underestimated. The man it landed beside was thrown violently to one side where he lay crumpled. The air was suddenly filled with stick grenades. One after another they clattered down onto the wooden duckboards.

Through luck or skill, or some combination of both, the German marines wiped out the Lewis gun crew in the first flurry of bombs.

Seeing that I ran forward to check if the gun, by some miracle, was still workable. A Lewis gun had tipped the scales in many a scrap. It didn't appear to be, but it wasn't the first time I regretted not paying more attention at Bailleul during the Lewis gun course. However, a new, more urgent problem clanged off my helmet and came to rest menacingly at my feet.

'Oh shit,' breathed the man who'd come with me – a mild understatement in the circumstances. But I was already bending at the waist, snatching at the long wooden handle that lay there like a child's rattle on the duckboard planks. I raised it back over my head and, with all my might, hurled it over the traverse and into the section of the trench still held by the enemy – where they would be massing before rushing us. I was angry and frustrated. Men were falling, the attack looked like it might be a fiasco, and there seemed nothing I and or anyone else could do about it. Almost immediately there was a flash and a bang, and I imagined that I heard anguished cries.

I glanced over my shoulder. The soldier was gaping at me. He had an odd look on his face. His mouth was half open though he wasn't actually saying anything.

Nor did I wait to hear what was on his mind. The first of the attackers rounded the corner, mere strides away. A single man, moving cautiously, the butt of his rifle nestled under his shoulder – prepared. Instinctively, I yanked up the barrel of the Lee-Enfield and shot from the hip in one rapid motion. There was no time to aim.

He landed a few feet away. And then I was too busy working the bolt to pay any further attention to him as two more grey-clad figures charged down upon me. A volley of shots from behind sounded and they too crashed to the ground, one after the other. The pile of bodies at my feet was now past my knees. Then another marine appeared and he too succumbed to the fire of the men behind.

'Sir, we have to pull back,' said the soldier. 'Before they try again.'

'Yes. Yes, of course,' I mumbled.

We'd been lucky, I realized. They'd only sent a few men to test the waters, sizing up our tenuous position. Equally certain was that they were preparing to erase it forthwith.

Cautiously we edged backwards to the rest of the platoon, but not before I grabbed the satchel bag with four potato mashers that I saw slung over the shoulder of one of the Germans. He wouldn't be needing them.

Without a word I handed them to Wallace.

'Thanks,' he said, 'we're almost out of bombs. But we need a little more help than that, MacPhail.' He cocked his head suggestively in the direction of the rear.

'No,' I said firmly. 'Don't even think about it. I'm staying here. I can't leave you like this. It's only a matter of time before the Boche stick their noses down that trench again, and there'll be a lot more of them next time.'

'That's our problem,' he said. 'You're here to observe and report back. Tell you what: forget about reporting back. Just find out where those bloody Highlanders of yours are hanging out and get them up. Tell them to hurry.'

Climbing over the parapet I caught a brief glance of Lieutenant Howard and a squad further to the west. Dawn was breaking. They were 20 yards away, fighting like madmen, surrounded by the enemy.

For a moment it was all I could do not to go to their aid. But then I thought of Wallace's parting words. "A" Company was in a perilous position and needed help. I felt the guilt tear at me, then I turned away and rushed in the direction of the wire.

Fortunately I was able to find the sally port again. Once through I paused. By any measure I ought to have kept going south. I'd been ordered by no less than Colonel Hayter to keep headquarters informed how the attack was progressing. The fact that "A" Company had grabbed a stretch of Regina Trench was certainly worth reporting. And south was where I'd find battalion headquarters. Once I reported they would surely send men forward to help – assuming there were any left to send. From there I could rush over to 13th Battalion HQ, see what was holding them up, and impress upon them the urgency of moving forward. It was the proper course of action. It was what Sam Stiles would have done. It was probably what any officer would have done. But in the time it took to do all that, "A" Company would be lost, and the toehold in Regina, too. Of that I was convinced. The information I'd brought would have been as good as useless.

I turned east towards the 13th Battalion and followed the wire. The sound of machine gun fire intensified.

I began to run.

As long as I kept running any Germans in the trench would have a hard time hitting me – unless they had an MG-08. In which case all they had to do was pull the trigger and wave it back and forth once or twice. But I needed to find the Highlanders.

Strangely, other than the bodies in kilts that I was beginning to encounter, I couldn't find a single one. After 50 yards I misjudged it manoeuvring between two shell holes, and stumbled, falling heavily to the ground. Winded, I looked up and was astonished to see one of the bodies I'd taken for dead, virtually in front of me, moving. He was an officer and was propelling himself toward the rear on his back, one hand clamped to his stomach where his innards threatened to spill out.

I stood up to go to him.

The sound of the machine gun burst came out of nowhere. It was probably three or four hundred yards away, yet it registered in my head like the clanging of a fire engine bearing down at full speed. My stomach throbbed empathetically as a cloying feel of panic draped itself over me.

Before I had time to think any more, a searing pain shot through my thigh and I gasped – more from the surprise than the pain.

Then someone wound up, put his back into it and applied a baseball bat to my left shoulder.

Involuntarily I winced, staggering from the force of the blow. My leg was feeling none too strong and it buckled as I stepped backwards, attempting in vain to catch my balance. As I fell, the thought came to me that my premonitions about the Somme had been absolutely right.

Dundas and so many other men had met their ends here. That my turn had come was not so very strange.

CHAPTER 12

8th of October, 1916
Regina Trench, northwest of Courcelette, France

'He's gone,' said a distant voice. 'Just look at him.'

I blinked my eyes a few times in rapid succession.

'Nah, I don't think so,' said another voice, this one closer by. 'I could have sworn he twitched, Reg. I'm sure of it.'

'Doesn't look like he's twitching to me.' The first voice had joined the second, a few steps away.

'SIR, are you there?' The voice thundered in my ear.

Vigorously I bobbed my head up and down.

'See, I told you. Nothing.'

'Strange.'

'Come on, let's go.'

With an effort I reached out and waved a hand to get their attention. But they were already making a run for the next hole and I was too late, and they didn't see me. With an effort I cried out, 'No. Wait!' They ran on and dove into a hole ten feet on. I felt like screaming, though for some reason the words wouldn't come.

I awoke. My heart was pounding, my entire head bathed in sweat despite the cold. Then I remembered what had happened.

Once I had established to my satisfaction that all my limbs were attached, that I was in point of fact neither dead nor even in imminent danger of dying – not from my present wounds – I had crawled into a nearby shell hole and closed my eyes. For only a brief moment I assured myself. Apparently, though, I'd dozed off. Not that that was a surprise. Even as a small boy, sleep was how I'd coped with setbacks, feeling revitalized and fit the next morning.

Now, as my senses returned, the overriding sensation was not so much one of revitalization as having had the caterpillar tracks of the Crème de Menthe grind out slow peregrinations on top of me. I was, however, alive. This train of thought inevitably led down other paths and I began to consider the seriousness of my wounds. As I did so they immediately started to ache… terribly. Some learned scholar no doubt had a name for this effect; and if I hadn't been so pre-occupied gritting my teeth I might have recalled who it was.

Gingerly I probed at my shoulder with a finger. Beyond ascertaining that the cloth of both tunic and shirt were torn, wet, and clotted with blood, I was little wiser about the extent of my wound, although it hurt like hell. As to my thigh, I could plainly see in the fabric where I'd been hit, right on the flabby front, halfway between knee and hip. And I felt a similar tear in the trouser leg at the back, where the round had exited. Which was definitely good news. Had it been shrapnel from a Woolly Bear it would have left an exit wound as big as my fist. As fortunes go, that mine had been determined by an MG-08 meant it still had a certain vague sheen to it, unlike that of my old Company Sergeant Major who'd lost both his legs and his life to a shrapnel shell the April before last. On the quiet nights the grisly sight of him still haunted my dreams.

Luckily both wounds didn't appear to be bleeding. To make certain I fished out the gauze field dressing I'd taken to carrying and tied it tightly around my thigh. The shoulder would have to wait for someone to do it for me. There wasn't a soul in sight, however, not even the officer with the gaping stomach wound. He'd pulled back like the rest of the 13th Battalion – those that still could.

There was some scattered shooting going on in Regina Trench and that made me think of Lieutenant Wallace and the remnants of "A" Company. I'd promised I'd get help, so there was nothing else for it. I rolled from my back on to one side.

A piercing pain shot through my leg as I got to my knees, and I bit down hard on my lip so as not to cry out. The last thing I wanted was to draw the attention of some Navy sniper from Hamburg with time on his hands and a full five rounds in his Mauser carbine.

The bullet hit me in the head.

That is to say it clanged off the side of my helmet. I knew it was the side because I felt the impact and yet I was still upright. Quickly I collapsed back into the hole, my heart pounding something terrible.

Half-heartedly I tried a few more times that afternoon to crawl to the rear, but was spooked on each occasion by a rifle or a machine gun going off. On top of which I could barely move my left arm and I was feeling rather weak. I finished the last of my iron rations sometime around noon and decided to wait for darkness. The only members of the 13th Battalion in the vicinity were as badly wounded as I was. Neither they nor I were in any state to save Wallace and "A" Company.

With darkness came the ignoble retreat. It was every man for himself, every uninjured limb pulling and pushing as best it could over the cold, muddy terrain. Those who could walk were labouring at each step, all willing themselves a few feet further to the next hole, and then on to the next. From everywhere it seemed, men had emerged and were stumbling and crawling to the rear and safety. Above, banks of clouds, lighter in colour, slowly shifted across a darkened sky, not as dark though as one would wish. Every so often a star shell or a flare exploded in a furious blaze of light. Then, for a fleeting instant, I saw the ground to all sides pulsing with movement – before everything froze. Once the flare fizzled out, or the star shell wafted off to the east, the creeping and the crawling through Death Valley resumed.

After many hours, though it was probably no more than 500 or 600 yards distant and consequently less than a ten-minute walk, I finally reached a trench. Once it had been theirs, but more recently it became ours and it turned out to be one of the North Practice Trenches, a short jaunt northeast of Courcelette. It was just off the left of the Dyke Road. I knew it for the 13th Battalion had its headquarters nearby.

Very soon after dropping over the parapet I was entrusted to a couple of burly stretcher bearers. For a moment as they dressed my wounds I contemplated asking about the attack, but thought better of it. Deep down I already knew what they'd say. It had been a day of failures all round – not solely on my part.

What I couldn't figure out was why anybody would reasonably expect to get a different result doing exactly the same as the week before. Same geography, same tactics, same opponent. Only the men were different, and that only because most of the first bunch weren't around to give it another go. But then I was the wrong person to ask; I understood very little of what was going on here at the Somme. Dundas was surely dead. Scores of others in the 10th Battalion were either dead or wounded. We hadn't even led one of those mad charges across No-Man's-Land, yet half the battalion was in the ground or in the hospital. And there were plenty of battalions in the Canadian Corps who were worse off than us. After today there'd be more beds to fill and graves to dig. No doubt Generals Haig and Gough would be able to explain the finer points of the strategy employed. I didn't see them turning up here to do it, though.

9th of October, 1916
Courcelette, France

Very early the next morning, or very late that night – depending on how you looked at it – the stretcher bearers dumped me carefully, albeit unceremoniously, onto the ground. Both sighed as they straightened up, shaking out their arms with evident relief. I'd been a heavy load.

Neither was theirs the only onerous experience. Being stretcher borne turned out to be worse than I expected, and I spent most of the short trip with my eyes closed and my teeth gritted. In no time my shoulder had gone from numb to a searing pain, aggravated at every bump, and with every turn and stumble. Not that I blamed the stretcher bearers, the ground was muddy and treacherously uneven. They'd managed it with aplomb.

'You'll be fine, sir,' one said reassuringly. 'Someone will be with you soon.' And with that they were gone. They had more to do before the night was out.

I lay in a row of ten men, perhaps more, one stretcher laid out beside the other on a patch of slick ground next to the Dyke Road in what I took to be Courcelette. As always it was hard to tell for certain, most of the landmarks being rubble.

After some minutes resting, staring up at the night sky with the stars twinkling beyond and practicing my breathing, I felt better; well enough that I stole a glance around at my surroundings. To my astonishment I spotted a familiar figure.

He was loitering amongst a group of soldiers gathered on the road. Don't ask me how or why, but Captain Sam Stiles was standing there.

At some sixth sense his head perked up. He turned away from the others and looked in my direction. I watched him. Then I raised my good arm and he bounded over.

'MacPhail! Is that you?' He stood over me, peering down. 'I thought it must be,' he said. 'How are you feeling?'

'Oh, just dandy,' I muttered.

Whereupon his eyes trawled up and down me. He winced.

'That bad, is it?'

'Not at all,' he said unconvincingly. 'Can I do something?'

'Water,' I croaked. 'Do you have some water?'

He reached for his bottle, got down on a knee, and with one arm raised up my head while the other poised a canteen at my lips. I gulped at it greedily. The water tasted of petrol. This wasn't at all unusual here at the Somme, the army viewing a tin can as a tin can and therefore readily interchangeable, regardless of its provenance or previous employment. Still, I don't think I've ever tasted anything as fine as that first mouthful Stiles poured me.

'Thanks,' I grunted when I was done, water still dripping down my chin. I let my head fall back, winded from this small exertion.

'Here, let me help you,' he said. 'You may feel better sitting up.' Before I could say anything he had gripped me firmly under the armpits and was beginning to lift.

'AARGH!' I cried out, pain shooting through my shoulder.

'Oh, sorry,' he muttered. 'I didn't realize.'

I didn't respond, my eyes closed against the pain which slowly began to subside. I felt so terribly, terribly weary. A little sleep wouldn't hurt, I thought. Everything seemed all jumbled up in my head, thoughts swirling round in a furious melee, each flitting by so quickly that none made any sense whatsoever. Thankfully they soon faded away.

I don't know how long I was out for.

Out of the eddying smoke, the deep bass notes of the big howitzers sounding in the background, I heard a tinny voice pipe up: 'He's over here.'

Let me collect his things, first,' the voice continued. Clumsy hands fumbled around me.

I forced open my eyes, confused. My vision was blurred. Stiles was leaning over, bent at the hip, his fingers prising open my tunic pocket. I felt the hand reach in. The beating of my heart became very loud, and as if the barn doors to my brain were thrown wide open the mist upstairs began to spiral away.

'Would you look at this,' Stiles whispered pensively. 'Whatever do we have here? Aren't you full of surprises, MacPhail –'

I blinked. The night air was clear and all at once I could see perfectly.

Stiles was peering into the small bag that I always carried in my breast pocket.

'Hey!' I cried out and pitched forward in an attempt to grab it from him. Then it felt as if someone buried a bayonet in my shoulder. I fell back, groaning. My leg was trembling, and it hurt too.

'Don't you worry, MacPhail,' Stiles said, smoothly, tucking the bag away in his own pocket. 'I'll take it in safekeeping for you. You wouldn't want someone at a casualty station to pilfer *this,* would you?'

Before I could answer a stretcher bearer pushed his way past Stiles. 'Excuse us, sir. We're going to move him now.' Another man appeared at my feet.

They wasted no time.

'Christ, it'd be easier carrying the ambulance to him,' said the man to my rear. He was speaking to the one holding my feet, who had his head turned in profile, and was grinning exuberantly; until he noticed me glaring.

The witty one called out: 'Captain, would you mind helping us out?'

Stiles did as he was asked and grabbed one side of one end. It was no particular surprise that it was the lighter end, but circumstances as they were this wasn't a moment to criticise. Very slowly the procession shuffled down to a crossroads where a motorized ambulance was parked. There were three Autocars, all waiting in a semi-circle, motors grumbling away. With a 'one-two-three', and grunts all round, they lifted me up, headfirst, onto the wooden bed of the ambulance and slid the stretcher over the planks until it banged up against the back of the hold. Someone threw a blanket over. A second stretcher was pushed in beside me and five walking wounded were helped up, to sit where they could.

'Good luck, MacPhail,' said Stiles, a curious look in his eye. 'Don't worry, I'll guard it with my life,' and he patted his pocket. With a loud *crunch* the driver put it in gear and we lurched off.

Reaching Albert, the ambulance swung into what looked to be a courtyard. When they lifted me out I recognized immediately where I was. There was an old brick schoolhouse at the bottom of the court-yard. It wasn't far from the cathedral and was best known these days as the chief dressing station.

Quickly, I was carried inside and gently laid on the brick floor of what appeared to be an outer room, the garlicky smell of acetylene gas quite overpowering. The windows were all taped shut. Through the half-open doorway to the inner room, very bright lamps shone, so this explained the need for fuel oil.

Several feet away an older man in uniform – one didn't see too many old men near the front – was giving a drink of water to one of the wretched, moaning bundles lined up in rows on the floor. Concentrating on my own misery I paid him no further heed until he appeared bending over me, with his white collar and equally white hair. Then there was no getting round who it was: Canon Scott, the chaplain from my own division, a friendly and tireless gentleman who was as apt to appear beside you in a front-line trench doling out cigarettes and kind words, as leading a battalion in hymn at a Sunday service in the rear.

His face was calm and reassuring. 'What's your name, Lieutenant?' he asked.

'MacPhail, sir. Malcolm MacPhail.'

'You must be an island man, then. You're from Prince Edward Island?'

'No, sir. I get that a lot, though. I'm from Alberta as it happens.'

'Then you're a fortunate man indeed. I've always longed to see the Rocky Mountains. They must be majestic.'

'They are. Beats Regina Trench any time. In fact, I wouldn't mind seeing them right about now.'

He smiled gently, his dark eyebrows lifting in sympathy. 'I've always found, Malcolm, the Lord has a way of providing.'

I was on the verge of asking whether the Lord could provide an explanation as to what we were doing here at the Somme, when a man in the next row began to groan. Canon Scott excused himself and went to him.

I watched as he spoke a few words. But instead of offering water as I presumed he would, he called instead for an orderly who, to his credit, came remarkably quickly. This was not entirely coincidental; Canon Scott not only had God arrayed on his side, he wore the crown and pip of a lieutenant-colonel.

The orderly called out to one of his mates, then nonchalantly lifted the mud-caked blanket to look underneath. A quick diagnosis.

I shall never forget the look of complete and utter anguish that appeared on their faces. Canon Scott and the orderly went pale. The man on the stretcher, while conscious, noticed none of this. He was staring off at the ceiling.

The orderly lowered the blanket and Canon Scott turned his head away. When the second orderly arrived they promptly lifted the stretcher and stepped past me toward what I now presumed must be the dressing chamber. As they passed by a small rectangle of paper fluttered down. I reached out for it.

'Hey! You dropped something.'

Neither the orderlies nor Canon Scott heard me.

I glanced at what turned out to be a photograph. Not of the soldier's sweetheart as I expected, but of his parents, plain and earnest and serious, dressed in their country finest. Only then did I pause to think how young the lad was.

Astonishingly, after only a couple of minutes in the dressing room the two orderlies reappeared with the stretcher. Canon Scott trailed somberly in their wake. Instead of placing the young soldier back where he'd lain, they turned right, going through another doorway – one I hadn't noticed earlier.

The man to my right coughed. 'The dying room,' he said, then coughed again.

I glanced over at him but didn't reply. The boy's parents stared back at me.

My own turn in the dressing room came a couple of hours later – I was one of the last – and I was laid out on a white painted table under the glare of the lights and the attentions of a doctor in a blood-stained white apron. Promptly they injected me with something. While I was vaguely conscious I don't know how long I was there. It couldn't have been very long, even if it felt otherwise as the Doctor fished around in my shoulder with what looked like a long pair of tongs.

'Lieutenant?' The Doctor's face appeared right above me.

Hazily I looked up at him.

'You had some luck.'

'Easy for you to say,' I groaned.

'No, really. You have little bleeding and the bullet in your leg went straight through. Nothing appears broken. We cleaned it up and I expect it will heal fine.' He took my palm and placed something the size of a marble in it. 'And this is what I retrieved from your shoulder. I thought it best I remove it straight away if possible, and fortunately I was able to find it. To prevent infection, you understand.' Then at the sound of shuffling feet he raised his head. From the expression on his face I could see that his mind was already on the next case. 'They'll examine it again in the hospital,' he said. 'Good luck, Lieutenant.' A brief nod to the orderlies and I was carried away; no time to mumble 'thank you'.

Afterwards I felt rather silly, and a little ashamed – many of the injuries at the dressing station were far more serious than mine – but my heart skipped a beat when for a brief instant I feared we were turning right into the dying room.

Later that day I departed the Somme.

As we drove south out of Albert, the ambulance hit a pothole that would have done any bush road back home proud. Briefly my head was launched upwards until it returned to Earth with an audible thud. While I had a vague suspicion that comments about my 'thick skull' weren't always meant as a term of endearment – on this occasion I was thankful for it.

The car shuddered violently from side to side as it came to more holes. It motored on, the tarpaulin at the back flapping open. Through the opening I could make out the billowing roll of the land beyond, the jumble of shell-torn brick buildings of Albert immediately behind us, and the heights of the great Basilica jutting out above them all. Fanny Durack hadn't moved an inch, bless her soul. Not that I had expected any differently.

No. The war would go on. The only question was: would it be with or without me?

PART TWO

CHAPTER 13

12th of October, 1916
No. 8 General Hospital, Rouen, France

Awakening, I rolled to my left and discovered that the bed beside me that had very definitely been occupied when I went to sleep early last night – hospitals not being hotbeds of activity much past 6.30 p.m. – was now very definitely empty. The sheets were ruffled, the white enamel bedpan still resting on the floor close at hand next to the end where it had gotten rather a lot of use in the brief time I'd been a neighbour. As the occupant of the bed was barely able to wheeze out a word edgeways, one of the nurses had confided to me in a low whisper that he'd been gassed. Although I'm a complete neophyte when it comes to things medical, even I could have told her that. I'd seen men die from gassing and the sight is a ghastly one. On top of which, I'd had a few lungfuls too many of the stuff myself, up in the Salient last year. I knew excruciatingly well what it felt like. I didn't envy the poor bugger lying there in the clean sheets, sweat pouring off him, every half hour retching horribly and gasping for breath. The oxygen they sprayed over him for five minutes at the hour, every hour, seemed to have little effect. I barely slept the first day on his account.

Now I had the feeling he wouldn't be returning. That was probably for the best: given the agony the poor fellow was in. As if to confirm my suspicions, one of the French lady folk employed to help the sisters with the many menial tasks bustled over a few minutes later.

'*Bonjour, monsieur,*' she chirped, radiating a beaming smile, which did me good. Then she set out about stripping down the bed, her cheeks reddening at the exertion.

'*Et le petit dejeuner?*' I enquired hopefully. My French was never better than when addressing matters of the stomach. For the first time since arriving in Rouen I actually felt hungry.

'*Oui, oui, c'arrive,*' she replied, a full toothed grin lighting her face.

'*Merci, mademoiselle.*'

She blushed at the compliment; me thinking her a young lady rather than the middle-sized, middle-aged woman of a working background she so obviously was. This may very well have been the one and only occasion in many years that a slip of my tongue had turned out all right. French was a more forgiving language than I'd perhaps assumed.

English in any event was not my strong suit.

'I understand you've recovered,' growled the whale of a matron, appearing scant minutes later. She had a broad Welsh accent, an even broader bottom, and a general air about her that could have chilled the Sahara. Much like the water tins that seemed to emanate from everywhere, so too with the nurses. Just my luck they'd shipped this one in straight from the North Pole.

'Not exactly,' I grunted. 'It hurts like h…' I swallowed the rest. On the very brink of the precipice, I realized the perfectly suitable and entirely appropriate word on the tip of my tongue would heat things up unbearably on the ward. I was still in her bad books for the language I'd used when they'd rolled me back onto the bed upon my return from the operating room.

'My shoulder. It hurts.'

'You were asking for breakfast,' she said accusingly.

'Yes, well… by my reckoning it *is* morning.'

She glared at me.

I stabbed a finger in the direction of the array of windows that ran along the entire opposite wall. 'I always find the sun coming up to be a sure-fire indication.'

'There's no need to get smart with me, young man.'

'No ma'am,' I whimpered, my growling stomach assuming command before my mouth did more serious damage. The funny thing was, she wasn't entirely mistaken; I *was* feeling better.

No. 8 General Hospital is the largest of Rouen's hospitals, and Rouen – a small city on the Seine not far from the Normandy coast – is famous for its many hospitals. That and its many churches, the most notable of which, the Notre-Dame Cathedral, was reputedly in much better shape than its counterpart in Albert. I hadn't yet seen it to confirm, but at over 100 miles from the front it seemed plausible. While I didn't know anything about the city's proximity to cemeteries, these two attributes nevertheless made Rouen an ideal locale to waver between life and death. Not that I was in any danger of the latter, not according to the doctor.

'They did a commendable job at the dressing station,' he told me, after painfully probing around at my various wounds soon after I arrived.

I sighed. Everyone was telling me how wonderfully fortunate I was. Meanwhile I cringed from the pain every time I shifted sides.

'I don't simply mean removing the bullet from your shoulder,' he continued. 'More often than not it's a shred of fabric or some other foreign object that is carried along with the projectile and enters the wound that causes infection, and is the real danger. But whoever looked after you did fine work. Your shoulder will require some time to heal, but there's nothing more I can do for you at the moment. You need to convalesce, Lieutenant.'

'So Blighty's out of the question?' I said wistfully.

He shook his head. 'We'll have you fit and on your feet before you know it.'

'Wonderful,' I muttered, a scene of the muddy, bullet-swept approaches to Regina Trench, dense coils of gleaming new concertina wire flashing before me.

The doctor must have realized the bitter-sweet nature of this news – to anybody who looked it was plastered all over my face – for he added: 'I can't do anything about that, Lieutenant. War demands a great deal from us all. However, with any luck you'll leave here healthy and with your limbs intact. I can't say that for a goodly number of the young men I see.'

'No, sir. I mean, yes, sir,' I said, sighing. 'It's just been a long war, that's all.'

'So it has,' he replied thoughtfully, 'so it has.' He looked away. 'It's been a very long war indeed.'

Whereupon I was wheeled to my bed and my first acquaintance with the matron.

From down the long cavernous hall, filled with four seemingly endless rows of beds, each covered in crisp white sheets, and from each protruding a head and a leg or an arm, most of these appendages wrapped tightly in white dressings, came the squeaking wheels of the stretcher cart. Another arrival.

'We have a much nicer bed for you, here,' I heard the nurse say as they grew nearer. 'Until a spot opens up on the officers' ward.'

Curious, I tilted my head to look. Nobody had offered me a place on the officers' ward. Not that I could remember, and I'm quite convinced I would have.

Leading the way was the sister, dressed in a blue dress of thick serge with white collars and broad white cuffs, a white apron to her ankles, her dark locks all but invisible under a flowing white headdress that trailed over her shoulders. White was a colour they were fond of in hospitals – rather less practical where I was coming from.

Then I saw the modest boulder that passed for the soldier's head, as it and he were pushed into view, the curly brown of a thick moustache and beard exactly as I remembered. I gasped.

'*Sacré bleu!*' boomed the voice. Half the heads in the ward looked up in alarm. 'Mac! What the devil are you doing here?'

'What am I doing here? That's a long story, Benoît. But to make a long story short, I think I'd simply had my fill of the Somme. So I figured what better place for some peace and quiet than Rouen?'

Benoît began to laugh. A hearty rumbling laugh that came from deep within. The sort of laugh that invariably made you laugh yourself, the tepid joke that started it long since forgotten. Soon I was doubled over in mirth, and that proved a mistake, for then I was peeling over in pain. The sister had gone to DuBois, who was clasping his side and grimacing too.

'That'll teach you both to behave,' said the nurse sternly, her sparkling eyes giving up the game.

For a few moments after, it was quiet as the nurse rearranged his sheets and he settled in.

At length I said: 'They didn't offer me a spot on the officers' ward.'

Benoît gazed over. 'What of it? Where would you rather be, 'ere with me or dere with them?' I never realized how many words in English began with "h" or "th" until I heard them being massacred wholesale.

I pretended to think about this. 'Depends on the food,' I said finally.

He sighed. Then glanced furtively around and began to rummage underneath his sheets.

'Careful,' I hissed. 'If you twist a rib, the matron's going to blame me.'

'Have a taste of this, Mac. You need to relax.' He stuck out an arm the width of a telephone pole and almost as long, and shoved a dull metal hip flask into my hand.

'Benoît, it's not even eight in the morning.'

'Have you eaten?'

'No.'

'Well, then – '

The reasoning behind this train of thought was not entirely clear – something French Canadian, I suspect. Perhaps it was customary to cleanse one's system with a stiff drink before breakfast, having gorged on beans in lard the previous evening. Were it that I had.

The logistics of transferring the flask from bad arm to good under cover of the sheets, and subsequently unscrewing the metal top with one hand alone, all without turning the bed into a distillery vat were formidable: formidable but not insurmountable.

'Ahh,' I said, as the whiskey bit at my throat. 'It's good stuff this. Thanks Benoît.'

'*Un petit apéritif,*' he clarified. Scotch whiskey followed by oatmeal porridge were a combination not well appreciated in the world outside Quebec's Eastern townships.

I took another nip. 'I got it in the thigh and the shoulder. What about you?'

He lifted the sheets so I might see. His midriff was bandaged in enough white to wrap a mummy several times over with plenty left for the rest of the ward. He could have been hit in any one of a dozen different organs, but the simple fact he was lying there suggested the bullet hadn't pierced anything vital. Certainly not his stomach. Benoit DuBois was a man who enjoyed his food and I would have heard otherwise.

'Machine gun?' I asked.

'*Oui.*'

'Regina Trench?'

'*Oui.*'

We didn't say anything after that. We just lay there, staring at the ceiling far above, thinking. Neither of us was soon going to forget Regina Trench. Then I asked him whether he happened to know what the casualties were.

He replied so quickly and so self-assuredly he made it sound like he knew it for a fact.

'A couple of thousand,' he grumbled.

'That many?' Things had not gone well, but that was a big number for a few hours of fighting over a few thousand yards of trench. 'Where'd you hear this?'

'It's true,' he insisted. 'The brother of the man beside me visited. He's a clerk at Corps Headquarters and tallied the numbers himself.'

I whistled. 'The bean counters in the rear may not find that very many, but that's three battalions. Three battalions out of the eight that went in. And for what? The wire was uncut. Christ, the artillery hadn't even touched Regina Trench.'

'They say we showed too little "dash".'

'Too little dash!?' I fumed. 'And who's "they"? I suppose this comes from the staff types of the Reserve Army who dash between dining hall and padded chair, then to a bed with a real mattress in it?'

Breakfast arrived to improve morale in the trenches. However, as was so often the case in the real trenches, fortunes fluctuate quickly. We were to be treated to a mid-morning visit from the matron. Not that there was any warning, she just turned up.

To my surprise she ignored me. Instead, she addressed her attentions to Benoît, which surprised me even more. I would have been relieved by this turn of events were it not that I was intrigued, and frankly completely bowled over by the sight of the old battle-axe ministering to Benoît.

'Is everything all right?' the matron asked solicitously. She bent over him like a concerned mother, firmly tucking his sheets in. It was fortuitous she did, I thought, lest the flask tumble out. That would have spoiled the mood in a flash. On the other hand, it may not have.

'*Merci, madame. C'est très gentil, Pauline,*' rumbled Benoît.

Then the strangest thing happened, Matron Davies blushed.

Benoît smiled, a big smile full of the exuberant *joie de vivre* that characterized him. She patted primly at his sheets, stiffened her back, and said, 'Do call if you need anything. That's what we're here for.'

I squelched a groan at this – or thought I had – and was met with an icy glare.

'Yes I will,' said Benoît. 'Thank you again, *Madame.*'

After she left I began to sputter. 'Pauline… *Merci, Madame…* How on earth did you do *that?*'

'Do what?' Benoît looked bewildered.

'What! You just wound that grumbly old polar bear round your little finger. You're calling her by her first name for Pete's sake. I'm lucky if "Pauline" allows me a bed. If it was up to her I'd be washing dishes for my breakfast from a cot in the kitchen.'

'Mac, you must remember all the rivers back home? The ones where the water's current is far too powerful to swim against it?'

I nodded. 'Sure. So what you're saying is that I should go with flow and let her walk all over me?'

'*Non.* All I'm saying, Mac, is don't get so wound up. She has worries of her own, so try not to trample on her little garden. A bit of respect goes a long way.'

'I've no problem with that, only she's been trampling all over my carrots ever since I got here.'

Benoît sighed, wearily.

CHAPTER 14

16th of November, 1916
No. 8 General Hospital, Rouen, France

The hospital was an attractive, three-storey building of white brick and stately windows, with a steep shingled roof and a profusion of chimneys, built in a U shape around a central courtyard. At the far end of the courtyard was the main entrance hall and its many dressing rooms and offices. The two wings to either side were, for the most part, where the patients found themselves, though multiple huts and tents were scattered throughout the grounds including a sizeable white one in the courtyard whose purpose I hadn't yet determined. I had a vague suspicion it might be the morgue so didn't enquire too closely.

Fronting the hospital and the courtyard was a broad patch of dirt and gravel where the road ended. There, ambulances could pull in to discharge their loads, turn, and return to whence they'd come. There were no ambulances this morning, only a couple of black Vauxhall staff cars, pulled up one abreast of the other, though not so as to block the way. On the far side of this strip of gravel was a modest park of sorts, with green grass and a goodly number of real trees – not the stumps I was accustomed to. Many feet and a lot of rain had taken their toll on the grass, however, and the trees were uniformly barren at this time of year. The overall impression was a dreary one, particularly as the weather had turned distinctly chilly the past few days, the sky sulking behind a sullen grey shroud from dawn till dusk. Winter was feeling its way along, an inevitability of nature that neither side had yet figured a way around – though someone at General Headquarters was undoubtedly on the case.

I rolled up the collar of my greatcoat. The air was cold and damp, penetrating deep into bone and marrow if given half a chance. But I was determined to get a short walk in before returning to the cloaking, oven-stoked warmth of the officers' ward. As the doctors had promised, my leg was healing well. I had a limp, and for that a cane came in handy, but I was pleased at the progress I was making. Exhorted by the nurses, I persevered in my twice-daily strolls, come rain or shine, or my shoulder acting up as it had been. The doctors were right about the shoulder too. Most days it didn't hurt much. I often brought along a newspaper to read on my ambles so that I might sit on a bench at the halfway mark and listen to the birds overhead whilst reading about a war that seemed deceptively far away. Today the news from London had warmed the very cockles of my heart.

As to the comfortable officers' ward, which I had to admit was a step up from the general ward, I had DuBois and his old-world Gallic courtesy with the matron to thank for that. I teased him that she must fancy him, and she might well have, despite the yawning gap in background, age, looks and overall congeniality. I'd grown quite fond of DuBois myself; he was an easy man to like. They say people gravitate towards those whose qualities outshine their own, and that would have explained the matron's interest in him.

The crunching of a vehicle caught my attention. It was crawling forward over the gravel heading towards the courtyard, a black staff car with a soldier in cap manning the wheel, and somebody of importance warming the back seat. It surprised me therefore to see that "somebody" was somebody I knew. And while his importance was modest – limited primarily to the confines of his own head, even if he did outrank me – the odds were high I was the reason behind his visit to no. 8 General Hospital.

Hesitating, I contemplated taking refuge behind a tree; after two years in the trenches you develop a certain instinct about when to keep your head down. But then I remembered what he'd stolen off me so I limped my way over to the car in a quick march.

The soldier driving had gotten out and was stepping smartly round to open the passenger door.

I shook my head as I approached. 'Let me,' I said, coming between him and the door. With my good arm – the Fritz gunner had hit his mark but at least he had the courtesy to nail me on the left – I yanked at the door handle. Then peered inside.

'Hello, Sam,' I grunted. 'I suspected you might show up here at some point.'

A flitter of surprise passed over his features, but he recovered well. 'Ah, Lieutenant MacPhail. You're looking remarkably fit,' he said as he stepped out, nearly planting his cane through the foot of my good leg. Unlike mine, his stick was purely decorative.

'Wonderful to see you,' he enthused. 'It's only been a month. Yet here you are up and about like the best of them.' As he went on to straighten his tunic, I could see him calculatingly taking stock. His smiling mouth kept up pretences, while his eyes surveyed me more closely to assess my true condition. It's the sort of calculating behaviour that tends to infuriate me – like when someone mocks you to your face but thinks they're doing it so cleverly you won't notice. For the first time in months I had a sudden urge to sharpen my bayonet. Stiles often appealed to that side of me.

Instead, I kept the bayonet sheathed, smiled and said, 'How nice of you to come and visit.' I wasn't going to put my mouth in it this time; not if I could help it.

Stiles was all charm and bonhomie. 'Oh, it's the least I could do. After all, you were one of my *boys* in the platoon so I couldn't very well not come by and see how you were faring, could I? I'm off on leave to Paris, as it happens. Thought I'd drop by on the way to visit. By God, MacPhail, it's good to see an old face. I hope they're treating you all right.'

According to the sign on the outskirts of Rouen, Paris was 138 km away: to the east. A detour westwards via Rouen was like cutting through Belgium from Germany to get to Paris. All of which confirmed that Stiles's motives weren't any purer than those of Von Schlieffen. I showed some teeth, hoping they weren't so gritted as to ruin the overall effect and told him they were treating me splendidly.

'Is there somewhere we can talk?' he asked.

'We can go back to the ward,' I offered. 'It's warm there, and quite comfortable for a hospital. With a little luck I might even be able to rustle you up a chair. You'll have to promise you'll be nice to the matron though.'

Stiles looked thoughtful. 'I was thinking of somewhere more private.'

'In that case…' I paused and glanced around. 'In that case, there's a fine bench I know –'

He hesitated momentarily, then nodded. 'It'll have to do.' He reached back into the car for his greatcoat. In that I couldn't blame him. November is not the ideal month to visit Rouen.

We established ourselves on the wooden bench, cold and damp, our feet resting in a puddle of mud on what purported to be the park lawn. It was not exactly the Plugstreet trenches where we'd first met, though the weather, mud and company lent it a certain vague similarity. The air was fresh and clean, however, and there weren't any Fritzs out for my head, which makes all the difference in the world.

For a couple of minutes we batted the ball of casual conversation back and forth like the old trench mates we were. Until the topic of the war surfaced and he told me the latest.

'Isn't that something,' I said. 'So the new boys managed it?'

'Yes. Took them three tries, but the 4th Division finally captured Regina Trench. They grabbed it a few days ago in a midnight assault. They may be new but they've earned their spurs the hard way.'

'That they have,' I agreed. 'And yet the offensive keeps going? I would have thought winter might finally put an end to it.'

'Not yet. It appears their next objective is to be Desire Trench.'

'You say "their". Where's the 1st Division, then?'

'We've been moved to the Vimy sector, along with the rest of the Corps, so we're out of it for the time being. The 4th Division is the only one of ours still at the Somme.'

'Ah, ha. So that explains you being on leave.'

'That's right. *Carpe Diem* as they say,' Stiles began plucking assiduously at some invisible lint on his trousers, so I knew there was something else he wanted to share. I looked at him expectantly.

'Just spit it out,' I said finally.

He eyed me with surprise. 'Well, I suppose this is as good a time as any. I wanted to tell you there's a good chance I won't be around when you return to the battalion. That's why I thought it best I see you as soon as possible.'

'Oh?'

'A staff position has come open.'

'You don't say?'

'Yes, it's with the 3rd Division. Look, I know you're going to rib me about abandoning the division. But they're a good bunch and I'm told I've got an excellent shot at it.'

'You surprise me. I always thought you were more of a man of action. Hopefully you won't find staff work terribly boring.'

'Nice of you to say, MacPhail. But you should realize staff work is becoming more and more crucial in this war. You might think about that yourself. You know how hard it is to stand out in the trenches. There's so much bloody drudgery involved. Not to mention wet socks day in, day out.'

At this I felt the vein in my forehead throbbing. Thoughts of crawling into No-Man's-Land to a listening post while Stiles manned the dug-out crossed my mind. I didn't say anything however. But the rolled-up newspaper in my greatcoat pocket did catch my eye. It was *The Times* from London, dated only yesterday, fresh from a Channel boat.

Casually I tossed it onto the bench between us. It wasn't so much an afterthought as a shot across Stiles's bows and his career plans. The paper was still open to the page I'd been savouring:

THE RESIGNATION OF SIR SAM HUGHES

A CONFLICT OF AUTHORITY

(FROM OUR CORRESPONDENT)

OTTAWA, Nov. 14.

The resignation of Sir Sam Hughes, Canadian Minister of Militia, has created a great sensation in political and military circles.

The official *communiqué*...

I felt like the fisherman watching the pike as it first glimpsed the lure sparkling amongst the weeds. Stiles glanced down absentmindedly. Then he blinked and looked again, more carefully. The concerto of tapping fingers on his thigh ceased.

'Do you mind?' he asked, pointing at the paper.

'Nah. Go ahead.' He snatched it up and began to read.

It was all I could do not to smirk as his eyes raced down the column.

'It was about time the Prime Minister got rid of the old bugger, don't you think?' I said.

At first Stiles didn't appear to hear, but then his head jolted up. 'What do you mean by that?'

Which was when I realized that while I was quite certain the Minister was a potent ally in Sam's quest for promotion, he didn't know I had long since made the connection. It was probably best that it remain that way. 'Oh, nothing,' I mumbled.

'Yeah, well. Keep your thoughts to yourself,' he shot back.

Stupidly all I'd done was rile him up. He sighed irritably and thrust the newspaper away in a jerk of his arm. It landed in the pool of mud.

'I think it's time that you and I get down to business, MacPhail,' he muttered.

'Business?'

'Yes, business.' His hand went to his pocket and retrieved the small felt bag he'd taken from my pocket only a month before. With a show of it he placed the diamonds halfway between us. I reached out to grab them, but he was much quicker. He snatched them away, dangling them at eye level for a spell before tucking them securely away again in his greatcoat.

'I wondered when you were going to get around to that,' I said.

'I *was* going to propose that we split them: fifty-fifty. No questions asked.'

'Split them! They're mine and you pinched them.'

'See, that's what I meant about no questions. Many people – justifiably – would wonder how it was that a junior lieutenant in the Expeditionary Force would be carrying around a fortune in diamonds.'

I felt myself reddening. 'That's really none of your damn business, or anyone else's. I'll have you know it's all above board.'

It was Stiles turn to smirk. 'I suppose you heard that a lot when you were a lawyer?'

Fuming, I didn't reply. For once I didn't know what to say. I hadn't told anybody about the diamonds, not even Roy Dundas who knew the circumstances and would have understood completely. However, Roy was buried somewhere in the Somme mud, so it wouldn't have done any good even if I had.

'On reflection I'm thinking sixty-forty might be more equitable,' Stiles said, watching me keenly. 'If I hadn't taken them into safekeeping they would surely have disappeared. So this puts you quite a bit ahead the way I see it. You should be thankful.'

'You know,' I sputtered, 'I never put you down as a common thief. But I suppose this is all about advancing your career somehow?'

He sighed. 'No, nothing like that, although it won't hurt. Look. Just to show you I'm a fair type, we'll leave it at fifty-fifty. But watch your tongue, MacPhail. You're talking to a superior officer.'

I clenched my fists together. My shoulder was aching something terrible.

'Yes or no, MacPhail? Those are the choices available. You've a quick tongue, I'll grant you that, but clever words won't do you much good this time. What's it to be?'

'NO,' I exploded. 'They're mine. You know it and I know it, and that's the only thing that matters.'

'Not entirely...' said Stiles evenly, a grin emerging. 'There's a little something that matters even more. You know the details far better than me, but isn't there a saying in that old profession of yours about possession being nine-tenths of the law?'

I stewed. Stiles beamed. Just as Von Schlieffen had had his way for a stretch in '14, Stiles was having his in '16. I suppose I felt like the Belgians had then.

After a few moments he clapped his hands on his knees and sprang energetically to his feet. 'Think about it. I really must run. Paris is waiting, you know,' he chortled. 'But don't fret, MacPhail, I'm a reasonable man. I'll be in touch.'

I watched as he slid gracefully into the motorcar. With an imperious chop of the hand he directed the driver to move out. This seemed rather superfluous; I don't expect the driver thought he'd settled into the backseat solely to admire the upholstery. The car turned in a neat circle on the gravel and puttered away towards the City of Lights, leaving me utterly in the dark as to what I should do next.

CHAPTER 15

28th of November, 1916
No. 8 General Hospital, Rouen, France

'So you see, they belonged to this fellow from home I knew, Harry Hobson. Harry was a bit of a scoundrel, truth be told, and apparently he'd snatched the stones in a heist before the war.'

'This Hobson he stole the diamonds…' said Benoît slowly, looking at me for confirmation. I nodded vigorously. 'Then he just gave them to you when he arrived in the trenches?'

'No… Not precisely.'

Benoît frowned.

'He was killed at Mount Sorrel last June, when we took back the hill. Machine gun got him. As I knew his father rather well I collected his belongings, fully intending to send them home.'

'And that's when you found the diamonds?'

'Exactly! There'd been rumours, and I'd had my suspicions. Still it came as a bit of a shock when I opened the bag. They weren't exactly something I could package up along with a postcard and the message: Your son is dead. P.S. Here are the proceeds from when he knocked over the Doll's Block. So I kept them.'

This was a mildly sanitized and considerably shorter version of the story, but there was no need to confuse DuBois with all the myriad twists and turns. As it was it had taken me the better part of two weeks before I concluded that I needed to confide in somebody. Benoît was the only candidate I could think of.

'So you took this fellow's things, eh, kind of like Stiles took yours?' For all his plodding girth, there was nothing lumbering about Benoît's tongue; even if 'things' came out sounding like 'sings' in the French-Canadian version of the word.

'Yeah, well, I wasn't dead when Stiles was rifling through my pockets,' I said sourly.

Too late to sound wholly convincing, I added: 'Besides, I'm not saying they're mine, all I'm saying is they're definitely not his. I told you about Stiles. He's the sort who's probably bought out half the rue de Rivoli to make sure he looks the part ahead of his big promotion to the staff.'

DuBois took a crunching bite of the apple he was holding and began to chew with gusto. There was little evidence that the wound in the region of his stomach had impaired his appetite in any way. 'You could just forget all about them,' he said eventually, wiping the trickle of juice from his beard with the back of a hand.

I frowned. 'What! And let him get away with it?'

'No.' He smiled wryly. 'No, I thought you might say that. But have you given any thought, Mac, to what you plan to do if you do get them back?'

I sighed. 'No, not exactly. If I'd known what to do with them in the first place I wouldn't have been carrying them around all this time, would I?'

Benoît turned back to his apple.

The ward was full that afternoon. It was not long after lunch and it was dark and gloomy, and the wind was screaming, sheets of rain pelting at the windows. Half the ward was in no condition to go anywhere, and the other half had unanimously decided to forgo their afternoon stroll for a game of cards inside. All hoped the pretty new nurse might happen by on her rounds; she had caused somewhat of a stir yesterday afternoon when she'd sauntered in, with a saucy bounce to her step, and a curviness to her figure that even the tent-like apparel prescribed for nurses could not suppress. Grown men, a great many of whom were married – officers that the other ranks looked up to for wisdom and as examples of courage under fire – became dithering idiots at the sight.

Once I would have had my own foot in my mouth, but that was before Kathryn. All I still had of her was the memory and a weathered sepia photograph I entrusted to my billfold – from after our marriage, and before the tuberculosis that had claimed her. By chance I'd been staring at it when Miss Ecclestone entered to dazzle those assembled. Thus fortified, I managed to keep my head while the others lost theirs.

Our billets were on the top floor, just under the eaves, which explained the low, angled ceiling. It was warm, stiflingly so, but the atmosphere was one of good cheer. It made for a pleasant contrast with the November storm wailing outside. I glanced down to the far end of the room where the card game was underway, from where I could hear Benoît's thunderous laugh. I was sitting in a simple wooden chair with one leg languorously perched on the bed, a couple of pages into a tome as thick as a telegraph pole. One of the other officers had lent me the book when I'd complained of having nothing to read. Appropriately it was entitled *War and Peace*. I had no great desire to read about the former having just escaped it, but it seemed fitting for the times. The lieutenant had assured me it was wonderful entertainment.

At the far end of the room, where the game was in full flight, there was a sudden ruckus. Chairs screeched and it sounded like everyone who was able was hastily getting to his feet. I smiled. Even a round from a trench mortar was less likely to get a soldier in a tear than the appearance of an attractive-looking nurse. I looked up.

It wasn't Nurse Ecclestone. I did see a nurse, however, the matron herself – lurking behind the newcomer, beaming – at her obsequious best. The newcomer was a senior officer, one I knew well enough to recognize at a hundred paces. It was Major-General Louis Lipsett, better known as the commander of the 3rd Division.

Quickly I took my foot off the bed and threw *War and Peace* onto it. The bedsprings groaned at the exchange.

Watching I saw the general exchange words with several men. Each of whom, judging by their broad smiles, seemed delighted he'd made the effort. After a minute or two with the card players he glanced over his shoulder at the matron. She lifted an arm and pointed down the room, seemingly straight at me. Or was it my imagination? The general's eyes followed her lead and appeared to hesitate momentarily at the sight of me… but then he was talking to the matron again.

General Lipsett began to walk down the ward, down the parquet floor with its herringbone motif, the hard soles of his leather boots knocking loudly. Gone was the animated buzz from minutes before. The ward was full but every head was unobtrusively tracking the general's progress, and the few mouths that did speak, did so in whispers. Every few steps Lipsett halted, leaned over and made what I assumed were polite enquiries of interest of each of the men still bedridden.

By now I was on my feet. I'd been trying to walk without the cane the last several days, and so far with success. Nevertheless, I held on to the back of the chair to be certain; it wouldn't do to crumple in a heap in the presence of the general.

With each step he made the list of possibilities explaining the general's visit shrank – until he was a mere ten feet away and only a single one remained. He'd come to see me. *But why?*

Naturally my first impulse was to think of the bag filled with diamonds, but I quickly dismissed the thought. Stiles wanted them for himself, so he had no reason to go blabbing the story to everyone and his brother. And even if he had, and someone in the army had felt obliged to investigate, I don't think they would have sent a major-general. That applied to every other reason I could think of. Generals were many things, but errand boys they most certainly were not. If any general were to come visiting I would have expected it to be General Currie.

'Good afternoon, Lieutenant,' said Lipsett amiably. He had his cap off and so did I so there was no need to salute. As saluting never came naturally this was fortunate.

'Good afternoon, sir,' I responded. It sounded a trifle stiff, even to my ears. That wasn't the only thing that was stiff; I was standing as ramrod straight as might reasonably be hoped for from someone who'd played target to a Fritz gunner's MG.

'Thank you,' Lipsett said to the matron. She hesitated, strangely reluctant to take her leave. Either she was awed by his company, unaware of the army concept of having been summarily dismissed, or wanted at long last to see someone put me in my place. She just stood there at his side, gawking.

General Lipsett wiped at a brow glistening in sweat. As his parted hairline was almost as far back as the crown of his head, this was a sizeable terrain to dry with a single hand. Admittedly it was very warm. I offered him my handkerchief.

'Thank-you,' he said, when the mopping was done and he handed it back. On a whim I offered it to the matron, jiggling it a few times in her face until she reached out to grab it.

Lipsett's head turned. He was clearly surprised to see she was still there. I wasn't surprised as much as annoyed. Suggestively I raised an eyebrow at her. Normally this would have been far too subtle a hint for the old goose, but with both of us staring she reddened and stammered, 'Very well. Should you need anything, General, please let me know.'

He nodded gently.

The general was not a particularly large man, and with his bushy eyebrows and matching fair moustache – the latter trimmed very neatly – you might describe him as having a sympathetic air. He was popular with the men. But then you'd do well not to overlook the gold-embossed red lapels, the line of coloured ribbons on his chest, or the crossed sword and baton adorning both epaulettes. Commissioned officer or not, a lieutenant learned very quickly to appreciate his lowly rung in the chain of command. As my father liked to explain ahead of our summer walks in the mountains: 'Remember, lad, appearances can be deceiving. A bear may appear harmless, but you must never forget his claws and that he can run a lot faster than you.' Of course, in my current condition a turtle would have given me a run for the money. But I happened to like General Lipsett.

His attention was now focused on me. 'You're wounded,' he said, 'why don't you have a seat?'

'Thank you, sir, I'll take the bed. You can have the chair if you'd like.'

It was an offer he accepted. With a squeal, and what was probably a very ugly mark left on the polished wooden floor, he inched the chair up closer to where I was sitting; so close he was sitting directly opposite me.

'How are you faring, MacPhail?' he asked. 'You look well, I must say.'

I hesitated, debating whether I should lay it on thick in order to stay on in Rouen for a few extra months. But Lipsett was not an officer to be mislaid by smokescreens. I put on the stoic face he would expect and told him: 'Under the circumstances I feel pretty good, sir. I'm already on my feet, albeit a little wobbly at times. The doctors assure me I'll be as good as new in a month or two.' I paused and scratched my head. 'I suspect they may just want to be rid of me.'

Lipsett's mouth broke into a shallow smile. 'Yes, well, let's hope they get their way.'

I frowned.

'You're probably wondering why I'm here,' he said.

'Well, sir, a few minutes ago I would have replied you were here to visit our wounded. Which technically speaking you still are.' I glanced down at my arm which hung limply in a white sling – 'to protect your shoulder,' the doctor had explained. 'But I can't escape the notion you've actually come to see me, and not necessarily my wounds. I don't think you would have made the journey to Rouen on a whim – although they tell me the city's not unattractive – therefore I suspect you must have something on your mind. For the life of me, though, I can't figure out what that might be, sir.'

'Hmm,' Lipsett replied. 'You're correct about it not being on a whim. As it happens I'm on my way to Le Havre to greet a visiting party of Members of Parliament come to see the division. However, I do have something on my mind, or more properly, something I'd like to get off it. I want to ask you something.'

My eyes widened.

'A spot has come open on my staff. I know many of you in the front line don't think overly much of the staff. There's a tendency to greatly underestimate their work. But I think the campaign at the Somme demonstrated how very, very important it is.' I began to vigorously nod, thinking of the flawed bombardments, the spotty communications, and above all the tactics that neither "spotty" nor "flawed" could ever begin to describe. For all the vast military organisation at the Somme there were dozens of things that had been flubbed – without even counting the multiple muck-ups at Army headquarters. 'If the men in the battalions are to succeed,' Lipsett continued, 'everything must be done to ensure that the plans and preparations are top notch. General Byng has told me repeatedly that he's determined to professionalize the Corps, and I wholeheartedly agree. For my part I want to ensure I have the right men in the right positions. Which is why I'm here.'

Suddenly the lights went on. 'Ah, so you want to ask me about Captain Stiles, sir,' I exclaimed, though wasn't entirely sure when I said it how the general had made the connection between the two of us. I couldn't help thinking what a delicious irony it was that I was to help in vetting Stiles for the cozy position he so desperately wanted. His fate was in my hands. The meeting was taking an unexpected turn.

'Who?' Lipsett replied, looking puzzled. Then he shook his head. 'No, it's much simpler than that. I would like you to join my staff, MacPhail.'

'You would?'

'Yes. I realize you'd have to change divisions, although that shouldn't concern you terribly. General Currie suggested your name, oddly enough.'

'He did?'

'Yes, he told me you had a… how did he phrase it? An "enquiring mind" was the expression, I believe. From everything I've seen of you I agree. That's what I'm looking for in my staff – officers who are able to think for themselves. On top of which you're a fighting man, Lieutenant MacPhail. You know how it is at the front. Many of the young chaps they send me are really quite brilliant, but they lack practical experience. As we both know, what looks fine on paper doesn't necessarily look the same on the battlefield.'

'No, sir,' I mumbled, a host of thoughts tumbling through my head.

Just as I began to digest this news, he told me something else that surprised me even more.

CHAPTER 16

17th of December, 1916
London, England

I strode through the gates of Buckingham Palace at a little past 10.30 a.m.

To the handful of bystanders and newspapermen who were watching it may have appeared more of a limping gait than a stride, though my new brown leather boots positively gleamed (the old ones were quite beyond salvage the cobbler had assured me in between sorrowful shakes of his head, leaving me in little doubt that my pocketbook would soon see action). My uniform had an unusual crispness to it, as if it and I had never seen the trenches. Apart from the limp my shoulders were back and my chest was puffed, and I'm pretty sure I wore the glimmer of a repressed smile. It wasn't every day I was to be presented to the King.

Before me, crossing the paved palace courtyard, were a scattered file of others, hurrying so as not to be late. Most were in their uniform best, though a few steps in front I saw a couple of ladies in stern ankle-length black dresses and matching hats, one holding the hand of a wide-eyed young boy in a white sailor's suit.

The doors to the palace were open, soldiers of the cast-lead variety standing guard to either side. I entered and began to ascend the wide, red, carpeted staircase. Gold glittered from the intricately-wrought stair railings, and even the wainscoted walls were trimmed in the stuff. On the landing ahead there was a tall columned archway, beyond which the stairs continued. Huge portraits adorned the walls to either side. Buckingham Palace was everything I expected it to be, and I suppose that's a good litmus test of any palace.

At the landing a spritely lad of eighty or so in a tailored frock coat greeted me and enquired if I had a coat to leave, or a cane, or perhaps something else? A closer look and I would have thought the answer was obvious. But people probably hid all sorts of things, in all sorts of places, upon entering Buckingham Palace. On the other hand, at his age he may not have seen me at all, let alone the cane I didn't have in my greatcoat pocket. I handed him my coat and he motioned me on.

Onwards required more climbing. At the top of the final flight of stairs another man was there to greet me, similarly attired.

'Good morning, sir,' he said politely. 'What are you to receive?'

'An M.C. they tell me,' I replied. Whereupon a third man asked me my name. Gravely, he let his finger trawl down a list until he came to what he was looking for, then nodded in approval.

I was ushered into a room where maybe thirty or forty others stood waiting. A distinguished-looking colonel with white hair and a white moustache appeared not long after. Solemnly and precisely he told us what we were to do.

We stood milling around, waiting in awkward silence for it to begin.

'So, what's it to be?' I asked the man to my side, an Imperial lieutenant.

He smiled. I think he was a little nervous, too. 'An M.C.,' he replied. 'And an Albert Medal.' His was the lilt of the Welsh matron, Miss Davies.

In the knowledge that a single rotten apple in the Welsh barrel didn't mean the rest were spoiled I smiled back at him. I guessed he was a couple of years younger than I. 'Not many people receive an Albert Medal,' I said. 'That's for life saving, isn't it?'

He nodded. 'One of the men dropped a lit grenade in the mud during training. They say I dug it out and tossed it away before it went off. It all happened very fast.' He looked almost embarrassed.

'Yes, I think for most of us here that holds true. You're barely conscious what you did. At the moment itself you react before you have a chance to think. Which is probably a good thing; otherwise you might not do anything. But I'll bet your mates appreciated your reflexes.'

'I'm William Morgan,' he said, offering me his hand.

'Malcolm MacPhail,' I said. Before I had a chance to ask him anything else the ceremony began, and the first man was summoned. 'Good luck,' I whispered to Morgan when his turn came. It was some time before I heard my own name called.

'Receive the Military Cross. Lieutenant Malcolm MacPhail,' bellowed the colonel.

I walked across the room and through the door into a smaller chamber. King George V was in full ornate, dressed in the uniform of a field-marshal, watching me. I took a few steps in his direction, paused, bowed, and advanced the final two steps. For some reason my heart was pounding. Ironically, I couldn't recall being so ill at ease rushing the strongpoint at Mount Sorrel in the first place.

Off the King's left flank an immaculately turned-out officer held up a purple cushion, on top of which lay what I presumed was my medal.

The King snatched it off with rather less ceremony than it was presented and stepped over towards me. I stood at attention; the thought occurring to me rather belatedly that it was best if I kept breathing.

He was short, the King. Having seen him once before on a horse, this surprised me. Otherwise he looked much as he had then, with a neat grey beard and the profile that was famous throughout the empire. Deftly he pinned the medal to my tunic.

'You appear to have been wounded in your action?' said the King.

'Not exactly, sir.'

The King frowned. He'd seen me limp in.

'I made it through the attack all right, sir. Unfortunately, I wasn't so lucky in what came afterwards.'

The King nodded and gave me his hand and a sympathetic look. Having considerable experience in such matters, he thereby diplomatically terminated the conversation. I can't say I blamed him.

I took two steps back, bowed, and after a sharp right and a few paces, it was all a blur until I was once again standing in the busy street outside the palace gates.

I looked around. What was it about London and pubs, and me? Every leave I found myself whiling away the hours in a dark-panelled drinking hole, or at least until it closed, which seemed to happen every three hours – morning, noon and night – barely enough time to finish your drink. I might have said the same about the tailors, though strangely they never seemed to close. But unlike the pub the hours spent at a tailors were an exercise in drudgery and a full-out assault on my pocketbook, albeit a necessary one. Where privates could get away with polishing their buttons for the occasional parade, officers were held to higher standards. Or so I was told. I hoisted my glass to the barkeeper; it was already seven o'clock so I had little time to lose.

'Well, I'll be darned,' I heard as the bartender set a frothy one down in front of me. 'If it isn't the illustrious Lieutenant Malcolm MacPhail.'

'Don't tell me,' I said, without looking, 'You're on leave again.'

Stiles shrugged disarmingly, then pounded me on the back with great enthusiasm. 'That's a surprise seeing you! What are you doing here, anyhow?' He barely had his fingers in the air and already the barman was bustling towards him, holding an overflowing pint served as it should be: with no froth at all. Henceforth I'd let him order, I decided.

I grunted. 'The King sent for me.'

'Ha! Always the comic. Cheers!'

Sam Stiles was not exactly who I would have dreamt up as ideal company – far from it – but I wasn't displeased to see him. London was a big city, and not knowing a soul it could feel rather lonely. A familiar face, even one who'd rob the shirt off my back if it suited his purposes, was still a familiar face. Particularly on a day like today, when there was no one else with whom I could share the tale of my adventures at the palace.

'Seriously, Sam, what are you doing in London? How much leave can one man possibly have?'

'This wasn't exactly leave,' he replied. 'My father was in town, so he sent for me. He's visiting with Sir Max Aitken.' I must have let my puzzlement show. 'You know, he's the one who runs the Canadian War Records Office, where all the war reports and photographs come from,' he added. 'He's also an old friend of the family. He's to be given a peerage in the New Year. Apparently, he'll go by the name of Lord Beaverbrook.'

'Ah, ha,' I said. 'So strings *were* pulled?'

'Don't be so naïve, MacPhail. I don't think they're making him a lord simply because Mr. Lloyd George snapped his fingers. Canada may be the senior Dominion, but we're still only colonials to most of them at Whitehall,' said Stiles breezily, oblivious to the fact I'd actually been referring to him and his leave – not Sir Max. I noted with interest, however, that the Stiles family's circle of influence apparently extended to the new British prime minister. It was precisely the sort of thing Roy Dundas had always warned me about.

'So. What's your story?' asked Stiles, setting down his glass. It was the better side of half full, but only narrowly.

I took a gulp myself. Then I reached for the copy of the London Gazette that I had acquired that very afternoon, with the intention of sending it home to my parents along with a long overdue letter. They would be very pleased, I thought. I folded it open to the page in question. 'Right hand column,' I said. Stiles began to read.

Lt. Malcolm William MacPhail, M.C., Can. Infy.
For conspicuous gallantry and devotion to duty in rushing an enemy strongpoint single-handedly. He showed great courage and determination throughout, thereby materially assisting the operations.

'It was in June, when we took back the hill,' I explained. 'You were convalescing or something.'

'You're a hero,' enthused Stiles. Nonchalantly he threw the paper onto the bar top, smack in the middle of a puddle of water. Alarmed, I grabbed for it. 'Show me your medal,' he said.

I pivoted in my seat so he might see. For no good reason I'd left it on.

He eyed it carefully and I sensed that he very much wanted to reach out and touch it. I turned away.

'One thing…' he said slowly. '… MCs only go to officers, and you weren't an officer at the time, were you?' It was precisely the sort of arcane army regulation that Sam Stiles was well versed in.

I grinned. 'Some kind soul in the battalion antedated my promotion to June 1st, rather than June 17th. I think the colonel may even have had something to do with it. So technically I *was* an officer when the battle took place.'

Stiles shook his head admiringly. He was always keenly interested in unorthodox tips that might help advance his career. 'That calls for a drink, I'd say.' Before I could respond he was waving to the publican, and all I could do then was cheer him on.

We spent a pleasant hour chatting, reminiscing like pals, two trench mates reunited away from the trenches. He'd long since given up trying to pull rank I noticed, reconciled to the fact that to me he would always be Sam or Stiles. That didn't stop him trying to put a certain distance between us by calling me by my last name or my rank. But he was genuinely fascinated to hear my account of the morning at the palace. Not once did the subject of diamonds come up. Benoît had convinced me the diamonds weren't so terribly important. They weren't mine to begin with. Only – and this thought kept returning – they didn't belong to Stiles either. That's what had rankled. What still rankled.

I was pondering whether I should broach the subject when suddenly he asked: 'So when did you hear?'

'To be honest I'd forgotten clean about it. It was so long ago. Even when they first informed me back in the Salient that my name was put up, I never expected it to amount to anything. You can imagine my surprise when a few weeks ago General Lipsett turns up out of nowhere.'

'General Lipsett?'

'Yes, he dropped by in Rouen, at the hospital, to tell me the news.'

'Major-General Lipsett came by the hospital? You can't tell me he travelled all the way to Rouen simply to tell you that you were to get a medal?' In other circumstances, and less buoyed by ale, I would have noticed the danger signs; the narrowing of the eyes; a certain awkward terseness to his speech. But I didn't notice. I drained my glass, and with somewhat of a light head motioned that he should order another. For the first time since the Somme I was feeling good about life.

'Well, yes,' I said. 'Although actually he came for another reason.'

Stiles was listening attentively but said nothing. He just stared. Even when the bartender set down two fresh glasses in front of our noses his gaze didn't waver. It was only at that moment that I realized this might be a delicate matter; uncharacteristically he had said nothing about his own appointment to the staff. But by then I was already well into No-Man's-Land, with nowhere to go but straight ahead, and damn the wire.

'The general asked me to join his staff,' I mumbled.

'Join the 3rd Division staff?' Stiles's face whitened.

'We'll be colleagues,' I said softly, a feeble attempt to pour oil on the waters. But even as I said it I knew deep down it wasn't true. After a pleasant evening I suppose I was trying to avoid a nasty denouement.

Stiles was clenching a fist and looking like he was poised to ram it down my throat. 'I wondered why I hadn't heard anything…' he muttered. Turning, he glared at me. 'Here I thought you were a friend.'

At this my eyes opened in disbelief. I may have had several of the Burton Brewery's finest in me, and so had he, but to say we were friends? What did he think? He'd rolled me of my belongings when I was lying on the ground, half unconscious after soaking up the worst of a Maxim machine gun.

'I tell you in complete confidence that there's a position open on the 3rd Division staff, and what do you do? In no time you worm yourself into a position where you can snatch it yourself.'

'Snatch it? From no. 8 General Hospital?'

But Stiles was open to neither reason nor logic. He began angrily shaking his head. 'You'll pay for this MacPhail. Just you wait and see,' he snarled. Abruptly he got to his feet.

'Will you be finishing that?' I said, pointing at his untouched glass. 'You don't mind if I drink it, do you?'

Stiles perched his cap on his head, and snatching his greatcoat turned to the door. All without saying another word. A cold draught of wind blew through the opening as he stepped out into a chilly winter evening in London. He didn't look back.

Sam Stiles had all the signs he was beginning to feel about me what I felt about him. I had a suspicion I wouldn't be seeing a bag of diamonds anytime soon. But at least I had a trinket of my own. I glanced down admiringly at the cross hanging from my chest.

Sighing, I took a sip of beer. It tasted good.

CHAPTER 17

5th of January, 1917
Near Verdun, France

'Come along then, Lieutenant. We don't want the entire delegation standing around waiting for you,' shouted Major Hammick over his shoulder. Hammick, attached to one of the 1st Division's artillery brigades, was shooting forward in pursuit of the brass hats and Major-General Currie. After a busy first day yesterday the French had stepped up the pace.

'No, sir,' I sighed, keenly aware of the company I was keeping. Hammick was by now a city block ahead. I hobbled after him at speed in the direction of the waiting Renault staff cars, in the backs of which a half-dozen generals were settling in. The motor cars bore a striking resemblance to Paris taxis. There was a spot reserved for me in one of them, in the open air front seat next to the driver. It being January, and I being a Canadian and therefore acclimatized to a little nip in the air, some smart subaltern on the French staff had undoubtedly concluded this neatly solved the seating problem. I guess I should have been grateful I wasn't consigned to the rooftop luggage rack.

I piled in beside the driver, an exhaust of freezing white breath preceding me. '*Bonjour*,' I said loudly, thereby drowning out the sound of my chattering teeth. '*C'est froid.*' The driver cocked his head and looked at me oddly, but didn't respond save for an almost imperceptible nod. I don't think it was my accent, nor even the frigid cold. Perhaps officers in the French Army simply didn't converse with the other ranks. On the other hand maybe this soldier *had* been a Parisian taxi driver; they were never known to talk much, let alone to mere passengers.

Of the more than twenty officers in the party, I was the most junior by a considerable stretch. There were quite a number of majors and a smattering of colonels, but generals predominated. I don't know what on earth had possessed General Lipsett sending me here.

When I reported to 3rd Division headquarters a few days after Christmas, I was given a day or two to settle in and meet the others on the staff. At which point the general sent for me and promptly told me he was shipping me off to Verdun in the first week of the New Year. As Verdun constituted arguably the worst battleground of the entire war this came as a rude shock.

'General Byng has asked General Currie to accompany a group of British officers to Verdun on a fact-finding mission,' Lipsett went on to say.

'Oh?' I replied. 'So the battle's definitely over, sir?'

'Yes, MacPhail,' he sighed. 'Has been for a couple of weeks if you'd been reading the papers.' I had, but other than extolling the great victory, nowhere had I read that the blaze wouldn't reignite. After all it had been raging for ten months running, give or take. Lipsett continued. 'Sir Julian is most interested that we learn from the French experience, so he's asked the general and a couple of others to join in the visit. I've spoken with Currie and he's graciously agreed to have you in his party.'

So, I was to be General Lipsett's personal representative. That had a certain ring to it. Naturally it was more complicated than that. Unofficially I was to be Lipsett's man in the field; officially, I was tagging along with General Currie as lackey, or whatever the current army term was – Stiles would have known, he was fond of a lackey or two himself. That had less of a ring to it.

Lipsett looked at me appraisingly. 'Do you think you're fit?' he asked.

At that stage I might have hemmed and hawed and told him the unvarnished truth; that I occasionally felt like an eighty-year-old waking up with arthritis and a dislocated shoulder. But I had no intention of missing my plum opportunity to serve at headquarters. That much I had learned from Stiles, even though it meant I was to become what I'd so often ridiculed: a staff officer. The alternative was to return to the trenches with one of the battalions. 'No question, sir.' I said firmly.

The car now hit a bump in the road and I reached out a hand to steady myself. On a whim I looked behind through the glass partition, into the passenger compartment.

Major Hammick sat with his back facing me. Across from him was General Currie in animated discussion with the two artillery men squeezed in on the narrow back seat: a Major Brooke of the Royal Artillery, and Lieutenant-Colonel McNaughton from Corps headquarters. After what I'd seen at the Somme it was no particular surprise that two-thirds of those attending were gunners. They could certainly use some extra tutoring.

For a moment I observed them, until the general lifted his head and his eyes caught mine, whereupon he nodded tersely. Embarrassed I turned away and pulled up the collar of my coat against the chill. Last night the mercury in the thermometer outside our billet had fallen to well under zero.

8th of January, 1917

A light dusting of snow covered the slope of the hill and the open treeless plains to the northeast beyond, giving it an almost pastoral quality. I say "almost" because the ground was otherwise barren, and even the snow did little to conceal the mottled nature of the terrain. Little near Verdun-sur-Meuse was unscathed. From a safe distance through our field glasses we had earlier viewed what remained of the famous forts to the north at Douaumont and Vaux. The German lines were too close for a more intimate reconnaissance. The French were understandably wary of losing a squad of British generals whilst in their care; that would do the *Entente* irreparable harm. A few exceptions aside, I'm not convinced the Allied cause would have suffered unduly.

Today was the final day of our visit. Near the crest of the hill at the lookout overlooking the Meuse, the desolate ruins of the city in the foreground and the battleground further off, the generals were clustered around one of the interpreters. A well-known French general stood a few paces in front of them making sweeping motions with his arm, pointing out the salient features of the land and explaining how the counter-attack under General Nivelle had retaken Douaumont. This was why we were here; not to hear of the months of desperate stalemate, but rather how the crushing offensives in October and December had pushed the Germans back with carefully-planned creeping barrages that trapped them in their holes while platoons of men, specially trained for the purpose, swept down upon them before they could react.

'It must be one of the most glorious victories in the history of the wars of the world,' I heard General Currie say to General "Curly" Birch of GHQ only yesterday, after yet another visit to yet another headquarters. I wasn't able to hear Birch's reply.

We'd seen no shortage of headquarters: from Corps HQs to divisional HQs, to brigade HQs, down to what I imagined was a platoon HQ. This last had little to recommend it, and our guides early this morning were unusually antsy about shepherding us away as quickly as possible. However as was common this trip, General Currie was not to be rushed. He'd cornered a young officer and was peppering him and the interpreter with all sorts of questions – the answers to which didn't sound as if they were entirely in accordance with those of the lieutenant's superiors. The others in the party had looked on, amused.

Presently I stomped my feet and furiously rubbed my hands together. The last time I'd had to do that I'd been in the trenches.

Normally I would have been very interested to hear General Mangin's briefing, but there was no room for other observers, and certainly not those of the more plebeian variety. Therefore I waited with the rest of the party, at a distance, contenting myself in the knowledge they all outranked me and weren't invited either, their feet probably as cold as mine.

Major Hammick looked at me and motioned I should come over. He was standing with Major Brooke and Lieutenant-Colonel McNaughton.

I went over to them and nodded politely.

'Have you found it worthwhile, sir?' I asked, addressing myself to Brooke. 'The visit, I mean.' Hammick I'd gotten to know but Brooke's role in this party was most peculiar. He was only a major, came from the 17th Divisional artillery, yet his own divisional commander wasn't even present. Furthermore I couldn't help noticing he was spending considerable time with Currie and the Canadian contingent.

'Yes. Yes, it's been intensely interesting,' Brooke replied, enthusiastically.

He was on the verge of saying more when McNaughton interjected. 'It's a junket,' he growled. The colonel had been standing to one side and was obviously bored for he joined the discussion with relish. A serious looking man, only a few years older than I, McNaughton had keen penetrating eyes and a countenance that on occasion made me think of the pet lion he was reputed to keep.

'Come now, sir,' said Brooke. 'Surely you must admit you've heard *something* new. The French appear to have mastered the creeping barrage. And look what a success it's been. The infantry and the artillery will be working together in future as never before if we can follow their example.'

'I've heard what *not* to do in organizing an efficient artillery service,' he grumbled.

When every part of you is numb it's not long before that inevitably spreads to the brain, or so I told myself afterwards. 'Well, sir, as a veteran of the Somme that seems a trifle harsh given that we have some organizing to do of our own,' I said.

Although the colonel had more likely than not been responsible for one or two of the bombardments I was referring to, he took it gracefully. Either that or he didn't catch my meaning. 'Trigonometry, Lieutenant, it's a question of trigonometry. That and applying a few other scientific methods.'

I think he saw scepticism in my look – actually I'd been racking my brain trying to recall my high school math lessons for some hint of what he was talking about – for he embarked on an explanation of sorts.

'The French fire was terribly imprecise. They were improvising the entire time...'

'On the contrary, sir,' said Brooke, heroically grabbing the baton and saving me from embarrassment or worse, 'their initial barrage was planned most carefully.'

Before long the three of them – Hammick had joined in – were engaged in a vigorous debate. To think I always assumed that all gunners ever did was shovel oversized shells into a big barrel and pull at a cord. Apparently there was more to it than I realized.

The day and our programme was to conclude with a visit to Souilly, at the headquarters of General Nivelle's legendary Second Army.

Souilly itself was unremarkable, an austere and dreary town of utilitarian brick and stone buildings, cut through by a thoroughfare consumed by mud, the latter having long since encroached upon the adjoining *trottoir* as well. Souilly's attraction lay in the fact it was far to the south of the battlefield and consequently wore none of its scars, nor suffered the devastation we had witnessed all week. That was what had commended it to the generals who'd directed this months' long campaign.

Army headquarters was located in the Mairie, a two-storey grey stone block in the centre of town, which demanded attention for its sheer solidity, if not its beauty. Two rows of five large French windows were arrayed on the façade, those of the first floor pleasingly rounded at the top – all marked by grilles that appeared from a distance to be white crosses. It made for a pleasing symmetry to the eye, an effect only slightly diminished by an ungainly stone staircase the size and contours of Fort Douaumont that had to be scaled before one reached the heavy oaken door.

Général Guillamat, a stubby, round-faced figure with a kindly look and a flowering grey walrus of a moustache greeted the party as we pulled up. Nivelle had been promoted to command France's armies in the North and Northeast in the wake of his success. Therefore the Deuxième Armée had passed to Guillamat and he welcomed us with enthusiasm. Once past the general and the guard of honour, we trooped up the stairs and into the former city hall.

Inside a surprise awaited.

'*Général, pouvez-vous me suivre s'il vous plaît?*' said the spectacled and highly starched adjutant to General Currie.

Currie – not one to whom French comes naturally – appeared to understand the request that he follow. McNaughton raised his eyebrows at me. Not because I was in the know, only that I happened to be walking beside him and he was as intrigued as the rest of us. Like a gaggle of goslings tied to the mother goose, McNaughton, Hammick, Brooke and I went in pursuit of the general. While the others in the delegation veered off left into a large room at the front, we were led to the back, our boots clacking noisily down the marbled hallway.

Inside the rather cramped office stood a French general, cap-less, hands behind his back. Behind him was a table covered with a colourful thick tapestry, overflowing with papers and maps. Short cropped hair, small dark eyes, and sagging jowls astride a severe little moustache, the general looked less the victor of Verdun than a man with the weight of the world on his shoulders. At the sight of us however his eyes brightened, and the dour expression softened a touch.

'General Nivelle,' I heard General Currie say.

Even without the hint I would have recognized him. You couldn't read a French newspaper the past months without seeing his likeness.

There was no interpreter, but Brooke – his knowledge of the language acquired as a child brought up in France – sidled up to Currie, to intervene if called upon. It proved unnecessary as Nivelle spoke admirable English. Despite the gaping difference in rank – a commander-in-chief being a wholly different animal than a divisional commander – both men soon developed a rapport of sorts. After several minutes Nivelle signalled an end to the conversation by wishing us well, expressing the hope that we might have learned something useful that we could put into practice. Then he shook each of our hands, before accompanying us down the hall where he met the others and gave the final lecture of the visit.

When it ended a lunch was served. While of a simple nature, consisting of an assortment of cheeses, meats and breads, no French lunch is complete without a glass or two of the country's finest. Or in my case one or two more. I reckoned I would sleep it off on the long journey northwards.

'It seems to me, that too many "victories" like the one at the Somme and we risk losing the war,' I was saying. The "junior" ranks had adjourned to the *trottoir* and I was holding forth on matters that lieutenants are traditionally advised to avoid. I was quickly reminded of that.

'The lieutenant would do well to remember his position,' intoned a stiff voice off my starboard quarter. My senses not entirely dimmed, I quickly straightened and assumed the position: salute and all. 'Yes, sir,' I said pertly.

Major-General Shute of the 63rd (Royal Navy) Division acknowledged me with a cursory flap of his hand, and an excellent overview of his bulbous nose as it pivoted towards me before tacking to return to more congenial company. Major-General Deverell was at his side.

A gassy praise of the lunch and the '*hospitalité Français*' followed from Shute, and the two generals strolled towards their cars, and out of earshot.

'What a shit,' I mumbled to myself. My choice of expletives was not entirely coincidental. Shute had acquired a bit of a reputation in the British Army. I'd learned of it in Rouen at the hospital where a lieutenant from Shute's division regaled us with a ditty by a fellow officer that left us rolling in the aisles. Apparently it had come about as a result of one of the general's latrine inspections. The last verse was a particular favourite of mine – more so of late.

For shit may be shot at odd corners
and paper supplied there to suit,
but a shit would be shot without mourners
If somebody shot that shit Shute.

General Currie came bolting down the steps, his eyes gleaming. He was positively chomping at the bit to get back to headquarters and report his findings. Knowing a little of him and General Byng, I had a feeling we'd be dancing to a different drumbeat forthwith.

'Do you think the Navy will be setting a new course too, after this?' I asked Hammick.

He rolled his eyes. He'd witnessed the altercation with Shute. 'No. He doesn't strike me as the sort to go to the bother.'

'A junket in other words,' I said sourly.

'Yes, for some of them I'm afraid it was.'

Instead of sleeping the long journey back to Arras, I spent the first couple of hours thinking. It was something General Nivelle had said. There was one word I couldn't get out of my mind: *bientôt*. Soon. He'd said it in French, which was maybe why I hadn't attached any significance to it at the time. 'Perhaps there are profitable lessons for you that you will be able to employ in your future operations,' he had said to Currie, before adding a split-second later, *'bientôt'*. No, it was not *à bientôt*, or "see you soon". I was quite certain. It was just the single word, and it could mean only one thing.

Suddenly this visit was cast in a different light. The French commander-in-chief was aware of something that was going to unfold, and soon, too. Equally it was apparent we were to be in on it. I would have thrown out a few fishing lines to General Currie but he was in the back seat, dozing. I should have been following his example.

However General Lipsett might know something. I would think about how best to approach it.

CHAPTER 18

20th of January, 1917
Hermaville, France

It was to be several weeks before I learned more.

Together with a few others, I arrived early at the 3rd Divisional Training school, only a modest walk from the château down past the church and along the frost-covered rue de L'Eglise. I was anxious not to be late. At 11 a.m. there was to be a demonstration of the platoon formations we'd recently adopted from the French.

'Why don't you attend?' General Lipsett had said, when he saw me in the hallway late yesterday. 'After all, you're the only one from the division who learned about it firsthand at Verdun.' I needed no encouragement.

It made for a welcome diversion from writing movement orders, which to a large extent is what I had been doing since arriving back at the division.

Naturally I understood the need for them. Getting 12,000 men in and out of the line on a regular basis requires a lot of preparation and organisation; trench reliefs to be carefully coordinated; billets and headquarters in the rear to be arranged, transportation where necessary. I was beginning to understand why it was that we marched everywhere – it was too darned complicated to come up with an alternative. It seemed a never-ending chore. While I appreciated a real bed, a roof over my head (especially a roof as grand as that of the lovely Château d'Hermaville), and three square meals a day, I caught myself yawning on more than one occasion. The GSO 1, Lieutenant-Colonel Hayter, had caught me too. Only yesterday.

Hermaville was a sleepy agrarian village, in the western hinterland of Arras, where I don't think much of any note had happened in the centuries prior to the war. Nor had things really changed in the interim. The front was a day's march to the east. However the meandering dirt lanes of Hermaville were undoubtedly livelier than they had been, houses and farms teamed with billeted soldiers, headquarters rotated in and out of the château, and a wide variety of other army units, including training schools, took root in the immediate vicinity.

The divisional training school was established at a farm on the fringes of the settlement. With its many barns and sheds, and a vista of tree-lined fields surrounding it on three sides, it was ideal for both classroom and practical training. Furthermore, someone had gone to considerable effort to defile this idyllic scene, transforming it into a battlefield complete with trenches and wire. I stood looking at the biggest of these fields.

Haltingly, feet stopped beside me. A haze of breath cut through the chilly air. 'So, MacPhail, what's it all about?'

I looked at him, puzzled. I had had nothing to do with today's demonstration.

'You were there weren't you?' Major Meredith insisted.

Since returning from Verdun I'd acquired a curious measure of respect as the divisional expert on matters French. Not only had Lipsett pumped me dry – though he'd stared at me blankly when I hinted the information might be useful in our 'forthcoming operations' – one or two of the battalion GOCs had accosted me with questions about the visit. As had the other staff. Meredith too was referring to Verdun. This past week the reorganisation had been the talk of the division. There were quite a few changes required for what General Currie had in mind. As with all change, that inevitably brought doubters.

'Sure,' I allowed. 'I was there, sir. You really should see the new platoon structure as an extension of a few things we tried ourselves at the Somme. Instead of the grenadiers and the machine guns working beside the infantry in their own companies, now they're integrated. If there was one thing the French repeated time and again, it was that the platoon leaders are the only ones able to react when required. But they need the bombers, machine guns and scouts at hand to do so.'

'Sounds a little risky to me. Who will control the battle?'

'That was rather the point the French were making. You were at the Somme, sir. After the first few minutes of an attack no one in the rear is in control. Even the company commanders are sometimes at wits end. Crashing wave after wave of men into a wire barrier according to some predetermined plan hasn't proven a gigantic success.'

'Put like that...' Meredith rubbed at his chin, thinking.

'That's not the only thing the French told us. Were you able to attend one of General Currie's lectures, sir?'

He shook his head in regret. 'I wanted to.'

'That's too bad, sir. As the general explained, the other major lesson is that every man must be thoroughly trained and rehearsed in the work he has to do. Let the platoons take the initiative, but make sure they're able and prepared to do so.'

'Fascinating,' said Meredith.

Whether he truly found so or not, the point was a moot one. A large staff car crunched up the lane.

Punctually, a few minutes before eleven, General Sir Henry Horne of the First Army had arrived.

When I first heard he was coming I half expected "Bungo" Byng to be accompanying him. But our Corps commander was absent, leaving affairs in the capable hands of General Lipsett and Colonel Hayter. In addition to the school OC and a battalion commander, a whole assortment of other worthies were present, as well as a few unworthies such as myself. The observers threatened to outnumber the platoons they were observing.

As this was the first opportunity I'd ever had to scrutinize a full general and an army commander at such close quarters, I made the most of it.

'That's quite a nose he's got,' I mused as we watched General Lipsett making the introductions.

'Lieutenant!' hissed Meredith.

Silently I went back to my observations.

As a Brigadier Horne had fought in the desperate rearguard action of 1914. He must have done well for they made him a Major-General. After a "mixed" outing at Festubert – weeks after the attack I'd helped carry the bodies of his men out of No-Man's-Land – they sent him to the Middle East for a spell and another promotion. His tenure at the Somme was equally "mixed" from all I'd heard. The Welsh certainly didn't care for him overly, not after Mametz Wood. Somebody obviously felt differently, however, for before long they'd given him an army to command. It just so happened we were in it.

'These are two members of my staff, Major Meredith and Lieutenant MacPhail,' said General Lipsett, as he guided our Army Commander along.

I threw up my arm in a salute. Meredith was a full second quicker on the uptake. Viewing the two of us from the rearguard position, Colonel Hayter's sagging, doleful eyes had a look of resignation to them.

'Gentlemen,' Horne said gravely. He looked straight at me, then proceeded to give Meredith the once-over. A quick glance was the intention. But his head darted back to look again, as if his eyes were deceiving him. With the crooked glimmer of a smile, he allowed Lipsett to hurry him on.

Meredith threw up his hands in bewilderment and looked at me. 'What?'

I pointed at his cap.

He took it off. 'Damn,' he said. The sizeable twig perched there rolled off. 'Don't you dare say a word, MacPhail.' I shrugged. 'You might have mentioned it earlier,' he muttered.

Meredith probably thought otherwise but one of the attractions of the Château d'Hermaville was that it was surrounded by trees, striking even in winter.

For all Meredith's embarrassment, I think what struck General Horne most about his visit to Hermaville was the final assault on the trench. Even I was struck by it and I'd been involved in the real thing. I wondered if he had.

Two grenades went off and a Lewis gun erupted. Then another joined it. When everyone was certain the machine gunners and bombers had done their bit – no medals being awarded for those quick off the mark during a demonstration with live ammunition – the riflemen surged forward to seize the trench. Seldom in the annals of this war had a victory been so decisive, or so predictable. All the same, it was a nice piece of theatre, with precisely enough drama to keep a general entertained whilst informing him also.

Curious, I sidled over to where the post-battle action was.

It was crowded. I wasn't the only one who wanted to hear what, if anything, General Horne had to say. Without using my elbows I couldn't get within ten yards of the inner circle. So I decided to employ a different strategy and went to stand by his staff car instead. The driver looked at me inquiringly and I nodded in return. As I was clearly not there to polish the hood ornament, and feeling somewhat self-conscious from the regular glances he threw in my direction, I pulled out a notepad and made as if I had some important scribblings to consign to it.

'Nothing seriously amiss, I trust, Lieutenant MacPhail?'

Lipsett, Horne, Hayter and a clean-shaven major whom I took to be the General's adjutant, were walking towards me. 'No, sir,' I said hurriedly. 'It went very well.'

'The preparations were thorough enough for your liking?'

Out of the corner of my eye I could see General Horne watching bemusedly.

'Most definitely, sir,' I said, my cheeks colouring.

Lipsett turned to Horne. 'The lieutenant accompanied General Currie on his visit to Verdun. So he has more than a passing acquaintance with the platoon tactics we're using. He's reminded me on several occasions that the key to success is in the preparation,' he said, with a wink.

'Did he indeed?' Horne replied. His eyes were kindly as they alighted on me. 'The young man may prove a useful asset to you in the coming period, Louis.'

To which Lipsett raised his eyebrows but said nothing.

Walking back to the château shortly afterwards, replaying the exchange in my head like a phonograph needle stuck in a groove it couldn't get out of, I was certain General Horne had let something slip. Just as General Nivelle had. Yet if there was something coming, the question was what? A few possibilities came to mind.

If I hadn't been so preoccupied thinking about what those were, rather than the task at hand, I'm certain I wouldn't have made the mistake.

CHAPTER 19

22nd of January, 1917
Hermaville, France

A short, spectacle-endowed and freckle-faced soldier whom I didn't recognize presented himself before me. His entrance into the room where I and five others were bent over our desks had not gone unnoticed. First, he wrenched open the door – one of those solid oak designs that had been all the rage amongst French castle owners of a certain generation – only to let it fall shut again with a deep thud. Then he'd stepped on Cassidy's pet terrier. Through it all I'd kept my nose down.

Only now he was standing in front of me. 'The colonel is asking for you, sir,' he said in a nervous staccato burst.

'Just give me a moment,' I answered, 'I'll be right with you.' I had a couple of things I wanted to complete.

'You'd best come straight away, sir,' said the soldier. His voice had an urgency to it.

Alarmed I looked up.

'I'm sorry, sir, but he told me to hurry.'

'Yes, yes, of course. I'm coming.'

Luckily, I didn't dither.

'What the blazes have you been doing, MacPhail?' thundered Colonel Hayter. He was standing with both hands parked on his hips, awaiting my arrival. Hayter was a Canadian but had served much of his career in the British Army, leaving him with an oddly-affected accent, each word spoken clearly and precisely. On this occasion his words erupted in a blistering tempo. The colonel was not a man easily riled, so I had a foreboding this might be serious.

'Sir?'

'You sent No. 2 Company of the Divisional train to Cambligneul!?'

I shifted on my feet. 'It's possible, sir,' I mumbled, trying to recall. The problem was it was a little like trying to remember your sixth move in your third chess match, four days ago.

'They were supposed to go to Estrée-Cauchie. I had their commander on the telephone this morning and he's livid, and rightly so. They spent hours last night mucking around and had to march back another two miles along the path they'd just come, simply because you sent them to the wrong place.'

My cheeks began to colour and I tried to look contrite. There was not much I could say in response. I felt like a complete idiot.

'I've a good mind to send you down there to explain in person,' growled the colonel.

I hung my head. 'I'll go if you like, sir.'

'What! And have them lynch you? Do you realize the paperwork that would cause? There'd be an inquiry. Some poor sods would be up on charges and I'd have to find a plot somewhere in which to throw your sorry remains.' Violently he shook his head. The worst of it was, I could see the disappointment on his face. I know he'd spoken favourably of me to the general in the past. He may even have been the reason why I was on the staff to begin with. 'You were a lawyer, MacPhail, you should be used to a few small details. This work is not exactly crafting the Magna Carta.'

'No, sir.'

It wasn't the worst of disasters, but it was very, very sloppy. There was no question about that. It was the sort of sloppiness that reinforced every scathing preconception an ordinary solder ever had about the staff. And I knew precisely what the colonel was thinking. Sloppiness at another moment might prove disastrous. He dismissed me with a curt wave of his hand.

Which is why when the call went out for volunteers for an urgent task early the next morning in the front line, my finger shot up. Only later did I learn I'd volunteered to accompany a raid. I don't think I would have reconsidered even if I had known.

23rd of January, 1917
Watling Crater, west of Neuville-Saint-Vaast, France

It was bitterly cold and the sun hadn't yet emerged when I encountered the first of the party of RCR towards the rear of the Folie section, 1000 yards east of the crossroads at Neuville-Saint-Vaast. Accompanying them I made my way down the communication trench towards the assembly point. The footing was treacherous from the rain, the snow, and all the traffic this part of the line saw. The raiding party was roughly thirty strong, an average-sized force as these things went, divided into three groups led by three officers. To my delight and astonishment there was a familiar face amongst them.

'Benoît! My Lord! I assumed you were still in Rouen,' I said.

He seized my hand and proceeded to squeeze the very life out of it. 'I might have been too,' he replied, with a wicked grin, 'if the doctor hadn't caught me with one of those pretty nurses. He declared me fit for immediate service.'

I pulled a long face. 'Tell me it wasn't the matron?'

'No, no, not her,' he said, and his teeth flashed again. 'So, Mac, what's this all about?'

'What makes you think I know? I may be on the staff…' At this the words shrivelled in my mouth. The potentially temporal nature of my appointment filled my thoughts as they had much of yesterday, a relief to close my eyes last night. I coughed and ploughed on: 'You know more than I do. All I was told was that the gentlemen at headquarters are anxious to hear the results of the raid. Seeing as how the intelligence officer is on leave, well… Well, that left me.'

'Hmm –' said DuBois, in the sort of tone that could have meant anything. For someone so ebullient, he could be terribly taciturn at times.

'Look, they said the purpose was to inflict as many casualties as possible. Hopefully you'll grab a prisoner or two so we can make some identifications, which is probably why they sent me. Surely you read the orders?'

He looked at me with guileless eyes, the sort you never would have expected on such a giant of a man. 'Does that mean you're not coming with us?'

In all honesty I hadn't planned on going as far as I had. I'd been lamenting the fact I hadn't remained at battalion headquarters with a few sandbagged logs overhead, and the promise of something warm to drink. The further you went down the trenches the less hospitable they became. That I was expected to write and deliver a report was one thing – no one said I had to provide the content to fill it.

DuBois stared at me expectantly.

'Of course, I'm coming,' I said breezily. 'Did you think I was going to sit here in a dug-out and sip tea?'

DuBois said nothing.

A little before 7.30 a.m. – ZERO Hour for our planned incursion into Fritz's current abode in this small corner of the Artois – I took a very cautious peek over the parapet. If I was going to put my life on the line it wouldn't hurt to do a little reconnaissance. It was definitely lighter, though not yet fully light. A large sign was posted incongruously in front of the German trench. The words on it were clearly legible even from this distance: *Cut out your damned artillery. We too are from the Somme.*

'Have a peek,' I said to Benoît. 'Fritzie seems a trifle on edge.'

He took a hurried glance. '*Tant pis,*' he muttered darkly. 'Wait 'til I'm in the artillery –'

For some reason Benoît had taken a serious disliking to our foe. Even getting shot, shelled, and gassed daily most in the trenches were philosophical about it. Or fatalistic. It was sometimes hard to tell the difference. Not Benoît. He'd never met a Fritz yet he didn't want to put his bayonet in.

Seeing as how the German sign said nothing about raids we proceeded apace with our preparations. Right before leaving Lieutenant Gray came rushing along the trench in a great tear with some important information. 'Remember, fellas, the withdrawal signal is when I give two Gs on the bugle,' he told us breathlessly. I looked at DuBois, who nodded understandingly. It was a fortunate thing C party was in his hands; I couldn't tell a G on the bugle from any other letter. In fact I don't think I even knew they had letters until then.

We entered the enemy line through the Watling Crater, a monstrous hole in the ground, the result of a mine the German tunnellers had exploded under our trenches. As the crater was now occupied by them, their efforts to gain a few yards had clearly been successful. Equally clear was that our artillery and trench mortars had made it a Pyrrhic victory; their plaintive sign was proof of that. The post, a woeful barricade of sandbags in the left rear of the crater wasn't heavily manned. The lone sentry was quickly disposed of. Barreling down a narrow sap for fifty yards eastward, we reached their front line, midway between the intersections of two communication trenches known as Fodder and Forge.

Slowing we came upon the main fire trench. The party in front had come to a near standstill. The lead men were checking for sentries and defenders willing to brave the box bombardment of trench mortars and field guns that was pounding away not far to the German rear. The coast must have been clear for the line of men began to move. I saw the first of them turn and set off northwards at a fast trot. We followed but DuBois took us in the opposite direction.

It was a strange sensation once again being in a German trench. Yet these were unlike any German trenches I had ever seen. Once neatly revetted with woven branches lining the walls and a fence post every few feet to anchor them in place, the revetting was in shreds. The walls were crumbling away in many places with nothing to hold the dirt in place. Of the bathmats there were but a few. They weren't in great condition either. Our artillery had evidently played heavily over these parts. Uncharacteristically our foe had not made the needed repairs. The trench was a mess.

We moved down it in single file as fast as we could, a slippery inch-thick veneer of half-frozen mud underfoot and obstacles aplenty. Benoît had insisted I take up the rear, a bomber or two and a few bayonet men leading the way. Having got me here in the first place I think he was suddenly conscious of what he'd got me into.

The man in front stopped abruptly. It was all I could do not to run into him. The man behind me had no such luck. He hit me square from behind. It was only because I'd braced in anticipation that I kept my balance and didn't send the whole line of dominos tumbling over.

'Jesus,' I cussed, then bit my tongue. The bombardment was loud, but here in the trench every sound was strangely amplified to my ears. The winter air could be like that.

'Sorry, sir,' mumbled the soldier.

I grunted. Observing the men ahead reaching for their bombs I pushed my way past.

When he spotted me DuBois threw a glance in the direction of the dug-out entrance. The dug-out was well built, heavy logs to either side, with a thick timbered roof covered with sandbags. Fritz may have let the trenches go, but his dug-outs were first class. There wasn't an enemy soldier in sight.

'There may be more than one entrance,' I said softly. 'Let me take a few men forward and we'll cover that one too. In case they try to make their escape.'

This thought obviously appealed to him. He grinned. 'Like rats in a hole,' he said.

'Something like that,' I replied. He handed me a smoke bomb. I didn't mention that dug-outs occasionally had not just two, but sometimes three entrances. I suspect he probably knew. But if you're going to stand around plotting strategy the battle is usually lost. Better to go on with it. So we did.

Sure enough we discovered a second entrance a few feet around the traverse.

I threw up my hand to signal a halt. Sergeant Ross brushed up beside me and glanced around the corner, hurriedly retrieving his head. He held up three fingers.

I nodded.

They were standing there, smoking cigarettes. I suppose they figured all they had to do was take a half step to one side and slide down the ladder if the shells came their way. Not that the one that got you ever afforded you that kind of forewarning. They'd been at the Somme too, so they ought to have known. They were playing the odds. Which on this morning were stacked against them.

Ross looked behind at the others who'd come with us. I could see on their faces he had their undivided attention. Once again he held up his hand with three fingers extended. The soldiers stashed their bombs away and took hold of their rifles. All with bayonets attached. I stuffed the smoke bomb into a pocket and pulled out the big Webley revolver – without bayonet. I guess they assumed officers could do it by force of personality alone.

Sergeant Ross looked at me.

I gave him a thumbs up.

Again he held his three fingers in the air so all could see. This time they counted down.

We rushed them in a silent charge. Unsurprisingly they spotted us almost immediately, scrambling for their weapons which were leaning against the trench wall, together with a big pile of metal helmets and gas masks. The smoke and the frosty air from their breath billowed around them.

The man furthest from the dug-out was the first to react and he pulled the rifle up horizontally at waist level as if to aim. It was a mistake on his part. Sergeant Ross bored into him at full speed, a foot of cold iron leading the way. The second man's reflexes were worse. He got a bayonet in the gut without even raising his rifle.

The third man was a different story. He too was trying to get his rifle in position, to aim at me; something I try to avoid at all costs. While I could have pulled the trigger this would have done two things. First, a Webley is not a weapon of stealth. Stokes mortars may have it in a one-on-one contest, but at close range a Webley makes a considerable racket. Secondly, one of the main reasons for this whole raid was to secure prisoners and identifications. Turning this soldier into Swiss cheese with .45 calibre-sized holes would put paid to that idea. There was a third possibility – fortunately one I didn't spend much time considering – that I'd miss completely.

Instead I extracted my trigger finger, grabbed the revolver by the long, blue steel barrel and took a final step. While he was still fumbling I chopped the heavy wooden grip down hard on his head. He fell at my feet. But I was given little time to admire my neat work.

'Sir?' said Ross. What sounded like bombs going off could be heard near the first entrance. Benoît was most eager to get on with it.

'Have a look,' I instructed.

He scrambled down the ladder a few steps, then pulled aside one corner of a heavy curtain. It was a gas blanket, not dissimilar to what we used ourselves. I bent over and peered past him down through the opening. Far at the bottom a faint light shimmered. Voices could be heard. Bottom must have been thirty feet underground.

I glanced at the pile of helmets and masks lying there. 'Smoke first,' I said.

Quickly Sergeant Ross climbed back up and directed one of the soldiers to take his place.

On our signal the soldier wrenched open the curtain. He scrambled back up the ladder as if his life depended on it; which it might well have done. I looked down at the no. 27 grenade I was holding. It seemed innocuous enough, a hand-sized metal canister dabbed in drab olive green. A thick brass rod protruded from one end. Extracting the small pin from the rod I extended my arm and let it fall. The sergeant and another man tossed theirs down at almost the identical moment.

There were thuds and a flash; the phosphorous had ignited. Sooner than I expected wisps of white smoke, acrid to the nose, curled back up towards us.

The voices below had become shouts. Ross waited. He'd plainly done this sort of thing before. He knew that as the smoke from the bombs steadily smothered the chamber the Germans would be desperately seeking an exit.

'Some Tickler's artillery would be just the thing,' I said, referring to the newly improved and highly explosive old favourite. Once fashioned by hand from jam tins, the latest factory-built versions were highly effective at blowing up dug-outs.

'We just have these,' he said, and showed me a Mills bomb clasped in his fist.

For a brief second I was afraid he'd left it too late. There was a scuffle of boots madly clambering up the ladder from below. But then he said, 'NOW!' His arm and two others reached out and dropped their grenades down the shaft. They went off in rapid succession, modest bangs that weren't any more impressive than fire crackers, though sounds deceived.

Wary that someone might start firing up the hole towards us – blindly, but no less lethal for that – we took a cautious look. From the dark well leading to the dug-out floor, tendrils of smoke issued forth. There was nothing to see. However, we both heard the tortured moans.

The pile of helmets again caught my eye. There were more than ten of them. Perhaps even fifteen.

'We really must go,' I said to Ross. 'On to the next before they're on to us.' No more than a minute – maybe two – had elapsed. As suggestions go it was laid on thick and while it was his unit, not mine, it takes a brave soldier to disregard the suggestion of a superior officer. The sergeant, accustomed to the relentless momentum of a raid, knew as well as I did that if we were to have any hope of catching others in the next dug-out we needed to move fast. Neither of us wanted to encounter a whole platoon fresh from breakfast with helmets on and rifles ready.

Ross looked sceptically at our erstwhile prisoner. The man had risen to his knees in the interim. He looked to be nursing a very tender head.

'You go ahead. I'll take care of him,' I said. Something that was easier said than done. This particular Fritz appeared to have had his fill of war. On top of which he could barely walk. That left me employing the usual devices of a revolver prodding him in the gut, while my other arm was clamped around his side so he wouldn't collapse. We weren't fast but at least we were moving. Benoît nodded his approval as he raced past with the others.

By the time the Fritz and I reached the second dug-out, the deed was done. Some of the soldiers had already left for the next.

'Ça va?' inquired Benoît, breathing heavily.

'It's fine,' I replied. 'I'll wait with him back at the turnoff. You go on. Don't worry, everything's under control.' To emphasize I stuck the barrel of the Webley in the man's ear.

When Benoît turned away, so did I. Only then did I see the man staring at me, with plaintive eyes and a pallor coloured white.

Quickly I retrieved the revolver from his ear and shook my head. 'No, no. As long as you do what you're told, you've nothing to worry about.' He looked doubtful. 'Kamerad?' I said.

Emphatically he bobbed his head up and down. *That* he did understand.

My calming words notwithstanding, I watched him like a hawk. I remembered well the tale from Courcelette when the captured but still haughty German Oberst assured one of ours that his side would never think of firing upon the bearer of a red cross. Yet when colonel and cohort were sent to our rear without escort under those very auspices, his mates promptly did precisely that. They wiped out nearly half of them. Of course it was always possible the colonel wasn't popular with his own side. Nevertheless, the principle was a useful one. Ask the French. They didn't trust the Germans much either since their sweeping right hook through Belgium, Luxembourg and the north of the country.

For this and other reasons sitting around waiting had its downside. At least running you were preoccupied, with no time to think things you shouldn't, or hear the many noises that might set you wondering. Every noise was a potential harbinger of trouble. At the approach of multiple footsteps down the trench, trouble was foremost in my mind.

'Shh,' I whispered to the prisoner. I indicated he should move to the opposite wall.

If they were German I reckoned they'd spot him first rounding the traverse. That would give me a precious extra second, maybe even the element of surprise. The prisoner was accustomed to my menacing theatrics with the revolver for he quickly did what I asked. Then I got down on one knee and nestled in tight against the trench wall. I held the Webley extended in a two-handed grip. Six rounds were all that I had. If worse came to worst it wouldn't be enough. Earlier I'd thought of taking one of the German carbines, but with all the hassle of getting the prisoner moving, I'd clean forgotten.

Three of them rounded the bend almost at once. Stared at the prisoner, then noticed me.

'*Oupelaï!*' exclaimed the first, suddenly grasping the game.

I lowered the revolver. 'Jesus, Benoît. You sure know how to get a man's wind up.'

At that moment two blasts of a bugle sounded.

'Were those Gs?' I asked.

DuBois nodded.

'You're certain?'

He smacked me on the back of the helmet. 'Move it, Mac. We're heading back.'

Back in our own trenches the mood was one of relief, mingled with mild elation. Barely twenty minutes had passed since we set out. To me it felt considerably longer. Benoît was wearing a grin that could have bridged a canal. Not only had his party bombed four dug-outs and taken a prisoner, they'd escaped without a single casualty.

'I think we caught them at breakfast,' I said. 'It's the only possible explanation.'

'A man has to eat,' rumbled Benoît, displaying an unusual degree of empathy for our enemy. Few men valued a good meal… any meal… like he did. 'You have a few tidbits for your report, eh?' He smiled.

'I think so,' I replied. 'A few odds and ends about the state of the trenches, the wire, the dug-outs. I'll interview the others, naturally.' Then I pointed at the prisoner. '23rd Reserve Infantrie Regiment. Nothing new about that, of course. But that they're still here may be news in itself.'

'How do you know these things, Mac?'

I frowned.

'His regiment, and so on.'

'Well for one thing I read the intelligence summaries.'

Patiently he waited for me to continue.

'Even if I hadn't, the 23 on his shoulder boards is a pretty big clue –' I raised an eyebrow.

Benoît glanced over at the prisoner seemingly to confirm, then grunted.

'I was thinking,' I said. 'When we were waiting around for the raid to begin, you mentioned something about the artillery?'

'Yes. They're transferring me.'

'What?'

'It's true.'

'For some reason I never pictured you as a gunner, Benoît.'

He looked down. 'I requested it.'

'You did! Whatever made you do that?'

'It was either the artillery or the Flying Corps. And I've never been one for heights.'

'No,' I said, contemplatively. 'I imagine you're probably right about that.'

'Do you think so?'

'Well I don't see one of those contraptions getting off the ground with all of you aboard. They're flimsy enough as it is. At least this way when they stuff you down the barrel there'll be a few hundred pounds of gunpowder to help you on your way.'

DuBois grimaced. The strange thing was I couldn't imagine what either he or the army was thinking. If ever a man was born to be an infantryman it was Benoît. With the possible exception of the Crème de Menthe he was the most intimidating object I'd ever seen on a battlefield. This transfer was all a bit of a mystery. Apparently, he intended to keep it that way.

One aspect of Benoît's sudden career shift, at least it was voluntary. That couldn't be said for my own prospects. If I didn't get back in Colonel Hayter's good graces I might very well be the one assigned DuBois's place. Whether I liked it or not.

CHAPTER 20

24th of January, 1917
Château de Hermaville, Hermaville, France

'I read your report,' said the colonel evenly. We were in a lovely second-floor room of the château, the frost-covered trees outside visible from any one of three imposing windows. He sat relaxed, his hands clasped together on his desk. I stood before him "at ease", feeling anything but, concentrating on such immediate priorities as breathing.

'Sir?' Seldom had I polished my buttons and buffed my uniform as I had today.

'It was quite a success the raid.'

'Oh, yes, sir. More than a hundred enemy casualties all told. For obvious reasons we couldn't count them all, but from what I witnessed I don't think it's an unreasonable estimate.'

'Their trenches were a mess, you wrote? I find that impossible to imagine.'

'As did I, sir. But while their trenches were a shambles, their dug-outs were first rate. Which I guess leads to the most important lesson.'

At this I saw I had Hayter's full attention. 'Go on, Lieutenant,' he said.

'No matter how heavy the barrage, there's no way our artillery can touch them in those deep dug-outs, sir. We could shower them with high explosive for a week. And even with the new fuses they're still invulnerable.'

'A lesson, you said?'

Thoughtfully I bit my lip, wondering whether I should continue pressing forward. But I'd already committed. Hayter was drumming his fingers on the desk, watching.

'It's another example of what we saw at the Somme, sir. Not forgetting about the French experience. It seems obvious that the only way we can take trenches like these are if we can catch the Boche still in their dug-outs. Of course that means the infantry and artillery must coordinate like never before; our men need to be at the dug-out entrances before the last shell is fired.'

'Hmm,' said Hayter noncommittally. 'Anything else?'

'Alternatively, we could schedule all our attacks at breakfast, sir. That might work.'

The colonel blinked, the drumming of his fingers stopped, and he glanced at me sharply. He had his mouth open, on the verge of replying, when to the rear I heard the hinges of the door squeak. Hayter's whole posture stiffened. If you're a lieutenant-colonel that can signify only one thing, so I followed his lead.

'Oh, don't let me interrupt,' said General Lipsett. 'Continue as you were, gentlemen.'

A wry grin came to Colonel Hayter's face. 'The lieutenant was just explaining the strategic importance of breakfast,' he said.

'Was he now?'

With that there was nothing for it but to repeat my whole account in considerably more detail. I didn't expect the general had read my report. As a precautionary measure I omitted any references to breakfast.

'Most interesting,' said Lipsett when I was done. His face gave nothing away. But nor was I being peremptorily dismissed, so it seemed a reason for cautious optimism. There hadn't been many of those this past week.

After an interval the general glanced at the colonel and the colonel glanced at the general. General Lipsett said: 'Have you told him?'

Hayter shook his head.

'Well, I'll leave you then. Thank you, Lieutenant. It was most informative.'

'Yes, sir.'

'Perhaps on the next occasion you can enlighten me with your thoughts on breakfast.'

He left before I could read his expression. I looked at Colonel Hayter. 'Tell me what, sir?'

'There's a new man arriving tomorrow from England who is going to join the staff. He's a captain and I've decided to have the two of you work together.'

I felt myself frowning. 'I don't really require any help, sir. Besides, I thought the staff was complete?'

'It is,' he replied, 'but we have a major operation coming –' He saw me twitch and quickly added: 'You'll hear about it soon enough, MacPhail. At the moment I can use every man I can get, and this fellow comes highly recommended. Naturally at some stage I'll need to re-evaluate staffing numbers,' he said smoothly. 'But we're getting ahead of ourselves.'

Impassive eyes stared back at me.

'I see, sir,' I said, not seeing much of anything except that my position was more precarious than I had feared. That the new man outranked me was also not a good sign. Rank carried its privileges and one of those was that in any kind of contest senior officers invariably bested junior ones.

Hayter saw all of this pass across my features, or he must have suspected it, but he didn't say anything more.

I stiffened and came to attention. 'Will that be all, sir?'

'Yes. Carry on. I wanted to let you know in advance. Seeing as how you and he will be working together. Thank you for your report, Lieutenant.'

Sam Stiles was at his personable best when he barged into my personal broom closet at the château. Any rancour he may have harboured had long since evaporated in the wake of his triumph of manoeuvre behind the lines. That I was furthermore to be his adjutant must have tasted as sweet as the fruit those young French girls, the Sweet Nells, were always selling.

'Our paths cross again,' he said jovially.

He'd come straight from the colonel and was therefore not in the least surprised to see me. I was more than a little surprised to see him. With his habit of popping up at the strangest moments I should have been prepared.

'Yes, so it would seem,' I grumbled. I did my best not to sound bitter. 'I do recall telling you back in London that this might happen.'

'You did?'

I nodded. 'You didn't believe me at the time.'

'Water under the bridge,' he said, with a flourish of his hand. 'The important thing is that everything worked out in the end.'

I forced my lips into a smile. To give Stiles his due, I hadn't believed my own words either. Yet here he was. Roy Dundas would have found it all a great lark.

Dundas. I hadn't thought about him in a long while. And now that I had, I felt guilty that I hadn't done so before. I wondered if anyone would think about me once I was buried in the mud somewhere. Likely not. But then if you spent your time thinking about all your friends on the wire somewhere, a trip to the asylum was a near certainty. Better to rail about the cold pork and beans, and the water in your boots.

'Alright MacPhail, let's get started,' said Stiles with uncharacteristic zeal.

From a height I dropped an inch of paper onto the empty desk I presumed would be his. The colour drained from his face.

28th of January, 1917

Colonel Hayter had not exaggerated the need for another man. All the same I couldn't help noticing that with Stiles's arrival my own workload *ceteris paribus* had actually increased. The Latin was a term used in economics that the banker Dundas had taught me. It meant "all else being equal". All else being equal Captain Sam Stiles was proving himself to be a major drain on the division's resources. It made one wonder what the colonel had been thinking taking up London's offer of a new man.

A few days passed and matters worsened. Stiles signed off on the 8th field ambulance being sent to Mont-Saint-Eloi instead of the 8th field engineers. Fortunately, Major Meredith caught it before things got out of hand, but I caught the blame.

Stiles carried on as if nothing very much had happened. While I wasn't even involved in the balls-up I had the distinct impression an accusing finger was pointed squarely in my direction. When Colonel Hayter shot me a look in the hallway that could have sunk the SMS Kaiser, I was certain of it. After that, recognizing the brittleness of my armour, I took to checking all Stiles's work and doing much of it myself – in addition to my own. Sam found this an ideal solution. 'It makes sense for you to occupy yourself with all the minutiae,' he said. 'I've always been better at the big picture.' When I asked what the 'big picture' was at the moment, he brushed me off and left for an early lunch. Lunch may have been what he was referring to.

Of a major operation there was no sign. I was still shunting units around the immediate vicinity, from the line to relief billets, and back to the line again. There were no orders from Corps headquarters or even a hint that we were to pack up and move elsewhere. However, when I learned that the Corps commander was to visit the divisional training school that very morning I was convinced we would finally hear more. Stiles reiterated – twice in the event I hadn't understood the first time – that I was simply far too busy to attend the demonstration – the obvious parallel with his own attendance somehow escaping his attention. I covered for him while he flitted with the senior ranks. But unusually for me I made a point of seeking him out upon his return that afternoon.

'So. Hear anything new?' I asked.

'General Byng expressed himself very pleased with how the training was going.'

'Really? You must feel gratified,' I said.

'Gratified? What the dickens are you on about, MacPhail? I had nothing do with the demonstration.'

'All the units turning up where they were supposed to. For a general, Bungo Byng seems a swell guy. But he might have been a little peeved had the field ambulance mustered for the display of platoon tactics today.'

Stiles groaned. 'Details, details, details. No wonder you've become a clerk.'

I let it pass.

'Have you seen this?' I passed him the latest intelligence summary.

He rifled through the pages, all four of them, then frowned. 'What am I supposed to see?'

'Two raids by the PPCLI in twenty-four hours. And another by the 49th Battalion. Patrols every night –'

'So?'

'Don't you think it might suggest something?'

'Have you had your lunch? You're rambling worse than ever, MacPhail.'

At that my stomach growled. 'Here we have the entire Corps assembled in front of Vimy for months on end. Ever since the Somme actually. It's freezing cold, there's snow on the ground, yet we're raiding multiple times a day. The engineers are busy constructing new subways in the Thélus section...'

'Good for them,' interrupted Stiles. 'What did you expect they'd be doing? Digging latrines? As you said yourself, we've got four divisions to move around and it's not as if we're in the safety of Hyde Park. My head's not as thick as yours; I feel a lot more comfortable with thirty feet of dirt above it. Be grateful. With all the tunnels they've built we could probably hide an entire battalion or two.'

'What did you say?'

'About your head or the battalions?'

'About hiding a battalion or two.'

Stiles hesitated. You didn't get to be a captain from nothing in the space of two years on the strength of a well-preened moustache alone. It required a certain ability to mingle with people who mattered, where you might hear things that mattered. Only it didn't do to blather what you'd heard to every boob crossing your path. After a moment of consideration it appeared my stature hadn't sunk that low. 'That's what I hear,' he said carefully. 'Thélus is not the only subway. They say there are plans for more. What of it?'

I didn't respond. I was thinking. Vimy Ridge. *Could it really be?*

CHAPTER 21

13th of February, 1917
Trenches northeast of Neuville-Saint-Vaast, France

Most nights this month a frosty stillness had cloaked the front lines, the crack of a single rifle shot abrupt and unusually chilling, the sound travelling for miles. Trench flares whooshed upwards, sputtering into a sickly white light, their long shadows swaying ghostly over No-Man's-Land. This night the temperatures had softened. By early morning when I arrived near the front, a thick mist was hanging over the fields, the long grey slope of the ridge that normally dominated the view to the northeast barely visible. Rising above the mist, however, the darkish contours of the crest line could be seen.

Two weeks had passed. Two weeks in which nothing of any real interest crossed my desk. And that surprised me. The intelligence summaries – longer by the day it seemed – were interesting, but there wasn't the slightest mention of an attack on Vimy Ridge. Nor anywhere else for that matter. In the meantime Stiles was doing his level best to ingratiate himself with the colonel, which came down to me doing the work while he sang his own praises. Not that I ever doubted his abilities in that regard; he had a palpable knack for it.

The chance to go out to the line to (hopefully) collect prisoners after a raid was a welcome break in this routine. In fact I'd jumped at the opportunity. So keen had I been in offering my services that both

Major Meredith and Stiles eyed me with a mixture of surprise and suspicion. 'I mean, if there's no one else to do it…,' I mumbled quickly. 'I'll go, of course.'

I was to meet the raiding party as they filed to the rear along Grange Tunnel, one of the principle communication paths that led from the road to the front line. Nearer the front a new subway was being built further eastwards. And Stiles was right, there were a lot of tunnels under construction. All along the western slope of the five-mile long ridge, tunnellers and engineers were busy carving and extending the deep passages in the chalky underground that underlay this part of France.

Partly my enthusiasm about this errand was down to curiosity; I'd never been in one of the tunnels and I wondered what they would look like.

Once through the entrance my small party disappeared into a subterranean passage vastly more elaborate than I anticipated. The tunnel was neatly chiseled in the rock, electric lamps lighting the way. One quickly lost sense of time, and even whether it was night or day.

This section of Grange Avenue close to the road wasn't as deep as the tunnel further along, the sentry informed me, but the chalk walls and the ceiling – high enough that I didn't need to duck, but low enough that stooping seemed appropriate – were imposing. They'd certainly hold up to a few good stomps from above, although whether that included a direct hit or even a close miss was unclear to me. Nevertheless, this passage hewn through the rock did its duty admirably against the bullets, stray or otherwise, likewise against the shards of Krupp steel that Fritz spewed in wearisome abundance. A further benefit to the tunnel was that it concealed everything from the prying eyes on the ridge. Fortunately, too, for the activity was considerable.

'Excuse us, sir,' said a soldier, politely. I stepped hurriedly to one side and observed as he and his companion, dressed lightly for the weather, trotted past carrying a long beam of wood on their shoulders. He brushed the sweat from his brow as he passed. The traffic in both directions was so heavy that after the better part of a mile dodging working parties, I eventually summoned the two men who were with me and we went and sat in a small dank alcove carved in a wall, to await the raiders. Next to me was a switch point and a thick coil of telephone wire. That was another advantage of the tunnel; there were few worries down here about a German shell disrupting communications.

This time I hadn't made the mistake of arriving too early, neatly avoiding the risk I'd be invited to accompany them.

The first I saw of the raiding party was an officer, apparently badly wounded, being helped along by two privates in kilts; one wearing a red-cross band on his arm. I'd seen an advanced dressing station a few alcoves down. But it was a bad omen. The Royal Highlanders or Black Watch, better known to me as the 42nd Battalion, had departed at 9.15 a.m. While there'd been a barrage planned, and the Stokes, rifle grenades and machine guns had been in close support, a daylight raid magnified the risks tenfold – no matter how many times the parties had run up and down the practice trenches.

Standing, I watched as they shuffled by. In close pursuit trooped a single file of men. Exactly fifty of them had gone off to storm the German line between the Durand and Patricia craters. Faces weary, streaked in grime, the expressions were nevertheless ones of exultation not despair. With relief I concluded that the venture had been a successful one, and a broad smile came easily to me. It broadened even further when I spotted the two officers. Their badges indicated that they belonged to the artillery.

As they came abreast, I reached out to the nearest of them and snatched at his sleeve. 'Benoît.'

Startled, he recoiled from my touch. His whole posture tensed like that of an animal cornered, his hand reaching to his side for the revolver or the trench knife. Then he finally saw me and his eyes widened. The stress and anger blew away like gas caught in a stiff wind, and his grin lit the gloom of Grange tunnel.

'Mac!'

'What's going on?' I said. 'This isn't your battalion? You're not even wearing a skirt, although you've certainly got the figure for one.'

'*Non,*' he said slowly. 'My transfer to the field artillery came through.'

It took me a second or two to digest this. Failing to discover any plausible connection between his answer and my question I said: 'And the first thing the field artillery does to welcome you into their ranks is send you out with the infantry? I thought the whole idea was the artillery shovelled eighteen pounders into a breech as quickly as possible, yanked a cord and left the real war to the rest of us.'

Benoît rolled his eyes. 'Mac... come on... Real war? You're at headquarters.'

'Speaking theoretically, then.'

'We were actually here to observe and report on the barrage,' said the lieutenant at Benoît's side. 'Only one thing led to another and before I knew it we were caught up in the action.'

'It's funny you should mention that,' I said, staring pointedly at Benoît. 'I had that identical experience not two weeks earlier.'

'Smythe here shot two Hun,' said Benoît, neatly cutting a full semi-circle around what I'd just said, 'and wounded a third.'

I looked at the lieutenant. Nothing about him marked him out as an experienced raider. He was a good three feet shorter than DuBois. Not that an impressive stature helped any. 'Malcolm MacPhail,' I said, and gave him a hand. 'I thought you artillery fellows were only skilled with the larger calibres?'

'It was a Webley,' he said.

'Ah, the field gun of revolvers.' I looked at Benoît. 'What about you?'

'I think I got one, too.'

His eyes flashed, so I didn't doubt him for a minute. When it came to the Hun, I was glad I was on Benoît's team... whichever one that was at the moment.

We talked for a minute before duty intervened. In my case it was the arrival of two downtrodden Germans who, it later become known, were from the 5th Company of the 23rd R.I.R. In Benoît's case it was Lieutenant Smythe tugging at his sleeve. He shrugged apologetically.

We resolved to meet soon. Before anything came of that, a new piece of the puzzle regarding our future operations fell into place.

16th of February, 1917
Bruay, France

Earlier we had passed them in the motorcar as they lined up on the Bruay-Division road. The entire 7th Brigade was present, all four battalions. They were interspersed with a few corps units and were in marching order, officers mounted on their chargers, pennants flying, awaiting the signal to begin. It would make for an impressive display. Given the exalted nature of our visitor that was the hope. Only after it was complete did I come to realize that it was not merely a show for the sake of show; the high and the mighty were vetting what the Empire's colonies had mustered.

I stood not with the soldiers in their carefully cleaned uniforms, rifles resting on one shoulder with bayonets fixed, but with a selection of the divisional staff a half mile down the dirt road. A half dozen of us were arrayed in file, one beside the other in the knee-high grass behind, so as not to overshadow our guests who stood close to the road. Off our immediate left were a roughly equal number of French staff officers, including a colonel. To their left were the real dignitaries.

Major-General Lipsett was present to command the parade. Beside him was the hero and hope of France, General Robert Nivelle, in all his crisp finery here to take the salute.

Being about as far down the totem pole as it was possible to be in such company I had taken up position on the extreme right. However, with all the gold braid jostling for space it was all I could do not to be pushed out of sight behind one of the trees that lined the road.

'That must make for some sort of record,' I said to Lieutenant Atherby. Atherby had snatched the spot beside me before I cottoned on to the fact that he was consigning me to the outer bleachers.

'What's that?' he asked, rubbing his hands together. It was partly clear this morning, and as a consequence cold enough that my teeth were chattering. Our trench coats we'd left at headquarters in the interests of decorum.

'Two commanders-in-chief visiting in two days' time,' I said.

'Field-Marshal Haig yesterday and then General Nivelle today?'

I nodded. 'It makes you wonder.'

Getting no immediate response I continued: 'Think about it, Allan. There are probably 200 divisions on the Western Front, maybe more, and by chance the two most senior British and French generals on the entire front drop by in rapid succession. We haven't had this much brass visit since the war began.'

'It never really occurred to me there might be something behind it,' Atherby said thoughtfully.

'That's probably why they have you counting boots in the quarter-master's office,' I said, with a grin.

Good-naturedly he shrugged it off. Neither of us was sorry, how-ever, when the marchpast began and we had the excuse of movement to warm up a little – if only to throw up our right arms in salute at intervals.

The RCR and the Royal Highlanders and the others marched past in smart step looking as if they had never seen a battlefield, let alone been in the trenches a few days before. They did it with a swagger that can only come from men who'd seen battle. No matter how much they practised at Shorncliffe there was no way to teach that. Perhaps that was what Nivelle and Haig had really come to see.

When it was done General Nivelle introduced General Lipsett to his staff, and naturally Lipsett reciprocated.

Reaching me Lipsett began a cursory introduction until Nivelle interrupted, saying softly, 'Good morning, lieutenant.'

'Good morning, sir,' I replied.

Nivelle chewed at his lip, no doubt trying to recollect how he knew me. 'Your trip to Verdun was rewarding I hope?'

'Yes, sir, it was. Most rewarding.' Then a strange urge came upon me and I said, 'You should know you can count on us, sir.'

His eyes widened, and he dipped his head to me without respond-ing, whereupon I saluted again and he moved off with General Lipsett.

They stood there afterwards, not twenty feet away, Nivelle and Lipsett, talking.

Atherby said something and I hushed him silent with an angry wave of my arm, but try as I might I could hear nothing of what they were saying. Until a fluke of the air interposed.

'But can you do it, General?' asked Nivelle. 'That is my concern.'

Lipsett said something in reply, although I couldn't hear what. Then he spotted me watching and with a graceful gesture motioned to General Nivelle that they should move on.

It was an odd choice of words he'd used: 'Can you do it?' Especially from a man who'd cracked a hard nut or two himself, like Fort Douaumont. Commanders-in-chief aren't renowned for their doubt-ing characters; if anything a little less confidence might have spared the rest of us a great deal. So that narrowed the field considerably.

I was convinced there was but one nut to which Nivelle could be referring. I did wonder, however, when they were planning on telling us.

CHAPTER 22

24th of February, 1917
Béthune, France

I waited for Benoît outside the elegant wrought-iron gates of the Compagnie des Mines de Bruay, a location chosen not by happenstance, nor for the grandeur of the magnificent administration building standing prominently behind the gates, but solely because our headquarters were situated there. And had been for a couple of blissful weeks. When not being overrun by Germans, coal mining had the air of being a lucrative endeavour.

The sentry outside examined me with undisguised interest, there not being anything remotely of interest in the street or the square opposite. I nodded, then proceeded to ignore him, leaning against one of the fence's imposing pillars of white stone and red brick – a pattern popular in northern France – hoping Benoît wouldn't be long. My stomach was grumbling and he'd promised a dinner fit for a king.

Several cars motored down the street towards us and with the approach of each I straightened up, eager to greet my boisterous French-Canadian friend, only to see all but one carry on past. It puttered through the gates with two officers in the back whom I didn't recognize, from one staff or the other. But no Benoît. After fifteen minutes had passed even the lorries began to attract my attention; one never knew with Benoît. A mule train would have equally interested me by that stage, only I didn't see one of those.

From the north a motorcycle rounded a corner at speed and tore up the pavé, hastening in our direction; a despatch rider with a message of vital importance. The sentry and I stood back as he careered around the corner *enroute* to headquarters. However, he didn't race through the gates as anticipated, but came to a screeching halt of burnt rubber, gasoline fumes, and thick clouds of dust.

The driver peeled back his goggles. 'Sorry I'm so late, Mac.'

'Where'd you get the wheel from?' I asked.

'Borrowed it,' he replied, and winked. I had my suspicions what that implied, but mindful of what had killed the cat, I didn't ask further and got on the back. Or tried to. With 200-plus pounds in front there wasn't a lot of saddle room left. I claimed what little remained, stuffed my cap into my tunic and grabbed hold of Benoît's waist with both arms; if I was going down with the ship he was going down with me.

'*On y va?*' he asked.

'Let's go,' I said. 'I'm starving. This had better be one hell of a dinner, Benoît.'

I heard him chuckle and he threw the throttle wide open. We turned left and roared off towards the north again. Conscious that General Lipsett might be gazing out a second-floor window, I buried my head in Benoît's back. By the time I looked up again we were already out of town.

The road to Béthune was a pleasant one, undulating and unspoilt, the area having seen little of war. I'd taken it on several occasions, a relaxing ride of roughly six miles or twenty minutes by car. Benoît cut a third off that, I saw next to nothing, and my hunger pangs were replaced by a jumpy sensation I typically only feel before going over the top.

We pulled up in the bustling Grande Place and he parked the wheel. A whole corral of sleek chargers of the variety preferred by officers of a certain rank and breeding was tethered nearby.

'All I said was that I was hungry,' I grumbled, as I unwrapped myself from the seat. 'A few extra minutes wouldn't have mattered.'

'Are you hungry or not?' he said. Without waiting for me to quibble further, he motioned I should follow. We headed across the cobble-stone square. Béthune was a town I knew well and liked. Its shops and restaurants were always open and well provisioned, its ancient

Spanish belfry and many old buildings charming, and the thousands of soldiers from England and colonies who passed through daily took eager advantage of all. I'd had a few meals in Béthune in the past, though none so memorable as to remember them.

But Benoît knew a place.

'The Café du Globe,' I mused, reading the giant white letters that ran across the entire façade between the first and second storeys of the building.

'Mac, your cap.'

I put it on. Benoît inspected me, then wearily shook his head. He took the cap in both hands and formed it as he thought it should be, then plopped it back on at a jaunty angle. 'Better.'

Two immaculately groomed Imperial majors were making for the door.

'Is this the sort of place you pay in gold bars?' I asked. Or diamonds, I thought to myself. They might have proved useful at a moment like this. Stiles, however, was keeping that little bag of gemstones under lock and key, well away from my view. I hadn't even bothered to ask. When the prevailing wind is blowing in your face, it's no moment to open the gas cylinders and charge forwards. Until I had an angle I'd wait. With types like Stiles you *always* needed an angle.

'*Viens.*'

Benoît held open the door. Then motioned for me to take off the very cap he'd set on my head not thirty seconds before. I walked inside to a haze of smoke and the sight of at least thirty British officers, all of whom outranked me. There was more golden glitter in the Café du Globe than the whole Yukon Territory.

'*Une coupe de Champagne, monsieur?*' asked a woman in black, magically appearing at my side.

'One franc,' whispered Benoît in my ear.

I reached for the glass.

The problem with champagne I soon discovered was that it tends to go to your head, particularly on an empty stomach. My natural inhibitions however were roundly outflanked at one franc per glass. With each new glass my voice rose another decibel or two till it was quite loud even by the raucous standards of the Café du Globe. Fortunately, Benoît had a well thought-out *plan de campagne.*

'Let's go,' he said suddenly, while I teased out the last drops of what possibly was number four.

'I thought we were going to eat,' I protested. I could smell the food and I was ravenous.

'We are,' he said, whereupon he settled the bill and hurried me out. Countenancing no further discussion he marched, and I followed, across the square and around the corner to the Hotel de France.

'It's a favourite of Canon Scott,' he said, before bustling me inside.

There we had a meal I'm not likely to soon forget, discovering along the way a new reason to admire the dear Canon.

Dinner began with a filet of white fish accompanied by young potatoes, all in a delightful cream sauce. As it was mid-February and not exactly the season for young potatoes, I had inwardly scoffed at the pretentiousness of the menu. But reconsidered after my first mouthful. I took a sip of wine, and reconsidered again. Benoît had engaged in a lively discussion about the choice and I worried that his Québécois accent had undermined any chance of a decent bottle, particularly as we ended up being served something the label described as Pomerol; to my ears it sounded like a cough syrup, or a new variety of German gas. One sip confirmed decisively it was neither. Quickly I took another.

'Not bad,' I said, coming up for breath. I think I may even have licked my lips. Benoît was applying himself with gusto to his plate, now nearly empty. 'So how's life in the artillery?' I asked, making an effort to be sociable.

'*Pas mal. Pas mal,*' he responded, washing down his last mouthful with a gulp of the dark, plummy-coloured nectar, before refilling our glasses. 'There's a man at Corps headquarters, Colonel McNaughton's his name. He's into something very new called counter-battery work, and I'm involved with that. I'm the brigade liaison.'

'Really? But counter-battery work, you say? Isn't that a fancy way of saying shooting at the enemy guns? That's hardly a new idea, Benoît.'

Firmly he shook his head. Even the arrival of the main course, a whole battery of mouth-watering *côtelettes d'agneau* surrounded by sweet green peas, didn't distract him from his discourse. 'Oh no, this is very advanced, scientific almost. The colonel has a whole variety of hush-hush techniques we're using to identify the Boche guns. You see we've never been able to figure out where they all are. But if we can do that, we have a good chance of destroying them. That's what the colonel says. I don't need to tell you what a difference it would make in an attack if we could suppress their guns.'

'Yes, I can see how that would help,' I said, trying hard to hold his eye without succumbing to the intoxicating aromas wafting up from my plate. 'By chance I met your Colonel McNaughton at Verdun. Seemed like a smart chap. Quite opinionated, but very smart.'

'What about you, Mac? How's headquarters?'

'I attended a demonstration recently on shooting a Lewis gun from the hip,' I said.

Benoît took a bite of his lamb. Still chewing he said, 'I can see where that might be useful at headquarters.'

I sighed. 'Yes, well, General Byng also visited today. Inspected the 8th Brigade in the forenoon.'

'Oh?'

I lowered my voice. 'We're to attack Vimy Ridge, Benoît.' Benoît looked up. He'd stopped chewing so I knew I had his undivided attention.

'Don't say a word to anyone but General Byng's working on a plan of operations. I happened to see a list of questions from HQ on General Lipsett's desk. Most referred to the ridge and it was marked "most urgent". The two of them talked for the longest while after the parade. Afterwards General Lipsett even took me aside and asked again about some of the details from Verdun.'

'It could mean anything, Mac.'

'Perhaps,' I said. 'But I don't think so.' Then I told him about the other pieces of the puzzle I'd put together. It was what we lawyers liked to call circumstantial evidence. While a court of law didn't put much credence in it, most everybody else believed in the law of coincidences; which is to say – the more there are, the less likely they're coincidence.

When I was finished, Benoît whistled softly.

'See what I mean?'

'Vimy's a fortress,' he said, rubbing at his beard, dinner temporarily overshadowed.

'Let's hope you're wrong about that.'

'The French already tried…'

'Yes, I know all that, Benoît,' I said, interrupting. 'They tried in '14 after the Germans first took it. Then once more during the second Artois offensive in '15 at the same time they succeeded in capturing the Lorette Spur. And later again that same year. Each time it was a bloody defeat. The Imperials didn't have much success at Vimy, either.'

'How bad was it then?'

'The casualties? All the attacks? Something like 150,000 men.' Benoît shook his head then drained his glass. 'That's only what I heard,' I said quietly. 'Maybe it wasn't that bad.'

Our pleasant evening out in Béthune was rapidly acquiring the atmosphere of the Last Supper.

But fortunately Benoît was of a sterner character and had done his apprenticeship in the trenches; what was a concern for later, was most decidedly not a concern at present. With an imperious wave of his arm and a few well-chosen words to the waiter he ordered a second bottle of wine to accompany the strawberries and cream. Suitably regrouped, we settled back in our armchairs to enjoy the after-dinner cigars.

Which was when I told him about Sam Stiles, and his miraculous reappearance as my superior at 3rd Division headquarters. 'The worst of it is, Colonel Hayter said he'd be re-evaluating the staff numbers after the next operation is complete. Frankly there's not work enough for both of us. Not unless this attack thins out the ranks considerably. And as you're probably going to tell me in a moment, casualties at headquarters don't tend to be high.'

Benoît was devoting himself to lighting a cigar. I wondered if he'd even heard what I said. He blew a long, lazy stream of smoke up to the chandelier above. 'Why didn't you say something earlier?'

I shrugged.

Then he laughed. Which took me aback. 'Here I thought it was this attack that was bothering you so, Mac. *Mais non.* You worry you're going to be a platoon lieutenant again.'

I sputtered as if to say something, but he held up his hand. 'Listen, Mac. If you want to stay where you are you need to take action. *L'attaque à outrance.*'

'Attack to the bitter end? Do you think so?'

'Of course. What are you going to tell Colonel Hayter: you sharpened more pencils last week than Captain Stiles?'

'*L'attaque à outrance* didn't work out so well in '14,' I grumbled. 'For the French, at least. And I'll have you know I do a little more than sharpen pencils every day, Benoît.'

He stubbed out his cigar. 'Does the colonel or the general ever hear about it?'

'Not unless I screw up.'

Benoît nodded triumphantly. 'Exactly. You're invisible, Mac. Invisible lieutenants always lose to captains, especially prominent ones. Sam Stiles is very prominent. You, my friend, need to take action.'

I grunted reservedly.

'Of all people, Mac, you must know how long the average lieutenant survives leading a platoon?'

Tersely I nodded.

'Well then? What are you waiting for?'

Dinner had been a marvel, the Pomerol a highlight. The conversation less so as the evening wore on. Afterwards the winding ride back to Bruay in the pitch dark astride a motorcycle driven by a drunken French-Canadian worried me less than it ought to have. My mind was awhirl. Although it may also have been the drink.

PART THREE

VIMY RIDGE

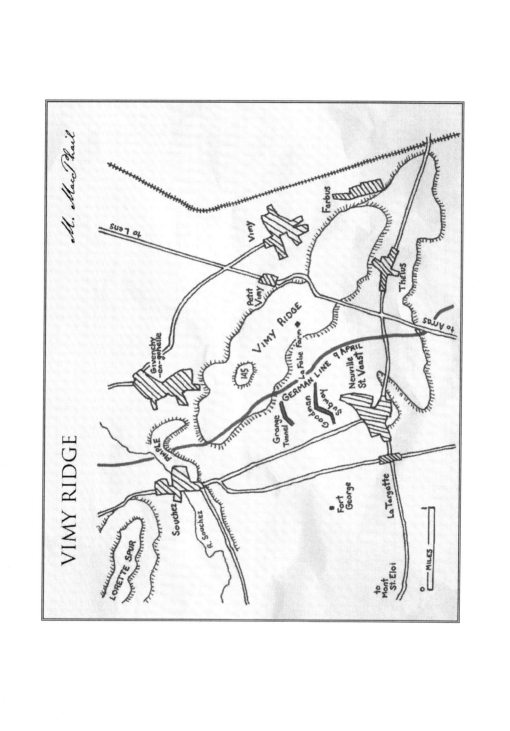

M. MacPhail

CHAPTER 23

3rd of March, 1917
Mont-Saint-Eloi, France

'The operation orders are complete?' inquired Stiles. I was surprised he even knew about them. They were for our move back to the front-line trenches, which wouldn't happen for more than a week.

'Yes, they're complete. I gave them to Colonel Hayter an hour ago. I told you but you had your head in some paper or other.'

'You should have insisted,' he said.

'I thought you weren't interested in details?' It was the sort of low intensity bickering and one-upmanship that had come to define our relationship.

Major Collum poked his head around the corner. 'Do either of you two speak French?' he asked. Collum was the new man to the staff since Major Meredith's transfer – Meredith was off to become a brigade major. By some accounts Collum was a bit of a stickler, although with a Military Cross he'd patently not spent his entire career battling paper and pedants.

'Yes, sir,' I piped up. This was an exaggeration, but not a wild one given Stiles's command of the language. After two years in France he'd hadn't graduated much beyond '*oui*' and '*non*'. Even that was a trial – for both listener and speaker. Stiles senior would probably have disapproved, anyhow, even if Stiles junior had shown the least aptitude for languages.

181

'Excellent,' said Major Collum. 'We've located a man who lived at La Folie Farm and I want someone to take a statement from him. We need to know everything we can about it.'

'La Folie Farm?' said Stiles.

'A Boche strongpoint on the ridge,' I replied. 'One of the strongest actually. It's a couple of hundred yards north of the Schwaben tunnel, if memory serves.'

'Yes, yes, I know that, MacPhail,' he snapped. 'The lieutenant sometimes imagines he's the only one fighting this war,' he said to the major.

The major frowned but went through the motions of a wan smile. Then he turned to me. 'If you'd get down there today, it'd be much appreciated, Lieutenant. The man's staying in Mont-Saint-Eloi. I'll have them give you a car from the pool and you can try out the new plank road on the way. Word is they finished it only yesterday.'

A car. A whole day away from Stiles. It was a "little bit of Heaven". That was how the boys had once loving called the Vimy sector having departed the Somme. At the time it seemed an appropriate description, much as it did today. The threat of a shell on my head if the Germans inaugurated our new road in their inimitable way was an acceptable price to pay. However, a bit of heaven, no matter how little, was denied me.

'I'll accompany you,' said Stiles.

'Oh, that won't be necessary, sir,' I said pertly, keeping up appearances for Major Collum's sake. The more pips, crowns or swords on a man's shoulders, the more such things tend to matter. I certainly didn't need additional headaches.

For all my studied politeness, my protests were to no avail. Stiles was determined.

That was how I found myself navigating the newly-completed plank road to Mont-Saint-Eloi with a nervous Captain Sam Stiles muttering instructions beside me. 'A little left... not too far... watch your speed...'

Ground which had been frozen solid the past two months was thawing in recent days, the rain showers quickening the process. A thick veneer of mud already glistened on the road bed and I knew it would worsen in the weeks ahead, so the miles of rough-cut planks were no idle luxury.

Stiles yelped, 'Watch it, MacPhail!'

One of the horses from a two-horse team pulling a limber had slipped off the planks and fallen in the mud onto its side. A crowd of men were gathered round trying to right the situation and the horse.

'I'm not blind,' I said, applying the brakes. 'I see them.' We slowed and came to a stop at a safe distance. 'However, if you don't stop that dithering we're the ones who are going to be in the mud. I need to concentrate on the driving. These planks are plenty slippery.'

Sourly Stiles pursed his lips.

The three-mile road from Mont-Saint-Eloi through La Targette to Neuville-Saint-Vaast, and our lines beyond, was desperately needed. Even the hopelessly unobservant observed each night that the roads in the vicinity were clogged with traffic, an endless stream of supplies, water and, most of all, ammunition. All making its way forward. Countless hundreds of lorries – and I'd heard tell an astonishing 50,000 horses – were employed for the task. There were reservoirs, pumping stations, and mile upon mile of pipelines being built to quench their thirst and ours. Sadly, for the poor creature ahead, these endeavours had come too late.

'We can't afford to sit here all day,' said Stiles, impatiently slapping his hand on his thigh. 'Major Collum is expecting us back.'

'We've only been gone forty minutes,' I said.

'MacPhail!'

I opened the car door. Standing on the running boards I leaned out. I could hear from the nature and number of the profanities the answer to my question before I asked it. 'You fellas gonna be long?' I hollered.

One of the men – I think it was the driver of the team – turned and looked ready to fire in my direction. Until he saw that I was an officer. 'We think it may have broken its leg, sir,' he shouted.

I waved. Then plunked back down on the seat. 'They say patience is a virtue,' I said. 'Tell me, though, seeing as how we appear to have some time on our hands, whatever happened with that raid two nights ago? The big one from the 4th Division. 1700 men involved. From the fact that everyone has their mouths zipped I gather it wasn't a huge success.'

183

'It was a fucking fiasco,' said Stiles. Coming from someone so attuned to the proper language for communicating both victory and defeat it was a shocking admission. I sat up straight.

'It was?'

'They waited so long for the right wind in order to release the gas that the Germans knew they were coming. They likely knew the entire plan by that point.'

'Oh?' I said solemnly.

'The Boche were lined up waiting for them in the trenches when they crossed No-Man's-Land. And then the wind shifted. So on top of it all they gassed themselves. Who knows what the final casualties will be. But the OCs of both battalions involved were killed. So, no, it's not something anyone wants to talk about.' A long pause. 'You do catch my gist, don't you, MacPhail?'

I sighed, then nodded. 'Yes.'

A revolver went off. Startled, both of us whipped our heads round to look through the windscreen. The man with the revolver, the horse team driver, looked like he'd been shot himself. He stood there with the pistol hanging listlessly in his right hand, staring down at what he'd done. But others were already busy untangling lines, cutting them where they had to be cut and calming the second horse. Soon the limber was plodding forward, the same driver doing his duty, attempting to recover his spirits, but with only half his team.

With their backs in it was surprising how quickly the men had rolled the corpse of the horse over and tugged it off the road. Horses are big, lumbering, heavy animals. But they had worked it out. An arm waved us urgently forward and I put the car in gear. Daylight was no moment to be driving in range of the enemy guns, and definitely not to be standing still. The men realized that.

I couldn't help but stare at the animal as we puttered by in first gear. It was a fine creature, a gorgeous chestnut brown, its hide still gleaming despite the indignities it had endured, its blood-matted head careless feet from the planks. Unless someone ran into it, it would be days if not weeks before it was buried. Maybe not even then. Left to rot.

Approaching Mont-Saint-Eloi I spotted the gaunt and shell-torn white twin towers of the great Abbey perched on the hill. They were famous once and I suppose still are. Despite Fritz's best efforts.

Before the village we came upon a proliferation of heavy guns lined up in rows, hub-by-hub so close together were they arrayed. They were hidden from sight in a sunken road that may well have been Roman. The centuries had passed and the Roman grasp of the local topography had not lost any of its pertinence. It might well be different in a few months from now after the topography was twisted by the hand of man. Never before had the world seen the destructive qualities of a modern barrage, one that transformed forests into virtual deserts, and towns into quarries of broken stone where bricks were pulverised to dust.

If only the gunners could do the same on the ridge when the time came, I thought grimly. Then we might not have so much to fear from strongpoints like La Folie Farm. The artillery men spoke confidently. But I recalled all too well their promises and good intentions at the Somme. For all the unceasing thunder and the mountains of shell casings afterwards, the uncut wire and the untouched trenches were what I remembered.

We located our refugee in the town centre, sharing a back room with two others in a tumbledown house that had escaped the German guns, but not the passage of time nor the lack of any visible maintenance. Inside, matters were different and the house exuded a warmth, though that might just have been the coal stove in the kitchen stoked to repel a second ice age. After ascertaining our business, the elderly landlady invited us in and rushed to bring us a drink. Coffee she didn't have, she said, but perhaps *un verre de vin*? Gratefully we accepted. We stripped of our coats, which we threw over the back of the hard wooden kitchen chairs, while she went in search of our man. Stiles and I took turns glancing enviously at the black enamel pot on the stove, simmering away with its heavenly aromas.

The man appeared forthwith. Before leaving us to our devices – reluctantly I could tell – the landlady shot him a tender look that made me think it was not simply for the few francs a month she had taken him in.

'Monsieur Dasort?' I asked.

'*Oui.*'

I stood and, after nearly sending his tumbler of wine flying, so too did Stiles. We shook hands and I introduced us in my best French, consisting of short crisp sentences and even shorter words, and explained why we had come, or a sanitized version thereof.

Monsieur Dasort was a vital old fellow endowed with a crop of unruly white hair and matching moustache, roughly three times my age, half my height and with twice my vigour.

I think he was flattered by the attention; two foreign officers (I question whether he recognized our ranks except to know we were officers) coming all this way with the sole purpose of visiting him. And not displeased with a little company on an otherwise dreary winter afternoon, notwithstanding the godly lunch awaiting him.

Dasort was a widower he told us, a veteran of the 1870 war against the Prussians. The injustice of it rankled still for he spoke in harsh words about the Germans. In his shoes I would have been more exercised by the fact that forty years later they were literally knocking down his door. But current events he took in his stride, a pragmatic and unruffled view of the world that typified the French in my experience. I glanced over at Stiles. Understanding next to nothing of the conversation he had taken up a dreamy examination of the wallpaper stripes on the far wall.

Under the table the point of my boot caught him midway between ankle and shin – hard. He grimaced and looked my way. I glared at him. The message was clear, I think.

'*Alors, La Ferme de Folie,*' said Monsieur Dasort. Stiles was listening attentively.

Enthusiastically I nodded.

'La Folie Farm was originally a château, two storeys high, with two deep cellars each approximately thirty feet by fifty feet, vaulted roofs, with one entrance to a cellar on the southwest side of the building and the other entrance approximately at the centre of the building on the northwest side.'

Immediately I began to ask about the cellars, thinking of Mouquet Farm at the Somme and the infernal maze of tunnels and machine-gun nests that the Boche had constructed underneath. Whole battalions had fallen before it was finally captured.

Fortunately, the old man spoke slowly, and enunciated well, and only twice did I have to ask him to repeat himself. He told us in detail about the new château built a few hundred yards north, and about the woods that surrounded them – not thick for the most part he said, although I suspected once our guns were finished it wouldn't matter if they were. Stiles proved himself indispensable by replenishing everyone's glass with wine at intervals. I couldn't help noticing that the intervals for Monsieur Dasort were generally half those for either Stiles or myself.

Well past noon the landlady poked her head through the doorway. As I'd heard everything I could possibly think to ask regarding La Folie Farm, and much I hadn't until the old man volunteered it, I beckoned her in. She took up station behind Monsieur Dasort and placed a wizened hand on his shoulder, smiling at us, while he responded by patting her hand. Then she invited us for lunch and a broad smile broke out on my face.

Suddenly however Stiles understood French. 'No, MacPhail, we have to go. The major is waiting.'

I pulled a face. 'C'mon. The war's not going anywhere in the next hour or two.'

'No. We have to go, Lieutenant,' he said, in his serious voice.

'Fine,' I said petulantly. 'Have it your way. Just don't expect me to stop if you suddenly need to pee.'

Back in Bruay Stiles was in fine form. Despite himself I think he'd rather enjoyed our little outing. There was not much to enjoy in this war so the hours away from it were precious. For the most part he hadn't been the worst company, I had to admit. Set your expectations low enough and anything will tend to surpass them.

'Listen,' he said. 'You did all the work. Let me write up the report. Your notes are in English, right?'

'Of course. Really? You'd do that?'

He shrugged. 'I know you sometimes think otherwise, but I'm not so bad, MacPhail.'

'Alright,' I said, tired after a long day and pleased at this unexpected relief from what otherwise would have been a long night. 'Thanks, eh.'

He nodded and I forgot about it until a day later.

We were at our desks when Major Collum entered. 'Excellent,' he said, looking at Stiles. 'Colonel Hayter was very pleased with your report on the interview.'

Stiles beamed. Collum noticed me watching and gave a fleeting smile in my direction. 'That's all gentlemen. But, well done, Captain.' Then he left.

A silence fell that might have been mistaken for the imminent approach of a gas cloud.

'Look, MacPhail. I know what you're thinking...'

'Forget it,' I said. 'Just forget it.'

Benoît was right. There was no way I could compete with the wiles of a Sam Stiles at headquarters. I had to get out in the field if I was to stay out of the field. It was the same sort of twisted logic that had led to this war. Philosophers probably had theories on the subject. I wished I'd read some of them.

In disgust I shook my head, then applied myself to the papers before me.

CHAPTER 24

9th of March, 1917
Bruay, France

'Damn it,' I said, replacing the telephone receiver.

Stiles put his coffee aside, looking up despite himself.

'That was the quartermaster's office. The tents and shelters didn't arrive at Villers-au-Bois and it doesn't look like they will, either. Not soon anyhow. It's fortunate I checked.'

'So?'

'So, the dispositions will have to be changed. We can't very well send men there tomorrow and have nowhere for them to billet.'

Stiles, who was never noticeably quick on the uptake – barring the occasions in which blatant self-interest attracted his full attention – must have found my explanation clear for I saw the clouds in his eyes parting. 'No we can't,' he said. 'Good thinking.'

In light of recent experience and thinking that Stiles would seize upon this fine piece of staff work as a personal triumph and serve it up as such, I quickly added, 'I'll find an alternative and write up new orders. Then I'll bring them over to the colonel.'

'Yes, do that, would you?' He sipped at his coffee.

There was no protest. No offer to 'help out' or take command. It was not what I had expected.

By early afternoon – having skipped lunch and ignoring the

resultant plaintive protests from my stomach – I had worked out an alternative. It was a mad scramble. Shuffling around twelve battalions of a thousand men each was no easy matter. Then I had new orders typed up and brought them personally to Colonel Hayter.

I tapped on his door. Impatiently I poked my head around. 'Sir?'

'MacPhail?'

'I discovered there was a problem with the availability of billets at Villers-au-Bois, Colonel. However I've arranged alternate locations and had an appendix to the operational orders and a new march table drawn up. I hope you find them adequate, sir.'

'Fine,' he said brusquely. 'Toss them on the table over there, would you?'

I hesitated.

'Was there anything else?'

'No, sir,' I said. Whereupon I beat an undignified retreat.

'What's with the colonel?' I whispered to the corporal outside.

'You caught him at a bad moment, sir. He's terribly preoccupied with the Prime Minister's arrival.'

As I puzzled over this, I stumbled into a whistling Sam Stiles sauntering down the hallway.

'How was lunch?' I grumbled, realizing then he'd totally outflanked me. The colonel was in no mood to hear about details, no matter how fine the work, and Stiles must surely have known.

'Superb,' he said. 'I had some time, so I went to a little place in town. Say what you want about the French, they sure know how to cook.'

He began gently dabbing at his moustache with the fingers of one hand, while I fought off the urge to go in search of the *flammenwerfer* that was never around when I needed it. 'Everything is in order then, Lieutenant? New dispositions all ready?'

I nodded in the affirmative.

'Excellent.'

A little before 5 p.m. the divisional staff was hurried outside to line up in front of the mine owner's château, which was where we toiled. The RCR had turned up with an honour guard, and they were already positioned in two meticulously straight rows, hard faces which had learned first to drill and only later to fight. Like all of us the *Shino boys* had matured into real soldiers.

Prime Minister Borden and two other prominent members of the government arrived soon after in a posse of large staff cars that ponderously rounded the gates and eased into the square. There was a bark from the regimental sergeant, followed by a hard thud as boot heels came together in unison. The weather had reversed its earlier course, and the light drizzle from this morning had turned to snow. It came down in large flakes, spiralling lazily to the ground, coating our hats and tunics. No stranger to snow the Prime Minister took a slow glance at his surroundings before donning a black bowler.

General Lipsett stepped forward and saluted. He was greeted with a handshake and what looked to be friendly words. Then, entourage assembled, the delegation passed slowly along the ranks of the assembled soldiers before coming to the motley brigade which manned the lines behind the lines.

The Prime Minister walked past me without a second glance, his curly white hair covered by the bowler, his thick dark moustache wearing the weather of the day. While I'd voted for him and could understand how a busy man didn't have time to greet each soldier individually, it was galling that he immediately headed towards Sam Stiles. General Lipsett, accompanying him, took it in measured stride. Colonel Hayter, who was tasked with the introductions, said: 'Sir. This is Captain Stiles. A fine officer of the division's operations staff.'

At this, a sound not dissimilar to a walrus snorting emanated from my end of the row.

The Prime Minister however was already in full stride and all eyes and ears were on him. 'But Sam and I know each other, Colonel,' he protested. 'So that doesn't surprise me. It is Sam, is it not?'

Sam did his best to blush. 'Yes, sir.'

The Prime Minister turned to his side. 'Rogers, you know the family. This is little Sam!'

Robert Rogers, a man with considerably more hair between lip and nose than graced his steeply sloped head, said, 'By George, it is. How are you Sam?' Rogers turned to the Prime Minister. 'Not little Sam anymore, Sir Robert.'

'No. No, indeed.'

To General Lipsett he said, 'A very fine staff you have, General. My compliments.'

It was all I could do not to sigh. Walrus imitations were out of the question.

15th of March, 1917
Bruay Training Area, Houdain, France

That my petty troubles at headquarters were no more than that, I was reminded a few days later. It was a live-fire exercise in which the entire 7th Brigade was to storm the taped trenches under the watchful eye of the brigadier, General Lipsett and the Corps commander. The trio was no less impressive for the absence of General Nivelle, Field-Marshal Haig, or the Prime Minister.

Anybody who knew anything knew by mid-March that we were to seize the ridge. It had somehow become common knowledge without so much as a single order being issued by General Byng, a matter-of-fact news item that had passed from brigadier to battalion colonel, to company major, by which time the newest draft would have had to have his ears stuffed with cotton wadding not to have heard. Even then one of his buddies would have good-naturedly plucked it out in order to relay the message, with a few details unknown to the generals added in. Such was the nature of trench rumours. Only this was no rumour.

Initially it surprised me that the secret had been allowed to spread to 100,000 men in the space of not much more than two weeks. Though when I thought about it, I realized the Germans must have known deep in their hearts for at least a month or two. They'd have noticed all the activity. The massive dumps of shells being built; the balloons and the aeroplanes buzzing endlessly overhead undaunted by their own circuses of colourfully-painted machines of prey; the relentless activity from dawn till dusk in our support areas, and most particularly that which took place after dusk. They'd certainly have noticed our daily bombardments and the frequent nocturnal excursions into their trenches, Mills bombs in hand. Other than the 4th Division's bloody stumble at the beginning of the month, holding the line was no sinecure for a Prussian or a Bavarian in Gruppe Vimy in the early months of 1917.

For the first time since I'd been in the army someone had decided there would be no pretences about secrecy. The men involved would be informed so they too could be prepared. That was the point of today's exercise. These were the lessons of Verdun being applied. In no time a full-scale plan of the ridge had been constructed, just down the road from Bruay at Houdain.

'My bet is they'll take it,' I said to no one in particular, a couple of my peers from the staff milling about. We were standing several feet back of the jumping-off trench, the carefully prepared course outlined on the slope of the modest hill opposite.

Someone laughed. 'What makes you think so?' said another, sharing in the joke.

'Yes, why do you think so, Lieutenant?'

Aside from the obvious that this was a practice assault and therefore missing crucial elements such as an enemy barrage and a tempest of machine-gun bullets, "Bungo" Byng himself was watching. Whatever points for improvement the Corps commander might discern he hadn't come to watch the home team lose. Of that I was quite confident. I was equally confident I couldn't say any of that.

Fighting Mac, otherwise known as Brigadier-General Macdonell, had me fixed in a fiery stare. The story was legendary of how the brigadier, out walking in No-Man's-Land, was shot in the arm by a German sniper. Instead of ducking, he stood tall, waved a fist of his good arm at his tormentor and fired back with a burst of Gaelic curses. Whereupon the sniper nailed him in the second arm. To say the brigadier had a temper was a wee bit like saying the French had a spat with the Germans. Based on the same story some simply called him Batty.

'Well, sir,' I said, my brain turning over furiously, 'your brigade has been training intensively and I imagine they know their stuff.' Macdonell didn't as much as blink. 'In addition to which I don't really think any of them would want to face you if they didn't succeed.'

For a moment I wondered if I'd gone too far. Then Macdonell

grunted, in a pleased kind of way. 'No, laddie, I don't reckon they would. What's your name?'

'MacPhail, sir. Malcolm MacPhail.'

'MacPhail... Malcolm MacPhail...' He let the words roll thickly off his tongue, savouring them. Ironically, Macdonell was about as Scottish as I was, a generation or two in between, but he liked to revel in his roots.

'Carry on,' he said amiably, and then carried on himself towards the group of generals and senior ranks assembled to observe the attack. I was about to turn away when I noticed Stiles standing amongst them. He was in between Colonel Hayter and a major from the Corps staff, both of whom were listening attentively.

'You missed your big opportunity, Mac,' Jarvis said, interrupting my thoughts. 'You could have asked the brigadier about the time and date of the attack instead of hounding us incessantly.'

'Hounding you? Most of you crowd barely know the time of day, let alone when Z Day will be. Why would I hound you?'

Jarvis was right about one thing; the odds were decent that Macdonell would know. Other than Lipsett and Byng, and they weren't taking piercing questions from nosy young lieutenants, no one else did. At least no one in the 3rd Division. I'd spoken to quite a number. It was a secret that was being held very close to the chest.

Shortly after, the attack commenced.

With a roar to waken the dead the soldiers clambered out of the jumping-off trench and began charging across the broken terrain. There were hundreds of them. Having never seen an attack from this angle it made for an uplifting sight, considerably more uplifting than the angle I was accustomed to. The attractions of a spot on the staff had seldom seemed so obvious.

From aerial photographs, updated regularly with information from patrols and raids, an exact replica of one sector of the ridge had been fashioned. The taped lines further up the hill marked out the German trenches. Where I'd foolishly assumed there was to be no shellfire, a line of officers on stomping horses simulated our creeping barrage, an artifice that was intimidatingly effective as anyone who has ever stood a few feet from a prancing four-footer can attest. Various coloured flags took the place of machine-gun posts, strongpoints and other features.

We'd long done similar things for raids, but not on such a grand scale. The bullets and bombs were real enough, too. As it had rained and the ground was rapidly thawing the mud was an exact replica of the real thing.

As I predicted, the 7th Brigade carried it in the end, rushing the white-taped lines in small groups. No waves of men advancing shoulder-to-shoulder, though half the officers and NCOs were judged to have fallen and others were forced (for the practice) to take their place. At the tape they skipped the hand-to-hand fighting. That and other specialist topics were the subject of the afternoon's training. Not that clobbering Fritz at close quarters required much additional training; it sometimes seemed we'd been doing nothing else the past two years.

I glanced over at the generals. General Byng, well prepared for the mud with lace-up boots that went to the knee, his hands thrust deep in the pockets of a thick trench coat, stood talking with General Lipsett. Lipsett was pointing to some feature of the course. Neither gave any outward sign whether they approved or disapproved of the efforts made.

They were still talking as they slowly sauntered by, oblivious to all and sundry except each other. Following them came the brigadier and the brigade major – who to my delight turned out to be none other than Major Meredith – and a handful of others.

Meredith nodded and Macdonell winked when he spotted me. He for one looked pleased with his brigade's performance. 'So, young MacPhail, you had it right,' he said loudly.

At this General Lipsett stopped in mid-stride. Byng turned to face General Lipsett, who was staring at us a trench width away. Byng said something to Lipsett, and Lipsett replied. Then just as suddenly they turned away and resumed their stroll.

'What was that all about?' said Stiles, slipping up from behind to stand beside me.

I shook my head. 'Beats me.'

'Oh, I forgot to mention it earlier. Colonel Hayter was looking for you.'

My eyes narrowed. 'He was? What about?'

Stiles shrugged. 'Might be something trivial. But then again, maybe not.' This last with a smarmy grin.

CHAPTER 25

15th of March, 1917
Bruay, France

Late that evening – it was nearly 10 p.m. – Colonel Hayter finally tracked me down. I'd had no success finding him as he flitted from one thing to another, told on each occasion to return at a later, more convenient moment.

Therefore I jumped to my feet when I saw him step into the small, former maid's bedroom that Stiles and I used as an office. Stiles had already called it a night and gone in search of a bunk. Hayter sized me up for a second, then said: 'Captain Stiles tells me you're bored with your duties on the staff.'

My first reaction was to gulp. My second was to sputter. 'Sir, that's not exactly what I said…' I protested. In fact, I hadn't said anything of the sort to Stiles, or to anyone else, but before I could say that Hayter waved me silent.

'Coincidentally your boredom comes at an opportune time, Lieutenant. You must know by now that we're busy planning the final details of the division's assault on Vimy Ridge. General Horne approved General Byng's plan for the Corps last week.'

'He did?'

'Yes, but that's neither here nor there as far as you're concerned. What is important is that we know exactly what the Germans are up to in the section of the ridge assigned to the division; which units they have in the line and in reserve; how strongly they've manned their trenches; the condition and locations of their dug-outs and strong-points. And, of course, the state of their wire.'

'Leave nothing for granted. Naturally, sir. But isn't that where the intelligence section comes into it?'

The colonel nodded. 'Normally they would. And they are. But they're a little overwhelmed at the moment. There's a great deal to do. The Camerons are taking a patrol into the German line early tomorrow morning. They tried a few hours ago but it didn't work out, so they're having another go. Seeing as how you've done it before, MacPhail, I'd like for you to accompany them. Don't misunderstand me, I'm not looking for you to throw bombs into dug-outs. What the general and I need are the pieces of information the others may miss in the heat of the battle.' He paused. 'Assuming it comes to that – a battle, I mean. I think you understand.'

I indicated that I did.

'Excellent. Oh, and a prisoner would be useful, MacPhail. Keep that in mind.'

Benoît would be pleased. It had taken me barely two weeks, but thanks to Stiles's machinations I was heading into the thick of it. Already I was more visible. In and of itself that was no reason for celebration. My name and service number jotted in the daily war diary, followed thereafter by a short service and a white cross in the ground out by Cabaret Rouge was a form of visibility I hoped to avoid. I wondered if Benoît realized that the course of action he'd advised was as likely to get me killed as confirmed in my position – and sooner rather than later. That afterwards Colonel Hayter and General Lipsett might say what a jolly good fellow I was, was no consolation whatsoever.

'I guess I'd best try to catch a few hours' sleep before I leave, sir,' I said.

'Oh, I don't think you'll have time for that,' replied the colonel. 'They're going in at 3.15 a.m.'

He looked at his watch. I looked at mine. 'That's only in five hours,' I said, alarmed. 'I'll get going.'

Hayter turned to leave.

'One thing, sir.'

'Yes.'

'When is Z Day?'

The colonel smiled. 'I don't know, Lieutenant. But even if I did, you don't think I'd tell you, do you? Especially seeing as how you're going into the enemy lines.' He made a show of looking at his watch again. 'In *less* than five hours.'

16ᵗʰ of March, 1917

East of Neuville-Saint-Vaast, France

The Cameron Highlanders, or 43ʳᵈ Battalion as the paperwork more commonly identified them, held a portion of the line on the left of the La Folie section, east of Neuville-Saint-Vaast, and west of the Bois de la Folie whence the section took its name. I caught up with the patrol at a little after one in the morning. They were 21 in total; 19 men led by two officers: Captain Hamilton and Lieutenant Geddie.

'Welcome,' said Captain Hamilton. 'Headquarters telephoned to say you were coming.' The captain didn't look overly enthusiastic at this latest development. Though with his weak chin, sagging eyes and broad forehead he was genetically predisposed to looking a little downcast. Not to mention it being a very early morning. I tried not to take it personally.

'So, what you do know about our little do, Lieutenant?' he asked.

'Not much, sir,' I replied. 'I was told that you were taking out a patrol and I was to tag along.'

Hamilton looked increasingly forlorn.

'I do have some experience,' I said, by way of reassurance. 'I wasn't always a staff officer.'

'We'll be going in between the Vernon and Commons craters,' said Lieutenant Geddie. Geddie was a most serious-looking young man with a silly little toothbrush moustache – a variant of facial hair growth I've never entirely understood, not that I ever understood moustaches. But I always thought that if you were going to burden yourself with one, the least you could do was have some hair in it. 'It's close to where we tried last night,' Geddie continued.

'You can't mean the patrol a few hours ago?'

'That's right.'

I frowned. Then realizing that might leave the wrong impression I said, 'It's just I figured they'd have rounded up new men for the second inning.' Neither Hamilton nor Geddie said anything. No wonder they looked so serious. 'I'll do my best to be of some help,' I added.

I wouldn't have sworn to it, but I had the impression that Captain Hamilton winced.

Our front line all along the western edge of Vimy Ridge was known as the "crater line". This particular stretch was chock full of them, one beside the other. Sizeable though shell craters could be, these were the cavernous holes that resulted from underground mines being detonated with hundreds of pounds of ammonal, leaving depressions twenty-five feet deep and a hundred wide. Most dated from the period early last year when the British took control of the Vimy sector and the French departed for Verdun. The engineers soon discovered that the Germans had embarked upon an ambitious mining programme and set about to countermine it. Someone told me that many of the tunnels we were using were first excavated during that battle of the tunnels.

The Camerons however were suffering the after-effects. In addition to the obvious problems associated with having big holes on your doorstep commonly filled with enemy machine gun and other posts, there was a particular difficulty in the 500-yard by 500-yard quadrant the cartographers labelled as S.28.a. Here the earthen lips of the craters, like the upturned rims of cup saucers, were high enough to prevent direct observation of the German front-line trenches immediately behind them. While the Germans couldn't see our trenches either, their mates with machine guns and the snipers a couple of hundred yards back and further up the slope had an unobstructed view of the Camerons.

Consequently, risky midnight expeditions to learn more, and observation posts on the crater edges were daily fare for the Highlanders. The looming attack only raised the stakes.

'One positive thing about the second time,' I remarked to Lieutenant Geddie as we departed, 'at least you know the way.'

Tersely he nodded, in no mood for my light-hearted flippancy. Not that I was feeling particularly relaxed myself as the hour for the raid approached, for that was what it had become.

'No, Lieutenant, it's a *raid*, not a patrol,' Captain Hamilton had interrupted, when I began ruminating about the desirability of bringing a prisoner back. It wasn't entirely a question of semantics. With a patrol there was always a chance of slipping back to our lines without a fight; a raid implied the fight was a given.

Hayter may not have thought he was sending me to bomb dugouts. However, on the off chance they'd be needed, and having been apprised of the actual nature of our outing, I stuffed my pockets with four Mills bombs and scrounged up a Lee-Enfield complete with bayonet. The Webley was my reserve card. If the Western Front teaches you anything, it's that anything can happen. And ten yards into No-Man's-Land nothing is certain, so it's best to come well prepared. Barring one of those Mark I tanks that was always missing in action when you needed one, I figured some high explosive, a bayonet and an ample supply of .303 rounds were the next best thing.

We turned left out of Vernon trench and entered into the fire-trench, which ran roughly north-south parallel to the ridge. After 75 yards we resumed our course eastwards turning into a narrow, winding observation sap that protruded some distance in the direction of the enemy trenches. Near the end of it we took the left branch. Then climbed out into the middle of No-Man's-Land on a quartet of ladders resting against the trench walls, left there for that purpose.

Slipping through the prepared gaps in our own wire we headed east, across the muddy ground and up the slight slope, towards the shadowy form of the ridge.

Vimy Ridge extends for approximately 4 ½ miles from north to south, it's breadth less than half that. Of all the many enemy bastions on the Western Front, from the Belgium coast down to the borders of neutral Switzerland, this ridge was the one immutable and unyielding spike in the line.

The view from its crest was like no other, they said, with the possible exception of the Lorette Spur. Thanks to the French, Lorette was again in our hands. But without Vimy the entire Douai plain to the north with its coal mines and industry was a German province, a leech sucking the country dry. Not having seen either ridgetop I was inclined to believe the stories. Driving north from Arras the blueish grey escarpment of Vimy was visible for miles.

However, where topography and the vicissitudes of war had conspired against our side, from studying the maps I realized that we were blessed in one critical respect. Where the eastern side of the ridge overlooking the Douai Plain was steep, if not cliff-like in spots, the gradient of the western slope that we were to ascend was more gradual.

Gradual or not the ground was soft underfoot and treacherously slippery. The mud stuck to my boots in great clods as I walked. In the darkness it required considerable concentration merely to stay upright. Large holes and even craters loomed up suddenly. All the while some Fritz sentry could have spotted us and given the alarm.

It was a dark night, the moon veiled behind a thick down-quilt of clouds. While there were flashes and thuds from guns firing in various spots along the miles of the escarpment – there was seldom an hour when they weren't – I would have welcomed a little of that racket closer to home, if only to mask our own. Not that we were particularly loud. Hamilton had warned us twice before leaving. It was just that every insignificant noise, every rattle of someone's kit or the squelching of a boot as it came loose from the mire sounded painfully clear.

We skirted the north side of Vernon crater in two snaking, elongated files. After we were underway for some minutes, I spotted the underbrush tangles of the enemy wire ahead. Then an 18-pound shell tore overhead and went off with a boom and a flash in the rear. High explosive presumably, although it may have been shrapnel.

No barrage had been prearranged. This was to be a "stealth" raid. However, the timing of this bombardment couldn't have come at more propitious moment. Two of the Camerons raced ahead, heavy wire cutters in hand. The cutters proved superfluous.

Within minutes Captain Hamilton announced, 'We've found a gap.' Hurriedly the word was whispered down the line. Under the lead of a sergeant, the group made for the promised gap and I accompanied them.

Big it wasn't, no more than a few feet wide, but sufficient for twenty-odd men practised in this brand of skulduggery by night. When the day of the assault came this wire would need to be gone entirely if a battalion were to pass. The artillery had work yet to do. Still, it didn't seem a great deal to report to Lieutenant-Colonel Hayter.

Without encountering any opposition we came upon a post slightly in advance of their fire-trench. The Germans had attempted to raid
the Camerons' trenches twenty-four hours earlier and the battalion
was dead set on getting its own back. I was increasingly dubious that I
was going to learn anything of interest this night.

Ahead heads were shaking, our progress at a halt. The men were
lined up, nervously waiting in the dark, weapons – mainly bombs and
cudgels – in hand. Not a shot had been fired. Behind me someone
approached and I glanced back. It was Captain Hamilton. 'The post
appears to be empty,' I told him.

'Are they certain?'

He passed by to go to the sergeant. The sergeant must have relayed
the same message for Hamilton returned almost immediately. The
enemy post was little more than a hole in the ground, a barricaded
dug-out surrounded by wire. That it was deserted seemed a genuine
disappointment for the captain.

Nevertheless, he took it in stride and gave the signal to move on.
The entire party went forward and leapt over the parapet into the
main trench, expecting a fight. But there wasn't a Fritz to be seen, not
a single solitary sentry.

We set off to raid along its length. For weeks the field artillery
had fired daily upon the German front line, and this stretch had been
hard hit. That told only part of the story, however. As the Boche who
manned it were nowhere to be seen, it was a fair guess they hadn't
abandoned it but were sheltering underground in the dug-outs.
Within a few minutes my theory was put to the test and the file halted
at the entrance to one. I pushed past the others to the front.

A private was relating the information that the dug-out was empty.

'Bomb it just in case,' said Hamilton.

'Hang on a minute, Captain,' I said. 'If you don't mind I'd like to
have a look. They may have left some papers or something else of value
behind.'

'You do realize, Lieutenant, if there is someone down there we can't
help you?'

'Yes, sir,' I said. What I didn't say, but was thinking, was that catching a prisoner or two might be precisely the sort of thing to impress
Hayter.

'Hawthorn, you'd best go with him,' said the captain.

A lean, sturdy-looking fellow two-thirds my height appeared beside me.

'Alright,' I said. 'Follow me.' I handed the rifle to the captain and pulled the revolver from its holster and let it hang from the lanyard around my neck.

The dug-out was no different than literally hundreds I'd seen before. A few thick wooden joists to either side and overhead, wooden stairs leading downwards into the murky unknown.

Tentatively I took the first couple of steps, testing the broad wooden planks for creaks, then paused and cranked my ear to below. Nothing. I grasped the Webley in a firm grip and went on. Below it was dark, even darker than up above but gradually my eyes adjusted and I took it slowly until they did, one measured step at a time, listening acutely. I could feel Hawthorn coming behind.

Fifteen steps down and we were already many feet below ground level. But these dug-outs could go much deeper. I'd seen several at the Somme that were thirty-five feet underground. Some told of ones even deeper, so far beneath the surface that even the ground-shaking storm of the biggest bombardment was but a distant roar.

A German dug-out is in many respects a wonder of the modern world. Those for officers spacious, with panelled walls and hung in decorative tapestries, with head room for the likes of DuBois in the chambers below, electric lighting so common as to be unexceptional. I had a feeling this wasn't of that calibre, though even here the passage downstairs bore the mark of craftsmen. Rough-hewn planks adorned the walls, sawn so as to fit precisely, not a nail out of place; the mud, dirt and privation of the soldier's existence left up top. Which was rather the point I guessed, although sheltering from the shells ran a close second.

Another ten steps down and I paused again. There was a humid staleness to the air. I thought I heard something. However, listen as I might there was nothing to discern beyond my own laboured breathing, the sound of which was so disconcerting that I quickly pushed on.

The stairs came to an end. What appeared to be a small room beckoned off to my right. Cautiously I stepped down onto the plank floor and turned the corner, vaguely aware that somewhere far off a light was shining. When it came to me where it was, I felt my stomach churn. I pivoted right and looked down, knowing in my gut before my eyes could confirm it.

Hawthorn bumped up beside me.

'Watch out,' I said. 'There's another staircase!'

We'd reached what in essence was a landing. The dug-out was deeper still. In such circumstances it was no surprise they'd ignored the calls from above to come out. Perhaps they hadn't heard them, although I tend to think they probably had and hoped their deep bunker and a little patience would see them through. It might well have done were it not for my blasted inquisitiveness, and this mindless competition with Sam Stiles.

The young soldier in field grey stood a few steps down, barely five feet away. No helmet, tousled hair, a cherubic face staring up at me with round eyes, his shocked expression a mirror of my own. The eyes narrowed and reflexively the arm to his side jerked upwards in an underhand toss and I saw the object fly through the air. It hit me square in the chest. But my left hand was already in motion and I snatched it before it fell to the ground. Vaguely I was aware it was a potato masher.

The shot sounded like a cannon in the enclosed space. It came from behind the soldier, where comrades were waiting, dark shapes silhouetted against the shimmering light below. 'Argh,' croaked Hawthorn.

My finger fumbled briefly until it found the smooth, cold curvature of the trigger. I pulled at it roughly, then pulled at it again. And again. My arm was extended at full length, stabbing with each shot, not as they taught at officers' school or anywhere the finer points of marksmanship were cultivated, but with a desperate ferocity until exasperatingly the revolver only clicked in response. A Mills bomb whished past me and bounced down the stairs, exploding with a *BANG* and a flash of light. The blast of the air swept past me. Smoke and gunpowder filled my nostrils. Only then did I think to look at my other hand, and did a quick repeat, before the relief washed over me.

'Move it, Hawthorn, get going. Give me your pistol, I'll cover the rear.'

We sprinted those stairs in a time any Olympic hurdles champion would have been proud of.

Captain Hamilton and the others had heard the commotion and were waiting as we bounded up the final steps to the trench.

'They're there!' I said, breathing hard, although this was blatantly obvious without my flash communiqué from the front. The Camerons let fly with a half-dozen bombs. While Mills bombs are not ideal in the sense they don't have the explosive power of a jam tin, or the searing smoke of a phosphorous bomb, I noted with satisfaction the geyser of dirt that blew back up through the dug-out entrance. There'd be no one coming in our footsteps. With any luck they'd sealed it off.

As the dust settled I noticed Lieutenant Geddie staring at me, serious even by his standards.

'What!?' I looked round.

Captain Hamilton and a half dozen others stood there, gaping. Hamilton pointed at my left hand.

I lifted it. 'Oh, don't worry,' I said turning the wooden handle around so they could see. 'Look. The pull cord's still inside. Perfectly safe. I thought perhaps you fellows might have some use for it? Otherwise I'm sure it'll come in handy back at headquarters.' I smiled at my feeble joke, if only to mask the exhilaration I was feeling. It had been a close call.

No one said anything, but I saw the meaningful glances they exchanged.

The Camerons bombed a couple of more dug-outs after that. Briefly we traded bombs (pins out for the occasion) with some Fritzs who turned up to defend their trench. Roughly an hour after setting out, at 4.20 a.m., we returned to our lines. There were no casualties, save Hawthorn who was nursing a good Blighty although probably not sufficiently serious to actually get him there. He didn't appear to hold the whole episode against me.

The men and Captain Hamilton were by all appearances content with the results. I couldn't help thinking of Colonel Hayter. He would surely be expecting more than the few trifles I had to offer.

On cue as if he'd tapped into the landlines in my head, Captain Hamilton said: 'Unfortunately no prisoners, Lieutenant.'

'No. Unfortunately not.'

'If it's any consolation, at least you can report back you got a few of them. You're welcome to join us any time,' said Lieutenant Geddie, and he cracked a smile.

Grumpily I nodded.

There was one thing that was abundantly obvious about the night's action; if I wanted a bomb proof job, working on General Lipsett's staff wasn't it.

CHAPTER 26

22nd of March, 1917
Trenches east of Neuville-Saint-Vaast, France

It could have turned out worse, I eventually concluded. Given that I was still around that might seem self-evident, but I was actually thinking of my report.

Colonel Hayter barely glanced at the foolscap sheet I handed him: my findings from the Camerons' raid. Despite my best efforts to make it look more substantial – the benefits of a law school education – it didn't amount to much and I reckon he saw through the big words and generous spacing straight away. It may simply have been my handwriting that warned him off. Regardless, I wasn't called upon to explain the glaring absence of prisoners even though, by my own admission, I'd had one virtually in my grasp. Hayter accepted it as it was, and that was that.

Only for me it was not quite that simple. The first few nights, violent images tumbled through my mind. Before sleep felled me I pictured the young German lad and the expression he'd been wearing. I still had his grenade.

In the week that followed no further mid-night excursions were proposed. I don't think I saw Hayter more than twice, and the general not at all. Major Collum ignored me. There'd been raids and patrols – that was par for the course – but my services in the field went uncalled for. I suppose I should have been grateful, regardless of Benoît's advice.

However, the attack was coming very soon. It had to be. The more I thought about that, the more I worried whether we'd carry it, and what would happen if we didn't. Even if we did the casualties would surely be enormous. For the first time the entire Canadian Corps, four divisions strong, 100,000 men in total, were to be thrown into the fray at one time. From everything I'd seen of Vimy the situation didn't lend itself to optimism. As Benoît had said, the ridge was a fortress; ten times worse than anything we'd faced at the Somme. Little wonder General Nivelle had reportedly told Byng and Lipsett it couldn't be done.

As the big day approached, headquarters might therefore have appeared as the ideal location to keep my head down. But I couldn't help reflecting on friends, Roy Dundas first and foremost. Two years previously he and I came to the Western Front. Since then, he and most of the fellows I knew from the first contingent were gone; I was one of the few still kicking. What also kicked was the certainty that *they* wouldn't have been cowering in the rear.

In the meantime, a clear victor was emerging in the battle of attrition at HQ. Yesterday the colonel had commended Stiles on his 'superior' staff work. In all honesty it was a complicated series of inter-divisional reliefs, including one by the field artillery, while a group from the Corps heavy artillery had arrived to make demands of its own. I concluded he'd had help. Normally the help would have been me, but astonishingly he hadn't even asked. And no one else owned up. The only possible explanation was that he'd bought one or more of them off with a bottle of whiskey, cases of which were easily within reach for a guy with his connections and background – without even opening that little bag of gemstones he had squirreled away somewhere.

It was 3 a.m., overcast and cold. On the right of the La Folie section the 8th Brigade was moving in and the 9th out. The relief appeared to be progressing smoothly. As I'd arranged it that pleased me.

Briefly I stopped at the battalion headquarters of the 4th and 5th CMR, not terribly far from the tunnel entrance, and the red-white striped barber's pole that marked it.

Then I walked down the Goodman subway as the Mounted Rifle battalions ahead of me had done not long before, encountering weary eyes and boots shuffling back in the opposite direction. From the northern outskirts of Neuville-Saint-Vaast the tunnel extended for almost a mile. Pipes, bundles of telephone wire, even a small tramway ran down the corridor chiseled from stone, the entire thing lit by electric bulbs affixed to the walls. Every several yards small bays or whole chambers appeared to one side or the other, some of them quite large.

Sometime later I left the tunnel at the last of the fourteen exits, climbing up the ladder into a gust of cold sleet at a spot directly behind the fire trench. Pulling up my collar I set about down the line.

The men were already settling down, keen on a few hours' sleep, the sentries and the routine quickly established. A rote they were familiar with. All was well.

Spotting someone I recognized I stopped in the first fire bay and spoke a few words with him. He was a man I knew as a private from nearly a year earlier, long since a sergeant, and keenly aware of his greater responsibilities as his frequent glances from left to right attested.

The man's eyes suddenly bulged. It was as if I had the young Prussian in the dug-out before me. *But there couldn't be any enemy? Not here?* On the off chance, I turned abruptly, reaching for my revolver.

'Steady on, Lieutenant.' The tone was calm and measured. Spoken in the King's English.

'General!'

General Lipsett permitted himself a watery smile at our surprise. He was wearing a helmet and a trench coat, and in the dark shadows of the trench there was no one who could have suspected who it was until he was upon you. He asked a few simple questions of the sergeant, nothing of any special significance. But to show his interest, I imagine. Then he addressed himself to me.

'The strangest yarn came to my ears, Lieutenant,' said the general, arching an eyebrow.

'Sir?'

'I heard you were trading bombs with the enemy out on a patrol. Actually, as the tale went it was not so much trading as accumulating –'

'I wouldn't put too much store in such tales, sir. You know how quickly rumours spread in the trenches.'

He was quiet for a moment. 'Yes, I thought it might have been something like that.' He stared at me. 'I mentioned your name to General Byng recently.'

My eyes widened. 'You did, sir?'

'Yes, he was most interested to hear you'd been to Verdun. I told him I thought it was a very useful experience for a young officer, and not unrewarding for the division.'

'Yes, sir, I learned a great deal.'

The general nodded, then carried on down the trench, leaving the two of us shaking our heads.

'If I live and breathe,' said the sergeant. 'Isn't that something?'

'I had no idea,' I said. 'General Lipsett is fond of doing some scouting of his own but I hardly expected to see him here. Not at this hour.' And what to think of the general mentioning me to the Corps commander?

Later that morning, closer to a time most people readily associated with morning, I was trotting slowly past a copse of trees on a steed called Winnifred, on my second errand of the day. There was a gas alert on, so I was mindful of that, not to mention the considerable effort I was devoting to remaining in the saddle.

'Nothing to fear, Lieutenant. Your Grandma could ride Old Winnifred,' the corporal had assured me. Not that this did anything to assuage my concerns. Grandma was a fiery bundle of Scottish energy who could have tamed a grizzly while cooking up a breakfast of fried bacon. Neither of which were remotely within my skill set. Ironically, there were more than enough cowboys in the battalion I'd come to France with, but I wasn't one of them. As a young city boy I'd once had a nasty spill out for a pleasure ride on what was advertised to my father as a pet pony. I'm not sure what my father learned from the experience but ever since I'd kept a wide berth of ponies. Unfortunately wide berths were seldom an option in the army. Pressed between walking countless miles – there being no car available – and jumping aback the pot-bellied mare no self-respecting officer would dare to be associated with, I chose the mare.

A loud bang and the copse of trees a few yards off our left was suddenly enveloped in flame. The tendrils licked out at Winnifred and me on the road.

I ducked. Winnifred whinnied. Then rose up on her hind legs as wise little boys will tell you horses are wont to do.

Too late I grabbed for the pommel and felt myself sliding away, the reins ripped from my hands.

With a painful thud and a *splat* I landed full on my behind on the muddy road, my teeth rattling. The guns in the copse exploded again. Common sense would have suggested I cover my ears from the thunder but I was too stunned to do anything. As the shock wore off I found myself wincing in pain.

'Sir,' shouted someone. I smelled nothing but gunpowder. There was the taste of blood in my mouth. A soldier was hurrying towards me. 'Are you all right?'

I gritted my teeth and said something that was drowned out by another blast. Through the trees I could see one of the guns – a huge thing. From its sheer size, wheels as high as the average man, the rim of the stubby barrel thicker than an arm, I figured it to be an 8-inch howitzer. Smoke was curling up from the barrel.

The soldier, an artilleryman, was instantly recognizable due to his wearing a white flannel shirt with rolled-up sleeves while the rest of us were tightly bundled against the cold. He leaned over me. Vaguely I was aware that a car had stopped, its doors hanging open; the occupants heading my way.

'Sir! Are you all right?' repeated the soldier. More loudly this time.

'What do you bloody well think?' I groaned. 'Help me up and we'll do the Turkey Trot.'

'Ah. Grace to God for thick heads,' a voice rumbled. 'Listen to him, he's fit as a fiddle.'

At this I turned. 'I should have known,' I said wearily.

Another artillery man had appeared on the road and had corralled the horse. Reins in hand he was comforting Winnifred by gently rubbing her head in the way of a man experienced in such things.

Benoît in contrast had his hands on his hips and was beaming down at me as if he'd been the one who single-handedly held the Germans at the Marne in 1914.

'Help me up you big oaf,' I growled. 'And wipe that grin off your face.'

My shoulder, which had felt pretty good the past month or two, was aching. In sympathy my thigh joined in.

Benoît and the officer accompanying him bent over and lifted me none too gently to my feet. '*Et voilà,*' said Benoît, when the deed was done.

'Thanks,' I muttered, wobbling a little. My hand went to rub at the sore spot that was my back and I instantly regretted it. The palm came back coated in mud. Mud and blood were what had typified my time in France. Thankfully the guns had fallen silent, so finally I could hear myself think.

Benoît reached out a hand and placed it gently on my shoulder. The wrong one. I cringed. His face turned solicitous. 'Are you okay, Mac?'

I gave a nod of sorts. 'Nothing a shot from your canteen wouldn't cure,' I said.

A smile in return. He handed it over.

I took a deep gulp and coughed at the cure.

'Where are you headed?' he asked.

'To the Wynter group. The heavy artillery.'

'The heavies? You found them.' He motioned at the trees. 'Or they found you.'

'Christ,' I said. 'What was that all about?'

'A practice barrage I imagine.'

'Practice for whom? Me, them, or the Hun?'

'The Hun, of course,' said Benoît evenly, ignoring the jest.

I looked down at myself. It was as if I'd rolled in the mud prior to someone driving a limber carrying 8-inch shells across me – only to have to have it wheel round and repeat the job at speed.

Gingerly I bent over and picked up my helmet. 'Good to see you, Benoît.' His companion gave me an empathetic look and walked over to the gunners. 'So, how's life with the Arties?'

'We did a shoot yesterday,' said Benoît.

'Oh?'

'A counter-battery shoot,' he elaborated. 'We fired 162 rounds at eight different enemy batteries.'

'You did?'

He lowered his voice. 'Mac, the colonel believes we've identified most of the guns opposite.'

'That sounds like quite a coup. I suppose you're destroying them now as fast as possible?'

'Not exactly,' he said. I frowned. 'We don't want to let the Boche in on it. Not until we're completely ready and we're certain we've found them all. Otherwise they'd simply replace them. But you probably noticed, Mac, how active the guns are the past few days?'

'Now that you mention it...' Meaningfully I glanced at the copse of trees.

Benoît was not be waylaid. 'The preliminary bombardment has started. Not that you'd notice but only half our guns are involved.'

'No, I hadn't noticed,' I said.

'That's for the same reason. Not to tip the enemy off. But when ZERO Hour comes –' There was something distinctly menacing to the way he said it.

'Speaking of ZERO Hour, you must know when it is?'

He shook his head.

'Strange,' I said. 'It can't be much longer though.'

'No. I don't think so.'

With that we turned to the subject of my recent tribulations. 'So,' I said, as I wrapped up my story, 'Stiles has dug himself in at headquarters as firmly as the Boche have on that ridge there. I suppose I shouldn't complain. I was the one who signed up for the infantry in the first place. You can't very well expect to go to war and not be at war. And there'll be a need for some new officers in the battalions when this is all over.'

Benoît looked pensive. It was not an expression I readily associated with him. 'Maybe. Maybe not,' he said. 'But I wouldn't give up hope, Mac. Even the straight roads have bends. Not every driver, especially the fast ones, pays attention as he should.' Then he smiled at this wisdom.

I was just plain confused. I wanted to ask what on earth he was trying to say when his travelling companion called out. They had to move on.

'Remember, Mac, *à outrance*,' he said as he left.

Later that afternoon, after having settled my differences with Winnifred at the threat of turning her into chops for the nearest French division, I lumbered into headquarters. There I was the subject of some probing glances. Passing General Lipsett and Colonel Hayter, they paused their conversation and stared at me. Only after I nodded formally did they react with nods of their own. Stiles, who remarkably was wielding a pen and studying a sheet of paper, took the opportunity of my reappearance to rest both wrist and eyes.

'What the blazes happened to you?'

'I ran into the heavies you might say.'

'Ah, good,' he promptly replied, no further interest in me. I shouldn't have been surprised. It takes a certain breed of man to be so self-absorbed. 'The arrangements I made were satisfactory then?' he asked.

'They seemed to think so.'

'Excellent.'

I turned to leave.

'One thing, MacPhail, before you go...'

Wearily I cocked an eyebrow.

'Three intelligence officers from Corps headquarters visited me this morning.'

Had I not been dead on my feet I might have remarked that it was difficult to fathom what an intelligence officer, let alone three, could possibly want with him. As it was I managed a more neutral, 'Oh?'

He was observing me closely. 'They searched my quarters.'

'They did what? They can't do that!'

'Yes, apparently they can. They've been given new powers to root out enemy spies they informed me.'

'You? A spy!' I burst out laughing. Stiles didn't know whether to be pleased or displeased at this reaction.

Then a thought came to me. 'They didn't find...'

Firmly he shook his head. 'No, they didn't find those.'

'You and I need to have a chat very soon, Captain Stiles.'

'We will. We will. I haven't forgotten,' he said. 'When things settle down after the attack.'

He looked at me strangely and began to speak. 'You know, MacPhail, I thought maybe...' Then abruptly his jaws clamped tight, and a smokescreen blew in.

It was no mystery what he was thinking. He was wondering whether I was the one who had ratted him out, which I hadn't. But then who had, and why? The whole situation was anything but straightforward. Much like my tenure on the staff. Much like the outcome of the attack that must surely come any day.

CHAPTER 27

29th of March, 1917
Near La Targette, France

I couldn't have summoned up a clearer explanation for why a dozen patrols were required every day to reconnoitre the German trenches than what was playing out in the skies over the ridge.

'Oh, no,' murmured the lieutenant at my side. 'Look!'

Droning slowly, steadily, and in a straight line above the ridge was a reconnaissance aeroplane from the Royal Flying Corps, a two-seated pusher, model to me unknown. The photographs they took were invaluable. Most of what we knew about what the enemy was doing, the strength of his defences, his dispositions, even how successful the barrages were, was thanks to the aeroplanes – the observer that peered over the hill, the one Wellington at Waterloo never had.

The pusher was an ungainly contraption, its rear-mounted propeller set immediately aft of the cabin where the pilot and the observer sat, with bi-wings so thick it seemed a miracle it was aloft, an impression reinforced by the flimsy-looking fuselage of two-by-fours that contrived to hold the rear tail in place. To the rear of the cabin, and considerably higher than the observer, was the pilot's seat nestled under the fore of the wing struts where I imagine the view was better. The observer sat in the bulbous open-front nose. A Lewis gun was mounted there on a swivel, but due to its positioning unable to fire either below or behind; the Royal Aircraft Factory was presumably banking on a generous measure of providence amongst air crews. At the observer's disposition was a second gun. He had to stand to use that, and it fired up and only as far back as the top wing. Notwithstanding the impracticality of both arrangements, one wondered what the poor fellow was to do with either gun when he had his head buried in the camera sights. Judging from the steadiness of the flight path that appeared to be what was preoccupying him currently.

There were three of the enemy. They swooped down from a cloud above in a flash, flying in a 1-2 formation, their speed and agility dazzling in comparison with the ugly duckling of a scout plodding along. By this time the whole platoon, me included, was shouting, 'Behind you!'

The scout waddled on; rigidly straight so as not disturb the photography, the stopwatch running to time the sequence.

The lieutenant's face took on a determined air. He seized his flare gun and rapidly shot one off in the direction of the aeroplanes. It was mid-afternoon and we were some distance away, but they could hardly have missed seeing it. Not that a flare going up near Vimy Ridge was anything unusual. Although in recent weeks it did tend to be the Germans who were sending up an S.O.S as the latest barrage dumped on their heads. Platoons marching forward behind the lines were not encouraged to use flares.

The enemy planes swept towards the scout, diving fast. In fact they dove too far and I thought for an instant that the danger had passed. Then they pulled up on a dime. All three of them. Right behind and a little lower than the observation plane. I was evidently not the only one who'd studied the layout of its guns. The scout flew on… oblivious.

In the meantime I'd noticed something else. 'Isn't that the darnedest thing? Hard to miss them with a colour scheme like that.'

Distractedly the lieutenant nodded, his eyes glued to the scene in front. 'There's a whole squadron. *Jastas* they call them,' he said out of the corner of his mouth. 'Albatrosses mainly. They've been shooting fish in a barrel here going on two months. Now the cocky bastards have given themselves a red paint job. To rub it in, I bet.'

The lead plane of the three, the leader of the pack and hence accustomed to muscling aside the others, pushed forward until he was nipping at the underbelly of the scout and his nose turned upwards. I may have imagined it but I thought I heard the short burst of the machine gun. It took only a single one.

There wasn't any smoke or visible signs of damage but the scout plane fell into an alarming dive heading straight in our direction. We stood there on the road not far from La Targette, clustered together and unmoving, watching anxiously.

The motor of the scout plane was whining away in a loud repetitive rhythm as it passed overhead, descending fast. I looked for faces but saw none and I wondered if they would make it. There was a collective groan when the aeroplane disappeared behind a grove of trees 500 yards on. But no smoke, so maybe providence was with them after all. I glanced over my shoulder. And felt my stomach turn.

What I hadn't noticed until then was that the German machines, which I'd distinctly seen banking to return to base, had circled around and were again nipping at the scout's heels, rushing it to its grave. They came at us like red-scarfed banshees, sleek tubular bi-wings buzzing down the road from the east. Their whirring propellers bit the air with a renewed ferocity, morsels of fresh prey in their sights.

'Run!' I screamed. Unbidden the whole platoon was already scattering to the winds. The three planes bore down upon us, so low they almost dusted the ground. Everywhere men, and a few horses, were fleeing. The single dauntless lorry on the road had halted, its doors open as they'd been left.

I made a sprint for the fields.

A staccato cough. Small pinpricks of light came from the top of the cowling of the first plane. He was heading straight at me.

The first burst of bullets painted a tight seam down the road, splashes of mud marking their progress, but by then I was diving away. Away from the planks and headfirst into the sea of mud.

They roared past in an agitation of noise and a gust of wind, their motors growling, a higher more incessant buzzing than that of the scout plane. They taunted the earth for a second more before pulling upwards and soaring into the sky, already sharply banking.

An anti-aircraft gun started to bark, not far away. It was soon joined by another. White puffs of smoke dotted the sky around the interlopers.

Arrogantly, almost dismissively, the "Reds" continued their turn and climbed rapidly. Within a few breathes all three were obscured to eye and field glass by thick rolls of cloud that swallowed them up.

All we could do was shake our fists in response.

But of the platoon I'd been accompanying on the road to Vimy, somehow, only a single man was hit. The lorry was ready for the scrap yard. For the second time in a week I was soaked in mud. My uniform and my nerves were a right mess.

And the raid hadn't even begun. When Benoît admonished me to keep going to the bitter end I'm not sure he realized how bitter the path could be.

La Folie section, near Neuville-Saint-Vaast, France

'You're from divisional headquarters, you say?' said the sentry dubiously.

'That's right,' I replied. 'We're at Villers-au-Bois currently, General Lipsett in command. Perhaps you've heard of him?'

Not to be misled by this most favoured ploy of enemy spies the sentry looked me up and down.

'For Christ's sake,' I said. 'I'm here to report to the 4th CMR, not undergo a bloody uniform inspection. If you'd like to go into the Hun lines in my place, just say the word. No problem. I'll make certain the buttons that pass here are duly polished.'

At this the private grinned. 'Pass, sir.'

'About bloody time,' I muttered. Afterwards I regretted my terse words. The man was on edge as we all were. The attack could come at any time and the sentry wasn't the only one anxious about enemy spies. The wildest rumours were making the rounds. Some geniuses in the 4th Division had even trapped two cats which had drawn suspicion due to their frequent visitations of our trenches. Then there were the intelligence officers who had searched Stiles's belongings.

I was late when I finally reached the battalion. Only after asking at every traverse did I locate Richards and his men at the furthermost extremity of Vernon Trench, waiting to go along the sap to the crater of similar name, and points eastward. They were at the exact spot where I'd headed out to the enemy line with the Camerons a few weeks earlier. Which was why I had been the consensus choice for tonight's raid. Perchance I wasn't included in the committee. In fact, I suspect the colonel had intended this one for Stiles, but when Stiles found it on his desk it was alarming how quickly his mind could work.

'Hmm. Vernon Crater. Say, MacPhail, isn't that where you went out earlier?'

Cagily I said, 'Perhaps. I've been out all along the line. Why?'

'Oh, the colonel wants someone to go along on a battle patrol,' he replied. 'I think I'd better let you do it. Bowing to experience and all that.'

'Experience does count,' I said thoughtfully. 'A little time at the sharp end certainly doesn't hurt when the talk turns to promotions. It's hard to make a name for oneself dotting i's.' I could see I had his attention, dotted i's not being a particular forte of his. 'Are you certain you don't want to reconsider? I'd understand if you did.'

Stiles appeared to deliberate. Briefly I thought he'd swallowed the bait. 'You're right, of course. But you're the man who knows the ground, not me. I have to think of the greater good, MacPhail.'

Greater good –. I steamed. He probably didn't want to dirty the pair of leather boots which had arrived with the last mail, a present from 'Pops' in London.

Mine were still caked with mud and looked like they'd been on someone's feet since the Boer War. More to the point Stiles wasn't mistaken in what he'd said. I did know the ground. My involvement in such raids suggested however that knowing the ground was highly overrated compared to a strong underhand pitch and a plentiful supply of Mills bombs.

We followed the sap out towards Vernon Crater before debouching, this time to the right of it. I didn't recognize a thing despite having walked the terrain not 50 yards away. In the darkness it was tough to see much of anything.

Richards had divided his small party into two groups of four, each led by a corporal. One party was to lead and the other was to cover. At my insistence I went with Lieutenant Richards and the first group. All told it was an unexpectedly small number to send into the enemy's front line.

We followed a heading due east, towards the section of the German trench where it crossed what had once been a small road up the ridge. As we did so rain began to patter down; the day had been marked by showers of varying intensity. Thankfully the wind had shifted once more so there was no need to wear respirators. Out in No-Man's-Land you needed every faculty you had, and a canvas hood over your head with steamed-up glass goggles tended to impair most of them.

'What about the wire?' I whispered to the lieutenant.

'We brought a cutter,' came the reply. Richards was no stranger to trench raids.

Far off to the right in the direction of Thélus, a small hamlet on the southern half of the ridge, the skies flared ominously and a man-made thunder clapped after. Stone for stone Thélus was being systematically obliterated this final week of March.

I gave a nod and kept walking, each step laborious, feet sinking away in the wet earth. Strangely, I couldn't shake the feeling of being terribly alone. In the larger raids there was always a file of men to follow, someone ahead in a tin bowl hat to remind you that whatever the odds said you weren't on your lonesome. Often a barrage roared to distract mind and queasy bowels from the dangers that awaited out of sight. Tonight I saw only the dishevelled ground, an old fence post, a rusting loop of wire, and felt the intimidating mass of the ridge looming beyond. When I squinted I could barely make out the two men Richards had sent in advance, two shapes a trifle darker than the rest.

'Wire,' said Richards, after we'd walked 100 yards. I could see neither wire nor men signalling and I looked at him, intending to question this assertion. The lieutenant was a powerful man, burly with broad shoulders, a clean-shaven square chin and alert eyes. His was the sort of head they put on pedestals. 'We'll stay put until it's cut,' he murmured.

'Alright,' I replied. Both his tone and his manner were confident and I went down on one knee, the Webley grasped in one hand.

Richards waved an arm over his shoulder, beckoning. The man with the cutters went forward.

Of late I was concerned that with raids so commonplace sloppiness would set in – bravado taking the place of brains and common sense.

For all the bombardments and the relentless pinpricks of our nightly excursions, Vimy Ridge was no place to let down one's guard. Fritz was well aware what we were attempting and he was having none of it. Unless we could wrest it away, the heights of Vimy belonged to him. Fortunately, Richards was taking matters seriously.

'Wait here,' he said to me, before vanishing into the night.

When he returned a few minutes later, panting from his exertions, he signalled that we should move.

There was definitely nothing wrong with his eyesight. Shortly thereafter I too spotted the first thick belt of wire, and shortly after that wormed on my stomach through the narrow slit that had been cut in the coils. I caught one arm on the thick strands as I pulled myself along. The barbs tore a gash in my trench coat sleeve before I was able to disentangle myself.

Once through, a quick trot and we saw the parapet looming. Richards waved furiously to go to ground. He was taking no chances; if a sentry spotted movement or heard a noise foreign to his ears ten men stood little chance trapped between enemy trench and the wire barrier to the rear.

'Dawson,' he whispered to the corporal of the second party. 'Cover us from here. We'll see if we can force an entrance.'

The first group of six crawled towards the parapet on hands and knees. It was easily visible with the sandbags stacked three high to create a protective dyke. Several feet immediately in front of the parapet ran two strands of wire, staked to the ground with metal rods roughly three feet high. Sometimes when the artillery had played over a trench the wire was destroyed along with the parapet. When it wasn't, there were generally three options; cut it, try to step over it, or squeeze under it. Richards chose for the last. He motioned to us to spread out.

Before I got started I glanced both ways down the wire. As far I could tell there weren't any tin cans or other oddities hanging there; an old tactic used by both sides, intended to provide warning in the event someone tried to do precisely what we intended to do.

With my head in the mud I propelled myself underneath. It was all I could do to restrain the urge of rising up on both elbows for more leverage. If I did, my back would almost certainly catch on a strand. I pushed with my legs and clawed with my fingers. It was a relief when first shoulders, and eventually my body, emerged from underneath the wire and I could rise to my knees.

The private who'd started off with me was already through. He was on his knees peeking over the sandbags and down into the trench. The others were coming up behind.

'Boche,' he hissed over his shoulder. I slid up abreast of him.

What he'd seen was the top of a helmet. And now I saw it too. In fact there appeared to be three helmets. I signalled with my fist in the air to warn the others.

Then to the private I made the motion of throwing a bomb. He nodded and reached for the bag at his side, while I fished in my pocket for a Mills bomb.

There was a clank and a commotion behind. The last man had gotten snagged on the wire. The *Stahlhelms* abruptly turned and began moving in our direction. It would take them only a minute. We were out of time.

I pulled out the little pin and lobbed it. The private beside me did the same.

Not fifteen feet away the grenades landed in the trench. The noise seemed all the louder for the relative silence that had gone before. There was a rifle shot from further down the trench. Then four more. A flare sizzled into light above us. There were shouts of alarm.

Cautiously I peered over the parapet to see if I could assess the damage. All three of the Germans were down, lying on the trench floor. When I looked closely I thought I saw something else. Behind me I heard the last man arrive.

'The next bay,' I said, turning to the others. 'Check out the next bay. I need to have a look here.'

Someone protested that it was too dangerous. I think it was Corporal Martin. I dismissed it with an airy wave; it was my skin at risk and the raid was already at an abrupt end, regardless of anything I did.

There were more rifle shots. I climbed over the sandbags and slid down into the trench. It was a long drop, the trench a good eight-feet deep. When my feet touched the bathmats I ran forward towards the enemy soldiers lying on the planks, only then remembering to grab for my revolver. When I reached the Germans I was leery, worried that they were only stunned or perhaps lightly wounded, the chance for revenge unexpectedly within grasp. Many a man had been killed by a foe he thought was dying. But these bodies were twisted in such strange and contorted positions there was no possibility they were alive, no matter their wounds. I also saw that I'd been right; one of them was a subaltern. An *oberleutnant* (first lieutenant) if I wasn't mistaken.

It was to him I went. Leaning down I rolled over his body, aware as I did so that my hands felt treacly and wet. Down the trench at the next bay more bombs were going off. *Good for them.*

Hastily I felt at all his pockets, hesitated at the touch of one and shoved a hand inside. *Papers!* Quickly I stuffed them in my tunic. With heart pumping, I tore back to the spot where I'd entered the trench. It wouldn't be long before the trench was swarming with the enemy. The revetting in this section was intact and in excellent shape, and I made thankful use of it as footholds and handholds to scramble to the top.

'We're falling back, MacPhail,' Lieutenant Richards shouted when he spotted me. He appeared to be wounded. All along the German line flares were going up, their phosphorescent light glaring down until a gust of the wind blew them in a different direction, leaving only shadows. The rifle fire had markedly intensified. If only they knew how few we were. The Mounted Rifles and I had poked our heads into a veritable hornet's nest.

In the confusion and our haste to flee we brazenly stepped over the parapet wire, an awkward manoeuvre but not overly difficult for either Richards or myself due to our height – more so for the others – and scampered for the wire belt.

The voice of a sentry was bellowing from the trench. Instantly bangs and flashes erupted in the midst of the German wire. For 100 yards to either side they were bombing their first-line defences.

Which was not entirely absurd as it was through that wire barrier that we planned to leave. Ironically Fritz's plans were probably made in anticipation of our arrival, not our exit.

I dove for it. Richards, Corporal Martin and the last two men were in close pursuit. This line of wire was far too high, too dense, and above all too wide to merely step over. One of the covering party had staked out the small passage cut earlier and several of the men going through it were bumping up against each other. I was of no mind to wait in a queue as the stick grenades rained down. I'd chance it on my own.

Slithering over the wet ground with my nose literally ploughing a furrow in the mud, I hoped not to get hung up on a barb between the shoulder blades. I'd barely begun to crawl when I heard a bang as another bomb went off – immediately behind me. There was an anguished cry, followed by voices shouting. Had it been possible I would have looked. But the only thing I could do was keep going. Finally I emerged from the wire thickets and I looked back. At that instant the enemy trench boiled over with explosions. Rifle grenades! Our grenadiers in the nearby craters were providing support.

Then I spotted Lieutenant Richards. He was in bad shape. Corporal Martin and one of the men, Private Brazeau, were desperately trying to untangle him from the fierce clutches of the wire. The German rifle fire and the bombing had ceased.

With difficulty they managed it, and got both him and themselves through the coils, a nerve-wracking experience simply to watch. Without the rifle grenades they wouldn't have managed it. Nor without them would I have been standing around in the open while a few men attempted to fashion a stretcher from an old piece of duckboard so as to carry the lieutenant. It was an endeavour I could contribute little to so I took up a covering position. For all the lack of activity in the enemy line I was conscious how quickly that might change. Soon a stretcher was brought forward.

'Will he make it?' I asked Corporal Martin, after reaching the relative safety of Vernon Trench. Retaliation from the German guns hadn't come and I was hoping it wouldn't.

The corporal shrugged but didn't reply.

I grimaced.

'Did you find something worthwhile in the Boche trench, sir?' I reckon it was his way of reassuring himself that the night's outing had been worthwhile. The German casualties far outnumbered our own, so by any measure the 4th CMR could be proud. But the thing was, the neat sums made at headquarters didn't add up the same when you knew the men involved.

'These,' I said, brandishing the papers. 'I found these.'

'What are they?' he asked.

'I don't know yet, Corporal. But I intend to find out.'

CHAPTER 28

2nd of April, 1917
Arras-Béthune road, Neuville-Saint-Vaast, France

'So what did he say?' asked Benoît.

'Not much,' I replied. 'After I told him the map was of our own line he seemed to lose interest. He said he'd examine it later. The other papers were even less interesting to him.'

'The major is a busy man.'

'Yeah, well, I'm busy too, and I'll bet you dollars to dumplings Major Collum hasn't been ducking stick grenades of late.'

'Perhaps he'll put it in the intelligence summary, Mac. The colonel and General Lipsett might see it.'

'Perhaps,' I said, 'Although either way it won't be terribly helpful in the planning. It was a bit creepy, though, seeing it laid out like that on paper. To think the enemy has nearly as accurate a picture of our trenches as we do: which battalions are in the line; the number of men; the state of our trenches... They'd even marked whether there was any new work being done.'

Benoît shuddered. 'I hope they don't know that much about our plans for the attack.'

'No,' I said. I hadn't thought of that possibility but Benoît's remark was perceptive. If the German intelligence was so refined, who was to say they didn't know exactly what we were up to. The attack might turn into the very slaughter General Nivelle and others feared. 'Did you hear they captured a German officer a time back,' I said. 'He had an interesting story to tell. He said they were ready for us. More precisely he said that if we Canadians reached the peak there'd only be enough of us left to fill a rowboat.'

A sound not dissimilar to a growl came from Benoît.

As we'd agreed I found him in Gun Valley astride the Arras-Béthune road at one of the divisional field batteries. In the absence of any pressing tasks, and not having had leave since somewhere around the turn of the century I had asked for, and the colonel agreed to, some time to visit friends and tour the division – although I phrased it more workmanlike than that.

Unfortunately, I picked a rotten day for an outing. April was seeing a return to winter.

'Too bad you don't have a car,' said Benoît, circumspectly, peering through the door of the hut. Outside it was storming, the wind from the southeast growing progressively stronger, heavy gusts whipping up out of nowhere. Cold rain fell in driving sheets. As the temperature was falling too, I was quite certain that by nightfall it would be snowing. It had been a chilly walk from Souchez where an ammunition lorry had deposited me an hour earlier. I was grateful for the lift as it had saved me a much longer walk from divisional HQ.

'The roads were jammed this morning and with this weather a car would get us nowhere,' I said. 'Come on. I'll walk with you. I've only a couple of miles under my belt so far today. Besides, you're from Québec; doesn't it snow all year round in *La Belle Province*? A spot of rain shouldn't deter you in the slightest.'

The six 18-pounders lined up in a row outside began to bark.

'What the devil is going on?' I asked. 'The guns have been firing like mad all morning. Is this the final bombardment? Do you think we're going in?'

Benoît waited until the battery fired again before replying. I wouldn't have thought it possible but he was truly becoming an artilleryman, an ear for the rhythm of the guns. All I heard was a continuous concussion of noise that startled me every time it started up. 'I don't think so, not right away,' he replied.

'What are you doing here, anyhow?' I asked. 'I may not know much about the artillery but I do know that the field batteries are for knocking down wire or smashing a trench, not shooting up Boche guns. I thought you were busy with this McNaughton fellow and the counter battery work?'

'I wish I was,' said Benoît wistfully, reaching for his greatcoat. 'I'd like that. But it was a temporary assignment. The officer who is normally the liaison is back from leave. My current orders are to double check the battery and divisional stockpiles.'

I frowned. 'You're counting shells?'

Stoically he shrugged.

'Could be worse, I suppose,' I said slowly. 'You could be responsible for polishing them.'

Benoît stepped out the door into a blast of wind. I followed. The battery behind roared and too late I clasped both palms to my ears.

We didn't walk for long before we reached the ruins of Neuville-Saint-Vaast. As I'd suspected, the traffic was only inching along in mud churned into butter by the passage of thousands of wheels. Along the harder shoulder we made considerably better progress than the lorries. Even by day the roads out of direct sight of the ridge were busy. Several of the drivers waved to us, cheerfully offering a ride, which we bravely declined. Given the inclement weather it seemed brave. Though when I contemplated the thousands of rounds of small arms ammunition, bombs, or stacks of shells they were carrying, coupled with the possibility – albeit small – that a stray shell found them, they were the brave ones.

Neuville-Saint-Vaast, a small village possessing neither beauty nor seemingly inhabitants, lies at the mid-way point of the escarpment. Immediately opposite on the other side is the ridge's namesake, the village of Vimy. Surprisingly, it was the first time I'd seen the place from close by.

'Can you believe that,' I marvelled. We'd turned east at the intersection and were plodding through what had been the centre of the village. Prior to the fierce fighting of 1915 when the French wrested it from German hands there'd been actual buildings. Another couple of steps and we came into full view of a munitions dump. It was cleverly nestled amongst tumbling walls to either side. Everywhere rows of shells were on display, the largest ones upright on end and the others stacked a dozen high like loaves of bread. Men were unloading a lorry by hand with only the help of strategically placed planks, skillfully rolling huge 60-pounders down from the lorry bed and off to a corner of the dump. Camouflage netting was draped overhead to hide the dump from the observers on the ridge and any German aviators of an unusually adventurous bent who dared loiter above our rear areas.

'We have more than a thousand guns,' said Benoît. 'A heavy for every 20 yards and a field gun for every 10.'

I whistled. 'Let me guess, they eat shells like you eat breakfast?'

Benoît, who'd steadily taken on the appearance of a drenched rat since leaving the battery, grinned. 'That's how we're going to beat them,' he said. 'Big plates of high explosive and helpings of shrapnel.'

'I'm pleased to hear it, Benoît. As long as you don't tell me it's going to be a walkover.'

'*Non,*' he said, shaking his head. 'I'm not going to tell you that.'

We both had memories of the Somme, and before that Festubert and the Salient. Whenever the artillery had pronounced that all we needed to do was prance on over to the German lines it was invariably a moment to start reciting the Lord's Prayer.

When I spotted a second dump only a few minutes later down the same road, and still in the village, it dawned on me that I'd never seen such extensive preparations. General Byng was leaving little to the vagaries of chance. But then no one had taken a position like Vimy Ridge in two and a half years of war, so anything to improve the odds was welcome.

Once through the devastation of town we passed into the devastation beyond and turned left. We went northwards past fields and small stands of trees scarred by German shells. Through the rain and the mist the mass of the ridge dominated the view off my right shoulder.

All four divisions of the Corps were lined up in numerical order from south to north along the escarpment. The 3rd Division's frontage extended from the southern outskirts of Neuville to a line not far shy of the ridge's highest point, Hill 145, less than a mile to the north. Somewhere between here and there, there was a field gun battery Benoît wished to visit. We passed another dump, this one of truly astonishing proportions.

The rain had abated slightly, but the wind was still fierce. I put my finger to it to test the direction.

'You realize we should be wearing our respirators,' I said. I was speaking loudly so as to be heard.

'You first,' he replied.

The sight of all those massive shells and the thought of them crashing down upon our foe had buttressed my spirits temporarily. Ten minutes later those same spirits were buckling. The cold wind and the rain were cutting mercilessly through my wet clothes.

'Is it far, this battery of yours?' I asked.

Benoît said something over his shoulder. I couldn't hear enough to make sense of it. After goading him into this stroll through the elements I didn't dare ask him to repeat himself. My ostensibly fine idea of spending an hour or two chatting amiably while Benoît went about his rounds bore all the trademarks of one of Field-Marshal Haig's infamous plans. I pulled at my collar again.

On this road, in plain view of the ridge, there wasn't a lorry to be seen. A mule train passed but it was headed in the wrong direction, towards the dump. We were on our own.

'Wait!' I said urgently. 'Listen.' Benoît halted.

His expression was one of weary fatalism, the face that epitomised foot soldiers everywhere. Then he tensed. '5.9s,' he said.

Behind us in the desert of rubble known as Neuville-Saint-Vaast there was a boom. A cloud of black smoke billowed upwards. Then came the whistle of more shells. One after the other. They too went off with a crash. If only they didn't hit the dumps.

'4.1s, too, from the sounds of it,' I said. 'Let's keep going.'

The rain started falling again in abandon, only it was turning to sleet. For certain there would be snow tonight. Don't think about it and keep walking, I told myself. If there'd been an alternative I would have considered it.

Until suddenly one appeared.

A staff car came racing up the road from Neuville. Mind you, racing is a relative term. At the pace the two of us were walking Aesop's tale of the tortoise and the hare was a beacon of hope. With all the shells falling on the village the driver's desire to put some distance behind him was understandable.

Benoît had heard the high pitched motor, too, and had swivelled round.

We stood there beside each other. Caps tilted down low against the wind, our greatcoats not designed for the wet, and too wet by now to do much about the cold.

They must have taken pity on us. Despite the shellfire several hundred yards back, the car slowed as it approached. It ground to a halt beside me. There was a long pause before the back door swung open.

'Get in, gentlemen,' called a French-accented voice. I looked twice. There was no question the motorcar was one of ours.

Not wanting to tempt fate, or the impatience of the occupants, I put my head down and made a dive for it. Benoît tumbled in after me.

'Welcome, gentlemen,' said the bespectacled lieutenant-colonel sitting beside me.

'*Mais, vous êtes Français, monsieur!*' gasped Benoît. Whereupon I was relieved of any need to respond. The two of them began a rapid fire conversation. I did my best to be inconspicuous in the middle, vaguely conscious that Belgium had tried the same manoeuvre in 1914. Also conscious that it hadn't worked out so well, I was on my best behaviour.

The colonel wore the red-white-red armband of the Corps on his right sleeve, and it was most definitely a maple leaf adorning the cap perched on his lap – had it been any other sort of foliage I might have doubted myself. But his French was not that of Benoît's. Even I could hear that. The colonel certainly didn't look or act anything like DuBois. With dark hair, dark eyes, a sliver of a dark moustache and a Rock of Gibraltar nose, he exuded a dignified, almost scholarly air. The small, round spectacles helped. Benoît was so enthusiastic at speaking French I think he clean forgot the cavernous difference in rank between a lieutenant and a lieutenant-colonel. The colonel appeared to take it in his stride.

From what I could gather the colonel's name was Brutinel. He was in command of the Corps machine guns. This surprised me as he didn't look at all the sort to be found crouched down behind a machine gun, not that lieutenant-colonels were ever to be found crouched down behind machine guns. Benoît on the other hand would have been a perfect candidate, but he'd already volunteered for the artillery.

We didn't drive far before the car pulled off the road and parked in the shelter of a grove of trees. The colonel threw open his door and stepped out. There was no need to guess why they'd stopped here; a ringing chatter of machine guns sounded from the direction of the trees.

Moving through them I glimpsed the line of the ridge again. The only thing was, I could see nothing of the enemy, nary a wire entanglement or even a strongpoint. Furthermore, the barrels of the big machine guns were angled upwards and I didn't see any aeroplanes either. These were not the smaller Lewis guns I was familiar with but the heavy Vickers guns, settled on a metal tripod, a three-man team to ensure their proper functioning. One team was furiously replacing an overheated barrel.

I hurried to the colonel. 'Sir, if you don't mind my asking. What the devil are they shooting at?'

A thin smile emerged. 'It's a barrage of course.'

'A barrage? With machine guns?' I suspect the puzzlement was obvious in my voice. My understanding of how a machine gun worked was that you pointed at a target and pulled the trigger. These guns were pointed at the sky.

'It's called indirect fire, Lieutenant,' said Brutinel. Benoît beside me was listening attentively. 'It's a new technique we're applying, one we've borrowed from the artillery. We're targeting the road junctions and communication trenches behind the enemy lines. These guns, Lieutenant, can fire as far away as 2 ½ miles. That's well on the other side of the ridge.'

'Ah,' I said slowly, suddenly recalling a certain day at the Somme when I'd seen something similar, 'so they won't be able to bring up supplies or men –'

'*Exactement*,' said Brutinel, warming to the subject. 'Nor even repair their trenches. When the attack comes it won't only be our field guns providing a protective barrage.'

I was nodding furiously at the implications of this. Out of the corner of my eye I saw Benoît doing the same.

'Now, if you'll excuse me, gentlemen,' said the colonel politely.

'Remarkable,' I said to Benoît, once he'd left. 'He may be on to something our colonel.'

'Something for you?' he asked.

I frowned.

'If it doesn't work out at headquarters? The Emma Gees?'

'Perhaps,' I said thoughtfully. 'Perhaps.'

'Listen, Mac, I have to leave. But before I do. Why did you come today?'

'I told you. I was owed a few hours off. I thought it'd be nice to see a friendly face.'

Benoît shook his head. He may have come from a small provincial backwater on the St. Lawrence, but gullible he was not.

'It's a long story,' I said.

'Well, quickly then. As long as it's not too long,' he said, fixing me a serious look. 'I have work to do.' His bushy eyebrows were furrowed so thickly I might have mistaken it for a line of wire.

'I had a small confrontation with Stiles last night.'

He arched an eyebrow.

'He's become convinced I ratted him out to the Corps intelligence staff. They searched his quarters and his belongings a while back. Never heard of anything like it before or since. Anyhow, I thought he was past it, but for some reason he's now certain I'm the one responsible. Only I had nothing to do with it!'

Benoît began to laugh.

'I don't see the humour,' I growled. Then I noticed his face. It was beaming.

'No. Don't tell me. That was you?'

He didn't deny it. Actually he didn't say anything. His eyes did the talking.

'Why? How?'

'*Un gars*. A guy I know in the intelligence section,' he replied after a stretch. 'You told me the trouble you were having. One night this fellow mentioned the new powers they'd been given to root out German spies. Honestly, all I told him, Mac, was that I'd heard some things. But I couldn't be certain.'

'On the basis of that three of them drove down from Camblain l'Abbé to search through all Stiles's things?'

Benoît winced. 'Not entirely. I also gave him a bottle of rum.'

At this I had to laugh.

'You realize if they'd found the diamonds they'd be gone forever. And Sam would be pointing an accusing finger straight at me.'

'Ah, Mac, even if you had those rocks you'd be fretting constantly. Fretting, that's the right word, *non?*' I nodded. 'Stiles may be a captain but you can run rings around him anytime.'

'Hmm. I'm glad you think so. But he told me there's room for only one of us at headquarters. So you can guess who that's going to be. Connections are what count there.'

'I thought I'd be doing you a good turn,' said Benoît.

'Thanks for the thought. I appreciate it. Really I do. But I don't have a single friend higher up in the ranks. Rather the opposite. In fact I'm lucky the Prime Minister sacked the Minister of the Militia; he wasn't exactly my greatest admirer. I thought perhaps General Lipsett was sympathetic. Unfortunately all he's heard about me since I joined his staff is the paperwork I fouled up on. As to Stiles… Christ, it wouldn't surprise me if he had a direct line to the King.'

Benoît offered me his water bottle.

'No, it's a little early for that.'

'Suit yourself,' he said, and took a deep swallow himself.

'On second thought…'

As the liquid burned a path down my throat, Benoît asked. 'So what are you going to do?'

'The same thing I always do. Get on with the work, I suppose. Who knows what this attack will bring. At the rate things are going I may not even be around in a week. Colonel Hayter has me out on patrols every second day it seems.'

Benoît stared at the ridge. The machine guns had taken a pause. 'It's not going to be easy is it?'

It was the sort of rhetorical question that didn't really require a response. To the south a new salvo of shells fell on Neuville-Saint-Vaast. They were big ones. A black cloud formed momentarily above the village, until the wind whisked it away.

CHAPTER 29

5th of April, 1917
Enemy trenches east of Neuville-Saint-Vaast, France

Formally, the purpose of the patrol was to "to obtain identifications, observe effects of fire on trenches and dug-outs and ascertain if the enemy held the front line in any strength".

Informally, a mild panic had broken out. The patrol was but one manifestation of this. It began around lunch time.

'Have a look at this, sir,' said Corporal Reynolds. He was one of the fellows I knew best on the signalling staff. I'd popped my head through the door and signallers being signallers that didn't go unnoticed. Outside of my normal duties which brought me here multiple times a week, I made a point of stopping by at other moments, simply to swap stories and hear what they were hearing. I'd even been known to share a nut cake on occasion. It wasn't solely because I was hoping to hear something of interest, they were smart lads generally and conversation came easy with them, but it didn't hurt. Sometimes it even paid dividends. Such as now.

Reynolds thrust a signal into my hands. '2nd Division sent this out an hour ago to its brigades.'

The first line was sufficient to alert me that something unusual was happening.

THE CAPTURE OF PRISONERS ON OUR FRONT

WITHIN THE NEXT TWENTY FOUR HOURS IS OF VITAL IMPORTANCE…

Quickly I skimmed through the next few lines, which expanded on the first, until I reached the final sentence.

THE G.O.C. WISHES YOU TO REALISE THE SUPREME IMPORTANCE OF OBTAINING INFORMATION FROM PRISONERS AT THE PRESENT TIME EVEN IF CASUALTIES ARE INCURRED IN TAKING PRISONERS.

I made a clucking noise the signallers could have been excused for thinking came from the chicken coop down the road, the one beside the always well-provisioned artillery. But I was surprised. I'd never before seen an order in which a commander *a priori* excused the casualties. Afterwards was a different matter; the post-battle rationalisations had flowed richly these past years. But beforehand? And what could the "supreme importance" of corralling a prisoner or two be? As the 2ⁿᵈ Division held our right flank the answers were not solely of theoretical interest.

'What the dickens is going on?' I asked.

'Dunno, sir.'

'C'mon. You must know something.'

'No, sir,' he said. A pause. 'We thought you might?'

I shook my head. 'But I intend to find out. Thanks, Reynolds.'

I didn't get far when I spotted a man who might know. It was Lieutenant-Colonel Hayter.

'Ah, MacPhail!' he said loudly and waved an arm to indicate I should come to him.

'I was hoping to find you,' he said.

'Sir?'

'I need you to go out to the line. The 1ˢᵗ CMR have a reconnaissance patrol going out this evening. Everyone else I can spare is already in the field with the Camerons. They've got some raids on.'

'Yes, sir.' It didn't seem the moment to point out that Captain Stiles was available, twiddling his thumbs even as we spoke, or more likely enjoying a late lunch.

'What's it all about, sir?' I asked.

Hayter examined me, his hand thoughtfully rubbing his chin. I knew what was preoccupying him; he was debating what he could or *should* tell me.

'The RFC has reported that the Germans may be engaged in a general withdrawal.'

My eyes popped. 'That can't be, sir.'

But as I thought about it, it dawned on me that it was not so far-fetched. It certainly explained the strange signal Reynold's had shown me.

'No,' he replied, 'and that's what all the reports from the front line say. Nevertheless, the aerial patrols insist they're retiring. We can't risk a new Alberich.' He planted his eyes on me, an unusual intensity in the look. 'Are you familiar with Alberich, Lieutenant MacPhail?'

'Yes, sir,' I said. 'In broad lines.'

Operation Alberich in March had thrown the Allied command into puzzled disarray, even if the papers billed it afterwards as a great enemy retreat. Precipitously the Germans had withdrawn 25 miles from the two bulging salients in their line at the Somme to regroup at the new Hindenburg Line. In so doing they gave up more ground than had been captured in the entire five-month long battle. Behind them they left a charred country, wells poisoned, trees felled, the roads holed through huge mines and booby-trapped. Nothing was spared. Ironically the ground surrendered changed nothing in the strategic equation; although tactfully this was a line of thinking the newspapers did not publish. If anything, the German position was stronger afterwards; a straighter line; fewer divisions to defend it, and the well-engineered defences of the Hindenburg positions to hand. What might have been turned to advantage with a skilful thrust forward was not. It took nearly a week for French and British units to close the gap. By then it was too late.

'So you realize what the implications of an Alberich would be?' asked the colonel.

'All our preparations would be for nought, sir. There's a good chance they might even dig in on the reverse slope of the ridge.'

Hayter nodded. 'Precisely, Lieutenant. For a few hundred yards of gain we'd have to begin all over again. And we'd pay a heavy price simply to consolidate the new line, make no mistake about that.'

'I'll leave then, shall I sir?'

He gave his assent, but not without one final, pressing instruction.

Lieutenant Wier and party were awaiting me. The 1st CMR were holding the line at the divisional boundary with the 2nd Division, on whose front the alarm had first been raised. If there was something to be seen in the general area we would surely see it from here. I suspect Colonel Hayter had come to the same conclusion. General Lipsett and he were not content to sit on their haunches and leave it in the hands of the 2nd Division if there *was* something going on. The sooner they knew for certain the better.

'We're going to cross No-Man's-Land, circle the B.4 Crater, then reconnoitre the enemy line as far back as Flapper Trench,' explained the lieutenant. We began stripping ourselves of personal effects and I clicked a bayonet onto a borrowed rifle.

What I hadn't anticipated was that we were to leave in broad daylight, at 6 p.m. While this brought advantages from the point of view of actually being able to see something, I was more conscious of the accompanying challenges – dodging fire from a row of Mauser carbines and a Maxim machine gun foremost amongst them. But as no one else was grousing, who was I to roil the waters?

I did however speak several more words with Lieutenant Wier.

'A prisoner,' I repeated. 'We absolutely must return with a prisoner.' Wier looked doubtful.

'Look,' I said. 'If it was up to me we'd throw in a few bombs and leave them all moaning on the duckboards, but Colonel Hayter and General Lipsett want prisoners. In fact, they're adamant about it. My orders are very clear, Wier. We *need* a prisoner.'

Wier continued to look doubtful. Snatching a prisoner was a tricky business. More often than not Fritz declined our initial invitation and that led to harsher tactics, the results of which typically left the soldier in question lying on the bathmats and terminally indisposed to interrogation.

'On second thought maybe I'll leave the rifle,' I said, visions of me trying to manhandle a sentry to the ground whilst holding a

Lee-Enfield taking shape. 'I'll keep the bayonet, though. And a club… does someone have an extra?'

There was nothing to see in No-Man's-Land, not that that was terribly unusual. For the most part both sides huddled in their trenches with little regard for what transpired fifty yards further – so long as it didn't involve an enemy attack. Even sentries were cautious in poking their heads over the parapet unless strictly necessary. We quickly crossed over the ground to the crater, cautious there might be men positioned on either side of the lip. But there weren't.

The crater hole itself was cavernous and deep, so deep a large farmhouse would have fit effortlessly, its roof well below ground. The rocks and debris that had been propelled hundreds of yards into the sky when the mine detonated lay scattered around the bowl. At the very bottom some fence posts and rusted coils of wire could be seen. After the first day in recent memory with little rain most of the accumulated water had seeped away. A careful study confirmed that the Germans had too.

We headed for what Lieutenant Wier told me was an enemy post nearby. That too proved empty. On any another occasion this observation would have pleased me. Now however I sighed.

We moved on towards the front-line trench.

The thick wire barrier that once guarded the approaches was wrought asunder. Which is to say there was nothing left of it. Here and there a stake was still standing, solitary strands of steel filament poking from the pitted ground. The trench beyond was in bad shape and didn't appear to be manned. A handful of us moved along the edge.

Further back in the support line, the intersection of Fly Trench and Flapper Trench was completely blown in. A white signboard stood drunkenly marking the spot. I couldn't see that any efforts had been made to repair either trenches or wire. Night and day this week the shells had poured in endless streams overhead, and both the state of the trenches and the wire, and the obvious lack of maintenance, were tangible proof of their effect. Fritz was reaping some little of what he had sowed.

But of any Fritzs on the ground there was no sign. I was beginning to think that instead of the wild goose chase I half anticipated, there might be something to this talk of a withdrawal. At that thought I could feel my stomach tightening. I needed that prisoner.

'Sir!' said Corporal Tait and pointed. There were three men running eastwards down Fly Trench to the intersection with Flapper, heading for the safety of a deeper stretch. They'd evidently spotted us for they were making considerable haste. As there was little trench to speak of at that point we could hardly avoid seeing them. Tait began firing his revolver. After the fourth shot I saw one of them fall.

Then I heard Lieutenant Wier on my left shooting off his six-round clip as fast as he could pull the trigger. He was aiming at a sole man who'd exposed himself a ways down the front line. 'Prisoners…' I muttered sourly to myself. The 1st Mounted Rifles appeared intent on eliminating every single enemy soldier we came upon.

A salvo of rifle shots sounded from the direction of Flapper, 100 yards away. Flapper ran roughly parallel to the front line and appeared to be where the remaining enemy had entrenched. Hurriedly we ducked away. A few of the lads returned fire until common sense prevailed.

Scarcely a minute passed before, by chance or design, one of our heavy shells came whistling over and landed in Flapper Trench. There was an impressive fountain of dirt followed by black smoke. The rifle fire ceased immediately. A better opportunity than this was unlikely.

'Tait, I'm going to see if I can capture that man you brought down.'

'I'll go with you, sir.'

'Promise me one thing, first.'

'Sir?'

'Don't shoot him unless I expressly tell you to.'

The corporal grinned.

We ran overland to Fly Trench and the spot where I'd seen the soldier go down.

He wasn't there. But then the corporal put on a sudden sprint. After scanning forward another ten yards I saw the reason. A man was lying in the shallow depression of what remained of the trench. He was tucked up tight against one side, just another mound of field-grey mud. Fortunately, Tait had noticed him.

The man's initial reaction was relief. He said a few words in German as Tait approached, only to bite his tongue when he saw who it was – I imagine he was counting on his comrades coming back for him. They would too, so we had to be quick.

'You got him good, Tait,' I said as I bent down. The soldier had been hit in the upper thigh, no more than a hand's width from the groin. He was bleeding profusely, his trouser leg soaked in it. A Webley revolver for all its heft, or perhaps because of it, packs a heavy punch.

I dropped to my knees and, putting away my own revolver, pulled out a field dressing. We all carried one in our left tunic pockets. That was where the army dictated they should be carried, the reasoning being that when time pressed no one would ever need to search if they already knew where. Time was pressing now and I ripped it open with my teeth. I don't think that was entirely as prescribed.

'A quick tourniquet,' I said to the man. He nodded. Then to Tait: 'I think we may have to carry him.'

I didn't cut away the trouser leg or do anything else; there was no time for that. I simply applied the pad to the spot where the blood was thickest, wrapped the cloth straps around his leg and tightened it very firmly. A pained groan came from him.

With me to one side and Tait to the other, we shuffled back to the front-line trench as fast as we could. In our haste we literally dragged him. Several times he manfully stifled a cry.

Lieutenant Wier and the others from the party were waiting.

The lieutenant was examining me, his face a mixture of relief that we were back, and something else. 'I see you managed to get your prisoner, MacPhail,' he said. I don't think he'd been expecting very much from a staff officer.

'He's not entirely whole,' I replied. 'Luckily your resourceful corporal pegged him in the leg and not somewhere else.'

Tait beamed. He was only an acting corporal, so I was glad to put in a few words on his behalf. I'd once marched in his boots.

I turned to the prisoner. He wasn't big, stout rather. He had a thick moustache of a fashion that was all the fashion in half the German Army. The insignia indicated he was from the 262nd R.I.R. An interrogation in an enemy trench was unorthodox, and not usually advisable, but I needed to know.

'What's going on?' I said to him.

His eyes widened and he glanced suspiciously at Wier's revolver. But he said nothing.

'*Was ist los?*' I asked again. Those are the three most valuable words of German when posing a question to a prisoner. Unfortunately, speaking a few words and subsequently understanding what the prisoner is answering are two entirely different things. This fellow rattled off a sentence or two at such speed that my brain felt like it was peering through an impenetrable fog.

'A retreat?' I pressed him. My finger waved from left to right, indicating first our lines and then the German ones to the east.

He shook his head.

'*Ein Rückzug?*' I repeated, thinking he'd misunderstood.

'*Nein,*' he replied, and launched into an elaborate explanation.

The gist of it was that there'd been a relief. I was quite certain I understood that correctly. One regiment, or perhaps more than one, was replacing another. There was no general retirement. It was a matter of routine, something armies had done for as long as there had been armies. All the details would come out when he was fully interrogated, but that was the single, crucial fact.

Our operation could continue.

I sighed, the relief welling up. I wouldn't be the only one feeling that way; a lot of senior officers at various headquarters would be wiping the sweat from their collective brows. I wondered if General Byng would hear of this. But first I had to get this Fritz with a hole in his leg back to the rear.

Lieutenant Wier had witnessed the entire exchange, as had most of the patrol who were standing in a semi-circle around the prisoner. It soon became apparent that Wier had missed the significance of the prisoner's words, though he may not have understood them.

'We need to get back,' I told him. 'And quickly too.'

He shook his head. 'I want to get a closer look at Zwischen Stellung,' he said. 'To reconnoitre the wire.'

Which was understandable as Zwischen Stellung formed the next obstacle in the German defences. The trench was some 700 yards further up the ridge, a darkish line on the horizon visible from where we stood. However I was feeling a little testy after all the trouble I'd gone to. The lack of anything to eat since lunchtime didn't help.

'Look,' I said, in an exasperated tone. 'Every general in a twenty-mile radius is concerned whether the Boche are pulling back. Because if they are, our plans to storm the ridge are as good as worthless. Then it won't make a damn bit of difference whether Zwischen Stellung is wired or not.'

Seeing his expression I realized I'd gone too far. 'It's good news, Weir. The prisoner said they'd had a relief. There is no withdrawal, so the attack is still on.'

He smiled tepidly.

With that the reconnaissance patrol came to an end. Wier led us back overland all the way from the B.4 Crater to battalion headquarters. There the prisoner was gratefully received. To my astonishment we did it without a single shot being fired in our direction. Wherever the Germans were, they weren't manning the parapets of the front line.

It was late when finally I reached Villers-au-Bois and divisional headquarters, anxious to relay my news. In the distance there were flashes from the guns going off. Along the entire length of the ridge there wasn't a moment when the spark of an explosion could not be seen. The night air, even at this distance, rumbled and cracked from the sound of them. Nor were we the only ones shelling. Our line was taking a beating from guns of all calibres.

In retrospect I needn't have rushed back.

The colonel was nowhere to be found. Major Collum was out. I thought briefly of informing General Lipsett personally, until I was told that he too hadn't been seen. Frustrated and mildly dejected I left a concise handwritten report with the duty officer. He'd see to it that those who needed to be informed, were. The most important thing, I told myself, the attack was still on.

It couldn't be long now.

CHAPTER 30

6th of April, 1917
Villers-au-Bois, France

The next morning as I stood negotiating with the cook for additional servings of breakfast on what seemed to me the very reasonable
grounds that I hadn't claimed dinner the previous night, I was startled
to see another outstretched plate appear beside mine. I was even more
startled when the cook reached out immediately with a generous
spoonful of the bacon I'd been eyeing so enviously. Bacon appears in
varying shapes, sizes and degrees of crispiness at the front, ranging
from lightly overdone to having been left too long in a 6-inch howitzer barrel. But the cook had surpassed himself.

'You apparently worked up quite an appetite yesterday,' said the
plate's owner.

I recognized the voice. But I turned to face him to make certain.

Colonel Hayter smiled at me pleasantly. 'Good morning, MacPhail.'

'Good morning, sir,' I mumbled. 'And yes, sir.'

The cook dropped another piece of toast on my plate. 'Just this
once, Lieutenant.'

'Thanks,' I sighed, eyeing the pan with bacon wistfully.

'Have you heard?' the colonel said conversationally, as he selected
fork and knife. 'The United States has declared war on Germany.
Happened the beginning of the week.'

Before breakfast and a cup of tea, or better yet coffee, I tend to float in a state known in the animal world as hibernation. Even allowing for that, this was the last thing I expected him to say. 'No. No, I hadn't heard, sir. But that's truly wonderful news.'

It was. Having the Yanks on our side – I assumed they'd be sending an army forthwith – could make all the difference. Unfortunately it changed nothing in the meantime. Within a week there was a very good chance many of us would be dead.

'Do you mind if I sit with you?'

'No, sir, not at all.'

Hayter chose a spot at the unoccupied end of the long wooden table and I set my plate down beside his. There were only a couple of others eating. Seeing who I was with they refrained from the usual banter, all nodding politely before returning to their own conversations.

'Pass me some tea, would you?'

I poured Hayter a cup and took coffee myself. There were officers' messes I'd heard about that had waiters in white for such moments. While I suspect that might have been a tall tale originating in the trenches, it may not have been. Either way the officers' mess of the 3rd Division tended to the Spartan. The coffee and tea sat in two silver-coloured pots on the table. The one concession to anything more elaborate was a white tablecloth. Barring that frivolities were for special occasions only. It was then I realized that today was a special occasion – of sorts. It was Good Friday.

After a bite and a sip of tea the colonel spoke. 'I read your report, MacPhail.'

I felt a glow coming to my cheeks. Perhaps this would help bolster my standing.

Hayter went on, 'Yours wasn't the first report to arrive, but nevertheless it was a useful confirmation. It's very welcome to have multiple sources of information at moments like those. Thankfully it was all a false alarm.'

The anticipation drained out of me. I felt as buoyant as one of the enemy's sausage-shaped observation balloons as it rapidly lost air and altitude whilst one of our fighting machines raced towards it. In my head I replayed his words... 'Useful confirmation'. It didn't sound any better with repetition.

Aloud I said: 'Yes, sir, there seems little doubt. It was just a relief, the enemy aren't retiring.'

The colonel went on to ask about several details as he worked his way through the parapet of bacon, while I told him what I'd seen regarding the wire and the perilous state of the front-line trenches. He seemed pleased at that. He asked me to repeat the part when I said that not only the front line but also the Zwischen Stellung didn't appear to be wired.

'It was at a distance, sir, but you tend to notice those sorts of things. The lieutenant from the battalion wanted to examine it further but I'm afraid I insisted we needed to get back.'

'A pity,' he said. 'I would have liked to have known more. We don't want to get hung up on any wire, MacPhail.'

I declined his offer of a second cup of coffee, pleading work to do. The colonel had been amiable enough. It was just that I'd been expecting more and was feeling a trifle underappreciated.

Not that Stiles who'd taken up position at his desk opposite did anything to improve that feeling. In fact the first sign of any life from him was when he threw a stack of papers onto my desk with the wry comment that after slacking off for a day I needed to get to it. Apart from that we studiously ignored each other – in so far as that's possible when sitting two feet away.

Around dinnertime there was a flurry of activity. Runners appeared in the hallway and clerks barged to and fro. The senior officers of the staff bustled from office to office.

'It's on,' muttered Stiles.

Good Friday it might be, there were few thoughts devoted to penance at the headquarters of the 3rd Canadian Division in Villers-au-Bois. It was altogether too much to expect a sudden bout of repentance sweeping over the headquarters of von Fasbender's Gruppe Vimy on the far side of the ridge.

Half the staff appeared at my elbow. There were movement orders to be written and sent. Confirmations received. A thousand final things to be coordinated, and the i's dotted and the t's crossed, as tens of thousands of men and tons of materiel were set in motion. It would be a late night.

The order for the attack had been issued.

7th of April, 1917
Fort George, 1 mile northwest of Neuville-Saint-Vaast, France

Most of what I learned of the operational details came second-hand, staff lieutenants not ranking especially high when it comes to the dissemination of important information. If the time of the attack was still a closely guarded secret, there was little doubt about the date of the assault; if for no other reason than that the battalions involved were required to be in their assembly areas by Easter Sunday. I'd written most of those orders myself so it had stuck in my mind. Unprompted, even Stiles drew the inevitable conclusion.

'Easter. The eighth of April,' he mused. 'So it has to be Monday, the ninth.'

'Correct,' I said, unable to restrain the urge, 'In most months the ninth day does tend to follow the eighth.'

Stiles looked at me sourly.

'In leap years it might be different,' I added.

I was rewarded by a momentary look of puzzlement while he considered this.

Then I saw him reloading. Before he could unleash the counter-barrage I got to my feet and left for the signallers, pleading an urgent priority. Not that I much cared what Stiles thought or did. I'd taken Benoît's advice to heart and written off the diamonds that weren't mine to begin with. I'd also pretty much written off any hope of remaining where I was. With the possible exception of pilots, there were few positions more hazardous than being the junior officer in an infantry company. This being the case I had a feeling there would be great demand for lieutenants in a few days. There was little Sam Stiles could say or do that could top that. On the other hand, I mused, working at divisional headquarters was not exactly without its perils. So maybe it was for the best.

Some of the staff had moved forward early this morning to the advanced divisional headquarters that opened at Fort George. As they generally included the more important personages of the division – denoted by a profusion of gold stripes, pips and clean boots – the atmosphere relaxed markedly with their departure. Not that this presaged any relaxation in my duties. The mechanics of sending a division into battle are remarkably complex and I was deluged in work until late in the afternoon. Then came a telephone call that I should report to the advanced headquarters.

Fort George was a rather ostentatious name for an astonishingly large, deep, and dingy-smelling dug-out in the old trenches north and west of Neuville-Saint-Vaast. I wasn't sure if this was part of the famed Labyrinth of trenches the French captured in '15 at the same time as the Lorette Spur, however the dug-out was without question German. Which, assuming the occupants have fled, is precisely the locale I would have advised for a headquarters.

When I arrived at Fort George I descended a narrow stone staircase. The large chamber it opened upon was humming with activity. A group of colonels – battalion commanders I soon surmised – were getting their final marching orders.

I was in time to hear General Lipsett say: 'Tell your men this. It's some advice from General Byng. You shall go over exactly like a railroad train, on the exact time, or you shall be annihilated.'

As battle cries go it lacked the stirring oomph of Henry V's speech at Agincourt. On the other hand, it had an unmistakeable ring of authenticity to it. Never had a battle in this war been so thoroughly and comprehensively planned. I figured Byng was referring to the creeping barrage when he spoke of keeping to schedule; too quick and our own shells would do you in; too slow and the Boche would gladly take up the slack.

The plan itself was no masterpiece of grand strategy. All the mornings watching the battalions on the taped ground and studying the plasticine models had taught me that. The geography didn't lend itself to much other than a frontal assault.

The ridge would be stormed in a plunging, miles wide, straight-ahead thrust for the jugular – save one errant knoll to the north near Souchez, the Pimple, which would come later. A charge like so many others in this war. Precisely seven hours and forty-eight minutes had been allocated.

However General Byng's plans for Vimy Ridge differed from what had come before in almost every other respect. The men were told that when strongpoints appeared they were not to halt, but to move quickly past, on no account to check their advance – heresy to those imbued with the army orthodoxy of maintaining the unbroken line. Like waves surging round the breakers of a lee shore the Corps was to press forward regardless. That too had been one of the lessons of Verdun.

Finally, when the colonels departed, Colonel Hayter found a brief moment to speak with me.

'Thank you for coming, Lieutenant. I'm sending you and a couple of others forward as liaison officers tomorrow. If there are any organisational hiccups, and there may be, I'm trusting you to smooth them over.'

I swallowed. It wasn't as if he was asking me to spearhead the assault. But simply being in the front line would be plenty hazardous. The jumping-off trenches and the support line would be the first to feel the retribution from the German guns. I hoped Benoît hadn't been exaggerating when he'd described what the counter-battery guns would do.

That night, under the light from a searching moon, I went up top and sat on a parapet and drank the remains of a bottle of 15-year old Scotch I'd been saving for a special occasion. It seemed appropriate.

8th of April, 1917
Grange Tunnel, east of Neuville-Saint-Vaast, France

Easter Sunday dawned grey but clear and dry. It was a temporary respite from the rain, an opportunity to drain the trenches. In many places the mud was at knee level, which otherwise would be a misery for the troops arriving to huddle and await the attack. Easter church parades were cancelled, preparations for war scheduled in their place.

I walked from the Fort George dug-out, arriving in the forenoon close to Neuville-Saint-Vaast. There, scant miles from the front, the sound of the guns was truly overwhelming. From ahead and behind the noise came from every point of the compass. Overhead, there was a steady *whoosh* from fresh salvos from one of the many field gun batteries I'd spotted in the woods along the road; then the screeching rumble of a shell from a heavy howitzer intruded as it tore across. When a massive round from one of the naval guns mounted on rail cars north of Villers-au-Bois flew past it was as if the heavens split in two halves to make room. For a moment all heads craned skyward.

I made for the entrance to the Grange Tunnel. Nearby, or in chambers off the main tunnel, the attacking battalions of the 7th Brigade had established their headquarters.

'Two of my companies moved into a section of the tunnel last night,' replied Major Norsworthy to my queries. 'We've cleared out the assembly trenches as best we could.' Norsworthy was the OC of the 42nd Battalion. Although I'm sure he had a great deal on his plate, he patiently heard me out.

'Have you received everything you need in terms of supplies, sir?'

'Yes,' he replied. 'We'll be distributing ammunition, extra iron rations, bombs, sandbags and so forth later this afternoon. You can report, Lieutenant, that the Highlanders will be ready.'

It was a similar story at the other two battalions: the Princess Patricia's Canadian Light Infantry and the RCR. I didn't enquire of the 49th Battalion for they were in reserve. So far the preparations had gone like clockwork.

That it had owed everything to the care of the arrangements, on which many a late night had been spent. Beyond that the presence of the tunnel greatly facilitated those arrangements. Assembling troops and supplies was always a treacherous activity, not least because it was a sure-fire signal that an attack was imminent, allowing the enemy precious time to prepare. But at this moment under cover of the tunnels thousands of men were massing, hopefully unbeknownst to the jittery Fritzs opposite.

I'd heard said that many of the tunnels were steeped in history, stemming from the time of the Huguenots escaping persecution. 300 years later the Canadian Corps arrived in the Vimy sector. Since then Grange Tunnel had passed into the welcoming hands of the 7th Brigade whose interest in it was not in the least historical. However, thanks largely to their own hard labour, and under supervision of the engineers, the 1300-yard long tunnel had been enlarged and extended and fitted with the conveniences of modern warfare in mere months. Appropriately they were the ones who would make use of it.

All this I knew, but I was staggered to see the sheer number of soldiers who had gathered in Grange Tunnel. Along both sides of the chiseled walls they sat, with their khaki-clad backs to the sweating cold chalk, hundreds of them. Thousands even. Highlanders and Patricias. Yard after yard of soldiers until, after a hundred yards walking, I encountered men of Benoît's old regiment, the RCR. They too sat scrunched together shoulder to shoulder, talking amongst themselves. Their rifles were clenched between knees while their hands dealt out playing cards with a steadiness I found remarkable. One man was studying a map under the yellow glow of the electric lamp above.

40,000 maps had been distributed to the troops. Where maps in the army were the most precious and rationed of resources, begging and borrowing commonplace even at headquarters, General Byng was of a different mind as to their use and their value. Every man in the first wave had been given one. It was a sign of his confidence in them.

I went over to the soldier with the map, a pleasant looking fellow at first glance – until with a start I noticed the ugly red weal of a scar disfiguring one cheek. 'So, do you know the way?' I asked him.

He smiled. 'I have the map, sir, but I've been over those trenches so many times I think I could do it blindfolded.' Beside him the others were nodding in agreement, big grins shining upwards.

'When's it to be, sir?' asked one of them.

I hesitated, wondering if I should tell them – the biggest, most closely held secret of the attack – I'd only heard myself this morning, minutes before leaving headquarters. But the gears were long in motion and these fellows would hear soon enough.

'5.30 a.m.,' I said. 'In time to roust Fritz from his bed.'

One man studied his watch and said, 'Not too long now, fellas.'

'You probably didn't realize, but it's General Ludendorff's birthday today,' I said.

'The Fritz General? It's his birthday?'

I smiled. 'Yes indeed. The 9th of April. He'll be 53.' They grinned broadly.

'Good luck, and make it a birthday for him he won't forget, will you?' I said, before hastily stepping aside into an adjoining alcove. What turned out to be an entire company of Patricias was filing past.

The last of the troops were being ushered forward to their respective sections of the tunnel.

I retraced my steps and poked a head into the various battalion headquarters to see if all was well. It was, so I went in search of brigade headquarters to give my report. That proved easier than I expected. It turned out that 7th Brigade headquarters was in the adjoining room to that of the 42nd Battalion.

'Thank you, Lieutenant,' said Major Collum when I reached him. The line was a good one, it hardly crackled at all. 'The colonel asked me to tell you to stay forward. We may need you there. Keep in touch if there's anything important.'

With that the line went dead.

I left the headquarters and the brigade staff and returned in the direction of the tunnel. Night had fallen. As always it was the glowing flare of the explosions and the curving arc of a flare going up that marked out the ridge. Strangely however the tempo of the shells was decreasing. On the eve of an attack I had never witnessed anything like it. The night was cold but the shiver that went through me had nothing to do with the temperature. If only they weren't running short on ammunition was all I could think.

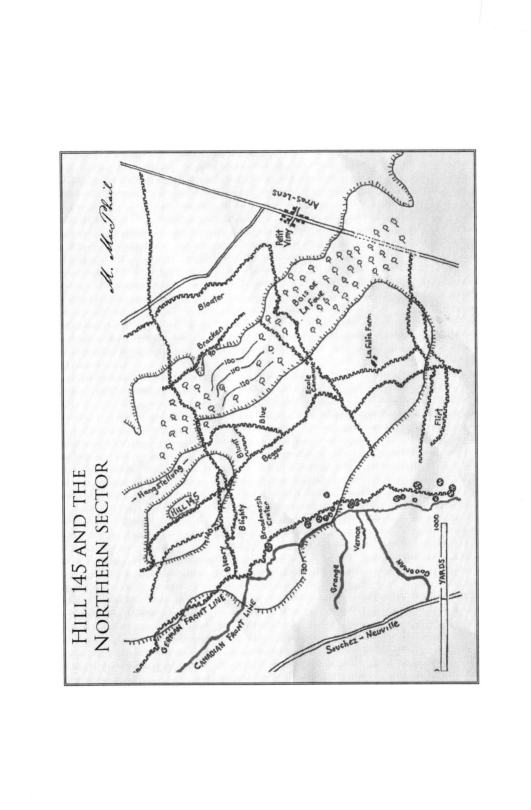

HILL 145 AND THE NORTHERN SECTOR

M. MacPhail

CHAPTER 31

9th of April, 1917
Vimy Ridge, France

Sometime after midnight men carrying large metal food containers appeared, and a hot meal was served as they passed, an overflowing ladleful and a piece of bread for each man. I partook with the others. I'm certain I wasn't the only one who barely noticed the contents of the mess tin, save that it was food.

At 3.30 a.m. the tot of extra-strength rum appeared. All noticed that and were grateful for the fiery trail that burned past tongues, down throats, and into stomachs caught somewhere in No-Man's-Land. "Liquid courage" some called it. The nomenclature wasn't inappropriate.

Past 4.00 a.m. sounded the order, subsequently passed down the line: 'FIX bayonets!'

Down that same line rippled a thousand dutiful clicks, one after the other. A dramatic pause… and then a final soft *CLICK* as the last obstinate rifle obeyed.

Ominously from above and in the distance a whistle sounded, its shrillness cutting through the fierce crash of the shells. It was German. Conversation ceased.

The officers on the stairs to the trenches waved their arms in excited consternation. Muffled curses to 'shut your trap' came from the sergeants. A long moment passed. A hundred anxious faces stared upwards, all senses tuned to what might follow. One minute and then another went by. Several minutes passed but nothing happened. The moment ended and a hundred men exhaled in chorus.

Then the signal was given. The men rose to their feet and began to shuffle forward, up the stairs and into the whistle of the wind and the patter of the rain, and the trenches that awaited. I watched them leave. But already new faces were appearing from behind, long columns of them.

The follow-up companies were arriving, taking up positions their comrades had only just left. Like them they settled down to wait before they too would debouche to the trenches when the show began.

As the minutes counted down, suddenly the fidgeting and nervous conversation stopped and anxious faces looked up. Mine was one of them. Down the tunnel the entire line of men was alert.

'What is *that?*' whispered a young soldier, echoing all our thoughts.

'That' was the sound of silence. The bombardment which had thundered unremittingly and without remorse for an entire week, a week of suffering for Fritz, had ceased abruptly. The guns were silent, the trench mortars still. A deathlike quiet had settled over the ridge. It was the single most unnerving sound I had ever heard.

I glanced at my watch.

When the agony of the silence threatened to become unbearable, finally the Emma Gees began to chatter, a rattling staccato that grew in intensity. There must have been hundreds of them. This was the barrage Colonel Brutinel had been referring to. An iron rain of more than 100,000 rounds a minute was falling on trenches, paths and supply routes – anywhere the enemy might be.

A minute later, at 5.30 a.m., the second hand ticked over one final time before standing erect. The assembled guns barked as one, a thunderous wall of noise that drowned out the machine guns. A wall of noise that surpassed anything at the Somme. Even deep under the chalk in Grange Tunnel the sound was overwhelming. I needn't have worried about the supply of ammunition. The attack was on.

Seconds later there was a gigantic *BOOM*. The ground shook and the lights on the chalk walls flickered uneasily. 'The mine in the Goodman subway,' an officer said to the man beside him. It wouldn't have been the only mine. There were several more, each mine dug at the furthermost extension of one of the tunnels. As they went off the assaulting troops would rush forward and emerge almost directly in the German line.

I went to the nearest stairs, the last set of three. Each staircase exited into a different trench. With my orders I could have remained safely on my behind with thirty feet of stone above my head. But with the attack underway there was no question of that. I had to see it for myself. My earlier qualms had disappeared, a feeling of something tremendous happening in its place.

Climbing the steps and emerging into the night air was the strangest sensation. It felt like I was climbing towards the darkest pits of Tartarus, storms of fire lighting the way. With each step the noise multiplied until, when I reached the level of the trench, it was deafening – too loud to think. The sky flashed in a violent thunderstorm of noise and light. The ground shook and trembled.

The lead platoons were nowhere to be seen so I proceeded down the duckboards.

'Sir, excuse us,' came the shout in my ear, and I moved to one side to allow them to pass. A fifty-man clutch of Patricias rushed by, laden down with shovels, picks, rolls of concertina and all the other gear the attack platoons had been spared. The second wave was getting into position. Then I spotted a narrow sap with an observation post at one end. There was a metal plate with a slit in it and I went to it and looked out.

I saw a staggered line of men, dark outlines against the explosions beyond, emerging from the muddy craters and shell holes, moving relentlessly forward towards the German front line. At that exact moment the churning maelstrom of the barrage lifted to settle 75 yards further. The Patricias were leaning into the barrage as far as it was possible to lean – any closer and they'd be in it.

Turning back to the trench I saw that it was packed with men, all heading out. On the elevated fire-step of the OP I also had a view further to the west and down the slope of the ridge, where the horizon glowed from the flashes of a thousand guns. A gust of wind caught me in the face and I recoiled at the cold sleet. Spring had turned into a snow storm. The odd thing was I hadn't noticed it earlier.

ZERO Hour had initially been fixed for Sunday, I'd been told. However as the 17th Corps on our right required additional time, it was pushed back twenty-four hours. In time for a snow storm as it turned out. But that might not be a bad thing I mused. Wiping the wet snow from my face I turned away. The wind was to the northwest, the cold sleet blowing straight into the faces of the German defenders.

I glanced again through the slit. A boiling wall of smoke and flames from the barrage filled my sight, but I could make out little of the men's progress. I would head back to the tunnel I decided. Perhaps there would be new instructions awaiting me there.

There weren't. In fact no one paid me the slightest attention. I was more invisible than Benoît could ever have imagined. I found a place to sit.

I wasn't there for ten minutes, maybe less, when a pair of bedraggled soldiers tumbled down the stairs into the tunnel.

Jumping to my feet I confronted them: 'Any news?'

'No sir,' they mumbled. If I had taken the trouble I would have noticed they were wounded. The attack had numbed more than my ear drums. The soldiers were preoccupied; providing a running commentary on the battle to a supernumerary lieutenant the least of their concerns.

'Well done, boys,' I said guiltily. 'Another 100 yards and you'll spot the dressing station.'

More followed, but the numbers weren't large – after the Somme one was a little inured to casualties. Nevertheless, it was encouraging.

Roughly forty minutes after the attack began a man bounded down the steps from one of the other exits and hurried to the rear. From the speed he moved at he was clearly not wounded so the only possible explanation was that he was a runner. I was prepared therefore when another appeared.

'Hang on,' I said, reaching out an arm to arrest his progress. 'The Black Line... How is it going?'

'We've taken it,' he said panting, his eyes elsewhere. I lowered my arm and off he went.

The Black Line was the foremost series of trenches back to Zwischen Stellung and Beggar Trench – the midway line of the ridge

– in addition to being the first objective of the day. General Byng's railroad was running on schedule.

I went to sit once more. Fidgeting, I realized as things stood I was simply taking up space. So I headed down the tunnel towards the various headquarters.

On some inexplicable premonition I chose that of the 42nd Battalion. They'd established themselves in a machine-gun post close to the tunnel entrance. It was really not much more than a couple of rooms in a dug-out, a handful of officers, and as many other ranks.

'OP reports the contact aeroplane was brought down, sir,' said a voice as I entered.

'No matter,' said an officer, 'We have ground observation.'

How the ground observers could see a thing in the dark and the driving sleet was beyond me, but I held my tongue and nodded at the lieutenant who took note of my entrance. Every few minutes a new report came, not all of them positive.

'Damn, Lieutenant Shum is wounded as well,' said Major Norsworthy. The casualties seemed modest thus far. But not in the ranks of the battalion officers; they were falling at a distressing rate.

I sidled up to the adjutant, Lieutenant MacLeod. 'Anything I can do?'

'No, I don't think so,' he said. 'The 8th Brigade is up on our right and in contact with the RCR. We've just heard that Corps believes all divisions are on the Black Line.'

'And the German barrage?'

'Appears to be rather weak,' he replied.

Benoît had been right. The counter battery work was paying off. 'So far so good, then,' I murmured.

Which remained the case for the better part of an hour. At any moment there would be confirmation whether the final objective, the Red Line, had been taken. But before it did a message was received from the battalion scout officer.

'What does he mean they're held up?' demanded Major Norsworthy of Lieutenant Auld. Auld was in charge of signals. On the table a large map of this section of the ridge was spread out, the faces around it alert and tense. It didn't take much mental acuity to conclude that there was a problem.

'His message doesn't say, sir. Only that the battalion on the left is held up. That would be the 54th, sir.'

'Yes, yes, I know that,' the major snapped.

Then one of the signals corporals entered from the adjoining chamber. 'I've got division on the line, sir. Colonel Hayter.'

'I'll go,' said Norsworthy. 'I must speak with him.'

I watched through the doorway as Norsworthy took the receiver and summarized the news to the colonel. 'I'd like to have a look myself, but I've lost a lot of officers,' I heard him say. There was a long pause. Midway through, he looked up. His eyes alighted on me. 'Yes, he's with us at headquarters, as it happens.' Another pause. 'Yes, I'll do that. Thank you.'

'MacPhail?' he called.

I went to him. 'Sir?'

'It appears 4th Division may be in trouble. There's no sign of them on our flank and we desperately need to know what the situation is. Unfortunately I'm a little short on men, but Colonel Hayter put forth your name. I'd like you to reconnoitre.'

He stared at me. Suddenly I grasped in all its enormity the nature of the problem. The 4th Division on our left was tasked with capturing the northernmost extremity of the ridge. Of the four divisions, the objectives of the 4th Division were the shortest in distance but encompassed the steepest ground, the dominating position of Hill 145 foremost amongst them. Without that hill the entire attack would be in jeopardy. Clearly Norsworthy feared the worst.

'Yes, sir. I understand. I'll leave now.' I donned my helmet and tightened the strap. I glanced at my watch. It was 8.15 a.m.

Exiting into the very trench I'd been in earlier, I set off in the direction the Patricias had, intending to make for Beggar Trench first. There I hoped to find Major Pease who was the senior Highlander in the field. Alternatively, I might find some signals linesmen who had new information.

By this hour it was long past dawn. The visibility was decent even if the weather was not. The sleet had ceased save for an unpleasant drizzle and there was a decided nip to the air. A thick grey veil hermetically sealed off both horizon and sky above. Under this shroud of smoke and cloud the view was remarkably clear for hundreds of yards in every direction. Greyish-white airbursts of shrapnel dotted the sky.

At one time not so very long ago there would have been woods to see, characteristic rolls in the ground, and other landmarks. However these, and most particularly the landmarks added more recently by our enemy, had been systematically erased. Churned fields of upturned earth replaced them.

I slogged past the crater line, each step an exertion due to the slippery mud, which alternatively dragged at my feet or threatened to send me into a nasty fall the moment I was making some progress. Only after I passed over the front-line German trench did I identify it as such. The trenches were so blown in by shell fire as to be unrecognizable.

Groups of men were moving overland, plodding methodically forward in file, with stretchers, machine guns and other gear resting on their shoulders. I hadn't practised endlessly on the taped trenches like the others, but Major Norsworthy had given me a small map, the same one the battalion had gone forward on. I hoped that would suffice.

I walked for approximately 200 yards eastwards when I nearly stumbled upon a body. Khaki, so I knew it was one of ours. Equally, from his posture, I knew this was not a man awaiting a stretcher. A few feet to his side were a couple of others. For the life of me I couldn't figure what had happened to them. There wasn't a machine-gun post or a trench in sight. Then the sad realization came bubbling up. Most likely it had been a question of misreading the terrain, too eager to keep pressing forward; an error of only ten yards was enough – victims of our own terrible barrage, the one plotted so meticulously by the clever Major Brooke I'd met at Verdun. I looked down at the man. As I turned away something made me look again and I recoiled in shock.

It was a handsome face, seemingly untouched by war. But I noticed the deep red scar disfiguring one cheek. There could be little question – it *was* him. A few hours before I'd spoken with him at length and he'd blithely reassured me all was well, as soldiers will do; that he knew the way blindfolded, while his buddies nodded their unreserved agreement.

For some reason the sight of him sprawled in the mud led to thoughts of Roy Dundas. There was no time for that now so I pushed them away into the dark recesses where I tried not to venture often. Gritting my teeth, I reached down and took the soldier's rifle. I like to think he would have been pleased I'd remembered him; that I'd chosen his rifle.

Another thought hove into mind. The soldier was from the RCR. The RCR however were on the brigade right, left of which came the PPLCI, and only then the 42nd. I needed to veer left.

As it transpired I veered too far left, but that served to acquaint me very quickly with the extent of the difficulties on the divisional boundary.

A bullet whistled over. When I caught my breath, I could feel my heart pounding. The rifleman must have spotted the bobbing of my helmet above the trench walls. It was a tough shot even for a sniper. However when someone's got your tin hat in his sights you don't dwell on those sort of considerations, you follow your first instincts and duck. Slowly I got to my feet. I kept my head down.

I'd been cautiously edging along, following the trench I'd found. It led northwest along the spine of the ridge towards the 4th Division. By now the 42nd Battalion and the rest of the 7th Brigade should be on the final objective, consolidating Blue Trench further east on the edge of the ridge's plateau. What I couldn't understand was that there wasn't a soldier to be seen, not one of ours, nor even one of theirs. Surely this was Beggar Trench? It had to be, I reasoned. I'd spotted the heights of Hill 145 ahead and Beggar Trench led straight to the hill according to the map. However by rights there should have been platoons of 102nd Battalion men, and those from the 54th too; they were to leapfrog through them.

'Jesus,' I exclaimed with a start as the implications of this hit me. The whole left of the 3rd Division was wide open! Major Norsworthy had been right to worry.

Reaching the junction with a cross trench I went down into a squat to study the map again. If the trench ahead was Blighty, I was far past the divisional boundary. Yet there wasn't a single 4th Division man to be found. Decisions had to be made.

I'd already walked too far. To keep going – assuming a sniper didn't get me first – would eventually lead to my own personal assault of Hill 145. As the hill was almost certainly still in enemy hands, that wasn't a battle I could win. I turned and went in the opposite direction. Eventually I'd run into the Highlanders. Better still some linesmen. I desperately needed to send a wire to the rear.

To my relief as I returned along Beggar I came to Blunt and encountered some of our soldiers. I'd missed them on the way in. From their insignia I saw they were 102nd Battalion. There were ten of them, led by a sergeant. They had a Lewis gun and a couple of the men were standing above ground, shovelling like madmen to rebuild the parapet.

'What the blazes is going on?' I said without preamble. 'There's not a man to be found on your left.'

Gravely the sergeant nodded. 'Yes, sir. We've had to refuse our left flank. The 87th hasn't come up.'

Ah, so that was it. The battalion yet further to the left was in trouble. They couldn't very well push forward and leave their flank exposed, so they were digging in along their left flank trailing back all the way to the Grenadier Guards of the 87th. This went a long way to explaining why I'd found no one forward. As was often the case, a problem for one battalion cascaded down the line until it was everyone's problem. 'Why haven't they come up?' I demanded to know. 'What's the holdup?'

'Dunno, sir.'

I stood there contemplating whether I should go in search of the missing 54th Battalion, or seek out the elusive linesmen, when a machine gun sounded. After a couple of close encounters with a machine gun you quickly learn to assess questions like; how far away is it? Is it one of theirs or yours? Is it aiming at you?

Tufts of dirt began flying from the parapet. Under the circumstances I didn't need to think long. One of the men who'd been shovelling fell. Then a second. The first tumbled into the trench with a thud, his shovel clanking after. The other lay prostrate a few feet from the lip of the trench, completely exposed.

I thought he was dead, but suddenly his arm twitched. The machine gun was slowly raking the whole junction from right to left. If I knew anything about machine gunners they would swivel and sweep back.

'Oh damn it to hell,' I cussed and sprang for the fire-step. Another scramble and I was on level ground reaching for the man's arms to drag him to safety. But by then the smooth traverse of the machine gun had ended. The firing paused. A vision of the gunner swinging the barrel in the other direction filled my head. Frantically I began pulling the man towards the trench. The machine gun chattered again. Bullets whizzed round. Desperately I yanked him on his back through the mud to the edge of the trench. Hands reached up to help. I leapt down.

For a moment I sat there in the mud in an ungainly heap, dazed, regaining my wits and my breath. Then shakily I looked up. The sergeant was watching. He saw the searching query in my eyes.

Very deliberately he knuckled his brow, but shook his head.

Eventually I reached some linesmen and a reporting centre a long way down Beggar Trench. There I was able to wire a terse summation of the situation. It ended with: DIVISIONAL FLANK IN THE AIR FROM BLUE TO PAST BEGGAR. HEAVY MG AND RIFLE FIRE FROM HILL 145. PLEASE ADVISE. It wouldn't have done to signal what I was really thinking: that the attack was wobbling. But men who understood would know. And react.

At least that's what I was counting upon.

CHAPTER 32

9th of April, 1917
Vimy Ridge, France

'Major Ewing!'

I had made my way forward to Blue Trench, which ran along the crest of the ridge overlooking La Folie Wood and the steep eastern slopes. As expected the 42nd was much in evidence, consolidating the Red Line to prepare for the inevitable counterattacks. A party was hard at work building a strongpoint on the brow of the ridge, a shallow ravine below. They couldn't have been at it for more than hour or two yet it looked nearly complete. There to my surprise I encountered the battalion second-in-command. Major Norsworthy had been sufficiently concerned to send his right-hand man forward.

'Hello, Lieutenant,' said Ewing. A cursory nod. He glanced at the Lee-Enfield over my shoulder. 'What have you learned?'

I told him, a more detailed and considerably less diplomatic appraisal of the situation than I'd sent by wire. 'Sir, there's a gap on your left you could run a division through,' I concluded by saying. 'Where the devil is the 54th?'

'Here, among other places. Major Pease found a platoon of them. They were on their objectives actually. However as you discovered the attack on Hill 145 appears to have failed. So the rest must be behind somewhere.'

'In other words, there's no one to stop the Boche if they grab their chance?'

He shook his head. 'I've ordered every available man to throw up a defensive flank.'

Someone was yelling. 'Stretchers, we need stretchers.' Both of us looked in that direction. The machine gun and rifle fire from the left was increasing rather than abating. The Boche in the trenches round the hill likely had nothing else to shoot at; in the absence of better they were enfilading us. 'Lieutenant Wattam is hit,' came a shout.

The major winced. 'In the time it took me to get back and forth from the Black Line we've lost three officers,' he sighed. 'I must return to headquarters, but I'd like you to remain here. Keep your eyes open, and see if you can round up some more boys from the 54th, would you, MacPhail?' The bushy eyebrows formed a question mark. I assured him I would.

After he left I went to the fire-step – newly constructed, for the old one under old ownership had been on the opposite side facing west – and stood up to take a look. A look was all I got. I saw trees, or the stumps of them immediately below, and the endless vista of the Douai Plain spread out in front. It was extraordinary. I could have stared at it for hours.

'SIR! Watch yourself, there's snipers in those woods. Their trenches are manned.'

With alacrity I slid back into the trench. With Germans to the north and east the only thing I could do with any degree of security was sit on the trench floor with my head between my knees. As that was most assuredly not what Majors Ewing and Norsworthy and others expected, nor even what I expected of myself, I went looking for the other Black Watch major, Pease. He was in command of the battalion front and had last been reported with some rifle grenadiers attempting to wipe out a squad of Fritzs with a machine gun. Judging by the fire we were taking it had been a temporary success, at best. I was barely away down Blue Trench heading north before a kilted soldier blundered into me. He stared, his eyes taking in my uniform. Most likely he was reassured by the fact I was an officer, even if I wasn't kitted out as adventurously as he. 'They're trying to turn our flank through Blighty, sir,' he said.

I whistled. It was all too probable. It was precisely what I would have done were I the German commander. Blighty Trench ran from east to west across the Ridge, crossing first Blue then Beggar Trenches at right angles. If they succeeded in rushing a few platoons down that trench, bypassing our front line, and then cut left there was no telling where that would lead.

Sending the soldier on his way with the strong admonition that he hurry and inform every officer and NCO he saw, I made alternate plans. It wasn't even a communication trench I picked. That would have meant far too long a detour. Instead I found a dangerously exposed track that led straight west back towards Beggar Trench. Despite the risks I headed down it. I was running, or the closest thing to a run as the wet and broken ground permitted. About that time it began to snow. Never before had I been so happy to see snow. The flurries were likely what saved me.

At the junction of Beggar and Blunt I encountered soldiers from the 102nd. There were considerably more of them than there'd been, and they'd obviously been digging in. A Colt gun was set up twenty yards down the trench to cover a broad swath from north to east.

'Who's in command?' I asked, panting, as I caught my breath.

'I guess I am, sir,' said one of them. A sergeant about my age stepped forward. He wasn't 102nd. The brass 54 on his shoulder was proof of that.

'Captain Jack's gone forward to have a look himself,' he said. 'He wanted to see if he could track down any more men. The battalion has withdrawn to here.'

I didn't know the captain in question but I understood what he was doing: consolidating his flank. That explained why there were so many more men. The remnants of the 54th were joining up with the 102nd. Unfortunately the withdrawal of the captain's battalion left the 42nd Highlanders in a bind.

The Colt gun began to rattle. Alarmed I ran to them.

'Germans, sir,' said a soldier, pointing. The dozen-odd rifles assembled at this spot were firing. On the skyline 200 yards away was a large body of men. That would be the flanking party the private had warned me about.

A bullet hissed past. The rifles increased their fire. I slung the

Lee-Enfield off my shoulder and leaning on the parapet began to fire myself. We were dug in modestly well, even a few sandbags in place. Of Blighty Trench little more than a shallow ditch remained, so we had the advantage of cover. And we had a machine gun.

A salvo of rifle grenades landed in the Germans' midst, popping noisily. My eyes shot to the right in the direction of Blue Trench. That would be Major Pease and his grenadiers. I turned back, took aim at the Boche party and fired. After a few minutes in which both sides briskly exchanged fire, the enemy began to withdraw. Their first probe, too tentative by far, had failed. But almost certainly it wouldn't be the last. The snow began to swirl down quite heavily.

Sometime after 10 a.m. I returned to Blue Trench, the ugliness of the ground transformed by a dusting of snow. I was not terribly surprised to spot the familiar features of Major Norsworthy.

He was standing outside the strongpoint, S.P. 7 as it had been dubbed. I suspected he'd listened woefully to his deputy's report and then raced forward to see for himself. His battalion was out on the proverbial limb and he knew it. I didn't waste words on small chat.

'Hello, sir,' I said. 'The 102nd are well consolidated around the junction of Beggar and Blunt, but the 54th have withdrawn to Beggar as well. There's no sign Hill 145 has been taken. Rather the reverse judging by the fire from there.'

'Beggar Trench, you say? That's impossible, I just took a patrol along it myself.'

'You might not have gone far enough, sir. They're well past our line at the corner of Blunt Trench.'

I could see him considering what I'd said.

'It's not really my place, sir, but I can't help thinking you could suggest to the 54th that they push forward to Blue? We'd have a little more flesh on the flank so to speak, if the enemy does come at us.'

'Yes, that would help,' he said thoughtfully. 'That would help indeed.'

An hour later I encountered Major Norsworthy once again. He looked grave.

'Is there news, sir?'

He chewed on his lip then handed me the signal he'd been reading. It was a message from brigade headquarters. They were sending him a platoon and two Lewis gun sections. But it was the first line of the signal that was troubling him: ENEMY ARE ADVANCING UP BOIS DU CHAMP POURRI, BOBBY, BOIKON AND FILLIP TRENCHES.

'They're counterattacking on the right, sir!'

'Yes,' he said glumly. 'It never rains but it pours.'

'Or snows, sir, as the case may be.' The ground was covered by a blanket of white, the sky heavy with low-hanging dark clouds that were slowly creeping over.

He ignored my lighthearted rejoinder and turned away, with instructions for one of his officers. However, whatever the enemy was up to it would be the RCR and the PPCLI that met them first, not the 42nd. When a short time later I heard the bombardment come down with a thunder in the neighbourhood of Petit Vimy where the enemy was reportedly assembling, I had the hope it might not even come to that. I didn't think I needed to remind him there were problems enough on the left without worrying about the right.

Yet later, as every man who could be spared entrenched along Blunt trench, the promised reinforcements arrived. Then another signal was brought in. A young fellow in a helmet two sizes too big came barreling around the corner of the dug-out and nearly did himself in on the low hanging beam of the entryway. He'd been warned about snipers I expect. With some considerable fluster he succeeded in handing the major a folded sheet of paper.

'Finally a little good news,' said Norsworthy to those assembled. 'The OC of the 54th has instructed his A Company to do their best to move up to Blue. He also says they've moved further down Beggar Trench in the direction of the hill.'

'Lieutenant?' I'd been turning to leave, intending to confirm these developments. I looked back.

'Come with me.' He stepped outside and I followed. The sun had peeked out, the snow showing signs of melting. We waited until we heard a couple of rifle shots. Then on the admittedly dubious theory they'd be reloading we rushed down the shallow sap to Blue Trench.

The trench was filling up with casualties. There were only enough stretchers for the most serious cases and the snipers were adding to the count with a fearful frequency. For many, a stretcher was too late. Not only was the sniping fierce from the direction of Hill 145 there were other marksmen on the battalion's doorstep. Just down the slope, they lay hidden in the undergrowth and behind logs.

'I want you to return to headquarters,' he said. 'I'm not convinced the urgency of our position is entirely clear to all concerned. The 4th Division needs to take action. We hardly lost a man going in, but we're being bled dry.'

I was about to respond that junior members of the staff were like children – to be seen and not heard – and my influence consequently not to be overestimated, when the buzzing of an aeroplane intruded. It was flying very low. The sound of its approach had been muffled by the brow of the hill as it swept up and over, otherwise we would surely have noticed it earlier.

Remembering my earlier encounter with things flying and German, I took no chances and ducked down. With a dignified delay the major followed.

The plane zoomed overhead. Before I could even unshoulder the rifle, it was already on the other side of the ridge and banking right. A couple of the men, more prepared than I, let fly with a futile shot or two.

'Isn't that the most exasperating thing,' said Norsworthy. 'They're going to know every single position we hold.'

'It's not the first I've seen this morning, sir,' I said. 'I wish someone would tell our own machines about them.'

It took me longer to reach the rear than I anticipated. The fire from the northern part of the ridge was regular and accurate enough that I wound my way with care over the battered trenches and through the sea of shell craters.

At battalion headquarters Major Ewing greeted me with a worried glance as I entered. Whereupon I reassured him that little had changed; the battalion was hunkered down, prepared for an attack, and anxiously awaiting relief from the enemy on the flank.

'I'm afraid there's nothing to report here,' he said, in response to my query.

'Well, what does the 4th Division have to say about it, sir?'

Ewing pursed his lips. 'When last we enquired they replied the situation was satisfactory.'

'Satisfactory!?' The words shot from my mouth. On the verge of a minor rant I had the presence of mind to belay further commentary. Rants from the lower ranks about one's superiors are to be avoided, even if I suspected Ewing agreed with me.

'You don't need to remind me, Lieutenant. I'm well aware it's serious,' he said.

That the situation was indeed being taken seriously was evidenced a few minutes later when reinforcements from the 3rd Divisional staff arrived. Only half the party could truly be considered reinforcements; the other half was little more than ballast. It was Major Collum and Captain Stiles.

'MacPhail! I thought you were forward?' said Collum. Stiles was eyeing me with a shocked look. It took me a moment before I realized it was the soiled and mud-encrusted state of my uniform that preoccupied him.

'I was, sir. I only just returned.'

At Collum's prompting Ewing summarized the difficulties on the left, and for a few minutes the two majors kept themselves company while Stiles and I looked on.

Collum turned to me. 'You've been there, MacPhail. Have you anything to add?'

Naturally I did. It's a habit of mine I've been trying to break. 'Only that if I were General von Falkenhausen, sir, I would send a battalion straight through the gap we've left for them.'

'It's fortunate then, MacPhail, that you're neither German, nor a general,' said Collum bitingly. This brought a fleeting smile to Stiles's face.

An hour passed. At 1.30 p.m. a new message arrived from Major Norsworthy. The situation was unchanged. He concluded with: I CONSIDER IT URGENT THAT 4TH DIVISION ADVANCE AND OCCUPY HILL 145.

'Bring this to Brigade immediately,' Major Ewing instructed the signals officer. We all looked at each other. No one said anything. No one had to.

'And to think the rest of the operations are proceeding well,' muttered Collum.

'They are?' I said. Beyond the sound of gun and shellfire to the south of the ridge I had heard very little, except that 2nd Division was at the village of Thélus.

'When I left both 1st and 2nd Division were almost at their final objectives.'

There was an excited shout from the adjoining chamber. A call from Division had come in for Major Collum. The man who'd taken it couldn't conceal his enthusiasm. He knew the situation.

We clustered around as Collum held the receiver to his ear. For the better of a minute he didn't speak. Finally he said, 'Yes, sir. I'll tell them.'

Faces turned to Major Collum. '4th Division is making arrangements for a new brigade to attack the hill at 4.30 p.m.'

'Thank God,' muttered Ewing. With that the atmosphere in the chamber lightened.

'I'm going back,' announced Major Collum. 'You'd best stay here, Captain Stiles. You'll be more useful in the field than at headquarters.'

At this I frowned. Stiles looked uneasy. 'But what should I do, sir?'

With exasperation the major stared at him. Then he snapped: 'Ask MacPhail. I'm sure he'll know.'

Against all odds I managed not to smirk. Stiles's face had transformed into a prune.

Quickly I addressed myself to Major Collum. 'I think we're needed most at the front line, sir,' I said. 'It could be especially important if there's any need to coordinate with 4th Division in their assault... Provided Major Ewing agrees, of course.' Ewing nodded vigorously.

'Well, there's your answer, Captain,' said Major Collum.

It was a solemn Sam Stiles who began the walk across Vimy Ridge. Even the unexpected sight of brilliant sunshine as we emerged from Grange Tunnel failed to spur him to words. We picked our way past the crater line, then dodged the innumerable shell holes near the intermediate line that were filled with water and occasionally a body or two. It was only after he stumbled on a broken fencepost half submerged in the mud and I reached out an arm to steady him that he muttered, 'Thanks'. It may have been coincidence but the sun disappeared shortly thereafter, not to reappear that day.

While he couldn't have anticipated this turn of events, I was taken aback by how well equipped Stiles was for a spell in the line. That included a rather unusual piece of kit for a staff officer. It was all I could do not to comment on it, so eventually I did.

'What's the Very gun for?' I asked. 'Were you intending to send up S.O.S. signals to warn General Lipsett if the paperwork wasn't in order?'

Self-consciously he reached for the flare gun protruding from his pocket. Briefly he let his hand rest on the wooden grip. 'Give it a rest, MacPhail. It's been a long day.'

'Come on,' I said. 'What did you expect?'

'I didn't expect that I'd be in the front lines of the assault. All thanks to you, by the way.'

'You're an officer in the army not the captain of the polo team, for Christ's sake. You signed up for war and here you are.'

'I did my time in the trenches,' he said indignantly.

'I remember that. As I recall you diligently guarded the dug-out while I crawled through No-Man's-Land in the mud to the listening post.'

Incredibly he had the audacity to grin. 'Don't tell me you're still sore about that?'

'No. But I think about it once in a while. Funnily enough I've concluded that's when I really became a soldier.'

The machine gun burst was at least 10 yards short but I dove for the ground all the same. When I looked up I saw Stiles lying beside me. From the rim of his helmet to the tip of his chin he exhibited a fine coating of mud.

'I forgot to mention. You should expect a bit of rifle and MG fire from our left.'

Nervously Stiles looked left.

I left him at Blue Trench in the hands of a sergeant who I knew wouldn't brook any unnecessary nonsense. As the Germans were shelling the front line, I didn't expect him to be troublesome.

Major Norsworthy was understandably delighted to hear about the planned attack. Even when 4.30 came and went with no sign of the promised show on the left, a message eventually arriving to say it was postponed by an hour, he 'understood'. But I heard him grumble when well past 5.30 p.m. the signal from the liaison officer at 4th Division headquarters reached him, stating that OPERATIONS AGAINST HILL 145 WILL BE CARRIED OUT TONIGHT. He would have grumbled more if the same signal hadn't said the division had made progress pushing forward. Theoretically the open gap had shrunk slightly.

That evening and most of the night was spent digging a defensive trench from the junction of Beggar and Blunt all the way back across the ridge to the Longfellow crater. Norsworthy didn't trust it and was taking his own precautions. I can't say I blamed him.

To no one's particular surprise the full-scale attack on the hill didn't materialize. Nor were the results of my late night foray along Beggar Trench inspiring.

'No sign of any reinforcements or battalions on the 54th's left?' asked the major. The sleet which had begun to fall not long before was turning to flurries again. Snow had settled on his helmet.

'No, sir. There's only the 102nd and the 54th forward, roughly 130 of them. Their left is still in the air.'

'Which means ours is, too,' he muttered.

A shell from a howitzer came screeching across, flashing brightly as it exploded. The deep concussion was as noticeable for what you felt as what you heard.

'A 5.9,' said Norsworthy, conversationally. 'They're straddling us by at least 20 or 30 yards, I reckon.'

'Yes, sir. Luckily. The right battalions seem to be getting it worse than we are.'

Around midnight things started to settle down. I was dead on my feet. I needed some rest. As there wouldn't be any better opportunity, I went in search of a dug-out. Down Blue Trench I found one where a group of Highlanders graciously allowed me to share a spot on their ground sheets.

I lay there for a minute thinking. About the day and the attack. And about Sam Stiles. I remember thinking how badly the Germans wanted this ridge, how they'd be plotting to sweep us from it – beginning at Hill 145. Then I must have fallen asleep. The next thing I recall I was sitting bolt upright, rubbing at my eyes. Held up close to my face were the luminous dials of my watch. It was 5 a.m.

CHAPTER 33

10th of April, 1917
Vimy Ridge, France

Another shell landed somewhere, not far off. I was fully awake by this time. Jumping to my feet with an energy that was most atypical of me in the wee hours, I heard more whistles and more bangs. Fritz was letting us have it.

Thinking this must be the prelude to the counter-attack, I ran down the trench and rounded the corner into the sap leading to S.P. 7. As I reached the strongpoint and ducked to enter, the trench to the rear was rocked by first one, and then a second huge explosion. The trench was well-manned so I feared the worst. However, if this was a softening up, much worse would follow.

'No, there's no sign of any Boche,' the Highlander lieutenant answered me. 'We had some reports of movement during the night, but nothing concrete.'

'What's that supposed to mean?'

'Only that Corps intelligence says there are very strong German reinforcements moving towards Vimy from Méricourt. But there's nothing local.'

'That sounds awfully concrete to me,' I muttered. 'Where's the major?'

'He's here,' said Major Norsworthy. Norsworthy had entered through the heavy timber doorway and unobserved by me taken up a position off my left flank. I don't think he meant anything by his choice.

Nevertheless, I felt compelled to ask.

'The left appears to be quiet,' he replied. 'Not like here. Fortunately the Boche registration on our positions is not so good. But I'm afraid there are considerable casualties in Blue Trench.'

The tension eased out of me. The Boche in my experience weren't the types to approach by stealth, so quiet was good. That being said the current deluge of steel and high explosive was anything but quiet, or good.

'I'd like you to take a closer look, just in case, MacPhail,' added the major.

'Yes, sir,' I said. The thought occurred to me that the major might know more than he was letting on, and I was to be the canary.

Leaving the strongpoint I came to the junction with Blue Trench. There I saw the damage wrought by the shells. One shell had been slightly long. Regardless, it had blown a fifteen-foot bite out of the parados. The other had fallen close to the first. It was as close to a direct hit as it was possible to be. *So much for poor registration.* A group of men were still poking and prodding through the debris. They'd give up soon; if there was anyone to be found they'd have found him by now.

A day earlier around noon the battalion sent a casualty estimate to the rear. 200 had been the sorry count. More than a man in four, most in the hours after 8 a.m. when the objectives were already reached and one could be excused for thinking it was simply a question of digging in. For a single battalion it was a lot of men. Heaven knows what today's report would reveal.

Down Blue Trench to the north I ran into Stiles hurrying in my direction. The shelling had awakened even him. He greeted me with an amiable, 'Morning', and appeared eager to talk.

'Morning,' I said in reply and kept going. Idle chat is never my strong suit; in the midst of an early morning bombardment I'm even less so inclined. There were encouraging signs the bombardment was petering out though.

Several hundred yards down Blue Trench I came upon a small squad of men from the 54th. They were holding the line at the point where it made a sharp jog to the west to intersect Blighty. All was quiet, precisely as Major Norsworthy had described.

'Any sign of the Boche?' I blurted out to the first man I encountered.

'No, sir,' he replied.

'And up the hill?' I indicated the heights behind him to the north-west. In the lightening dawn sky the modest bulge of the hill loomed on the horizon, partly concealed by mist but visible nonetheless.

'All quiet,' he said. 'We haven't heard a peep since last night when there was some fighting.'

'Really?' From the tone of my voice I think the soldier thought I was disappointed, but it was astonishment rather. I'd been so certain that the Germans would seize this opportunity to drive a wedge into the attack. But apparently – thankfully – I was wrong.

Carefully I studied the hill and the approaches to make certain. Look as I might I could spot only a handful of figures moving about. There were no signs of an attack, impending or not. Bavarians being Bavarians perhaps they first intended to finish their breakfasts. Which reminded me, I hadn't had mine.

A few words with the soldiers and I returned down the trench whence I came, positively ravished at the thought of tinned bully beef and hardtack. Overall, the attack yesterday had gone extremely well. But until the remaining German positions on the ridge and in the lines behind were taken, anything might happen. Until it did there was no harm in a decent breakfast.

The morning proved uneventful to the point of being remarkable. I puzzled about this until I met Major Norsworthy out on one of his regular inspection rounds. Then I learned that events were moving faster than I realized.

'4th Division took the trenches round Hill 145 last night,' he announced. But his face was so painfully expressionless and his voice so studiously neutral that the boisterous smile that had been gathering steam on my face died a premature death. The man hadn't been to bed all night so a little terseness was to be expected. But had something happened?

'Surely that's wonderful news?' I said hesitatingly. 'Is the hill cleared, sir?'

'Not yet. I expect it will be shortly. Finally we'll be relieved of that infernal sniping,' he said. Seeing my expression he must have felt a further explanation was warranted. 'What you must understand of Hill 145's defences, Lieutenant MacPhail, is that the reserve companies are all behind the hill in the *Hangstellung*. Unless they can be overcome, the hill won't be secured.'

'*Hangstellung?*' I mumbled.

'Yes. On the back slope there's a whole series of large, deeply-built dug-outs. Next to impossible to hit with the artillery. Make no mistake, they'll be full. I expect 4th Division will be taking them on soon.'

I nodded. Where this left the 3rd Division I wasn't entirely certain. I had little time to ponder the matter as a signal had arrived from Major Ewing.

Ewing had been to the brigade conference held an hour earlier. Orders from Corps HQ directed that all battalions were to push out patrols to scout the German second line. The ridge wasn't yet completely taken, but the attack was rushing on. General Byng knew as no other to relent was to give the enemy an opportunity to regroup. It wouldn't have been the first time the Germans had bounced an attacker from Vimy Ridge.

Back in 1915 one of the French colonial divisions had fought its way close to the peak, only to be unceremoniously rousted in a counter-attack. Two years later it seemed fitting that colonials once more – albeit those of the British Empire rather than the French – had scaled its heights. To a man I think we all felt that hell and damnation would strike before Fritz pushed us off.

The weather gods in any event were winking at us.

'It's like Christmas in April, eh?' I heard a soldier exclaim to the man beside him, with obvious delight. The man beside him sounded anything but delighted. He was probably from somewhere there wasn't much snow, although I was doubtful those existed in Canada.

'Next bloody time they send us into a blizzard, the least they can do is let us take our greatcoats.'

A fluffy white down, several inches thick, now decorated the ground and all about. The wet flakes had swirled down all morning and showed no signs of relenting. Decked out in matching white, the scout officer and his party were leaving to reconnoitre La Folie Wood and the trench behind.

Sometime after they left, Stiles and I and most of the remaining officers of the battalion gathered in the strongpoint. Confirmation had arrived that Hill 145 was definitely taken. An operation this afternoon was planned to capture the Red Line and the *Hangstellung*.

There was a commotion at the entrance.

A private was loudly demanding passage of the sentry, a few carefully chosen adverbs lending his case support. The man was from the scout patrol. His trousers were soaked to the knee, he and his rifle were wrapped in white, yet he looked sweaty, the frigid temperature notwithstanding.

'Where's Lieutenant McIntyre?' asked one of the officers.

'He got it in the arm and the head, sir. They're bringing him back, although we lost Private Savoy. There are a few others besides the lieutenant wounded.'

The full account soon emerged. They'd been caught by what they believed to be one of our own shells falling short, then a group of snipers down the hill had taken them under fire. Needless to say there wasn't a great deal of scouting done after that.

'Blast,' said Major Norsworthy. 'Division and Brigade are terribly anxious to hear what they found.'

Gently I coughed. 'Captain Stiles and I could go, sir. The snipers might not notice a small party quite as easily.'

Stiles was looking at me like I deserved a knobkerrie to the head. Given the opportunity I suspect he would have volunteered to deliver it. The major was more circumspect than critical.

'Hmm. Yes, that's quite possible,' he reflected. 'Would you?' His eyes fell on Stiles.

With the entire dug-out watching Stiles naturally agreed. In such circumstances it paid to do what was expected of you, and he knew it like no other. To my ears his assent wasn't entirely wholehearted, but Norsworthy appeared content.

'Outstanding,' he said.

'Can't you for once keep your trap shut, MacPhail,' groused Stiles as we left.

CHAPTER 34

10th of April, 1917
Vimy Ridge, France

The two of us were barely over the parapet, and cautiously working our way down the steep slope toward what remained of La Folie Wood, when the guns erupted. These were our guns for it was precisely 3.00 p.m. At 3.15 p.m. General Watson would be sending his reserve battalions forward to deal with the sore on the northern end of the ridge that had festered all of a day and half of the next. Eleven minutes of slow fire and four minutes of intense fire was the pre-battle prescription. Simultaneously the village of Vimy to the east of the ridge would be bombarded for an hour in the hope that we might then seize the railheads. There was no better way for the Boche to bring reinforcements forward than by rail.

'That should keep them distracted,' I mumbled to Stiles.

'Where are we heading?' he whispered back.

Wearily I shook my head. Had the man never studied a map in his life?

Roughly I pulled him down into the cover of some undergrowth behind a couple of trees. This little patrol was more dangerous than I'd admitted to either him or myself. There was no sense taking chances.

'Yes, you're absolutely right,' I said. 'It would be useful if you knew what you were doing. In the event I'm disabled you can lead the patrol.'

279

Stiles groaned. It was not as it was supposed to be between captains and lieutenants. That stage we'd passed long ago, like a marriage slowly gone sour.

'Look. You can see the Bois de La Folie on the map. We're approximately here.' I stabbed a finger at the eastern crest of the ridge. Further east entirely covering the slope of the ridge was the wood, helpfully illustrated with hundreds of little trees in case the significance of the French name escaped him. 'Through the wood at the very bottom of the slope, we'll emerge upon Bracken Trench. That's their first trench on the line between Bois du Champ Pourri and Petit Vimy.' Stiles looked puzzled. '*Champ Pourri* means Rotten Field, or something of the sort,' I explained. I knew it was the French pronunciation that had caught him up.

Stiles nodded solemnly.

I was about to add that it sounded like a property the Stiles family would be associated with, but sensibly refrained; no need to unduly aggravate the one man who could watch my back.

'I suggest we take as direct a route as possible downhill, then go along the trench for a bit,' I said.

'It'll be manned,' he replied. 'I can tell you that already.'

'Oh?'

'It certainly was yesterday when the patrols looked, so I don't see why it would be different today. The Boche are not going to abandon the road without a fight.'

He *had* looked at a map. The road he was referring to paralleled the eastern side of Vimy Ridge. Of course they wouldn't give up the road if they wished to recapture the ridge. Whatever else Stiles was, he wasn't stupid. It was something I tended to forget.

'Well, if the trench is full then we'll look for the weak spots,' I improvised.

'Quite the plan, MacPhail.'

We moved as quickly as we could, going from the cover of one tree to another, taking care to keep a distance between us. Two targets close together were far easier to hit than one. The ground was slippery, however. Snow and brush obscured the ground underneath. Circling a tree I stepped forward, concentrating on what lay ahead, feeling my way with my feet. The ground gave way. My foot just kept going, sliding down into a depression. Only by grabbing at the tree did I arrest my fall.

'You okay?' said Stiles when he reached me.

'Yeah, I'll be fine,' I grunted. My ankle was sore. Thankfully it wasn't sprained. Pulling myself to my feet I was preparing to take a tentative step forward when Stiles grabbed me by my arm from behind. He yanked so hard that I tumbled backward into the snow.

'What the…!?' I began.

'Shh.' He jabbed a thumb to the right. 'In front of the logs,' he whispered.

Immediately I saw what he was exercised about. Snipers. At least three of them, and not 50 yards away. Probably the very ones who had shot Lieutenant McIntyre earlier. They hadn't spotted us and we only saw them because we were slightly to their rear. From that angle the jumble of logs and branches they were hiding behind provided little cover.

One man was bent over his rifle butt, his head at the sights, the barrel resting on a log and pointed up the slope towards our trenches. Piqued by what had overcome the patrol, the grenadiers had fired off volleys of rifle grenades in revenge. To little effect, apparently. For a sniper, the Bois de la Folie was ideal terrain.

'Thanks,' I mumbled.

If it hadn't been for Stiles I would have stepped into the clearing. Barring a singularly unprecedented turn of good fortune, that almost certainly would have resulted in me being spotted by one or more of the snipers. A casual glance to one side would have been enough. Most snipers I knew didn't need more than a single shot. Definitely not on a 50-yard range.

With the snipers off our right, that narrowed the options considerably. Consequently I jerked my thumb left. Stiles nodded his agreement. When in doubt go the opposite way. Once we were out of sight we could resume our course.

Briefly I debated crawling. But eventually decided to risk it upright, albeit bent right over. This time I didn't rush, moving instead step-for-step, deliberately, with great care. No sudden movement or crashing of branches to alert their attention. The white smocks we'd borrowed from the patrol were a godsend.

The barrage on the ridge had reached a new and furious crescendo when we once more turned east. Soon the attack to secure the hill would be going in.

Steadily the incline of the slope lessened until it was virtually flat. The going became easier. As the barrage ended the edge of the wood loomed into sight. We crawled the final few feet to the tree line.

It was difficult to see much of the German trench, beyond what I guessed was the parapet. That would be Bracken Trench. I consulted the map. Behind it – 500 yards further – was the second and main defensive line, Bloater Trench. Bloater began at roughly the midway mark of the ridge, as measured from south to north, near the hamlet of Petit Vimy. It continued far to the north. The road was behind it. I didn't see any wire in front of Bracken. Bloater would be a different story.

'Let's take a look,' I said to Stiles. 'We'll never see anything from here.'

Stiles looked dubious. Between us and the trench was 70 yards of open ground. While the ground was by no means flat, and I saw one or two ditches, I could understand his hesitation. I suppose I just wanted to show him a thing or two about life away from headquarters. And let him experience what I'd been experiencing these past weeks – thanks in part to him. 'Come on,' I said brusquely.

We made it to the first ditch with little difficulty. Once I'd caught my breath I dared a peek over the lip. No signs of wire and there wasn't a German to be seen. 'Next ditch is closer by,' I said. 'It looks as if they may have pulled back.'

'Hmm,' said Stiles.

Within a minute we were lying in the snow again, and again I was peeking towards Bracken Trench.

'Not a thing,' I said. 'I think we should risk it.'

Two strides and we were there. After a wary glance we jumped swiftly down into the trench, landing with a clatter on the duckboards, our revolvers held ready. There wasn't a soldier anywhere. By now I was convinced I was on to something; this might lead to the breakthrough we were waiting for. Slip a few companies down the side of the escarpment and we could crash the second line, the soft underbelly of the Germany Army awaiting.

Bloater ahead was heavily wired, as I expected. But there would surely be a few guns that had crossed the mud of the ridge that could provide a barrage? There was also good news. 'Not a Boche in sight,' I whispered over my shoulder.

A crack sounded from directly behind me. It was unmistakeably a revolver. Unmistakeably a Webley. *Damn!* I spun round.

'He came from behind the traverse,' said Stiles. 'There's a dug-out.'

'A dug-out!' My heart began to beat very fast. I hadn't noticed a dug-out entrance. Why hadn't he said something earlier? 'Did you get him?' I asked.

He hesitated. 'I think so.'

A shot whistled past.

Then a stick grenade came tumbling through the air. We both ducked. It landed in the field behind where it went off with a bang and a fleeting puff of smoke.

'Two can play this game,' I growled to myself, and fumbled to pull a Mills bomb from my pocket. After all the raids I'd been on I was well aware how useful they could be. On the off-chance I'd taken a couple along.

There were shouts from down the trench. The sound of men gathering. A flare whizzed into the sky above Bloater Trench. A beacon of double red appeared far up in the sky. They were calling for an S.O.S. barrage. Another flare went up. In case there'd been any doubt the Bavarian Corps was requesting reinforcements. I pulled the little pin from the Mills bomb and lobbed it in the direction where I'd heard the voices. 'Run!' I shouted to Stiles.

With brute force we clambered up the revetments and pulled ourselves over the parapet. Rising drunkenly to our feet, and stumbling terribly in our haste, we ran for the first ditch where we dove for cover.

'Hang on,' I hissed at Stiles. He was already lifting himself to run further. I got on my knees and took the second Mills bomb, eyes locked on the trench behind. I threw it towards the spot we'd just departed. There was a bang. 'Okay. Now!'

Somehow we made it across the snow-covered field. We were almost at the tree line when I heard the crackle of rifle fire. A last spurt of energy and I tumbled into the undergrowth, Stiles landing nearly on top of me.

'Whew,' I heard him say. We lay there winded, our limbs in a tangle, my mind in a whir.

'It's not over yet,' I cautioned. 'Keep your head down. They may have a machine gun.'

They didn't. Or if they did, they didn't use it. That was probably our salvation for at 70 yards a Maxim machine gun is still only stretching its legs. Instead there was a scattering of rifle shots, each deadly in its own right, but not unduly worrisome crouching behind a wall consisting of three feet of shell-blasted oaken trunk.

The trench which I initially thought was deserted was crawling with activity. The activity that I worried about most consisted of the large group of soldiers that were rapidly crossing the field in our direction.

At the sight of them Stiles went to get up.

'Wait,' I said. 'There's a dozen of them, at least. We can't outrun them all, not while watching our backs at the same time. Here we've got some cover. And they haven't. We need to reduce the odds. Let's stay put.'

Stiles looked dour. But he crouched down and brought his revolver to bear, so he must have agreed.

'Make those shots count,' I said. Too late I realized it was the sort of irritating and utterly superfluous comment that would rile me like a red cape will a bull. It appeared to have a similar effect on Stiles.

'Said Custer at his last stand,' I heard him mutter. Followed by my name and an impressive selection of trench obscenities I never realized were so popular at headquarters.

Kneeling behind the tree I braced the revolver firmly against the trunk for a better aim.

At 30 yards, or thereabouts, we gave it all we had. Even with two six-cylinder Webleys and a quick reload in between, it could hardly compare to a Maxim gun. One of those could chew through that many bullets in three seconds. Nevertheless, the field was considerably emptier than it had been hitherto. After a minute or two of this my ammunition cache exhibited a similar condition.

When I saw that it was my last round a cold sweat broke out. I regretted now not having taken the Lee-Enfield. They were such cumbersome things fending your way through trees and into trenches, so I'd left it behind. Frantically I looked around.

'Do you have any Mills bombs?' I asked Stiles.

He shook his head.

'Bullets?'

'A couple,' he replied.

'Well, what the hell are you waiting for?' Then a thought came to me. 'Your flare gun. Where's your flare gun? You did bring it, didn't you?'

Stiles nodded.

'Give it to me.'

He hesitated, looking at his pocket, his hand hanging in mid-air. I glanced past the tree trunk. The Germans were only twenty yards away, the remaining group now charging in our direction. 'For Christ's sake, give me the damn thing,' I shouted.

Reluctantly he gave it to me. I reached out and snatched it away. 'Is it loaded?' I breathed.

'Yes.'

I rolled onto my stomach. With both hands holding the grip and my legs splayed out behind for better stability, I pointed the barrel at the soldier in the middle. 'On my mark,' I said. I heard a grunt. The soldier in my sights was a step or two ahead of the others. From the way the others clustered around him I guessed he must be an NCO. In fact I was counting upon it. A bullet zipped by. I took careful aim. Dead centre. I had a single shot and I had to make it count. There was no time for anything fancy. Another yard. Then another. I took a deep breath.

Then I squeezed the trigger. The pull on a Very pistol is considerably softer than that on a Webley revolver. A gentle tensing of my forefinger was all that it took. A sound issued from the gun more akin to a dull *plop* than a pistol shot. Beside me I could heard Stiles firing.

The flare raced forward like a firecracker, sizzling white as it went and hit the man square in the chest. The two soldiers to either side of him recoiled, grasping frantically at their faces, which was odd. But the NCO kept running… for a step… For an excruciating instant I feared the flare was a dud or had bounced harmlessly off. Whereupon his chest burst into light. I saw the flames flicker and grow. The flare hadn't bounced off, but through some vagary of chance had embedded itself in his webbing.

There were shouts and a most unnerving scream. The impetuous charge came to a timely end. A moment of indecision wavered momentarily over the small group, before they turned en masse and fled. Then came the whoosh of a shell overhead, and another.

It wasn't the S.O.S. barrage the Germans had requested. These were our guns. The shells were bracketing Bracken Trench with white airbursts from the shrapnel and soaring plumes of dirt from the high explosive. The forward observers had seen the German flares and fearing the worst had called down the artillery.

It was time to leave.

'Jesus, that was close,' said Stiles, as he strode up beside me. For all his dishevelled appearance I'd never seen him looking so fit. His eyes sparkled. He might make a soldier after all, I thought. Then dismissed the idea instantly.

'You know, Sam, I think it's time you and I finally settled the question of those rocks of mine, and their safe return,' I growled.

No response came and I glanced over at him. A morose look had appeared on his face.

'Don't tell me you spent them all?' I groaned.

He shook his head, too vehemently to have been lying.

'Well hand them over then.' To underline the message I held out my hand.

'You know I was planning to. But they're gone.'

'Gone?'

'You fired them away.'

Incredulously, I stared at him. 'I what...,' I began to say. Then the coin dropped.

'I always kept them stuffed down the barrel of that flare gun,' he said. 'Seemed like a good spot at the time.'

'You mean to say I fired ten thousand dollars' worth of diamonds into that Boche sergeant?' I said.

Stiles grimaced.

'Huh,' I said. Then I began to chuckle, at first softly.

'I don't see what's so bloody funny,' said Stiles, as I wiped the tears from one eye.

'No, you wouldn't,' I replied. 'But don't you think it's just a little bit amusing? Years from now there may even be a veritable diamond rush here on Vimy Ridge. If you plan ahead you could sell lemonade to the crowds.'

Stiles didn't appear convinced.

Diamonds notwithstanding, I was in high spirits as we climbed the steep slope through the Bois de la Folie. We veered well around where I guessed the snipers would be. Later I heard the three had surrendered soon after 4th Division cleared Hill 145 and the *Hangstellung*.

Were it not for my good humour I might have reacted quicker to the whistle. Nonsense, I told myself afterwards – being at one's sharpest wouldn't have made any difference. With a good ear and a reasonable sense of direction you could hope to dodge an Iron Pig or even a Jack Johnson, something I'd done many times in the past, but not a Whizz-Bang. The cruel irony of it was that I was fairly certain it was one of ours. Another short. There'd been complaints all day. But one couldn't possibly fault the artillery here at Vimy – not like at the Somme. Still, they weren't infallible.

That I'd heard the mid-air bang meant that I wasn't dead. So naturally I did what anyone would do and I turned to look behind. 'Stiles?' I said. I wasn't expecting anything in particular, and least of all what I saw, which was nothing. One minute he'd been there, plodding up the hill twenty feet behind me. The next he was gone. A freak roll of the dice that I was alive and he was not. I searched for him in the undergrowth. In a wide circumference I peered behind trees and stumps and in places where he might have dived for cover. Eventually on a patch of snow I found something of him. It was no more than a haze of pink. There was no hope, and I had no energy and no stomach to look further.

I trudged up the embankment to give my report.

CHAPTER 35

10-11 April, 1917
Fort George, 1 mile northwest of Neuville-Saint-Vaast, France

Shortly after I returned to the Highlanders on the ridge, a message arrived summoning Stiles and I to divisional headquarters. There was no need to reply there'd only be one of us. Nor were we the only ones with orders. The front-line battalions were informed they were to be relieved that evening. Major Norsworthy thanked me briefly, then plunged into the business of preparation.

By the time I reached Fort George, the single sentence into which my report to Major Collum had been condensed was already broadly disseminated at headquarters. Thanks to the wonders of modern technology and tireless work by the linesmen to keep the lines up as the enemy shells contrived otherwise, it had flown across the wired miles to the rear while I took the slow route through the snow, mud and assorted obstacles of the ridge – the latter blissfully no longer including sniper fire. They may even have discussed the report over dinner while I stood on the bustling road near Neuville-Saint-Vaast washing down mouthfuls of iron rations with fresh water from a newly-filled canteen.

Such however was the interest in that single sentence that not only Major Collum but also Colonel Hayter and General Lipsett assembled to hear the full and complete version for themselves. Were it not for my weariness and the gnawing feeling I had about Stiles, I would have been nervous. I gulped however when I saw General Lipsett appear.

'So you were actually *in* Bracken Trench?' said the colonel when I was finished. He seemed quite surprised at this.

'Yes, sir. If we'd seen that it was manned I dare say we wouldn't have been, but we didn't realize that until later. The enemy were all in dug-outs – probably because of our barrages.'

'When you say manned...'

'I saw at least an entire platoon, sir, and I suspect there were more.'

'Right,' said Hayter. He glanced meaningfully over at General Lipsett, who was watching inscrutably. Hayter and he had clearly discussed what was to be asked, the colonel appointed as interrogator. 'And Bloater Trench?'

'Well, sir, as I mentioned I didn't get a good look due to circumstances, but judging how quickly they got a flare up I'd wager that too was filled to the brim. It was definitely well wired.'

'Hmm,' said Hayter.

'Just as we've heard,' mused the general to the colonel. 'We're not going to dislodge the Boche with a patrol or two it would seem.'

'No, General,' replied the colonel. 'It'll have to be a full attack.' Then to me: 'It's a pity about Captain Stiles, Lieutenant. I know the two of you were close, coming from the same battalion –'

'Yes, sir,' I said simply. Colonel Hayter was an intelligent man, but he'd slipped off the duckboards with that remark. Nevertheless, I'd known Sam Stiles the entire time I'd been in the army. Our endless bickering and competition aside, it was strange to think he was gone. Never would I mourn him like I did Roy Dundas and others, but neither would I soon forget him. The diamonds were gone as well. That was definitely for the best; they'd only ever been a source of endless vexation. There were vexations enough at the front without another one.

'We'd best make a start with the preparations, Ross,' said General Lipsett.

The colonel nodded. Looking at me, the general cocked an eyebrow when I stepped from behind the table and he saw the state of my trousers. Briefly I thought he was going to comment. Then he said: 'Shall we let the good lieutenant tidy himself up and get some rest first?

Colonel Hayter grinned broadly. 'Yes, perhaps we should.'

Awakening early the next day my first instinct was to roll over and close my eyes once more. I'd forgotten what it was like to sleep in a real bed. Then I thought of the impending attack. Wearily I planted my feet on the ground and dressed.

Major Collum was waiting for me in one of the many chambers of the dug-out.

'Are there any developments, sir?' I asked.

'A warning order came in at 2 a.m.,' he replied. 'We're to prepare to attack the Bloater-Flower line tomorrow.'

'No surprises there, sir,' I said.

'I have a few things I'd like you to take care of,' he replied.

There were no surprises in that either. My day was shaping up to be a busy one.

At a little past eleven there was a frisson of excitement. A new wire from Corps headquarters was received. It noted that rail movements suggested the enemy was preparing to withdraw from the ground north of Vimy. After a more level-headed individual reread the signal, and dryly added that intelligence said there were no signs of immediate departure from this front, a sobered staff went back to work.

Past four General Lipsett returned from the vast Aux Rietz cave near La Targette and the afternoon conference at 2nd Division headquarters. The planned operation was postponed for twenty-four hours.

'What's that all about?' someone muttered. There was a lot of shaking of heads. Those that knew weren't telling and those that didn't were left to speculate.

That night the wind picked up from the southwest. The snow began to fall very heavily.

12th of April, 1917

'Christ, it's a bloody blizzard outside,' I puffed. I stomped my feet and shook off the last vestiges of snow from my hat. The simple denizens of this corner of Fort George, otherwise known as the 3rd Divisional General Staff, made the appearance of being amused.

In the deep dungeons of the redoubt designed to ward off the worst of the artillery, neither light, wind, rain, nor fresh air were known to penetrate. The last in particular was why I had gone out into the support trench in order to taste the early morning and clear my head of the cobwebs before plunging into what I was certain was going to be an eventful day. However, even in the shelter of the trench, my early morning reconnaissance soon ran afoul of arctic conditions similar to those that overcame Sir John Franklin and his expedition. The wind to my back was blowing an icy tempest. The Germans peering over their parapets to the west would be feeling it straight in their faces. That at least was a pleasant thought. I descended the stairs.

An hour later at 7.45 a.m. one of the telephones rang and it was promptly answered. 'Colonel Ironside for Colonel Hayter,' came the shout. Only neither Colonel Hayter nor General Lipsett were present. In fact there seemed to be no officer present except me. Or perhaps I was merely closest to the telephone.

'Sir, will you take it?' asked the signaller. I could tell he was most anxious to pass it on.

I uncrossed my arms and reached for the receiver. 'Hello, sir?' I said uneasily.

'Who is this?' An authoritative voice boomed down the line. Ironside was one of the numerous British staff officers to be found throughout the Canadian Corps. He was the GSO 1 of the 4th Division. Some opined he was brilliant. It was also said this was an opinion he wholeheartedly concurred with. After the disastrous raid in March when the 4th Division lost the best part of a battalion due among other things to a simple refusal to change plans in the face of overwhelming evidence they should, I was more sceptical. Not that I intended to tell him that. And the division's final attack on Hill 145 had undeniably been a great success, even if what had gone before was not.

'MacPhail, sir. Lieutenant MacPhail. I'm the duty officer at the moment. Neither the colonel nor the general can take your call at present, unfortunately.'

'Hmm,' came the growl. 'You'll have to do then.'

The line crackled. I'd never seen Ironside. It might very well have been his name that influenced the picture in my mind, but I saw a strong-jawed man glaring icily at the telephone as he dealt with the dimwit at the other end. I wasn't so dimwitted as not to know that I should watch my tongue.

'We've taken the Pimple.'

At this my eyes widened. I hadn't even known there was to be an attack. Although common sense would have suggested one had to happen sooner rather than later. The Pimple was not on the ridge proper but was a valley over, to the north. From its peak the north-ernmost part of the ridge could be both observed and fired upon. It was critical that it be taken. The intention had been to attack earlier, however the designated 10th Brigade was thrown in to clean up Hill 145.

'Congratulations, sir,' I said.

'Yes, yes,' said Ironside, impatiently.

Quickly I asked, 'Are there any other details that I can pass along, sir?'

'Inform your superiors that the objectives were gained and a number of prisoners taken, Lieutenant.'

I had my mouth open to ask a follow-up question when the line went dead. Ironside was a busy man I told myself. The news was certainly very welcome. And to think they'd done it in a snowstorm. In retrospect, it may well have been the final straw for the Germans.

I went in search of Colonel Hayter to tell him.

Shortly before noon a forward observation officer reported that a party had reached Bracken Trench – in fact the coordinates revealed that it was the precise spot where Stiles and I had briefly occupied the trench ourselves – which was when I realized something important was happening. As the afternoon wore on report after report was received, each as positive as the last. Our troops were in Bloater, then Buck, and soon other trenches. For this good fortune one possibility loomed above all others.

Nor was I the only one pondering if it meant what I thought it meant. There was no one who worried about a general retirement anymore. 'Could this really be it?' said Major Collum loudly an hour later. He was holding yet another signal in his hands. Heads looked up and the clerk who was typing stopped abruptly. The room became very quiet.

I cleared my throat and smiled. 'Yes, sir,' I said. 'I'm not a betting man, but if I was I'd wager we'd done it.'

13th of April, 1917
Vimy Ridge, France

On the morning of the fifth day of our attack on Vimy Ridge the enemy finally and unambiguously accepted his defeat. There would be no massed counter-attacks – no further resistance. He was withdrawing, albeit cautiously. One after another his positions behind the escarpment had emptied. Patrols were pushing forward unopposed.

I stood on the edge of the ridge not far from La Folie Farm – it was safe to do that now – with my hands on my hips, letting my eyes wander over the vista before me. After days of thick snow and frequent showers, the weather had cleared for the occasion, the visibility startling.

In the foreground past the wired fence posts on the very edge of the ridge were the stark ruins of Vimy and Petit Vimy and La Chaudière. Beyond them the Douai Plain stretched for fifteen miles to the north and the east. This was a sight no Allied soldier had seen since 1914. A view of a seemingly endless succession of farmers' fields, unmarked by war, gave to the north upon the rooftops of Lens. Around the city the enemy would no doubt be furiously adding to his defences. And yet there! A quarter turn to the east. Was it possible? Those must surely be the spires of the Cathedral of Douai.

An officer came and stood beside me. I didn't know him. The lieutenant was wearing the blue patch of the 2nd Division on his arm. He was grinning mightily and I grinned in return.

'An impressive sight,' he said. 'Feels good to be here doesn't it?'

'It sure does,' I replied.

'Looks like we've shown the Boche a thing or two, eh?'

'Oh, I think we've done more than that,' I said. It seemed impossible to think that this bastion which the Germans in their arrogance – it was easy to speak that word now – had been so convinced was impregnable had fallen. That it had fallen to those they so often derided as mere colonials – pretend soldiers – would be especially galling. This entire war everybody from the Kaiser on down had threatened to send us home in rowboats.

'I expect they're retiring to the Méricourt Line and the Avion Switch,' said the officer. 'To hold Lens.'

'As likely as not,' I replied. 'You wouldn't care to hazard a guess where we're going next?'

'No,' he laughed. 'But, you know, I don't think the boys will mind.'

I thought about this on the way back to Fort George. That the victory had been hard won was evidenced by the casualty figures. I'd heard them called 'light'. By the sanguinary standards of the Western Front and taking account of what we'd done I guess they were, but light they were not. They numbered in the many thousands, the final figure I dared not guess. Yet despite that morale was high. I could see it on the faces around. This was not the spirit-crushing "victory" of the Somme. This was real victory, the first in this war. Somehow it felt as if the tide of war itself had swung. And we'd helped swing it.

As if to illustrate, two lorries with standing room only came lurching past on the road. The soldiers were smiling and boyishly calling out to one another, in the best of spirits. A few wore German helmets. When they spotted me, an officer, walking in my lonesome alongside the fascines that kept the planks of the road from sinking into the mud they raised their helmets and gave a rousing cheer. I raised my helmet back and that garnered still more cheers. No, I reckoned. The lieutenant was right. The boys would go wherever they were told, and likely raise a cheer doing it.

'I've some mail for you, sir,' said the clerk, and handed me a pile of letters.

'Mail?' I looked at Benoît who shrugged. The last time I'd had mail seemed a lifetime ago, although it was closer to a week. Guiltily I tried to recall the last time I'd written any mail myself. That might well have been a lifetime ago. But after these years overseas my parents would be accustomed to my laxness. But what was this? One of the letters, also postmarked Calgary, was in a handwriting I didn't recognize. I gulped. My heart was beating as fast as it had that day in Bracken Trench with Stiles.

'What's wrong?' asked Benoît. He'd turned up at Fort George at roughly the same time I had, and after shaking the life out of what had been a perfectly healthy arm, we began talking.

'I think it may be bad news about my parents.'

'Why would you possibly think that, Mac?' he said, eyeing the letters in my other hand. 'But open it. No sense in worrying if you don't need to.' It was a sort of wisdom that masquerades as common sense.

So I did. I opened it. I could feel him examining me as my eyes raced down the single handwritten page. Then they returned to the beginning, or close to it. I read the letter again more slowly. It was a pleasant script, not difficult to read.

'I'll be damned,' I whispered.

'What is it?' Benoît could barely contain himself for his curiosity.

'You're never going to believe this. It's…' I couldn't find the words for what I wanted to say. 'The letter is from Roy Dundas's parents.' Benoît's dark eyebrows frowned. 'They received a letter from him at the beginning of the month.'

'A letter?' Benoît looked as if he'd seen the Holy Ghost.

'Yes, a letter. Appears he's not dead after all. Roy, God bless him, is in a German POW camp.'

'*Sacré Bleu*,' said Benoît.

I was grinning like a madman.

'This calls for a drink, Mac.' Naturally he mashed the words, but then that was an unmistakeable part of Benoît's charm. Much like his water bottle, which he was offering freely.

'You know, Benoît, I heard from a fellow today that when 2nd Division overran Thélus they found a German officers' dug-out complete with a fully-stocked bar and a staff of five waiters.' Benoît looked fascinated. 'At times like that I think you're in the wrong army,' I said.

'Excuse me, gentlemen.'

It wasn't so much the voice I recognized as the impeccably precise and polite language. I could see the canteen making a general retreat – if not surreptitiously at least rapidly – to Benoît's tunic pocket. It shouldn't have come as a surprise but I was relieved Benoît hadn't offered General Lipsett a drink.

'If you'd excuse us, Lieutenant DuBois', said the general. 'I'd like to speak with Lieutenant MacPhail for a moment.'

'Yes, sir.' Benoît disappeared.

'Colonel Hayter is responsible for the staff, as you know, MacPhail. However, I believe in keeping an eye on things myself. It's come to my attention these past weeks that you've spent precious little time at headquarters,' he said.

My natural reaction – anybody's natural reaction – was to explain. The fish in me was already jumping for the bait with an open mouth, when I checked myself. I hardly needed to tell the general what he must have known all along. Perhaps he'd even ordered it.

'No, sir,' I replied.

'What I find truly remarkable is the number of times that your name has come to my attention in the short span you've been on my staff. I don't mean simply reading it at the bottom of the movement orders.'

'Sir?'

'What I wish to say, MacPhail, is that I asked you to join my staff with a certain purpose in mind. There are men who are comfortable and skilled in ensuring that the details required to keep a division operating are dealt with efficiently. And there are men who can put a bayonet in a man. However, one doesn't necessary preclude the other. Occasionally even the staff requires a man who can do both.'

'Yes, sir,' I said, at a loss to think of anything else more appropriate.

'Colonel Hayter has mentioned you to me several times, very favourably on all occasions.'

'He did?'

'You look surprised.'

'It's just...' I hesitated. 'I was expecting Captain Stiles would be taking my place... at least I did until recently.'

'Stiles?'

'Yes, sir.'

'Whatever gave you that idea?'

I shrugged.

'No, I'm afraid both the colonel and I are of one mind on this. You won't be going anywhere, Lieutenant. The 3rd Division has claimed you as its own. I hope that doesn't disappoint you?'

'No, sir,' I said. 'Thank you, sir.' I felt the colour rushing to my cheeks, a silly grin breaking out.

'There's no need to thank me. You've carried out your duties admirably during this operation, MacPhail.'

'Sir.'

'However, the war isn't over quite yet, unfortunately.'

'No, sir. I'll get back to work.'

'If you would,' he said.

If I didn't know better there was a twinkle to his eye.

It was one of my better days on the Western Front.

AUTHOR'S NOTE AND ACKNOWLEDGEMENTS

From the Somme to Vimy Ridge, this novel begins and ends with two battles that each in their way shaped nations. The Battle of the Somme is forever engraved in the long history of the United Kingdom, the date of July 1st 1916 a painful wound, a day of infamy on which an unthinkable 57,000 soldiers fell. Through history books, literature, and film that single day has shaped how the country and even the world remembers the Great War. But the battle itself was an affair of many months, of many nations, and many individual battles. When Malcolm arrived at the Somme two months of fighting had passed. It was to go on for three more. By its end 24,000* of his countrymen had fallen, and countless others in the ranks of the other Allied nations.

The Battle of Vimy Ridge was both smaller and shorter, part of the broader British and French offensives at Arras and the Chemin des Dames. However, to this day, April 9, 1917 remains the bloodiest day in Canadian military history. Despite that it is remembered primarily as a stunning victory in a war when victories to that point were few, a milestone on the country's path to full nationhood. Vimy Ridge proved a welcome boost to Entente morale even though the front lines moved only slightly as a result. During the German spring offensives of 1918, defended by the Corps that had captured it, the ridge was the single unyielding anchor in the British line. General Ludendorff's plan of driving a wedge between French and British did not come to pass.

In no way have I done justice to all that happened in this momentous period. But then this is a novel and makes no pretentions otherwise. Malcolm's story is intertwined with the history, the fiction shaped around it. Necessarily his view is a limited one. As a young lieutenant I could only let him see glimpses of the broader whole. However I hoped in those glimpses or vignettes to convey the story of this phase of the war, and how it must have been for a soldier living through those times.

The attacks at the Somme in which Malcolm plays a role are emblematic of late 1916. This is the Great War of popular history. One can only imagine the excitement and optimism of the soldiers marching towards the Somme, before that slowly curdled after yet another gruelling "spell" in the trenches, or yet another attack. Until only weary resignation remained. Then having to pick themselves up in the wake of the battle and do their all to prepare once more for war. And finally, when it was over, the unmistakeable pride and joy, the feeling that they had truly accomplished something important at Vimy. This too was the Great War, if not always the war of popular history.

With the exception of Malcolm himself, Benoît DuBois, Roy Dundas, Sam Stiles and a handful of others, a great many of the characters in the book were real people. General Gough of the Reserve Army was one such character. He was to earn the everlasting enmity of the Canadians for his role in pressing the attacks of 1 and 8 October against their protests (Chapter 10). For all the famous "learning curve" of the BEF it took almost two years before he was sacked. Welsh Lieutenant William Morgan did receive the Military Cross and the Albert Medal on 17 December 1916 at Buckingham Palace (Chapter 16), while Sergeant Ross of the RCR was very much a pillar of strength in the raid near the Watling Crater (Chapter 19), even if some of the small details of that excursion owe more to me than to him.

For those who might express disbelief at the admittedly remarkable tendency for heavy rainfall or snow during Malcolm's forays to the front, I can assure you that the weather was every bit as treacherous as I have described. And for those who might speculate whether it was indeed the Red Baron who "strafed" Malcolm on the La Targette road (Chapter 27), I can say only this; Richthofen may not have done it, but the colour of his airplane and his presence at Vimy during the period in question make him a prime suspect.

The many raids Malcolm is involved in all happened more or less as described. That includes the 1st CMR patrol on April 5th (Chapter 29), the day of the alarm that the Germans might be engaged in a general withdrawal, even if patrol members would not be able to recall being accompanied by a certain staff officer out for a prisoner! Much of the detail about these raids came from studying war diaries, battalion histories and personal accounts, trench map in hand, trying to make sense of them – the information often incomplete, inconsistent and sometimes contradictory. Where the history ran out my imagination stepped up.

So, too, with the story of Malcolm at Vimy Ridge. The initial failure at Hill 145 (where today the stunning white twin towers of Canada's national monument stand), and the resultant open left flank of the 3rd Division, was the critical breakwater on which the entire attack might have foundered. The tale I have told reflects the fog of war which loomed heavy that afternoon and evening. Information was late to arrive and incomplete, and occasionally downright false. More often than not, units didn't know what was happening a couple of hundred yards to either side. The 42nd Battalion, for example, frantically built a defensive trench across the ridge that first night, fearing the worst. Only the next day did they learn that the 85th Battalion to their left had already taken Hill 145 in a bold bayonet charge without artillery support. Had the Germans not been dealing with problems of their own that afternoon, and their own fog of war, the history of the battle may well have been different.

I owe thanks to Dr. Gary Grothman and Diann Duthie for reading my first draft, steering me from my worst mistakes, and providing me with many invaluable comments and suggestions. My editor, Dexter Petley, did much to improve the book with his detailed and perceptive edits. Likewise, I must thank Ian Forsdike MBE for his diligence and keen eye in proofing the final version.

If you enjoyed reading *Vicissitudes of War* I would be extremely grateful if you took a couple of minutes to leave a review at the retailer where you purchased it. Readers put great store by reviews. For most authors, and I count myself amongst them, it is one of the best ways to have new readers discover your work.

In the event you haven't already done so, I encourage you to sign up for my email list at www.darrellduthie.com in order to receive advance notice of new publications (the next book will be out in 2021). On the site you can also find a variety of information relating to all the books in the series, including large-scale maps and other details. If you'd like, you can even get in touch with me.

Many thanks for reading!

Darrell Duthie
Amersfoort, September 14th, 2020
www.darrellduthie.com

* This figure includes the men of the Newfoundland Regiment (now a Canadian province, then a Dominion) who went over the top on July 1st at Beaumont-Hamel. Within the first 30 minutes nearly 9 out of 10 had fallen.

BOOKS IN THE
MALCOLM MACPHAIL WW1 SERIES

The books are numbered in the order in which they were written.
Each can be read on its own, however, or in chronological order.

Find them online at your favourite bookstore.
Also available as e-books.

Watch for the next book in the series coming in 2021.

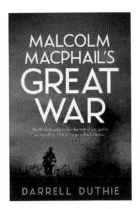 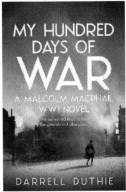 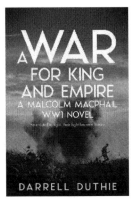

WRITING ORDER

Malcolm MacPhail's Great War – Book 1 (1917-1918)

My Hundred Days of War – Book 2 (1918)

A War for King and Empire – Book 3 (1915-1916)

Vicissitudes of War – Book 4 (1916-1917)

CHRONOLOGICAL ORDER

A War for King and Empire – Book 3 (1915-1916)

Vicissitudes of War – Book 4 (1916-1917)

Malcolm MacPhail's Great War – Book 1 (1917-1918)

My Hundred Days of War – Book 2 (1918)

Printed in Great Britain
by Amazon

62344583R00184